Connections Past

Jeneva's Journey, Volume 1

Faye & George Chamberlain

Published by Celect Project Services Ltd., 2021.

CONNECTIONS PAST

First edition. September 1, 2021.

Written by Faye & George Chamberlain.

Following the charitable nature of the main character, we will be donating a percentage of book sales to:

The Big Brother/Big Sister Organizations.

Prologue

One misty evening, Takoda Yassi and his daughter, Jeneva, strolled on the lush green hillside overlooking the valley of the River Lagan. They were celebrating her sixteenth birthday backpacking in Northern Ireland.

When they stopped to rest on a rock and admire the setting sun illuminating the horizon with pastel shades of orange, pink, and purple, Takoda pulled a rectangular black velvet box out of his backpack.

"Happy birthday, honey," he said, handing it to his daughter. "Your mother asked me to give this to you today."

Immediately, tears bubbled in the corners of the young girl's eyes and spilled down her cheeks. The box was tied with a beaded ribbon, which she gently removed and wrapped around her long ponytail. Inside the box was a beige leather bracelet with three circular buttons fastened on it, each with a different symbol.

Jeneva looked up at her father. "Do the symbols mean something?"

"I'm sorry, honey. I'm not exactly sure. Before your mom died, she had a vision of what your future holds. She instructed me to tell you that 'the symbols are an integral part of a puzzle that will guide you on a journey to your destiny.'"

Not a day passed that Jeneva didn't long for the opportunity to meet and spend time with her mother. It was her only selfish desire. Seemingly, an impossible dream . . . or was it?

<u>Author Quote</u>

The totality of our sameness is greater than the sum of our differences.

George Chamberlain

• • • •

<u>Acknowledgements</u>

Maggie Morris: Indie Editor
CY Studios: Photography
SelfPubBooks.com/LivingstonAtLarge: Cover Design

Part 1
The Bracelet
Chapter 1

Destiny's Child
Takoda Yassi was offered a prominent position at the Smithsonian National Museum of the American Indian. As a member of the Sioux Nation, he welcomed the opportunity to work with other native American historians. It was a wonderful opportunity to continue his research.

Once they were settled, Lynn took a volunteer job at an orphanage, where she found solace in caring for the parentless children, loving them as if they were her own. After years of trying to have children of their own, the couple had given up hope. That was, until the evening of Lynne's 37th birthday when she had one of her visions.

For nine months they'd anticipated this day with apprehension and euphoria. The doctor had warned them that, at this stage in Lynne's life, there could be complications. But the couple was certain their belief in Lynne's vision, their aspiration to be parents, and the Great Spirit would answer their prayers. Despite the odds, the pregnancy came to full term.

Moments after his baby girl came into the world, a glass-shattering cry sent a shiver up Takoda's spine. His little girl, Jeneva, would be a force to be reckoned with.

Her oval head was covered with black velvet curls, and her big brown eyes twinkled in the delivery room lighting. Lynne looked adoringly at her husband cradling their baby like a receiver holding a football. Her eyes filled with love as she reached out to take her daughter.

Suddenly, her arms fell limp at her sides. Takoda watched help-lessly as his wife's bronze complexion paled to an ash gray. The mon-itors that, a second ago, had filled the room with a serene, rhythmic sound now emitted spasmodic, ear-piercing shrieks.

"What's happening?" Takoda shouted at the maternity nurse as she went rushing out the door. Something told him this was bad, but his heart hoped it wasn't. Holding Lynne's hand, he felt powerless by her side. Her eyes languidly fluttered, then closed. He glanced back at the screens. *Do those flat lines mean her heart has stopped? Is she dead? Where is everybody?* Frantically searching for reassurance that his wife wasn't gone, Takoda headed for the door. Baby Jeneva was still sound asleep in his arms. He almost collided with the doctor and two nurses.

"Doctor! One minute she was fine, then she just closed her eyes. She's going to be all right, isn't she?" His voice and eyes were filled with desperation.

The short, elderly doctor didn't answer. He checked the patient for a pulse, then signaled the nurse to push the Code Blue alarm. The announcement came over the PA system, "Code Blue, delivery room three, Code Blue, delivery room three."

One of the nurses replaced the empty IV bag on the forked pedestal, and the other scooped the sleeping newborn from Takoda's resistant arms and steered him out of the room.

"I'll take her to the nursery." She disappeared down the hall.

Takoda returned to Lynne's bedside, taking her hand in his.

"Lynne, I'm here, my darling. I'm right here."

A husky male nurse, with tattooed forearms, hastily maneuvered the crash cart beside the doctor administering CPR.

Takoda watched anxiously from the other side of the bed. Before he knew what was happening, he was being forcibly piloted him out the door. Wrestling against the strong tattooed arms pulling him down the hall to the waiting room, he frantically called out, "Lynne—Lynne—Lynne."

Takoda heard the doctor's voice echo through the hallowed halls. "Clear!"

"You have to wait here, sir." The male nurse's voice was caring and gentle, not what you would expect from such a Hulk-like man. "Someone will be in shortly to follow up on your wife's condition."

Then, he disappeared down the corridor, leaving Takoda alone, wondering how he would ever go on living without his wife.

LYNNE LAY MOTIONLESS as the monitors returned to a rhythmic, *beep, beep, beep*. In her mind, thoughts raced out of control, and oblivious to the comings and goings surrounding her, she fell into a superconscious state. Her third eye chakra projected kaleidoscope pictures at lightning speed into her mind's eye. When she took control of her thoughts, the postcard-like snapshots were of her baby's future.

One was of her daughter racing through the halls of a museum; the next one showed her receiving awards; another showed her older, working alone in a lab. A much harder one to see showed her seated in a dark cave. The most vivid image revealed Jeneva standing with five people on top of what appeared to be a mountain. A unique phenomenon canopied over them in a half moon of the most beautiful colors imaginable. Lynne could sense the compassion and harmony radiating up from the smiling crowd that gathered below. And then, it was gone. Darkness fell over her.

Visions such as this were neither unusual nor frightening to Lynne. Growing up, she was exposed to many rituals and beliefs passed down by the tribe's elders. They influenced her interest in the afterlife and future events. She was always amenable to receiving mystical visions that came to her without warning, as they'd come to her mother before her.

WHEN THE DOCTOR FOUND him, Takoda was in the nursery, looking at his baby girl, with a tear-filled hankie in his hand. The doctor accompanied him down the hallway and advised him that his wife had just endured an amniotic fluid embolism, a very rare medical occurrence. And some of the amniotic fluid had gotten into her circulatory system, causing an allergic-type reaction; in this case, severe enough to stop her heart. He had ordered a blood transfusion, injected her with thinners, and applied electrical charges to Lynne's heart. They were able to bring her back. She appeared to be out of the woods, for the moment.

Standing outside the ICU, he placed a comforting hand on Takoda's arm.

"What she needs now is rest. I'll check in tomorrow, but she will need to stay here for a couple days."

After the doctor disappeared, Takoda placed his palm on the window and said a prayer.

When he raised his head and looked through the window, Lynne had opened her eyes and was waving him in. The expression on her face told him something had happened.

He rushed to her bedside, trying to remain calm. How beautiful she looked with her black hair draped over her shoulders. Her big brown eyes were weary but twinkled just as they had the day they met. Takoda admired her so and hoped their daughter would grow up to be just as caring as her mother. How could she not? Lynne was going to be a wonderful role model.

Before he sat down, she asked him to get her purse from the closet. Takoda got it and placed it in her lap. Once he was certain she was comfortable, he sat on the edge of the bed, waiting. She took his hand in hers and gave him that familiar grin that confirmed his suspicions.

"I saw our daughter's future," she said. "She's going to make great changes in the world, but she's going to need this." She pulled a rectangular black velvet case out of her beaded handbag and handed it to Takoda. Inside was a leather bracelet with three symbols on it.

He took the bracelet from the box and scrutinized it for a moment, then put it back in the case and into his breast pocket. The last thing he wanted to do at this moment was talk about jewelry. He had almost lost her and needed to know she was alright. Hoping to change the subject, he asked, "How are you feeling?"

"Better," she said and fixed her eyes on his. "The bracelet is an integral part of a puzzle that will guide her on a journey to her destiny."

Takoda nodded and assured her he understood it's importance. Clearly, it was no ordinary bracelet.

After Lynne revealed all the details of her vision and gave him explicit instructions as to when he was to give the bracelet to their daughter and what to tell her, she closed her eyes, and whispered, "I will always love you."

There was no reason to question what Lynne told him. He trusted her intuition completely and promised to help their daughter achieve her destiny any way he could. For hours, he sat holding his wife's hand and watching her chest rise and fall in peaceful sleep. When he could no longer ignore his nagging bladder, he kissed her cheek.

"I'll be right back," he whispered.

The nurse at the ICU desk gave him a nod when he pointed in the direction of the men's room. While he was drying his hands, he looked at his reflection in the mirror.

"You're a father. Imagine that!"

A sudden urge to see his daughter came over him. His eyes scanned the nursery. He spotted her lying under a pink card, "I'm a Girl, Jeneva Yassi." She was bundled in a pink blanket, sleeping like a lamb amongst the other pink and blue cocoons. He finally knew what it meant to be called a proud papa. He couldn't be prouder.

As he stepped out of the nursery, he heard the echoing call. "Code Blue, ICU." A vibrating chill permeated his body. Suddenly, he realized why Lynne insisted he give the bracelet to Jeneva. Not only had she seen their daughter's future, but she had also seen her own.

Takoda ran to the ICU, where he could only watch through the window the desperate efforts of the doctor engaging the defibrillator. Once, twice, three times. After the fourth try, the paddles were put back on the cart. The head nurse's eyes were apologetic as she shook her head at Takoda. Slowly, she pulled a sheet over Lynne's deceased body and turned off the whining monitors.

The pale green walls closed in around Takoda. His legs turned to jelly, and he crumpled to the floor on all fours, sobbing uncontrollably into his large trembling hands. His pleading words resonated through the abandoned hall. "No! You can't leave me. Your daughter needs you. I need you."

A gentle hand touched his shoulder. When he raised his head, he saw the head nurse looking sorrowfully down at him.

"Would you like to say goodbye to your wife?"

Without answering her, he reached for the windowsill and pulled himself upright. Then he turned away from her timidly, wiping his puffy red eyes on his sleeve and blowing his nose in his damp handkerchief.

The chilling air in the ICU made his body quiver. He approached the cloaked body. The room was completely silent now. No reassuring *beep, beep, beep* from the monitors. Takoda was surrounded by dead silence.

The nurse slowly pulled the sheet downward over Lynne's chest, revealing only her face. Takoda gasped when he saw that his beloved wife's brown skin was now a ghostly grey. He almost didn't recognize her.

From the other side of the bed, the nurse acknowledged his obvious jaw-dropping shock with a compassionate nod. She must have seen this moment many times before and would see it many times again.

"I'm so sorry for your loss. I realize you are in pain but if I could share something with you?"

"Of course." Takoda caressed Lynne's cheek as he listened.

"I grew up in the church. My mom was a pastor. When someone in her congregation lost someone, she would tell them, 'The best way to mourn the death of your loved one is to take care of the living who belong to them.' You must take care of yourself, Mr. Yassi, so you can take care of your daughter. She needs you to be strong. Stay as long as you like. I'll be at the station when you're ready to fill out the paperwork." She pulled the drapes to give him some privacy and closed the door behind her.

In his state of heartbreak, Takoda felt his own life fading away. He laid himself across his wife's chest, holding her in his arms.

"I can't do this on my own. Why? Why did you leave me?" He wept.

At the doctor's subtle cough behind him, he released his hold on Lynne and stood upright. He had no idea how long he'd been in that position, but the tingling in his arms and the stabbing pain in his lower back told him it must have been quite a while.

"Mr. Yazzi, would it be all right if we spoke in the hall? You can come back if you like. This will only take a minute."

Takoda dried his eyes and met the doctor outside the ICU.

The doctor craned his neck to look up at Takoda and spoke to him in a matter-of-fact tone. "I thought you would like to know what happened in there."

Takoda took a deep breath and responded with a nod.

"The clotting of a weakened pulmonary vein caused another major heart attack. Regrettably, despite the best efforts of the ICU team, we were not able to bring your wife back a second time."

His eyes softened as he put his hand on Takoda's arm. He was too short to reach his shoulder. He offered his condolences and walked away, leaving the widowed man slumped against the wall. The love of his life was gone. Takoda became both mother and father to his newborn child that day.

Chapter 2

R eminiscent Lunch
    At eleven thirty, Takoda stepped out of his Washington DC hotel into the busy street. His tailored pinstripe suit fit his six-foot-two frame like a glove, and his straight gray hair was braided down his back. Takoda had made a name for himself in the circle of researchers, philanthropists, and celebrities who were making a difference in the world. For over twenty-five years at the National Museum of the American Indian, he'd conducted research on the potable water supply for underdeveloped countries, for which he was recognized as a leader. A feature story about his efforts and findings appeared in an issue of *World Water Projects Magazine*.

Presently, his bags were packed, ready for his return trip to Sudan. He would be investigating the effects of newfound magnetic rocks at the confluence of the Blue and White Nile rivers.

This afternoon, though, he was looking forward to meeting with now twenty-six-year-old daughter Jeneva at their favorite seaside restaurant. Since she'd moved to Switzerland, they rarely had a chance to meet and discuss what was happening with each other's research. Both were devoting all their time to work and volunteering. Rarely did they socialize with anyone outside their research groups. He couldn't wait to tell her about his return to Africa, secretly hoping she'd consider joining him.

He heard the screen door of The Olde Marine Restaurant give its rusty squeak as he stepped inside. He panned the crowded room with the anticipation of a child on Christmas morning, looking for Jeneva. A disappointed sigh escaped his pouting lips. He hoped she was just delayed in traffic and would come hustling through the door at any minute. To assume anything else would be a negative thought, which he tried to avoid at all costs.

11

A bubbly hostess in a white frayed top and mini skirt greeted him and showed him to a table. He averted his eyes from the scantily dressed girl by scanning the menu and ordering a pitcher of iced tea. When she returned with his drink, he continued to keep his head down. Once she left, Takoda's thoughts returned to Jeneva.

Every time he saw his daughter, he was captivated by the resemblances to her mother. They wore their straight black hair pulled back with a beaded ribbon. And their eyes, those ebony eyes. Their warm and gregarious personality made anyone around feel at ease. Now that Jeneva was almost thirty, everything about her mirrored her mother at that age.

He couldn't help but wonder whether he'd told Jeneva everything about the mother she'd never have the chance to know. Like the many times Lynne didn't hesitated to help someone, even when she wasn't feeling well herself. And how she loved to organize parties or visit someone who was sick or struggling. It delighted him that his daughter was naturally following in her mother's footsteps.

Today was already predestined to be emotional, without bringing Lynne into the picture, so he decided not to mention her unless Jeneva did.

Before his emotions got the best of him, he turned his head to peruse the marina. The flagrant ostentatiousness of the oversized vessels made his blood boil. *Don't they know the extreme strife and hardship sustained by the less fortunate people around the world?* Apparently, they didn't care, but he certainly did.

JENEVA YASSI STROLLED nonchalantly along the pier at the National Harbor on the Potomac River, wearing her favorite sun hat and a full-length flowery sundress that flattered her figure. She stopped at the rail, closed her eyes, and lifted her head to meet the heat of the midday sun. She heard the harbor flags snapping and water splashing against the boats in the marina. When she opened her eyes, the spring sky was a blanket of blue, filled with squawking sea gulls circling and scavenging the boardwalk for morsels of discarded food.

The elite marina was jammed with everything from eight-foot dinghies to eighty-foot yachts. Several were occupied by their owners and friends, indulging in cocktails served in colorful glasses. Jeneva imagined they were toasting some accomplishment they achieved that week or maybe just welcoming spring. Only one person acknowledged her walking by and gave her a friendly wave, which she, of course, returned with enthusiasm and a smile. It frustrated her that most people seemed to be concerned only with themselves, with no interest in the problems or affairs of others. On Facebook, if you didn't have enough friends "liking" your selfies, you replied with a sad emoji. This was a real sore spot with Jeneva. She believed self-acceptance was more important than peer approval. She recalled telling her father; "If I could change one thing in this, me, me, me world; it would be for everyone to be more caring and considerate toward each other's feelings and less interested in flaunting themselves, their wealth, and their extravagant possessions." He'd agreed wholeheartedly.

Nearing the cedar-shingled restaurant at the end of the pier, she heard lively music filling the air. Her sense of smell was overcome by the mouth-watering aroma of fried onions, burgers, and hot dogs. She was not surprised that every table was occupied with sun worshippers enjoying their first outdoor lunch of the year.

Jeneva knew her father wasn't much for the sun, and it was a sure bet he'd be waiting for her in the comfort of the air-conditioned eatery, with a tall glass of iced tea at his fingertips. Maybe he'd already placed their usual order, the seafood platter for two. As she entered through the screen door, she spotted him, just as she'd suspected. He was sitting patiently in a corner booth, sipping his habitual drink, and looking handsome in his three-piece suit.

He appeared to be deep in thought and didn't acknowledge her presence until she placed her hand on his broad shoulder, immediately bringing him back to the present. He struggled to get his lanky body out from beneath the booth table. He gave her a warm, loving embrace.

Once they were both seated, Jeneva asked, "What were you thinking about with such an intense look on your face?"

"I was just thinking about the extreme inequities in the world. You won't believe the struggles the women and children in Sudan endure. They spend hours of their day walking for miles to a well and then returning home with water on their backs, just to survive."

Takoda turned his gaze to the window.

"It's so upsetting to see how the people in this harbor are spending millions of dollars frivolously just to float on top of the water and fill their lives with grotesque displays of conspicuous consumption, while others die from the lack of water."

Jeneva reciprocated with her own personal loathing.

"I can't believe how people are relentlessly looking for the wow factor. Rushing out to buy the latest, new and improved gadgets just to be recognized by their peers for what they have." She shook her head in disgust. It was apparent that the subject put a bad taste in both their mouths. Fortunately, at that moment, their lunch arrived to divert their thoughts.

Even though they were sitting across from each other, they struggled to hear what the other was saying. It seemed everyone around them was speaking in elevated voices. Cell phones rang obscure jingles and were answered with loud hellos. Children fussed and whined about not being able to get a Wi-Fi connection or their favorite food. She put her hand up to her face and whispered, "Those kids don't seem to appreciate what a privilege eating out in a restaurant with their family is."

"Attitudes sure have changed since I was a young boy."

"That's for sure. It blows my mind how accepting society is about it all. Whatever happened to good manners and respect for your parents?"

She reached across the table and put her hand on her father's.

"Which reminds me, congratulations again for receiving the American Ingenuity Award for your international work on water purification. You did me proud, Pops!"

"I'm pleased as punch you made the trip to be by my side last night, honey. It meant the world to me."

"I also came for Maddy's sixteenth birthday party. She and her dad are expecting me for dinner tonight." She caught a glimpse of disappointment on his face.

She suspected he'd been hoping to have dinner with her tonight as well. They both knew they had so little time left before they went back to their research projects.

"Can you put this in a card and give it to that adorable Little Sister of yours. Along with a hug if you don't mind?" He had pulled a hundred-dollar bill out of his wallet.

"Thanks, I'm sure she'll appreciate that you thought of her. She'll probably use the money to buy apps and music for the iPhone I'm giving her."

"Turning sixteen is a milestone in a young girl's life. Maddy seems like a different person from the one you met eight years ago when you two were matched up through Big Brothers Big Sisters. You deserve a lot of credit for those changes. I'm proud of you for being there for her and giving her guidance when she needed it."

"Thanks, Dad. She's been good for me too. Speaking of birthdays, I'll never forget my sixteenth, when you gave me this bracelet from Mom."

Even today, ten years later, they were both at a loss to put meaning and connection to the three symbols.

Takoda wiped the lingering sauce from his mouth and fingers with a moist toilette, then pulled a ticket and leaflet from his inside breast pocket.

"These are for a symposium being held at the Walter E. Washington Convention Center tomorrow. I'm going to be tied up in a few last-minute meetings before I head to Sudan, so I can't go. I think you'd find the topics quite interesting."

Jeneva picked them up with sticky fingers, gave the leaflet a quick look, and flashed him a mischievous grin. She was envisioning the Three Stooges putting on a dog and pony show for an audience of stuffed-shirt scholars.

"Thanks! I'll try to make it." She shrugged and slipped both in the beaded leather bag, which had been her mother's favorite.

There it was again, that feeling that her mom was beside her. It was Jeneva's turn to draw a blank gaze. Her father must have picked up on her sudden feeling because he reached over, placing his hand on her cheek. She blinked, then looked apprehensively into his eyes.

"Sorry about that. I sensed Mom was here again. She must have heard us talking about the bracelet. Sometimes I think she's trying to tell me something."

Although she knew her father understood and was doing his best to cope with his feelings of still missing his wife, she also knew he felt helpless to ease her pain and yearning for her mom's companionship.

Jeneva initiated the conclusion of their reunion feast with their customary holding of hands with a gentle squeeze. Both were aware of the loneliness they were destined to feel when they went their separate ways. The unspoken feelings of respect and admiration for the research each was doing would get them through it. That and probably a lot of video chats whenever possible. They wiggled out from behind the table and once again embraced with a father-daughter all-encompassing hug. They both knew it could be months, maybe years, before they saw each other again. Her father's eyes were full of conflicting emotion, and when he leaned down and placed a gentle kiss on her cheek, he said with no words how much he'd miss her. This brought a big smile to her face and a tug at her heartstrings. She reluctantly separated and turned towards the exit. Wiping a tear from her cheek, she opened the squeaky screen door and gave her father a backwards wave. She walked briskly down the marina boardwalk and into her first adventure.

Chapter 3

Takoda Yassi
The brittle boards of the pier creaked under his feet as he headed toward the parking lot. From the corner of his eye, Takoda glimpsed a small boy floating a toy boat. The boy sat on the swim platform of a Bluewater yacht anchored in the marina. Takoda smiled at his innocence but couldn't help wondering whether someday this child would also fall into the devil-may-care world of extravagance of his parents. The parents who were, at this very minute, laughing with friends on the upper deck, oblivious to their son's whereabouts. Takoda redirected his focus to the parking lot where he saw the car, he rented for his daughter drive away.

Splash!

The wake from a passing boat must have pulled the string out of the little boy's hands. In an effort to retrieve it, he'd lost his balance and tumbled into the gasoline-polluted water. Why his parents hadn't put a life jacket on him was inconceivable. His arms flailed like a baby bird taking its first flight. The mouthfuls of water he took in muffled his screams.

Takoda ran toward the slip. It was very apparent this child didn't know how to swim and needed immediate help. A quick glance at the upper deck confirmed the six adults had no idea what had just happened ten feet below them.

Time was of the essence, and it appeared he was the only chance this little boy had for survival. He slipped out of his loafers, tore off his suit jacket, loosened and tossed his tie. He pushed off the edge of the aluminum walkway with the ease of an Olympic driver. He surfaced thirty feet later, within arms-reach of the drowning boy, or so he calculated. Takoda looked around at the still water. The boy was nowhere in sight! Effortlessly, he upended his body and dove headfirst into the unknown depths. A narrow ray of sunlight squeezed

18

between the walkway and the yacht, illuminating a limp shadow descending in the murky bay. After a dozen powerful kicks, the weightless body was in his arms. As he broke through the surface, he bellowed for help.

Immediately, heads turned, and the chatter started. "Who's that man, and what's he doing to that kid?" "Where are his parents?" "Why didn't he have a life jacket on?" They left the comfort of their floating sanctuaries and made their way toward the water.

A small trolling boat with an elderly gentleman, probably returning from a leisurely morning of fishing, came to their rescue. The old fellow cut the motor as he came up beside them. Takoda instructed him to put his hands under the boy's armpits and pull him up into the boat as he pushed from below. Within a minute, Takoda had hauled himself into the tiny vessel. The old man appeared to be stunned.

"What are you waiting for? Start the engine!"

The man bowed his head and crossed his chest.

"I'm afraid it's too late. He's gone."

Takoda refused to believe his efforts had been in vain and started CPR on the lifeless child. All eyes were on the trio as the small vessel made its way dockside.

When Takoda stepped onto the now-crowded pier with the motionless child in his arms, he was thankful to hear screaming sirens getting close. He laid the boy gently on the aluminum boards and started compressions again. Suddenly, he felt someone brutally pull back on his shoulder and shove him aside. A man in a Hawaiian shirt and pressed golf-length shorts screamed a racial slur in his face and told him to get his hands off his child.

Takoda recognized his assailant. He'd been on the upper deck above the neglected boy's boat launch. It was apparent by the abusive tone and referral to his native heritage that this man did not appreciate that Takoda was trying to save his son's life. He saw only his skin color, not the man, or his efforts.

The father lifted his son's head. The boy convulsed, spewing water all over his father's canvas shoes. He was alive! Sighs of relief, cheers, and applause erupted from the bystanders. The ambulance attendants stepped in and ran a series of tests on the spot. They found no reason to take the little guy to hospital, thanks to his quick retrieval from the water. They did, however, recommend bed rest and constant supervision for the next twenty-four hours.

No one noticed Takoda, soaking-wet, retrieving his discarded clothes and now on his way to the parking lot.

Sitting in his car, the adrenaline rush was subsiding, but anger still vibrated inside him. He thanked God the boy was okay. It was the careless parenting and then the physical and verbal abuse toward him from the father that infuriated him. As a Sioux Native American, this was not the first nor would it be the last racial slur and prejudice he would be confronted with. For the most part, he chalked it up to ignorance and lack of education. He tried not to take it personally but with dignity, grace, and a smile. This tactic usually made the opponents scratch their heads in bewilderment and walk away.

Hard tapping of knuckles on the car window made Takoda jump in his seat. On the other side of the door, a man and woman smiled and motioned for him to put the window down. Before it was completely open, a hand extended inside the car, offering a congratulatory shake. The hand belonged to a jovial, older fellow, who was accompanied by an equally jolly, older woman, presumably his wife. Both sported jack-o-lantern grins. They told Takoda his selfless act had not gone unnoticed. With a pointing finger, the round-faced man told him he took a video of the whole thing from right over there. Takoda smiled at the two seniors and their excitement.

"Look here!" Mr. Smiley Face said, passing his cell phone in the car window. "It was my first time making a video, so it's a bit shaky."

Mrs. Smiley Face pointed in from behind her husband. "That's you! Saving that little boy. You're a hero! That father is nothing but an ungrateful jerk. You deserve a medal, sir!"

Takoda watched himself taking charge of the situation, then handed the phone back through the window. He thanked the couple for their kind words. He could still see them, smiling and waving goodbye, in the rear-view mirror as he drove away.

Much to his dismay, the video went viral, and people everywhere were talking about the "big Indian" that saved a little boy from drowning. Because of the power of the internet, it didn't take long for the media to locate him.

In the lobby of his apartment, he patiently tolerated the media's badgering, unwanted praise, and recognition for what seemed like an hour. He politely excused himself and left the building through the back door. After a strenuous hourlong jog, he was hopeful the reporters had left.

As he approached his apartment, he heard the telephone ringing. He unlocked the door and grabbed the handset on the foyer table. It was Jeneva. He had turned off the ringer on his cell phone at lunch, and with all the excitement since then, he hadn't noticed she'd been calling.

"Dad, I've been trying to reach you for an hour. Turn on the TV to the local news."

Flopping into his recliner, he clicked the TV on. The commentator narrated as a video showed what had happened at the pier. Apparently, several people had used their phones to capture his heroic deed. The reporter said the videos had gone viral within minutes of their postings. Every station in their syndicate was flooded with emails and phone calls. All of them commended the Good Samaritan and stated how appalled they were with the behavior of the father.

"OMG, Dad! You're a Hero! Thank goodness you were there! An experience like that could haunt a child the rest of his life. How could his parents be so neglectful of their son and disrespectful to you?"

Takoda sighed. "The important thing is the little guy is okay. He's young. Hopefully, he'll forget all about it. With any luck, the parents will at least put a life jacket on him from now on."

"You're my hero too, Dad!"

Once again, they said their goodbyes.

Chapter 4

J eneva Yassi

Jeneva lay down on the bed, reflecting on the many experiences she'd shared with her father over the years. How different they were, compared to the ones she suspected that neglected little boy had to look forward to.

Because of her upbringing, Jeneva understood her father's reaction to the attention the rescue was getting. It was about the well-being of others and the self-satisfaction one gets from helping others, not the expectation of gratitude. Ever since she was old enough, she and her dad had offered their services at food banks, soup kitchens, hospitals, and charitable events around the world. It was second nature for Jeneva to be aware of the not always obvious, inherent needs of others.

As a small child, she had accompanied her father to work at the Smithsonian. It was like going to school. While wandering through all the museums day after day, she'd developed the ability to remember everything she read. Little Jeneva was a sponge, soaking everything in and bringing all her questions back to her dad, who gave her answers in a way she was able to comprehend. When she was old enough to understand, her father gave her advice on life. One of his favorite quotations was 'Always be open to unexpected opportunities because sometimes, the journey is more important than the destination.' She liked that one and used it as an excuse to travel to exotic places.

Takoda had been privileged to attend the best schools and felt it important to afford his daughter the same opportunity. There was no doubt in his mind that Jeneva would excel at anything she put her mind to, and his money would be well spent. To broaden her knowledge and reinforce her interests, they'd traveled to several countries:

Spain, Poland, Italy, France, Germany, Britain, Scotland, and Ireland, exposing her to various lifestyles and cultures.

While in England, they boarded one of the thousand vessels in the flotilla being led down the Thames by the Queen's Royal Barge, *Gloriana*, during the celebration of Queen Elizabeth II's Diamond Jubilee. They watched and waved at the Royal family as they were ushered by on the *MV Spirit of Chartwell*. That was a trip she would never forget. She still had the plastic souvenir crown her dad bought her.

It was Jeneva's passion for travel and her concern for the well-being of people in distress that drew her to join Global Volunteers when she was twenty.

Haiti and the Dominican Republic were hit by an earthquake of such enormity that help from all available international aid organizations was needed. They coordinated the distribution of food and water to thousands of the homeless, many of whom were forced to live in urban makeshift cities constructed from found materials and donated tarps. The Global Volunteers, along with many other Good Samaritans, assisted with the adoptions and transport of parentless children to the United States and Canada. Jeneva had gone not once, but twice, to support the reconstruction after the catastrophic event.

Through volunteering with the Big Brothers Big Sisters organization, she hoped to inspire positivity in the lives of girls just like her, who also grew up without a mother to love and guide them.

School had been a breeze for quick-learning Jeneva. In most classes, she was bored to tears, so she took it upon herself to become an unofficial TA for her struggling classmates. She completed high school on the principal's honor role, was voted valedictorian, and given several awards for her services in the classroom and some off-campus charitable activities. Most of her continuing education was completed in Europe. She received her PhD from the University of Cambridge in England with a doctorate in quantum physics.

During her studies at Cambridge, she sat in on some of Stephen Hawking's study halls. She'd been intrigued with his description of the particle accelerator machines being the closest thing we have to time machines. At the time, she had little interest in time machines, other than the possibility of a connection to discovering a new energy source. Years later, her ambitions turned to finding a clean energy source that would be available worldwide. That's when she went to work with the European Council for Nuclear Research at the CERN Control Centre near Geneva, Switzerland.

The general population probably thinks these accelerators are quite rare or even fictitious, but there are actually forty-two thousand of them in existence. The machines have been used for a vast array of purposes, everything from tumor-destroying beams to fight cancer, better diapers, shrink wrap, and even more efficient fuel-injection systems for cars. These opportunities are endless; or, in science terms, infinite. She was grateful for the advantages she'd been given and what she'd accomplished because of them.

Jeneva glanced at the clock. She still had time to do some research before heading to Maddy's birthday party. Knowing her appetite for technology often distracted her for hours, she decided to have a quick shower and get dressed before delving into her files. After drying off, she dropped the towel and reached in the closet, throwing several possibilities on the bed. She decided on a floral-patterned sundress. As she stood looking in the full-length mirror at her shapely figure, she rolled her long black hair in a knot and attached the hairpin her mother used to wear. Satisfied that her open cleavage was just enough to encourage a second glance from Maddy's Dad, Brian, Jeneva pulled a file out of her beaded purse and opened it on the small hotel desktop.

The work she was presently doing seemed mundane and boring. She longed to find the key to helping preserve the world's resources, possibly in the form of a new, not yet discovered energy source. It needed to be something clean, inexpensive, and non-invasive to the environment. Optimistically, she hoped if she was patient, the answer would come to her. She closed the file and glanced at the symbols on the bracelet, a hummingbird, turquoise with gold flecks, and a sun and moon, side by side.

"Do you really hold the answer to my destiny?"

The clasp released, and the bracelet fell in her lap.

Chapter 5

Madison Cartwright

Madison's father hastily ushered his crying daughter out of the hospital room. At seven years old, she'd just said good-bye to her mom. Exhausted from months of chemo and radiation, breast cancer took Madison's mother's life that day. The little girl hadn't just lost her mom, she'd lost her best friend. They'd been inseparable. They went shopping together, took long walks to the park, and played on the swings. After cuddling under a blanket watching Saturday morning cartoons, they would sing songs while baking cookies.

Madison's lip quivered as she tipped her blond head and blue eyes up at him. "Daddy. Do you like donuts?" She wiped her dripping nose on her sleeve.

"Not really, why do you want to know that?"

"I can't tell you. It's Mommy's and my secret!"

"Okay, but if you change your mind, I'm sure Mommy wouldn't be upset if you told me." She was likely thinking about the Krispy Kreme tradition he knew she and her mom had on their birthdays where they "secretly" indulged in Krispy Kreme donuts and chocolate milkshakes.

Madison clung to his side while they sat speechless in the Washington DC hospital cancer ward. Life would be so different now with Madison's mom missing from all their family traditions. Madison's favorite was the Christmas toy drive. He played Santa, and she handed out gifts to the kids, dressed as an elf. The gift wrapping had been her mother's job. She had the knack for making each present, large or small, look special with colorful ribbons and bows.

Madison tugged on her dad's sleeve. "Daddy, who's going to wrap the presents for the kids?" She was thinking about the same things he was. He sensed sincere concern in her voice.

"I don't know, sweetheart. We'll find somebody. Don't you worry about it."

It appeared his little girl was over the initial shock of losing her mom, and he thought it a good time to remove her from the cancer ward.

On their way to the car, Madison divulged her secret to her father. They stopped for donuts and milkshakes on their way home.

AFTER THE PASSING OF her mother, Madison, who'd always known her place, used her manners, and given the utmost respect to her elders, became a holy terror. At home, she refused to do any chores or adhere to the rules her father put in place. As for school, her teacher began calling home with concerns. Madison wasn't completing her homework, and she refused to work with anyone on classroom assignments. One day, she told her teacher to, "Piss off and leave me alone." This was a shocking turn of events for everyone who knew this well-behaved little girl prior to her mother's passing. Madison was at the top of her class, a straight-A student, and liked by all her teachers and peers. Having traveled working charity events with her parents and being an avid reader, she'd seemed much older and wiser than her years. This young girl, who'd shown so much promise, was now on a destructive path and needed guidance. She needed someone to talk to who understood what she was going through. Someone who could put her back on the straight and narrow.

Brian feared her heart was broken beyond repair and that she'd never be happy again. He suspected she was dealing with the situation the only way she thought she could, by putting on a stubborn and fearless facade. Rather than accepting comfort from others, she pushed everyone away, trying to prove she was okay and didn't need anyone. All they wanted to do was talk about her feelings, and he suspected she didn't want to talk; at least not to them. It hurt too much. The loss of her mother had devastated her, and she was struggling to forgive her for leaving her.

The little girl's whole persona changed the day Jeneva Yassi came into her life through Big Brothers Big Sisters. This young woman understood the pain and the loneliness because she too had lost her mother. This connection would bring them together for a long, long time.

IT HAD BEEN OVER A year since Jeneva visited Washington DC. It'd been exciting to get all dressed up in formal attire and accompany her father to the awards dinner last evening. She was so proud of him. Tonight, would be the opposite. Tonight, would be very informal. She was on her way to visit her Little Sister, Maddy, who was celebrating her sixteenth birthday. It would only be the three of them, she, Maddy, and Brian. They'd eat mac and cheese with wieners, chocolate cake, and bubble gum ice cream, Maddy's habitual birthday dinner. When Maddy called with the invitation, she told Jeneva there was a sleepover planned for the weekend and she could stay if she wanted. Tactfully, she'd declined, having decided to attend the Symposium. Jeneva smiled when she thought of the squeals of young girls and loud music. It would no doubt send Brian running for cover.

During the drive to the party, Jeneva thought about her and Madison's first meeting. It had been eight years ago to the day. Madison had recently lost her mother to cancer. The Big Sister organization matched them up shortly after Jeneva turned eighteen.

The heavy front door had opened slowly. Inside, Jeneva saw a teary-eyed little girl sniffling. She smiled the biggest smile she could muster.

"Hi, Madison, I'm Jeneva. I'm so happy to finally meet you."

"Hi." A shy voice spoke to the floor.

Jeneva tried to get her to look up by asking, "What a pretty dress! Did you pick it out yourself?"

The little girl was wearing a pastel-yellow dress with matching ribbons tied in her curly blond pigtails.

There was no response, just a sniff.

"What do you say we go find your dad?"

Madison turned her head and bellowed toward the next room to ensure her father heard her.

"No way! I'm mad at him! I'm never speaking to him as long as I live. I hate him!"

Jeneva was shocked at the sudden change in the demeanor of the shy little girl.

"*Hate* is a pretty strong word. Why are you so mad at him?"

Accompanied with intermittent bouts of crying, she told her about the puppy her dad wouldn't allow her to have. Jeneva suggested that she couldn't stay mad at her dad and that he probably had good reasons for making her wait a couple years before taking on such a big responsibility. This infuriated Madison even more.

She raised her head, crossed her arms in front of her, and looked up at Jeneva with a piercing glare. "I knew you'd take his side. I'm so mad I could spit!" She abruptly turned her back on her new Big Sister.

Jeneva caught a glimpse of Madison's dad hiding in the other room. She assumed he was afraid his presence could make things worse after his daughter's outburst. It appeared it was up to her to calm the angry child.

She knelt to the little girl's eye level and held out a colorful birthday bag overflowing with pink tissue paper.

"Happy birthday, Madison. Would you like to open your present?"

Madison turned her head slightly to look at the package, but the rest of her stood steadfast, arms still crossed, lips still pouting.

"No! I'm too mad." She snapped her head back around.

Jeneva was perplexed, never having dealt with such attitude from a child.

"Well then, Miss Maddy . . ." Jeneva paused, waiting for a reaction. To her surprise, none came. "I guess I'll take it to the children's ward at the hospital and see if anyone there wants it."

The little girl turned around and pointed an accusing finger at Jeneva. "My name's Madison, not Maddy, and I hate hospitals!"

"Oh, why's that?"

"That's where my mommy died!" Her anger was coupled with sadness now.

Jeneva saw her briskly wipe away a tear. *This is turning into a disaster. Why on earth did I mention the hospital?* She stood up and quickly changed the subject.

"I have an idea, Maddy!" There was no rebuttal to the new nickname this time. "Let's make a list of all the things we can do together until your dad changes his mind and lets you get a puppy."

The birthday girl didn't say anything. She just stared at Jeneva with a suspicious look.

"We can do anything you want."

"Anything?" Her eyes widened, and a devilish grin appeared on her lips.

"I should have said, anything that your dad says is okay."

"Can we go to Krispy Kreme? I get a free donut today cause it's my birthday! Mom used to take me, right Dad?"

Brian was making his way into the room with a congratulatory smile directed Jeneva.

"Yes, she did, sweetie. What do you say we go eat supper, and then you can go for your birthday donut? Maybe I'll come too, if that's all right with you?"

"Really, Daddy?" But you don't like donuts!"

"Well, this is a special occasion. My little girl only turns eight once."

"Can I open my presents now?" She looked hopefully at Jeneva, then at her dad.

"Yes, you can," they both agreed in unison.

Jeneva's fingers were crossed behind her back. Buried beneath the tissue paper, there was a life-size toy puppy that walked and barked when you pinched the pooch's ear. This could go one of two ways; it would either be the perfect compromise, or all hell would break loose, and the mad face and tears would be back. The birthday fairy must have sprinkled moondust in the air because Maddy was ecstatic. She hugged the fluffy cocker spaniel to her chest.

"Look, Daddy! I have a puppy!" She squealed with glee.

Then she gave her Big Sister the biggest hug Jeneva had ever had from anyone. That day, a friendship was born between the two motherless girls that would last a lifetime. As the party of three sat down to eat mac and cheese with wieners, the little girl told her dad that she had a new name.

"It's *Maddy*. Jeneva gave it to me. Can I keep it?" Jeneva and Maddy both stared at him in anticipation.

"If you like it, I like it." Brian gave Jeneva a winning look of approval.

Later that evening, while Maddy was getting ready for bed, Brian expressed his gratitude for extinguishing the fire she'd walked into.

"I can't thank you enough. You're an angel." He gave her a father-ly hug. Jeneva started to blush and backed away just as Maddy came bounding down the stairs.

For the next eight years, Jeneva and Maddy had long talks on the phone regularly. Jeneva would tell her about all the places she went with her dad and the experiences with different charities she was working with. Maddy would talk about all the fun she was having helping her dad with his charity events through the firehall and at the hospital. The young girl also proudly reported that her grades were improving. Every Christmas, Jeneva would be there to wrap presents for their firehall Charity Christmas Party.

Chapter 6

Maddy's 16th Birthday

Jeneva made a quick stop at the grocery store to pick up a birthday card; which she signed from Takoda as promised; along with a chocolate cake and bubble gum ice cream. Pulling into the driveway in the suburban neighborhood, Jeneva thought she could picture herself living in the quaint bungalow. Lush flower baskets decorated the front steps of a manicured yard corralled by a white picket fence. She wondered whether, now that she was well into adulthood, Brian still considered her just his daughter's Big Sister.

At twenty-eight, Jeneva had no romantic prospects in site. She did find Brian very handsome and admired his charitable acts of kindness, and he'd done a commendable job raising Maddy by himself. So far, he'd been a perfect gentleman, and she respected him for that. He was thirty-four, which in her opinion, made him a probable candidate. After all, she already had a fabulous relationship with his daughter. It seemed like a natural progression.

"You're finally here!" Maddy raced full speed toward her. Even though she was eight years older than the day they'd met, her appearance hadn't changed much. She was a mere five feet tall, with long blond hair and a slender physique. They embraced, then walked arm in arm into the house. They went into the kitchen, placed the cake on the already-set table, and put the ice cream in the freezer.

As Brian's eyes met Jeneva's, she thought she saw something there, or maybe it was just wishful thinking. He came around the counter with open arms.

"Welcome back, Jeneva! We've missed you."

She thought she saw an unmistakable twinkle in his baby blues.

As she returned his embrace, she felt dizzy. Her legs turned to noodles, and she collapsed in his masculine arms.

"Are you all right?" The twinkle in his eyes changed into a look of concern.

"It's nothing. Probably just the heat." She shrugged it off.

With one arm wrapped around her bare back, he supported her limp body as they headed to the living room. Maddy walked on the other side with her arms outstretched, ready to help if need be. Jeneva, embarrassed, was finding it hard to compose herself and hide the schoolgirl infatuation that had overcome her. Brian insisted she relax in his recliner until dinner was ready. When he was convinced, she was comfortable, he instructed Maddy to keep an eye on her. He left the room and returned with a glass of water.

"Thank you. I'm okay." Blushing, she gave them both a big reassuring smile.

"Let's get this party started."

Brian went to the kitchen and came back with a bottle of ginger ale and three glasses. He called it pretend champagne.

They clinked their glasses in midair, toasting to Maddy's sixteenth birthday.

"Mazel Tov!"

Brian told Maddy that she could go to her bedroom and look for her present, if she wanted to, which of course she did posthaste.

He told Jeneva he'd bought her a flat-screen TV for her bedroom, selfishly hoping to avoid watching *The Voice* and *Dancing with the Stars*, two of Maddy's favorite shows. The opportunity to install it without her knowing had presented itself that morning. She'd left early to volunteer in the children's ward at a nearby hospital.

It was Jeneva who encouraged Maddy to share her story of losing her mom with other kids. Maddy was able to comfort them by talking about her emotional struggles and how she dealt with them. This was an enormous undertaking in the beginning. In a short time, however, it proved to be exactly what Maddy needed to pull her out of the downward spiral she'd been in and back to her happy, diligent, well-behaved self.

A glass-shattering scream echoed through the house.

"Guess she found it."

Brian sat in a matching armchair next to Jeneva, where he watched her intently. Was he looking for any signs of recurring dizziness, or was he noticing she was now an adult?

A look of disbelief still lingered on Maddy's face when she came running into the room. She plunked down on her father's lap and gave him a hug that would rival a boa constrictor's spiral squeeze.

"I can't believe you got me a TV! I love you, Dad!" Her eyes were gleaming with adoration.

He cupped her chin in his hand and looked proudly into her smiling eyes. "I love you too, sweetheart! I'm so proud of you for getting those exceptional grades, and all the volunteering you've been doing is very admirable. I thought you deserved something special this year." He pulled her close, and she put another choke hold on his neck.

Maddy turned her head and gave Jeneva a wink and an expectant smile. Jeneva took an envelope out of her purse and handed it to Maddy.

"It's from Takoda. He sends his best wishes."

She opened it, read the verse, and then waved the bill in the air and told her to thank him for the generous gift.

She batted her eyes and flashed her a big toothy grin. "Got anything else hidden in that big purse of yours?"

"Maybe. Have you really been buckling down at school and helping around the house?"

"Yes! I sure have. Just ask him." She looked at her father, who gave a nod.

"I even got an A+ in English last semester. Want me to prove it?"

Jeneva told her that she didn't need to right then, but she was interested in looking at her report card later.

"Here you go. Happy birthday, Maddy." Jeneva pulled a small package out of her purse.

The wrapping was hastily ripped off. No scream this time, just a gasp, as she leaped off her father's lap and into Jeneva's. She almost squeezed the breath out of her with a big hug and then planted a kiss on her cheek.

"Thank you! Thank you! Thank you! I can't believe you got me my own cell phone. I love it! Can you help me put your number and dad's number in it?"

"I'm sure she will, but we better eat first before everything's dry as dust." Brian offered Jeneva his hand.

The dialogue during dinner was dominated by the birthday girl's chatter about how much she loved her gifts. She proudly told Jeneva that she and her father baked six dozen cookies for tomorrow's charity bake sale down at the firehall.

"It was my idea to donate the money to the SPCA to help with the cost of a much-needed addition they were planning to build."

She wanted to know whether Jeneva could teach her to drive. Should she change her hairstyle now that she was sixteen? Where should she apply for a part-time job? When were they going to have a spa day together? Everything a young girl would ask her mother, Maddy was asking Jeneva.

Their initial meeting eight years ago had evolved into a mother-daughter type relationship. Even though they didn't see each other a lot, both knew what the other was up to through the magic of Facebook Messenger and long phone calls. It broke Jeneva's heart every time she left Maddy behind. This time would be even harder. It was going to be more than a year before she could get back to visit them, and she'd decided not to mention anything until the party was over.

During the meal, Brian had given Jeneva what she thought were a little more than friendly glances. She was even more hopeful after the ceremonial blowing out of the candles and eating of cake. He told Maddy to take the PVR up to her room and program in her shows while they cleared the table and loaded the dishwasher. While she was gone, their conversation centered mostly around the birthday girl and how much she had changed since Jeneva came into her life.

"I can't thank you enough for all you've done with Maddy. It's hard to believe it was eight years ago that you knocked on our door and introduced yourself as her Big Sister."

"I know. It seems like only yesterday. I don't see a puppy, so I guess she got over that?"

Brian laughed. "I couldn't have done it without your positive influence. You have been a wonderful role model, and she really listens to you. You've a saint." He set a small box in the palm of her hand.

"What's this?" Jeneva gave him a confused look.

"Just a little thank-you, from me to you."

She opened the box to see a small broach inside. The words, "Sainte Therese, Patron of Big Sisters" encircled a robed woman.

"It's lovely. Thank you." Jeneva gave him her biggest smile.

"I hope the religious connotation doesn't offend you. It's the Catholic coming out of me. It just seemed so appropriate."

"Not at all. I appreciate the sentiment. I'll pin it on my purse, so it goes everywhere with me." She timidly gave him a kiss on the cheek.

He took advantage of her closeness and gently pulled her into the clutches of his muscular arms. He gave her a quick assessing gaze to which she answered with a blink of her eyes, then he kissed her zealously.

When they realized Maddy was standing in the doorway, they separated. Both with guilty looks on their faces.

"Here's my report card." She handed it to Jeneva, giving her an approving smile.

After a thorough examination, Jeneva praised her for such wonderful marks and encouraged her to keep up the good work.

Before the tearful goodbyes, they entered Brian's and Jeneva's numbers into the new phone as well as personal ringtones.

It was almost eleven, and Jeneva was exhausted. It had been a long day. Her head was spinning with her hopeful thoughts of Brian and how much she was going to miss them both. If only she didn't have to work halfway across the world. She couldn't help wondering whether Brian would still be interested in her when she came back to Washington in a year, maybe two?

Chapter 7

Dexter Applebaum

It was six o'clock in the morning when Dexter Applebaum's plane touched down at Reagan Washington National Airport in Arlington, Virginia. He'd taken the red eye from Quito, Ecuador, in hopes of undisturbed serenity while he put the final touches on his symposium presentation.

Twenty minutes later, he was seated in the back of a town car on his way to his hotel. He planned to get a few hours rest before heading to a symposium at the Walter E. Washington Convention Center, where he was a keynote speaker.

He was taking a short break from his research, which he rarely afforded himself. Currently, he was researching and recording data on the solar physics of Sun-Earth interactions for the world scientific community at the Quito Astronomical Observatory.

Dexter was a man of preciseness. As far as he was concerned, there was a reason for everything, and he saw no reason to waste time milling around some rotating baggage dispenser when a well-organized carry-on would expedite one's airport exit. His check-in at the hotel was just as efficient, thanks to his post-trip internet planning.

At the hotel entrance, a uniformed fellow waited with his white glove on the gold-plated door handle.

"Good morning, sir!"

"Good morning to you, my good man."

Entering the hotel, Dexter saw a group of ladies standing in the lobby. They all turned their heads to ogle him making his way to the reception desk. His dark bushy eyebrows and dreamy bedroom eyes, along with the barber trimmed four-day-old whiskers, were beguiling to women. Their girlish whispers were not surprising; he was accustomed to the adoration of the opposite sex.

With a suave tip of his panama chapeau, he wished them, *"Good morning, ladies."* Which caused a response of breathy sighs and snickers.

He attributed his good looks to his mixed Inca lineage. Dexter's mother was predominately of Inca heritage, and his father was the grandson of a German immigrant to Ecuador.

His great-grandfather, Abraham, was originally from Germany but came to Ecuador to hunt Nazis after the Second World War. Before the war, he'd been a naturalist, and he fell in love with the biodiversity and unfeigned beauty of Ecuador and decided to make it his home.

His father Jacob was given an envelope at the reading of his father's will. Inside was a gold chain with a forget-me-not flower, encased in an amber pendant. Dexter's dad bestowed it on him one afternoon while they were relaxing on the lawn of their estate, sipping cognac. The family heirloom had been passed down to each generation. Whenever he traveled, Dexter wore it for good luck.

Dexter was born and raised in Ecuador and studied at the National Polytechnic School in Quito. He then took his postgraduate doctorate in astronomy, specializing in magnetic portals at Howard University in Washington DC. His family was very well off, affording him the opportunity to study abroad. Being a confident yet quiet individual, he sometimes struggled to interact with others. If you didn't speak with knowledge and understanding, he didn't have the time of day for you. Nor, if you showed signs of narcissism, were you worthy of his friendship. He didn't consider himself a loner, just someone who chose his friends with much scrutiny.

At the age of twenty-eight, Dexter's work took priority. Presently, he was at the height of his career and loving it. He didn't have time or interest in a romantic relationship, not to mention the commitment that went along with it. With his good looks and charismatic personality, he fancied himself somewhat of a ladies' man. If he so desired, he had no trouble finding a willing female companion to accompany him to social events or his bedroom.

Dexter possessed an inquisitive nature and was continuously thinking and challenging the norms. He was very work focused, almost to a fault. All of which sometimes caused him to come off as a cold person in the business world. Although lacking a bit in the sense-of-humor department, he was a kind, genuine, honest, and charitable-minded guy.

Settling into his temporary accommodations, he removed the neatly ironed clothes from his carry-on and hung them fastidiously in the closet. His CK boxers and socks were strategically placed in the top drawer of the bureau. He undressed, rolled his travel clothes, and placed them back in the suitcase which he slipped out of sight, under the bed. By then, the effects of the long flight had caught up with him, so he crawled into the king-size bed, naked, and fell asleep immediately.

The vibration of his Fitbit alarm summoned him out of his slumber. He sat up on the side of the bed and called room service for the speedy delivery of a sandwich and salad. While he waited, he took a quick shower, dried off, splashed on his favorite cologne by Hugo Boss, and put on his golf shirt and Dockers. When he opened the door, the same uniformed gentleman who'd opened the front door upon his arrival stood there. It appeared he was doing double duty today. The waiter/doorman thanked him for the generous tip and bid him a nice day. Dexter pulled out his notes and gave them one last perusal while he ate.

At the entrance of the hotel, Dexter stood anxiously waiting for a taxi. A tall, dark-skinned beauty in high heels, wearing a fitted flowery sundress and a bouncy wide-brimmed hat that concealed her face, jumped in front of him. Her large, beaded handbag slapped him in the groin when she pulled open the rear door.

She didn't notice Dexter's shocked expression.

"Sorry, hon. I'm running late!"

She jumped in, ordered the driver to, "Pin it!" then slammed the door. The driver followed the order and the taxi sped away.

Dexter stood there dumbfounded, shaking his head. "What the hell just happened?"

The doorman observed the whole thing and approached Dexter. "Taxi, sir?" He hid a snicker behind his gloved hand.

Chapter 8

The Symposium
    At the entrance to the Walter E. Washington Convention Center, a large billboard read:

Today We Welcome:

Alex Belle, Iridologist and Mechanical Engineer, Inventor of Visualization Technology

Dexter Applebaum, Astronomer, Specialty: Magnetic Portals Research

Amir Whitelaw, Archaeologist, specializing in ancient artifacts and pyramids

Jeneva sat on the edge of her seat while the first speaker, Alex Belle, explained how someone's visual thoughts could be read electronically and displayed on a monitor. Alex asked for a volunteer to come up so he could demonstrate the machine. There was no shortage of willing candidates, but in an effort to ward off any skepticism that the demonstration might be staged, Alex asked the moderator to pick the volunteer. A geeky fiftyish gentleman from row two climbed up onto the stage. Alex brought out a razor and joked that the first step required the shaving of the man's head. The audience laughed hysterically as the frightened man made a sudden attempt to exit the stage before realizing it was a joke. Alex attached the electrodes to various points on the man's head. He advised the observers that this was the prototype of the machine, and the final version would be considerably more refined. He told the man to close his eyes and visualize a simple, familiar image. All eyes were on the screen, which remained blank for about thirty seconds until, suddenly, a horse appeared on it. Alex paused the screen and asked the man to keep his eyes closed and tell everyone what he was thinking about.

"Midnight, my horse."

Alex said he could open his eyes. Mouth open and eyes wide, the shocked man nodded his head in disbelief. The audience stood and applauded enthusiastically.

The next speaker, Dexter Applebaum, strutted across the stage as if he owned the place, positioning himself behind the podium. With an air of confidence, he gave his audience the once-over, his eyes landing abruptly on Jeneva. He blinked. The woman who'd stole his cab, was here, sitting front and center. Her hand went to her mouth, concealing an embarrassed snicker. Dexter gave her a look of disdain and returned to his task at hand, seemingly back in full control of his thoughts.

Jeneva listened as Dexter explained how he'd made an accidental discovery during an experiment dealing with magnetic portals. He drew a comparison to the discovery of penicillin in 1928 when Sir Alexander Fleming returned from a holiday and found an obscure mold growing in a petri dish where he was cultivating staphylococcus. Fleming noticed that a short area around the mold, the agar nutrient, was free of bacteria.

Dexter told them the observation heralded the greatest discovery in the thousand-year history of medical science. And because Fleming had been concentrating on cultivating the staph bacteria, it was only by chance, along with his broad experience in bacteriology, that he recognized this as something more important than what he'd set out to find.

Dexter told the audience he too had been concentrating on the earth's magnetic fields when something totally unrelated to that experiment led him to the connection with the sun's magnetic fields and the flux transfer. He also intrigued the audience with details on hidden portals in the vicinity of Earth that were now being confirmed by NASA.

In closing, he shared what he called words of wisdom. "We should accept that the final discovery may or may not be everything we hoped for. Therefore, always take your time and observe the small discoveries that may happen by accident throughout our life's journey. For those could end up being more important than your original goal."

Jeneva was making notes, pondering the concept of magnetic portals, and wondering whether this was something she could use in her research of the particle accelerators. She was afraid Dexter Applebaum wouldn't give her the time of day after their earlier encounter outside the hotel. His so-called words of wisdom intrigued her as well. Definitely something her father might say.

The final speaker made his way center stage. He introduced himself as Amir Whitelaw, an archaeologist who recently participated in an excavation in Java, Indonesia. He reported that if this pyramid-shaped mound near Cianjur, West Java, was confirmed to be a twenty-thousand-year-old pyramid, it would be the oldest on earth. Pointing to the projected pictures on a large overhead screen, the slender man discussed the similarities and differences of pyramids around the world with their suspected initial construction dates and associated locations. With proud enthusiasm, he announced that his next excavation was going to be in his native country of Ecuador, at the Hummingbird Pyramid.

This subject brought back memories of visiting Egypt with her father, where they toured the Pyramid of Djoser and the Giza Pyramid Complex. Although she recognized them as structural phenomena, her interest ended there. She let her mind wander back to her own research and the possibility of magnetic connections, blocking out the remainder of the speaker's dissertation.

After the applause subsided, Jeneva made her way to the exit.

"Holy crap on a cracker!" she said under her breath.

Dexter was waiting for her at the exit, with daggers shooting from his eyes, straight toward her. She had mixed feelings about running head-on into this tall, dark, and handsome man. On one hand, she did find his talk very interesting and thought he might have some insight to offer her. On the other hand, she was mortified that he was the guy she'd pilfered the taxi from a few hours earlier. From the look he was giving her, he no doubt would have a few choice words for her. There seemed to be no escaping the inevitable. Surprisingly, she saw his demeanor change, and a warm smile replaced his pursed lips as she got closer.

"I don't think we have been formally introduced. I'm Dexter Applebaum, and who, pray tell, are you?" His seductive blue eyes leered at her like a sly fox eyeing his prey.

Jeneva detected a hint of sarcasm in his voice as he handed her his business card. She slipped the card in her sweater pocket, told him her name, and extended her hand, apologizing for her earlier behavior. He assured her all was forgiven. Would she join him and the other speakers for a drink?

He led her into a dimly lit room that smelled of stale cigars and old wood. She followed him over to a table occupied by Alex Belle and Amir Whitelaw and another gentleman sitting in the shadows. After their congratulatory pats on their backs for well-done presentations, they turned their attention to Jeneva, and she told them about her and Dexter's incident at the hotel. They all enjoyed a good laugh. Jeneva was thankful when Alex took control of the conversation, distracting the other gentlemen's focus from her.

Alex started by introducing the man in the shadows as Nelson Jones, partner and cofounder of the visualization technology they were working on. Nelson shook everyone's hand but stayed relatively quiet. It was apparent he was uncomfortable in the limelight, unlike his partner, Alex, who obviously thrived on attention. The phantom shadows masked Nelson's face, making it difficult for anyone to see him at first. Jeneva was certain his attempt to be inconspicuous probably came from his facial disfigurement. Earlier, he stood behind a curtain on the sideline of the stage during the symposium, out of the crowd's view. In an attempt to bring him into the conversation, she directed a question to him regarding the frequency of the electrodes.

Timidly, he answered her question. Her interest seemed sincere, and he started to open up to her, explaining the process they went through and the battles they lost and won to bring their invention from a dream to a reality. He seemed to find it easy to talk to Jeneva, even pulling his chair forward so they wouldn't have to raise their voices. This put him in full view of everyone in the room.

When Nelson excused himself to go to the men's room, Jeneva listened in on Alex and Dexter's conversation. They were comparing their ideas about magnetic fields and their effects on the earth.

She felt her cell phone vibrate, and Maddy's face appeared.

Chapter 9

Thank You for Your Service

Jeneva excused herself and headed to the hall.

"Hi, sweetie!"

"Jeneva, my name is Patricia, I'm Madison's Aunt. She asked me to call you. I'm afraid I have some bad news." The caller sounded distraught.

The woman explained that while combatting a home fire, her brother, Brian, had entered the house several times, trying to find a child. He'd given the boy the last of his oxygen in an effort to save him, sacrificing himself to extreme smoke inhalation.

Jeneva gasped for her own air and crumpled to the floor.

THE CHURCH WAS OVERFLOWING with bereaved people from the community and fifty or more firefighters from neighboring halls. The chief spoke on behalf of the team, commending Brian for his years of service and countless charitable hours at the hall and in the nearby communities. He told the crowd that the commemorative plaque, which he held in his hand, was going to hang alongside Brian's picture at the firehall, in honor of his selfless sacrifice.

There was a warm drizzle falling as Brian's sister, Patricia, and her husband, ushered Maddy and their daughter under the crossed ladders at the entrance to the cemetery. The saluting honor guard, in full uniform, stood frozen at attention as the family passed by. The now-orphaned Maddy was dressed in a black tunic dress with a pillbox hat and lace veil covering her bowed, sobbing face. One of the funeral coordinators rushed over and offered them umbrellas.

Jeneva waited for the procession of family and friends to parade under the ladders and take their places before she walked in. She spotted Maddy with her aunt and uncle. Under the circumstances, she was unsure of her place. Should she be with Maddy or leave her alone to be with her family? She watched Patricia, hoping for a sign to come forward and stand at Maddy's side. So far, there was no recognition of her whatsoever. It occurred to her that Patricia had no idea who she was or how important Maddy was to her or her to Maddy. Jeneva's emotions took over and she made her way over to them. She introduced herself to the couple standing with Maddy.

When Maddy heard Jeneva's voice, she raised her head.

"Where have you been? I've been waiting for you," she whispered.

She took hold of Jeneva's arm and snuggled into her side. After a reading of the firemen's prayer, the bagpipes bellowed "Amazing Grace," which caused the tears to flow like wine in the circle of mourners.

After the service, the parents of the boy who Brian gave his life for approached the chief and handed him a substantial donation for the firehall. The boy himself gave Madison a bouquet of flowers and a hug. There was a reception in the firehall after the burial, where lots of condolences were offered for the thirty-four-year-old firefighter and hero. The wives of the firefighters in Brian's station, made dainty sandwiches and squares that were devoured during shared memories of Brian and his selfless dedication to helping others.

Patricia approached Jeneva and asked her to follow her and Maddy into the chief's office for a private conversation. Maddy took Jeneva's hand as they walked down the hallway, leaving the noisy chatter of the assembly behind them. Patricia closed the door and leaned on the desk, allowing Jeneva and Maddy to sit side by side in front of her in the small, windowless room. She told her about the conversation her and Maddy had on the drive from the cemetery to the firehall.

"By the time my niece finished offering praises to your character and your good influences, I was hard pressed to find any reason I shouldn't allow her to spend the summer with her Big Sister. I understand my brother encouraged this relationship for the past eight years, so I'm not going to take her away from you."

"Thank you, she means a lot to me."

"Maddy will stay with us until the end of the school year, then, maybe, visit you in Switzerland if that's okay with you?"

Jeneva knew she had a lot of work waiting for her when she got back and wasn't sure this was the best time for a visitor, especially one that she knew would demand a lot of her time. Maddy must have seen the hesitation on her face because she piped up and assured her, she wouldn't be any trouble.

"Please, Jeneva, I'll cook, and clean, and run errands for you. Please say I can come! You did say you had a special room all ready for my visits."

Jeneva reluctantly agreed and thanked Patricia for the opportunity to spend time with Maddy. She promised to be in touch once she was settled back home in Switzerland.

Maddy wrapped her arms around her Big Sister. "Thank you for being here today and for letting me come to visit next month.

Jeneva saw a tear roll down Maddy's cheek as they got up.

"I'll miss you," Jeneva said.

"I'll miss you more."

Jeneva left the room and headed out of the firehall to her car. Once she was alone with her thoughts, her own feelings of loss overcame her. She was so worried about Maddy's loss of her father, that she'd supressed her own. The last time she'd seen Brian, she was convinced that a romantic relationship was in the making. She closed her eyes and pretended she was back in the kitchen, being held in his strong arms. She could see his boyish glances from across the dinner table and the nervous guilt when his daughter caught them together in an embrace. What if they'd been honest with each other the night of Maddy's birthday and expressed their feelings toward each other? Would he still be alive today?

Chapter 10

Think What You Like

After having a good night's sleep, Jeneva got up early, packed her suitcase, and snacked on a light breakfast. She was tying her hair up when the concierge rang to tell her that Mr. Yassi and their cab were waiting at the front door.

Takoda opened the taxi door for her. Before entering the yellow cab, she looked around. Was she looking for someone? Dexter perhaps?

In the airport terminal, a few passengers' heads turned when Takoda and Jeneva walked by. They made a striking pair. What onlookers observed was a gray-haired businessman, his arm linked with a beautiful young woman with the body of a runway model wearing an expensive tailored pantsuit. Scandalmongers might think she was a money-hungry dimwit with a sugar daddy trying to relive his youth.

Jeneva could sense the disgust in their disapproving glances. So, with a smug, flirty smile, she winked at one or two of them as she and her dad meandered through the aisles. They found adjoining seats facing the runway, which put their backs to the other passengers. They sat quietly watching the chaotic shuffling of planes on the tarmac.

After a few minutes, Jeneva said, "Did you happen to notice the looks we were getting?"

"I did. It felt like they were watching our every move, passing judgment without even knowing a thing about us. It's frustrating to me that people tend to imagine the worst. I can still feel their eyes burning a hole in the back of my head." He gave it a rub.

She leaned over and put her head on his shoulder.

"I'm gonna miss you, Dad." She gulped back a lump the size of a golf ball.

Takoda reached for his daughter's hand and gave it a squeeze.

"Me too." He planted a kiss on the top of her head.

A voice came over the loudspeaker, announcing that all passengers with small children and priority seating could commence boarding.

"That's me!" She stood up and shouldered her carry-on bags. The two walked toward the departure gate hand in hand.

"Okay, guess this is it." Takoda wrapped his arms around Jeneva. "Take care of yourself, kiddo, and don't forget to call when you get a minute."

"I will. You be careful in Africa." She tightened her arms around his waist.

Tears running down her cheeks, Jeneva turned and walked toward the gangway, giving her dad the backward wave.

TAKODA FOUND A SEAT by his gate and reviewed his flight agenda to Africa. After slipping the boarding passes in the pocket of his suit jacket, he pulled out a manila folder from his briefcase marked 'Nile River Research' from the case. In preparation for his trip to Sudan, he'd printed some notable information to look over before he arrived and took advantage of the time to review it.

Takoda was compelled to revisit Sudan when he heard about a recent discovery of unique rocks where the Blue and White Nile rivers meet to become the Nile River. A procedure using these ancient crystalline rock formations revealed their capability to disinfect polluted water. His years of research convinced him that ancient water-purification methodology could change lives in third world countries.

The thunderous roar of an engine on the runway made Takoda look up. As the big plane rolled forward, he looked out at the skyline. *After years of travel and research, looking for answers to many of the water problems in the world, could the Niles hold the secret I've been looking for?* he wondered.

After he'd boarded and was settled in his seat, he searched for the news on the small TV screen he'd pulled out of his armrest. The morning news was showing a clip from *Saturday Night Live*. Takoda couldn't help himself, and he laughed out loud. Most of the passengers had their earbuds in, watching movies or connected to their cell phones or iPads, and didn't notice his outburst.

One of the flight attendants stopped at his side. "May I offer you a beverage, sir?"

"Thank you, not at the moment. Maybe later." He asked that he not be disturbed while he took a nap. He returned the TV to the armrest, closed his eyes, and faded off to sleep.

When he woke up several hours later, a little boy was staring at him. He was in the line of passengers waiting for the toilet.

"Hey, mister! Are you a real Indian?"

Without hesitating, Takoda replied, "Well, young man, I am, but nowadays we are referred to as *Native Americans*. I'm from the Sioux Nation in North Dakota. Do you know where that is?"

Looking a little embarrassed, the boy shook his head and eagerly continued with another question. "Why do you have such long hair? Mommy makes me cut mine, so I don't look like a girl." He rolled his eyes.

Takoda chuckled. "When I was one year old, my mom cut my hair too. But when I grew up, she told me that the connection the Native Americans have with the earth is relative to the length of their hair. So, the longer your hair, the closer you are to the earth, which is very important to my people."

"You must be really close to the earth, cuz yours is really long."

Takoda asked him if he'd ever heard the term *Mother Earth*.

The youngster pursed his lips and said he hadn't.

"Well, I have respect for Mother Earth just like you have respect for your mother."

"Come on, Cody. It's our turn." The boy's father apologized for the interrogation.

"No worries." Takoda gave the man a reassuring nod.

On his way back to his seat, Cody raised his arm as he passed Takoda. "High-five, Native American?" He said, offering a big grin.

Takoda high-fived the boy and gave him a wink. Hopeful his story had educated him in some small way that would encourage the child to keep asking questions.

Takoda disembarked in Istanbul, Turkey, around seven that evening for his overnight stay. He'd board tomorrow morning at nine for the last leg of his trip to Khartoum.

The suite at the Crowne Plaza Istanbul Florya, presented a magnificent view of the sea. He arrived just in time to watch the breathtaking sunset falling into the ebony waters stretching beyond his balcony. He straightened out his cramping legs as he relaxed in the chaise lounge, closed his eyes, and nodded off under the glow of a dazzling crescent moon.

Takoda was one of those fortunate people who could rest for fifteen minutes and wake up feeling like a million bucks. Before long, he'd changed into his trunks and was off to swim lengths in the pool. After his vigorous workout, he put on the complimentary robe and headed back to his room to shower off the chlorine. He called room service and ordered a cheese and cracker plate to snack on before turning in for the night. A glance at his watch and a quick calculation of the time difference told him it was too late to call Jeneva. She'd be back at work. He made a mental note to call her before boarding in the morning.

Chapter 11

The Explosion
    Jeneva was grateful her flight home was uneventful and served a meal that would hold her till morning. The fridge in her apartment was empty, other than the bagel with cream cheese she'd grabbed before leaving the airport. She intended to eat it on the way to work the next morning. After all the comings and goings in Washington, she was ready to crawl into her own bed for a good sleep, even though it was only seven. She sat on the edge of her bed, kicked off her shoes, stripped down, and checked the voice message on her cell phone. It was from Maddy, letting her know she was settled in at her Aunt Patricia's and would call her again tomorrow to discuss her upcoming visit. Jeneva threw back the blankets and crawled into bed. She hoped to sleep off the jet lag before starting back to work in the morning.

THE BAGEL HIT THE SPOT, but she had a craving for a latte. Just as she was pulling out of the parking lot of her favorite café, Maddy's face popped up on the screen of her cell phone, and the theme song from *Friends* played.

    "Hey kiddo, perfect timing. We can chat while I drive to work."

    "So that gives me what, five minutes to talk your ear off?"

    "Give or take. How are you holding up?"

    "Things are good here. I'm sharing a room with my cousin, Taylor. She's fourteen, so I'm kind of like her big sister."

    "That's cool! I hope she's as good a Little Sister to you as you are for me. Things wrapping up at school yet?"

"I wish! Our teacher just gave us a big project on the environment. She told us about her friend Rachael and her twin sister who died in a forest fire. The whole class was in tears when she finished. It sure got our attention. I think we all have a better understanding of the effects society has on the environment after hearing that story."

"When we have more time, you'll have to tell me what happened. I'm just pulling up to the Center, so I'll have to let you go."

"All right, have a great first day back. Love ya!"

"Thanks. Love you too. Bye for now."

The CERN Control Centre was holding an open house in two days. They were celebrating their twenty-fifth anniversary of the experimental program of the world's largest particle accelerator. Specifically, the Large Hadron Collider, LHC for short. They assigned Jeneva the not-too-challenging job of flushing the LHC with boiling water and solvents to ready it for the upcoming ceremony.

Even with the full night's sleep, she was still a little out of sync from the time change, so she was quite content with such a menial task. All she had to do was flush and change the automated machine's fluid every hour, on the hour, for the next six hours. After the first wash out was completed, she set her alarm on her Fitbit to ring in one hour and laid her head on the counter.

Snap!

Jeneva's head jerked up from her catnap and she saw a spiral of smoke swelling through the center of the machine. Another *Snap!* Then—*Boom!*

Before she could get close enough to inspect the anomaly, she was cannonballed across the room. Her body looked like a horseshoe being pulled backward by a powerful magnet. The impact on the wall knocked her out cold. When she came to, the room was filled with smoke. Sweat ran down her cheeks, and her eyes burned from the acrid air, making it hard to see. Her clothes were damp. She hoped she hadn't wet herself. That would be embarrassing when they came to rescue her.

All of a sudden, excruciating pain hit her. She screamed in agony. She reached over and cradled her right arm, causing even more unbearable pain. Biting down hard on her lip, she tried to adjust the broken bone into a stable position. Another agonizing scream filled the lab. Shock was setting in, and she was losing consciousness. She talked to herself.

"Stay awake, Jeneva. Concentrate on your breathing. Deep breath in. Deep breath out. Hang in there. Help is on the way."

Desperate to stabilize her arm, she scanned the floor around her and found a rubber belt that was miraculously still intact.

"You got this." Jeneva was trying her hardest to stay positive.

Ever so gently, she put the belt over her head. The jagged edges of the separated humorous bone grazed against each other, sending a piercing wave of excruciating pain up her arm. She screamed through the agony, maneuvering the arm into the loop.

Breathe, Jeneva. Breathe! You're going to get through this! You can't give up! the voice in her dizzying head urged.

The horrendous pain in her arm quickly snapped her back to reality and the dire situation she was in. All the hurting and frustration came out in a reverberating shout.

"Help!" Despite knowing the lab was as soundproof as a bank vault on a Sunday morning, it seemed like the right thing to do, considering her situation.

Not five feet away from her, she saw the steel canister that held the solvent lying on its side, the liquid having spilled onto the floor. Across the room, the explosion had left pieces of steel and wires hanging in disarray. Jeneva squinted . . . small residual combustions were happening in the gaping hole of the machine.

Putting all her weight on her good arm, she struggled to stand up and get her balance, but the room spun, and her vision blurred. She slumped her back against the wall, cradling her injured appendage, waiting for her vision to clear.

The arcing wires flailed back and forth, like a den of angry snakes. She was frozen stiff, fearing for her life. The lab was starting to resemble a forest fire, with furious flames spreading spontaneously around the smoke-filled room. The extinguisher was halfway between her and the exit door, less than twenty feet from where she leaned. The bigger problem was the large filter, the size of a sofa, lying engulfed in dancing blades of red, orange, and blue. If she was going to escape, she'd have to put out the burning filter and get to the door before collapsing from smoke inhalation. Her chest heaved with every laborious inhale. Her throat was parched, turning her desperate screams for help into nothing more than meek whimpers.

The red emergency light started turning, and the alarm sounded with the urgency of an air raid siren. The bomb-like explosion was deafening, but the sudden shrill of the alarm sent a wintery chill all the way through her battered body. She lost her balance and folded on the floor, landing on her injured arm. A dagger-to-the-gut pain shot down her arm. She wailed in agony. With sheer determination, she stood and thrust herself forward, coughing uncontrollably and holding her arm at her side. Her ears rang from the roaring sound of the alarm, and her eyes burned from the toxic smoke. All strength left her good arm, and she collapsed face down on the concrete floor. Jeneva was losing all hope of being rescued. A deep gasp escaped her dry lips; her eyelids drooped, and her fatigued body surrendered to the peril surrounding her.

The overhead sprinklers kicked in, and the fire in her escape path was extinguished. But it was too late—she wasn't going anywhere. Without warning, a volcanic explosion shook the foundation of the laboratory. The windows shattered, releasing a cascade of glass, a large piece of which lodged itself in Jeneva's forehead. With a groan, the scorched ceiling joist buckled and let go, turning the floor into a gnarly mat of broken glass, burning boards, and splintered beams, concealing any evidence of machines or life. From beneath the fallen ceiling, spontaneous flames popped up. Billowing smoke escaped from every aperture it could find. Once again, Jeneva was sealed under a gray cloud of toxicity.

The lab where Jeneva, just ten minutes ago, saw the first wink of a spark in the Large Hadron Collider now looked like a battlefield. The sound of firefighters cautiously entering the lab reached Jeneva's ears. Unable to call out, she lay and waited for them to locate her buried under a mound of rubble. She must have looked dead because they checked her for signs of life before putting on her oxygen mask and a proper sling on her broken arm. It was decided that the head wound warranted her being emergency airlifted by helicopter to the University Hospital of Geneva. Before long, Jeneva learned she'd suffered a life-threatening cranial injury. The emergency ward was put on high alert, and a prominent surgeon was called in.

Chapter 12

G etting to Know You
 The doctors had reached Takoda while he was still at the airport in Turkey. He was told the humerus bone in her right arm was broken; she had sustained a concussion, and they were prepping her for emergency surgery to deal with the large piece of glass that was stuck in her forehead. Because of the delicate nature of brain surgery, and barring any complications, he was told that they estimated she'd be in recovery in about five to six hours.

Takoda listened intently, jotting down the address of the hospital. He thanked the caller and said he'd be there as soon as he could get a flight. He rushed to the ticket counter. The attendant was very sympathetic to his story and found someone to give up their seat in exchange for a two-hundred-dollar credit, putting Takoda on the next flight, taking off in forty-five minutes. The agent assured him his bags would be rerouted to the address he gave her by the next evening. He made a note in his phone to call his daughter's neighbor and asked her to watch for his luggage and take it in for safekeeping until he got there.

The flight took three hours and fifteen minutes. Even with the time it would take to travel from the airport in Geneva to her hospital, Jeneva would still be in surgery when he got to her. The whole trip, he thought of his daughter hooked up to life support machines that echoed a rhythmic *beep, beep, beep* on the bare walls.

A NURSE ACCOMPANIED Takoda to the waiting room, where he spent the next three hours in total disbelief and despair. When he could no longer tolerate the uncertainty, he went to the nurse's station to enquire about his daughter's surgery. She told him Jeneva was on her way to recovery, and he could see her as soon as the surgeon had spoken with him.

Ten minutes later, the weary surgeon clothed in pale green scrubs arrived and went through the details as he knew them.

"Monsieur Yassi, upon your daughter's arrival, the diagnostic team took X-rays and a CT scan to look for any interior damage or blood clots. The images showed a spiral fracture of the humerus in her right arm. She also has a large contusion on the back of her head, which has given her a major concussion. The most disturbing find was the piece of glass penetrating her forehead that was so deep it ruptured some of the frontal lobe brain tissue. It took the best part of five hours to set and pin the broken bone and remove the glass and suture the punctured brow."

He said the urgency of the situation had precluded the protocol of operating on a person with a concussion, which in turn, led to some complications, the worst one being cardiac arrest.

"It took almost three minutes, but the surgical team was able to revive your daughter's heart while the surgeon continued to suture the wound. She is presently in a coma and being kept alive on a life support system. To the best of my knowledge, she is in no pain. I am so sorry. Despite doing the best we could to save your daughter, there could be brain damage. It's doubtful she will ever wake up."

The devastating diagnosis brought Takoda to his knees. He held his head in his hands.

"No, this can't be happening to my Jeneva!" he cried out in desperation.

The doctor asked whether there was someone he could call.

"There is no one else. We only have each other."

The doctor beckoned a nearby attendant to help Takoda to his feet, and the three of them made their way to the recovery room. At the door, Takoda was warned of all the tubes and working machines sustaining his daughter's life.

Nothing could have prepared him for what he saw. Buried under blankets of white, with only a badly bruised face visible beneath her bandaged head, was his little girl. He slowly approached her bedside, lifted the sheet off her arm, and took her cool hand in his.

"I'm here, honey. Daddy's here."

An hour later, a nurse gently woke him when she came to check Jeneva's blood pressure. A phone was ringing.

"Monsieur, I think your daughter's phone is ringing. It is over there in the closet."

"Merci," he said, his voice hoarse from fatigue.

He opened the door and took out the large purse. The ringing stopped. He took the phone out, set it on the bed, and stuffed the purse on the floor at his feet. Once again, he took hold of Jeneva's hand and told her he was still with her. The cell phone rang again.

"Hello?" Takoda's said.

"May I please speak to Jeneva?"

"Is that you, Madison?"

"Yes. Takoda?" She was puzzled that he'd be answering Jeneva's phone when he was supposed to be in Africa.

"Yes, Maddy. It's me."

"Where's Jeneva?"

Takoda wasn't sure how to answer the question. Having not spent a lot of time with Maddy, he wondered whether she could handle what was happening and what was to come. After all, she'd just lost her father.

"Takoda! What's wrong? Where is she?"

He took a deep breath. In his calmest voice, he started to explain what happened and that she wouldn't be able to talk to her right now; omitting the possibility that she might never be able to talk to her again. Maddy took the news surprisingly well. Although, she did try to convince him that she should come for her visit early. He was able to talk her out of coming, assuring her he would not leave Jeneva's side, and promised he would call her with updates. After agreeing to give his daughter a kiss and hug from her, they said goodbye and ended the call.

Takoda sat through the night, holding his daughter's hand, reassuring her everything was going to be okay. Around eleven in the morning, the nurse finally convinced him to go home and rest, assuring him she'd call if there was any change in his daughter's condition. She overheard the conversation he'd had with Maddy and told him she would stay close so his daughter wouldn't be alone.

Takoda thanked her and reluctantly left his comatose daughter and went to her apartment. The neighbor must have heard him come in because she brought his bags to the door before he was over the threshold. He thanked her and decided not to elaborate on Jeneva's situation. Instead, he just told her she was being monitored and might be there for a while. To say any more was too painful right now.

Day after angst-ridden day, Takoda sat by Jeneva's side. Sometimes he read aloud, hoping for a reaction. He tried reminiscing about their many vacations, describing what the queen wore for her Diamond Jubilee celebration, the view they'd enjoyed in Ireland on her sixteenth birthday, and standing in awe at the bottom of the Grand Canyon after the helicopter ride. They'd shared so many great adventures and gone to so many wonderful places. There was no shortage of stories to draw from, but nothing fazed her motionless mind or body. As promised, Takoda called Maddy regularly. Sadly, always with the regrettable news. When Maddy confessed she'd booked her flight early and would be there as soon as school ended, he had to admit he'd be happy for the help in rousing Jeneva.

One afternoon, while he was resting in the chair at Jeneva's bedside, which he'd done daily for the past two weeks, he had a dream or a vision. He wasn't quite sure which.

He saw himself standing beside Lynne. She'd brought him along to perform a smudging on the father of a friend shortly before he was expected to pass on to the afterlife. Takoda was very familiar with the different rituals of his people, thanks to Lynne and her willingness to help so many people. That day, Lynne burned dry sage, producing a smoky cloud that she waved over the body to cleanse the mind, body, and spirit of the dying man.

Takoda's eyes popped open. He remembered Lynne explaining that this action was also used in healing rituals. There was no doubt in his mind Lynne wanted him to perform a smudging ceremony over their daughter.

On that day's call, Maddy told him she was packed and ready to go the next morning. They'd do the smudging together.

IN JENEVA'S ROOM, TAKODA lit the bundle of dry sage and blew out the flame, which started the smoke to waft in the air over Jeneva's body. He had explained to Maddy what the smudging ritual entailed and what it might accomplish, trying not to place too much hope in her heart, or his.

They took turns waving the smoky bundle back and forth as Jeneva lay unaware of the efforts being made to bring her back to the ones who loved her.

Over and over, they repeated the chant, "Come back to us, Jeneva. We love you. Please wake up."

The odor must have escaped into the hall because a nurse came rushing in through the closed door with a look of sheer terror on her face.

"*Bon Dieu*!" she cried, followed by a warning that whatever Takoda was doing must stop, immediately, or she would have to call security.

He could tell that there would be no pacifying the crotchety old woman with an explanation. He gave the area a final wave and distinguished the smoke in the bathroom sink. Satisfied with him promising this wouldn't happen again, the nurse left the room. She did, however, return with a can of air freshener and proceeded to spray a substantial amount of lavender fragrance around the room.

Maddy and Takoda sat on each side of Jeneva's bed, holding her hands, watching for the slightest sign that the smudging might have worked. But their efforts were in vain. Nothing was happening. With heavy hearts, they solemnly made their way out of the hospital.

Outside the revolving doors, Takoda asked Maddy what she wanted to eat. When she said she liked seafood, he couldn't help but think this was another of Jeneva's influences. Google Maps brought them to a steak and seafood restaurant a short stroll away. They sat across from each other, just as he and Jeneva did at the Olde Marine Restaurant a few short weeks ago.

While they waited for their food, Maddy asked Takoda to tell her more about the Sioux heritage and their beliefs and rituals. She asked about his upcoming trip to Sudan and what had led him to research ancient water-purification systems.

It was a good distraction from the disappointing reality they were facing back at the hospital. They ate and talked for a couple hours, getting to know each other and sharing stories of things they'd done with Jeneva and things they hoped to do when she woke up.

The waitress stopped by their table for the second time, insinuatingly pushing the bill closer to Takoda and advising him that her shift was over. He handed her a euro bill, apologized for keeping her, and told her to keep the change. With full bellies and hopeful hearts, they made their way back to the hospital.

The night nurse told them there was no change, so they each gave Jeneva a kiss goodnight and headed to Jeneva's apartment.

Takoda opened the door to the spare room and set Maddy's luggage inside.

"I think this is your room." He stepped back from the doorway.

The room had been decorated mostly in yellow, Maddy's favorite color, in anticipation of her visits. The single bed was topped with a floral bedspread and an oversized pillow in a matching sham. Centered atop the white dresser was a lovely bouquet of artificial yellow sweetheart roses.

"It's beautiful! Jeneva told me she made up a room for me, but I didn't know she went to so much trouble." She twirled around in a circle. "I feel like a princess."

"That's Jeneva for you, always thinking of ways to please. I'll be in the office. There's a day bed in there calling my name." He yawned and headed down the hall.

Maddy unpacked her bag and got into her pajamas, then went looking for Takoda. He was sitting on the end of the bed with his head hung down.

"Everything okay?"

"I was just thinking about Jeneva." He quickly wiped a tear from his cheek.

"I just wanted to thank you for a nice day, despite how sad it is, seeing her like that.

"It was my pleasure."

"Maybe Jeneva will join us next time. She loves seafood too."

"Sounds like a plan." Takoda lowered his gaze.

Maddy took a couple steps closer, and Takoda raised his head to look at her.

"Well, good night!" She looked shyly into his watery eyes. "Um .
. . I could sure use a hug."

He opened his arms. "Me too."

From his seated position, Maddy was able to put her arms
around his neck, and Takoda's arms reached right around her small
waist. The embrace lasted less than a minute but was just what they
both needed to close off the tiring experience of their day. He wished
her sweet dreams, and she went to her room. Takoda hoped her long
journey and her tiring day would make for an easy transition to sleep.

MADDY WANDERED INTO the kitchen, rubbing the sleep from
her eyes.

"Good morning, Maddy. How'd you sleep?"

"Like a princess," she said, opening the fridge door.

"I'm afraid the fridge and cupboards are bare. When it comes
to cooking, I'm no Gordon Ramsay. I'm more of an Uber Eats kind
of guy. I thought I would take you to one of Jeneva's favorite places,
Crêperie St. Pierre.

"That sounds terrific. I've heard of crepes but never tried them.
Give me five minutes to dress. "I can't wait to try them. Since Jeneva
likes them, I probably will too." Her words trailed off as she disappeared down the hall.

The quaint eatery was in Geneva in an old stone building on the
corner of a busy intersection. There was an outdoor patio nestled
in the fenced alcove. It was decorated with large potted greenery
and French flag banners. There was a chill in the air and threatening
clouds rolling overhead, so they found a booth inside. A painted
mural of the Eiffel Tower with a plate of crepes in the foreground
shrouded the deteriorating stone wall at the back of the small estab-

lishment. Above several pictures of the crepes being offered was a sign that read A Taste of Paris in the Heart of Geneva.

Takoda ordered a variety plate for them to share. Maddy fell in love with crepes; cream filled, fruit filled, vegetable filled. She tried them all. They agreed that they were the perfect food, good for breakfast, lunch, and dinner.

Sitting across from Maddy, watching her sample each rolled-up delicacy, Takoda pondered how alike the two girls were. Now that he was getting to know Jeneva's Little Sister better, he thought they both had such inquisitive minds, full of questions and eager to learn new things.

He couldn't help but smile when he thought about how Jeneva would often take him off guard with her quirky humor, never failing to make him laugh. In their short time together, he suspected Maddy was still honing her humor skills, or maybe she was holding back until she got to know him better. From the stories the young girl was sharing, it appeared Jeneva followed in his footsteps. Turning their experiences together into learning experiences and always trying to find some form of charity where they could volunteer. Maddy told him how her father, Brian, had raised her in much the same fashion by allowing her to help him help others at community events. She told him it was Jeneva who encouraged her to volunteer in the children's ward at a local hospital.

"She said by sharing how I dealt with the loss of my mom, I'd be helping other kids deal with their loss."

Takoda smiled to himself. *It's like having two daughters. Or is it a daughter and granddaughter? Can't be. I'm not that old,* he mused.

Chapter 13

Questions Answered

Jeneva had no sense of where she was or how long she'd been there. Her body felt like an inflated balloon, angelically floating across a cloudless sky. She was disoriented and confused, even suspected she might be dead. Her nostrils sensed a faint smell of smoke and some kind of herbal incense. She was quite sure her eyes were closed, but she thought she could see something in the fog that was moving toward her.

Although Jeneva had only seen her mother in pictures, the approaching figure looked remarkably familiar. As the ghostly shape emerged from the mist, her long black hair danced in an invisible breeze. The woman wore an elk skin dress with fringes dangling from the hem. A colorfully beaded headband with an eagle feather hung down one side of her face. This was the outfit Jeneva's mother was wearing in one of her favorite pictures of her. It was tucked securely in her wallet, traveling everywhere with her. Even in her comatose state, there was no doubt in Jeneva's mind. This was her mother.

Lynne reached out her hand to Jeneva and smiled a warm, motherly smile.

"Don't be afraid my sweet child. I am here to help you. I know you are struggling to solve the mystery of the symbols on the bracelet."

As their hands touched, a surge of energy infiltrated Jeneva's body. Despite her warm internal feelings, she became chilled with gooseflesh that covered her body like a second skin. She tried to talk, but nothing came out. It felt as if her voice box had been removed.

"Calm yourself, my dear. I am here to answer all your questions. Now, close your eyes, and listen to my voice."

Jeneva did as she was told. What happened next was truly astounding; a telepathic joining of mother and daughter, a transfer

71

of Lynne's memories into Jeneva's unconscious mind. Immediately, a surreal feeling of peace came over her body, mind, and soul as her desires and her need to know her mother were fulfilled. All the plaguing questions were answered.

"Open your eyes, Jeneva."

They made eye contact.

"As your father has told you, the bracelet will lead you on a journey to your life's destiny. Follow your heart and continue to help those in need. All will be revealed if you keep your mind open to what you see and what you hear. Know that I am always close by, watching over you. The bracelet is our connection. Wear it always. I have one other thing I want you to remember. Never be too focused on where you think you should go. It's easy to miss where you are meant to be."

She released her daughter's hand. Slowly, their fingers caressed each other until they hung separated in midair.

"Goodbye and good luck, my sweet child. Remember my words and never forget I love you."

As the mist wrapped around her departing figure, Lynne disappeared as stealthily as she'd appeared.

So many questions were answered and miraculously embedded in her mind, everything from her mother's favorite flower to her favorite candy bar. Jeneva was finally satisfied that she knew everything she needed to know about her mother. After all the wishing and hoping, her dream of meeting her mother had come true.

Chapter 14

She's Back

After their feast of crepes, Takoda and Maddy returned to the hospital and solemnly took their place on either side of Jeneva's bed.

Jeneva had been unconscious for fifteen days now and the doctors were losing faith that she would ever wake up. Takoda and Maddy remained optimistic and continued talking to her.

"Open your eyes, honey."

Jeneva's body remained still, but her brain was waking up. Was that her father calling to her? It sounded as if he were talking to her from across the Grand Canyon.

"Please wake up, Jeneva."

Then she heard a younger voice.

"Maddy, is that you?" No words left Jeneva's lips. But something was happening. "Dad, I'm here!" she hollered, but again, no words were audible.

"I miss you so much!" Takoda gave her cool hand a squeeze. He gasped when it squeezed back.

Suddenly, the monitor at the bedside sounded an ear-piecing alarm. Jeneva's eyes fluttered open, then closed, but not before they noticed a rapid zigzag line crossing the monitor's screen. The change in the monitor must have been noticed at the nurse's station too. The shuffling sound of someone rushing reached her ears. An impatient hand took hold of Jeneva's wrist, checking her pulse.

"What's happening?" her father asked.

"Well, sir, it looks like your daughter is trying to wake up. Keep talking to her. I'll get the doctor." Squeaky rubber-soled shoes rushed out the door.

Maddy ran to the other side of the room and took hold of Takoda's arms, pulling him down to her eye level.

"We did this. We brought her back. I knew it would work!" Maddy's voice was so full of excitement that Jeneva could imagine her bouncing on the spot with excitement.

"I think you may be right. She's trying to come back to us."

As they waited anxiously for the doctor's arrival, Takoda and Maddy continued encouraging Jeneva to open her eyes, gently squeezing her hands and caressing her cheeks, which were starting to warm.

The doctor finally arrived and checked her vitals. He told them her blood pressure and heart rate were that of a healthy young woman. As he was explaining what they should expect, if she did come out of her coma, Jeneva opened her eyes.

FOR THE NEXT COUPLE days, she was very weak and slept a lot. She had very little memory of the explosion and questioned her memory of seeing her mother. She asked her dad what he thought. He explained that the doctors had lost her on the operating table, and after three minutes, her heart started beating again. He suggested that might have been when Lynne came to her.

"It's a miracle you came back. You've been unconscious for fifteen days, and the doctors were losing faith that you'd ever wake up. But Maddy and I remained optimistic. We've been at your bedside, talking to you, every day."

Being an advocate of apparitions, he convinced Jeneva that she should believe in the divine aspect of things because not everything is science based and can be logically resolved. He encouraged her to trust whatever Lynne told her to be something worth remembering.

Jeneva had an overwhelming feeling the vision had come while she was fading in and out of consciousness during their smudging, and not in the operating room as her father suggested. She decided, when and where were irrelevant. The only thing that mattered was that she'd finally met her mom.

One afternoon, while Takoda was at work, the two girls played several hands of various card games to pass the time.

"What do you say we take a break?"

"Sure, I was tired of beating you anyway," Maddy teased.

"Can you grab my cell phone from my purse? I should check my messages."

Maddy rummaged in the beaded purse and retrieved a pamphlet along with the cell phone.

"What's this?" she asked, waving the pamphlet as she handed the cell phone over.

Jeneva nonchalantly told her it was from a symposium she'd attended before leaving Washington and returned her attention to her inbox. Maddy meticulously looked over the pamphlet. When she flipped to the back page, she jumped off the stool she was sitting on, causing it to topple over backward. Her voice filled with excitement as she stuck the folded sheet under Jeneva's nose.

"Oh, my gosh! That hummingbird picture looks the same as the one on your bracelet!"

A bit perplexed, Jeneva saw that it was indeed an exact match. How had she missed that? Then it came to her. She hadn't been paying attention when the archaeologist, Amir something, spoke at the symposium, and she hadn't bothered to look at the back of the brochure that day, nor since.

The girls went ballistic, waving their arms in the air and screaming simultaneously.

"The hummingbird! We found the hummingbird!"

Once they calmed down, Maddy searched the internet on her phone, and Jeneva read the pamphlet's back page. They both hoped to find the connection between the hummingbird on Jeneva's bracelet and The Hummingbird Pyramid in La Maná. The information Jeneva read on Amir said he was heading to Ecuador for his next archaeological dig, which turned out to be a couple weeks ago. Maddy read a report out loud that mentioned ancient artifacts had been discovered in La Maná, at the Hummingbird Pyramid.

"That must be why he's gone there."

"You could be right," Jeneva said.

Jeneva was ecstatic to finally have a clue to the meaning behind one of the symbols on her bracelet. She thanked Maddy for pointing it out and suggested it could be an important starting point to her journey.

"Journey? What journey?" Maddy scrunched her face inquisitively.

Jeneva hadn't told Maddy about her contact with Lynne. She thought it would be too much for a young girl who lost her mother, and recently her father, to comprehend. After dodging a multitude of questions, she decided she had no choice and tried to explain what she'd experienced. Rather than using the term *vision*, Jeneva kept it simple and called it a dream.

"Well! Life is a journey, and my mother told me to follow the meaning of these three symbols." She held out her wrist and pointed to them.

Maddy had noticed the bracelet on Jeneva's wrist on occasion. Jeneva had told her it was a gift from her mother, so she assumed Maddy had thought it was just a memento.

"Apparently, they'll lead me on a journey to my life's destiny. Isn't that cool?"

"Very cool! Can I come with you on your journey?" She grabbed Jeneva's hands, begging. "Please, can I come?"

"It looks like you already are. I can't wait to tell Dad."

For the next few days, the three of them brainstormed on the significance and meaning of the other two symbols. They mulled over the possibility that the half moon, half sun could be day and night. And the blue one with sparkly gold stripes, well, that one really had them stumped. The mysterious symbols gave them all something to talk about, which helped pass the time in the boring hospital room.

WHEN JENEVA FELL ASLEEP after eating all her lunch, Maddy and Takoda decided to go for a stroll. When they reached the family waiting room, they saw a woman holding her face in her hands, sobbing uncontrollably.

Maddy went to the cooler and poured herself a cup of water. Takoda headed straight to the woman and asked whether he could sit. She said he could. He introduced himself, and she told him her name was Crystal. Maddy watched as Takoda engaged the distraught young lady in conversation. From her vantage point, she overheard him say he noticed her sitting at the bedside of a boy in the room next to his daughter's. He asked what his name was and what had happened to him. She blew her nose.

"Benny was skateboarding without his helmet and lost control. He was thrown over the top of the wall onto the ground. The impact broke his neck and severed multiple nerves in his spine."

She dabbed at her red puffy eyes and blew her nose.

"If he wakes up, I've been told, he most definitely will be confined to a wheelchair. The doctors induced the coma to restrain his body, which will allow the nerves to heal and mask his pain."

Maddy listened intently as Takoda gave the woman a condensed version of what had happened to Jeneva and encouraged her not to give up. Crystal thanked him for taking the time to talk to her, and for sharing his story, and said she would try to stay positive.

Takoda stood up and headed for the door. Maddy followed close behind.

Once they were in the hall, out of hearing range, Maddy said, "That was a really nice thing you did. It reminded me of the way my dad used to deal with victims of fires when we would bring them food and clothes. He had a way of making them feel better despite their losses."

She hoped Takoda didn't notice her eyes moisten and her lip quiver.

"Thank you for that. From what I've heard, your dad was a very special man. I believe, it's the little things we do for others that could make a difference in their lives. Sometimes in ways we will never know."

"I sure miss him," she said, hooking her arm in his. "Can we go to the cafeteria? A nurse told me they have a soup and sandwich special."

They ate, then returned to Jeneva's room where they stayed until the supper tray of hospital food arrived. They said their goodbyes to Jeneva, promising to return tomorrow after breakfast.

THE NEXT MORNING, AFTER having passed the physical and mental examinations, the doctor agreed Jeneva could go home. He stipulated she was not to overexert herself, and most importantly, she must get plenty of bed rest and start gentle physical therapy on her arm. Takoda and Maddy were there and assured him they were more than happy to make sure the patient adhered to his recommendations.

In the weeks that followed, her father and Maddy had been true to their word. Takoda would drive Jeneva to her physical therapy appointments once a week and spend a few hours a day in her room working on his research, while overseeing her doing the recommended strengthening exercises. Maddy assisted Jeneva with showers and did the housekeeping, grocery shopping, and cooking. The doctor told them, along with lots of rest, nutritional meals were an integral part of the healing process. So, everything she purchased was fresh and organic.

After dinner, Takoda would leave for a brisk two-mile walk, five if he felt energetic and the weather permitted. Most evenings, they'd munch on popcorn or Doritos and watch TV or read. Occasionally, Jeneva airdropped her and her father's vacation pictures to the TV, and they joked that they were like those movie stars who travel around the world, doing charity work in third world countries. Maddy found it all very interesting and told them she'd like to do that someday.

Whenever Jeneva started talking about the bracelet and possibly going to Ecuador, Maddy and Takoda were quick to say it was too soon for her to even consider traveling.

Maddy stood tall, placed her hands on her hips and deepened her voice, "Before you can go anywhere, young lady, you have to get that arm healed. What do you say you get the pully going and loosen up those muscles?" Maddy offered her a hand and ushered her to the bedroom.

Since Maddy had arrived, the three were becoming quite close, like a family, doing everything together. At bedtime, the girls would kneel at their bedsides and include both their moms and dads in their prayers and wish for world peace. Takoda would stand in the doorway, arms crossed, watching with a proud fatherly expression on his face.

One night, after Maddy had gone to bed, Jeneva and Takoda were sitting in the backyard sipping wine and enjoying the fresh ion filled air after a rain shower had passed. She asked Takoda whether he'd consider taking Maddy with him to Africa for a while. He told her he'd consider it but didn't think her Aunt Patricia would approve. Jeneva pulled out her cell phone and called Maddy's Aunt to see what she thought of the idea. After establishing that she'd cover all the expenses and guaranteeing that Maddy would be home before school started in September, Patricia consented to let her niece go. She agreed it would be a distraction from losing her father and a once in-a-lifetime experience she'd never forget.

Over breakfast the next morning, Jeneva made the proposal to Maddy. At first, Maddy voiced her reservations.

"You need me here. With Takoda gone, who will take care of you?"

"I will manage just fine. Besides, you're supposed to be on vacation, not babysitting me."

"I want you to go with Dad because he has taken me on some pretty amazing trips, and we have some super memories. I guarantee you're going to come back with your own remarkable stories that you'll remember the rest of your life. Besides, thanks to the superb job you and Dad have done taking care of me, I'm doing better than the doctor even expected."

"Maybe so, but Aunt Patricia will never let me go to Africa. I begged her to let me come here, remember?"

"I remember, but I spoke to her last night and explained the situation. She was very understanding. She's calling you tonight to talk it over."

"Oh, all right. Only if you're sure you'll be okay." She placed her hand on Jeneva's cheek.

"I'll be fine, but we should go shopping and get you some new clothes for your trip."

"If you insist." Maddy gave her a Cheshire cat smile.

A few days later, Jeneva received a large manila envelope from Patricia. Inside was her written consent giving Takoda guardianship to take Maddy out of the country.

THE MORNING TAKODA and Maddy were to embark on the long trip to Khartoum, Jeneva's drowsy father entered the living room from the kitchen to relax with his coffee. When he passed a suitcase sitting at the door, he did a double take.

"Morning, sleepyhead." Maddy's cheery voice seemed to startle him. Maddy was sitting on the couch, showing Jeneva her straight-faced mug shot in her passport. "I'm all packed. Jeneva showed me how to frugally pack a suitcase, purchase a ticket, and check in through the internet. She says it's all part of the adventure and the fun of traveling to new places."

"Somebody's excited." Takoda took a sip of his coffee.

"I sure am! Jeneva told me the Smithsonian is flying us first class. I can't wait." She jumped up off the couch and ran down the hall to her room, arms stretched out like a child pretending to be an airplane.

Both Takoda and Jeneva shook their heads at the playful display of excitement. They loved that they were able to bring such joy to the young girl at this confusing time in her life.

The next hour passed too quickly. Here she was, waving goodbye to her Little Sister peering at her through the rear window of the taxi. Jeneva sensed that Maddy had similar mixed feelings about leaving as she did.

Jeneva had just started her morning physical therapy routine when the doorbell rang.

"Back already?" She opened the door expecting to see Maddy.

"Good morning, Miss. Yassi. I'm T. Parsons. I believe you are expecting me." He gave the hand of her weak arm a firm shake.

She'd forgotten about the call she received from the HR department at the CERN Control Centre yesterday. They needed to send someone over to discuss her accident, and she told them to come the next day. She apologized for her look of surprise and invited the gentleman to sit down at the kitchen table.

"Can I get you anything, coffee, tea, water?"

"No, thanks, I'm in a bit of a rush. The guys at head office are waiting for me to bring this issue to a close. If you don't mind, can we just get started?"

"Of course." She wondered what could be so urgent that it didn't allow for a cup of coffee.

The bald-headed guest unbuttoned his double-breasted suit jacket, placed his briefcase on the floor at his side, and pulled out a folder. He adjusted his thick-lensed bifocals to the edge of his nose, opened the file, and read the following letter to Jeneva.

Dear Miss Jeneva Yassi,

First and foremost, we want to offer our most sincere apologies for the injuries inflicted upon you and assure you everything possible is being done to safeguard against something of this magnitude ever happening again.

Official findings: It has been discovered that the first explosion was the result of the liquid being used to scrub the LHC. It rapidly transformed into a gas, and the sudden pressure release caused the first ignition. This, in turn, ricocheted throughout the electrical system, triggering the combustion. A chain reaction caused by the heated water particles from the sprinkler system, separating into hydrogen and hydroxide, acted as an accelerant to the alkali metal fire, sequentially, setting off the second, more ruinous explosion.

We are offering the enclosed remuneration of: Five Hundred Thousand Euros with our genuine apologies and best wishes for a speedy recovery.

Sincerely,

CERN Control Centre

HE SLID THE LETTER across the table along with a pen and the envelope that contained a check. She opened the envelope.

"That's a lot of zeros." She thought it an extreme amount for a broken bone, the odd headache, and a fading four-inch scar on her forehead.

"If you are satisfied with the amount, I need you to sign at the bottom, above your name. If you agree to accept the monetary settlement, you are also required to sign this 'Release of Liability' form."

He pulled another sheet from the folder and passed it to her.

Jeneva read over the form twice, to ensure she understood all the legal ramifications. The amount they were offering was, to say the least, more than fair and extremely generous, and she was eager to put the accident out of her mind and never speak of it to anyone. She picked up the check and stared at it in mesmerized disbelief.

"Miss Yassi!" His impatient voice startled her. When she flinched, it sent a sharp pain up her arm. A reminder of what this offer represented.

"I have to advise you that once you sign the Release of Liability, you can never petition for future medical bills, physical therapy expenses, punitive damages, nothing at all! This is it. five hundred thousand euros. Do you understand?" His tone was quite emphatic.

Jeneva stared at him, then back at the blank line awaiting her signature. She raised her eyes back to his.

"I understand." She signed both the acceptance letter and the release form.

After the folders were back in the black leather bag, the man stood up and reached across the table, offering her his hand.

"I wish you all the best." He then headed toward the door.

Jeneva stood and followed him.

"Thank you for coming. I will be in touch when I decide if or when I'm coming back to work."

Needless to say, there was no way she would ever consider returning to a job that she already found boring, but she didn't want to appear ungrateful. As the door closed, she turned, putting her back against it. Flabbergasted by her new-found fortune, she slid down to the floor. Her eyes opened wide as the reality of her windfall filled her head. *Now I have the means to go in search of my destiny.* With clenched fists, she threw her arms in the air and gave out an unrestrained, "Woo-hoo! Ouch!" then cradled her still healing arm.

Chapter 15

The Hummingbird Pyramid

The next morning from her bed, Jeneva noticed her duffle bag tucked in the bottom of her closet. It brought back memories of her extended stay in the hospital and the traumatic explosion that put her there. She slipped out of her bed, walked over, and picked it up. She was about to toss it on the top shelf when something fell on the floor. It was the pamphlet from the symposium. "Just when I forget about it, here it is again." Jeneva wrinkled her brow, pondering what it could mean. She tossed the bag back in the closet and went to the kitchen with the folded paper in hand.

She remembered that after she'd come out of the coma, she'd slept a lot and Maddy had kept herself occupied compiling information about the Hummingbird Pyramid and put it in a file folder. The day they took her home from the hospital, Maddy told her where she put the folder. But now, only a week later, her memory was failing her.

"Think, Jeneva, think!" she scolded herself. The most logical place would be on the coffee table in the living room, so she started there. No, not there. She went back to the kitchen and filled her coffee cup and sat down at the table. Bowing her head, she closed her eyes and rubbed her temples.

"Where did she put it?" She raised her head and scanned the room. She spotted something tucked between the fridge and the microwave.

"Aha! I found you," Jeneva said with delight. She jumped up, and rushing across the room, she had to grab the fridge handle to keep from falling over. After a minute or so, she regained her balance.

"Whoa! That was weird!" Then, she recalled the doctor saying her concussion might cause dizzy spells.

Jeneva tucked the pamphlet in the folder, slipped the folder under her arm, then slowly shuffled to her bedroom with one hand on the wall for balance.

"I'll look at you later. I think I need to lie down and rest for a while," she told the folder, placing it on the nightstand. As a rule, she wasn't one to give in easily, but lately, she was listening to her body, and right now, it wanted to lie down.

The ringing of Jeneva's phone woke her with a start, rousing her from a deep sleep. It was Maddy calling to let her know they'd made it to Khartoum safe and sound. She yammered on about the long flight and the excellent food. With unrestrained enthusiasm, the girl informed Jeneva that her father reserved a two-bedroom suite the size of her apartment. Maddy seemed to think every detail was worth mentioning, even the gold-embossed robes in the bathroom.

Jeneva felt sorry for her dad. She figured the teenager probably talked the whole flight, impeding his usual catnap, which she knew he relished on long flights. Before Maddy handed the phone to Takoda, she did ask how she was feeling and assured her she could come back if she decided she needed her help.

Takoda's conversation was much shorter.

"Just checking in to make sure you're feeling okay and remind you to rest as much as possible, and don't worry about us. I'm sure we'll get on just fine."

Jeneva told them both she was fine and ended the call before they asked any more questions. Still lying on her side in bed, she decided they didn't need to know about her little dizzy spell.

It had been nine hours since her episode in the kitchen, and she was feeling pretty good, all things considered. Not to instigate another dizzy spell, she stood up ever so slowly, grabbed her cell phone and the folder off the nightstand, and returned to the kitchen. She filled a tumbler with water and a few cubes of ice and settled into a comfy chair on her backyard patio. She tilted her face to the sky, enjoying the warm July sunshine on her face.

"Thank you. Thank you. Thank you."

This ritual of thanking the Universe was something she'd practiced ever since she'd read the book *The Secret*. Reading it reinforced her belief in the power of positive thinking and the importance of gratitude. She'd survived that catastrophic accident, and who knows what else she'd avoided by staying positive and being grateful. She'd tried to be grateful, not only for the good things in life but also for the bad, because they could lead to something unexpected.

Inside the folder, she found a dozen printed sheets, along with some pictures, and the symposium pamphlet. For the next hour or so, she combed through the information, occasionally glancing at the symbols on her bracelet. The hummingbird picture on the pamphlet was undeniably the same, but their connection remained a mystery.

The last sheet in the folder was covered with several pictures of the pyramids in the La Maná area. Beside the picture of the Hummingbird Pyramid was a smaller picture of a hummingbird and a white rose, which was labeled the national flower of Ecuador. It was identical to the symbol on her bracelet. Farther down was the contact information for those wanting to plan a visit to the pyramids, temple, or mine sites. It was also noted that tubing down the Calope River past the pyramids was available from May to November. A framed box in the corner caught Jeneva's eye. It described an opportunity to volunteer on the archaeological dig sites. They were looking for people to participate in the ongoing excavations of the pyramids, including the Hummingbird Pyramid.

After reading through the information, she envisioned the mystery and intrigue of her destiny finally unfolding right before her eyes. *Could this be what Mom was trying to tell me? Is this where I'm supposed to start my journey?* The excitement of it all sent a tingling sensation through her whole body. Jeneva closed the folder and went back inside her ground-floor apartment, where she slept for another eight hours. Thousands of colourful hummingbirds and the humming sound of their beating wings filled her dreams.

Chapter 16

The Woman Who Snatched the Cab

That evening, Jeneva checked the internet to confirm that the current time would be suitable for a call to Ecuador. She remembered that Applebaum guy saying he'd be traveling back there to do some astrological research on the upcoming autumnal equinox. Jeneva punched in *equinox* on her computer. It looked like the next celestial event would be around the twenty-third of September. She hoped he'd already be there, and maybe, just maybe, they'd have another chance meeting. But for now, all she wanted was Amir's cell number so she could solidify a volunteer position when she got to the pyramid in Ecuador.

"Hmm, where did I put his business card?" She tapped her index finger on her chin. Ever since the symposium, she'd wondered whether she'd ever reconnect with Dexter. There

was something about him that got under her skin. Without his help, she'd have to search for Amir Whitelaw, on her own. She hoped he'd remembered her.

Jeneva first checked in the duffle bag in the closet. Having no luck there, she went looking for her purse. So much had happened in her life in three short months. Since meeting Dexter, Brian had died in a fire, she'd attended his funeral, flown back to Geneva, survived the explosion, had an encounter with her mom, struggled through a lengthy recuperation, and her dad and Maddy had left for Sudan together. Her head hurt just thinking about it all. Thankfully, the large, beaded purse was in its usual spot, hanging on the coat tree at the front door. She took it to the kitchen and dumped the contents on the table. After rummaging through everything, to no avail, she sat down and closed her eyes and rubbed her temples again. *What did I do with it? What was I wearing that day? Did I put it in a pocket? The* answer didn't come, so she tossed everything back in her purse and returned it to the coat tree.

Her legs started to feel like rubber, and her head began to spin. *Not again.* It occurred to her that she hadn't eaten anything today, so she went back to the kitchen and made herself a bowl of soup, hoping the dizziness would subside after she ate. While she sat patiently waiting for the soup to cool, she tried to remember exactly what had conspired the day she met Dexter. She snickered when she recalled nabbing his cab. And then there was the embarrassment when he looked down at her from his vantage point on stage at the symposium. The touch of his warm, soft hand in hers when they'd introduced themselves and the masculine smell of his cologne made her weak in the knees. She closed her eyes and imagined looking into his sultry eyes, and it came to her.

Her sweater pocket. She'd put it there after she shook his hand. She hurried to her stacked washer and dryer in the hall closet. She slowed her pace when the light-headedness returned, and her legs softened like melting butter. Poising herself on the hall walls, stiff as an iron cross, she stared at the closet doors, waiting for her head to stop spinning.

Once it settled, a wave of panic came over her. Maddy might have put the sweater through the wash already. She swung open the door, and there it was, stretched on a drying rack. She reached in the pocket and pulled out Dexter's laminated business card. It was in almost perfect condition.

"Now where's my damn cell phone? This recurring memory loss is annoying." She leaned over the machines and saw it in the front pocket of her jeans. She quickly typed in his number and waited nervously.

"Applebaum here."

Her heart skipped a beat at the sound of his voice.

"Oh, hello! This is Jeneva Yassi. We met at the symposium in Washington. Do you remember me?"

"How could I forget the woman who snatched my cab from under my nose?" He gave a hearty laugh. "How've you been?"

Without going into too much detail, she told him about the accident and said she was well on her way to a full recovery. She told him the reason for her call was to see whether he knew how she could get in touch with Amir Whitelaw, the archeologist that spoke at the symposium. He told her they exchanged business cards that day in the bar, but he would have to call her back after he located it. Curiously, he asked why she'd want to speak to an archaeologist. Jeneva hesitated to tell him about the bracelet but decided the more people who knew about it, the more help she might have in finding answers. She divulged her dilemma of trying to solve the mystery of the symbols. Now was not the time to tell him about her vision and what her mom communicated to her. Dexter seemed genuinely interested in helping and suggested he might be able to give some input regarding the magnetic aspects of the La Maná area. Jeneva forgot his expertise was astrology and magnet energy. Before hanging up, he asked her to forward a picture of all three symbols, so he could investigate them in detail.

That went surprisingly well, she thought, after they'd said their goodbyes. *Looks like there's a chance we might be working together on this journey after all, Mr. Applebaum.* She snickered.

Two nail-biting days passed, and she hadn't heard back from Dexter. He'd probably come to his senses and figured she was on a wild goose chase. Admittedly, the same thought crossed her own mind, on more than one occasion. Lately, she questioned a lot of things that happened after the accident at the CERN Control Centre. It seemed so many things had changed in her life.

The next day, she finally got a text from Dexter. He included Amir's cell number and two words. Good Luck!

"Boy, did I peg him wrong!" She was a bit disappointed in his short, direct response. "Who needs you, Dexter Applebaum? Certainly not me!" Her infuriated words echoed off the walls around her.

On the inside of the folder, she wrote Amir's number and then called him. No surprise, it went to voice mail. He was probably working at the pyramid. Jeneva left him a message, detailing the reason for her call, and asked him to call back at his earliest convenience. In her head, she rehearsed what she was going to say to him when he called back. She didn't want the same brushoff that she'd received from Dexter.

Jeneva didn't have to wait long. Amir called her back within the hour. She decided to inquire about a volunteer position at the Hummingbird Pyramid only and leave its connection with the bracelet until she met him in person.

He was quick to tell her he did remember her and the discussion in the bar about her, the woman who stole Dexter's cab.

"Nice to know I'm so memorable."

When she asked whether he had any leverage in who was accepted as a volunteer, the archaeologist told her they preferred someone with some schooling in archaeology and/or previous experience on a dig. He did assure her he'd put in a good word if her name came up. Wanting to justify her qualifications and give him some reason to support her, Jeneva highlighted all her volunteering around the world and asked whether that would bode well when a decision was being made. Amir assured her it very well could.

"It can be a lengthy process. I recommend you submit your application ASAP."

Jeneva thanked him for the information and told him she looked forward to, hopefully, working with him.

In less than an hour, she completed the application with all the necessary questions answered and her personal history as a volunteer attached. For good measure, she noted that she was an acquaintance of the archaeologist on site. She drove to the post office, where the envelope was stamped and deposited in that day's outgoing mail.

Now came the hard part, telling Maddy and Takoda what she was up to. She decided to wait until she was accepted before marching into that battle.

Chapter 17

S econd Chances
Before Takoda and Maddy headed out along the bustling Al Qasr Street in Sudan's capital city of Khartoum, Takoda turned to face her with a serious look on his face.

"Is something wrong?" Maddy asked.

"Not at all. It's just that when Jeneva and I visited foreign countries, I always insisted she hook her arm in mine. Would you mind humoring me? I don't want to lose you in a crowd." He tipped his elbow in her direction.

"There's something else—if you ever feel you are in danger or if we get separated, call out *Ómakiya yo*, as loud as you can, and I'll come running. It's Jeneva's and my secret code word."

"Ómakiya yo? What does it mean?"

"It means *help*, in Lakota."

"Ómakiya yo. Okay. That's so cool."

Maddy was tickled pink to think he cared so much about her welfare. She was a bit intimidated by the enormity of the city and gladly welcomed the safety of his arm and the secret code word.

As they strolled leisurely down the sidewalk, sandwiched between old and new high-rise buildings, Maddy questioned him about this, that, and the other thing, listening intently to Takoda's responses and following up with more questions.

When one of Takoda's answers trailed off, Maddy followed his gaze. Up ahead, a suspicious character approached them with his hands stuffed deep in his pockets. He wore a faded baseball cap and a camo jacket with matching pants, both riddled with holes. His sneakers were ripped out at the seams, exposing his dirty sockless feet. His head was lowered, so all you could see was a veiled shadow of his face. An old worn-out backpack he had slung over one shoulder appeared to be empty.

Takoda gave Maddy a slight pull in his direction as the suspicious figure passed by. When Takoda and Maddy looked over their shoulders, they saw him look back at them and then turn the corner and disappear. Maddy was relieved that, because of all the traveling Takoda had done over the years, he had a keen sense for trouble. It looked as if it was averted this time.

Maddy resumed asking Takoda questions. Suddenly, she sensed something happening behind her. The stranger reappeared, grabbed her phone out of her back pocket, and was about to make a getaway.

With catlike reflexes, Takoda reached over Maddy's head and grabbed the arm of the thief.

"Hold on there, son. What's your hurry?"

"Let me go, or I'll call the cops," the bandit hollered, jerking back and forth, trying to escape the grasp of Takoda towering two feet over him.

"Go ahead. Why don't you use that phone you just took from my . . .?" He hesitated a moment as if unsure of what he was expected to call his daughter's Little Sister. "My granddaughter." He gave Maddy a wink.

"We all know that isn't your phone, so why don't you just give it back, and we'll talk about why you took it in the first place."

The perp stilled, obviously not sure what he should do. Takoda had a firm grip on his arm, and it didn't look as if he was going to let him go any time soon.

"Hey man! What do you care? Take the stupid phone and let go of my arm!" He tossed the phone to his captor, who handed it back to Maddy.

"Thank you!" Maddy said, facing the phone snatcher. She thought he looked about her age.

"This was a gift from my best friend, and it means a lot to me." She held the phone next to her heart. "How would you feel if somebody took something of yours that meant a lot to you?"

The kid stood with his head facing the ground, seemingly reflecting on the question. "Sorry. I-I needed a phone for my little brother. He's only five." His voice was a little shaky. He spoke to Maddy as if hoping someone closer to his own age would be more apt to show mercy on him.

"Ever since our dad died a few years ago, Mom works two jobs, so I'm mostly responsible for him. I want him to have a phone so he can call me if he needs me. He is recovering from a serious virus and can't get out of bed without help. He's at home all alone till I get there after school."

"Is that true, or are you just trying to make us feel sorry for you and let you go?" Takoda gave his arm a subtle squeeze, just to let him know he was still in control.

With watering eyes, the thief turned and looked up at Takoda.

"It's true, sir! Come to my house, and I'll prove it. It's only a block away, and you can see for yourself." The boy pointed up the road.

Takoda gave him a grave look, somewhat convinced of the boy's sincerity, then told him, "That won't be necessary. What's your name, son?"

"My name's Charles, but everybody calls me Chuck."

Takoda continued to engage the kid in conversation, subtly releasing his arm. His ploy worked. The boy didn't move. He just stood there with beseeching eyes, darting back and forth from the girl to the man. Maddy looked at Takoda with wide-eyed trepidation, to which he gave her a wink, reassuring her everything would be okay. She trusted him totally but took hold of his arm just the same.

Takoda told the young man it was his granddaughter's first visit to Khartoum. Although, when he was here before, there hadn't been time for any sightseeing. He asked if he would be interested in making some money by being their city tour guide.

Chuck's expression said he couldn't believe his ears or the fact that Takoda would want anything to do with him after he just tried to steal his granddaughter's cell phone. Sometime while they were talking, he'd let go of his arm, without his noticing. He seemed torn between running and hearing Takoda out.

"That is, assuming you know your way around this city." Takoda tilted his head and raised one intimidating eyebrow.

"Yes, sir, I sure do. Every other weekend for the past two years, I've delivered pizza from Debonairs. Sometimes while I'm waiting for orders, I read the tour magazines they have in a rack by the door. So, there is a lot I know about the main attractions."

The suspicious character Takoda was worried about moments ago had changed into a totally different person. It seemed that the boy was not what he appeared to be at first glance, but a product of a situation he was trying to fix the only way he thought he could.

Takoda looked at Maddy. "What do you say? Should we give this young fellow a second chance?"

The boy's story seemed believable and touched her heart.

"Yes, I think we should. Besides, I have my phone back, and he did say he was sorry. Maybe he can earn enough from helping others to buy a phone for his brother. What do you say, Chuck? Is that something you might want to do?"

"Ah, what do you mean, helping others? I thought I just had to show you guys around?" He flipped his finger back and forth in their direction.

"Well, Chuck, we aren't the only tourists in this town. I'm sure there are lots of people who would pay for a good tour guide. Let's see how you do today, and maybe we can help you find a real job. That is, if you're up for it?" She gave him a questioning look.

Chuck was flabbergasted. This could be a real game changer. If he played his cards right and proved himself to these two, who knows, maybe he could quit the pick pocket business? He wasn't real comfortable stealing anyway. The thought of getting caught and his brother not knowing where he was, weighed heavy on his mind.

"Where do you want to start? I recommend Sudan National Museum. It's recently been revamped. I heard they imported three temples from Egypt. I haven't seen them, but I read the reviews, and they are supposed to be really something," Chuck said.

They followed their guide through the bustling streets. The young man guided them passed high-rises, traditional homes, handicraft shops, and into the museum, answering their questions with a convincing air of confidence. He told Takoda, if he was a fan of cars, he would really enjoy their next stop.

Takoda suggested they take a break for a bite to eat, maybe at the place Chuck delivered pizza for. When they arrived at Debonairs, there was a line up out the door. Chuck told them to wait on the patio and he would see whether he could get them in.

While Takoda and Maddy waited for Chuck to come back, they agreed the story he told them had merit after all and they were right to take a chance on him. When he emerged from the restaurant a few moments later, he took Maddy's hand.

"Come with me."

A pretty waitress directed them to a booth at the back of the crowded room. Chuck thanked her by name, and she gave him a look that made it obvious she was smitten with the handsome young man. They finished a large of what was proclaimed to be *The Best Pizza in Town*. Despite their full bellies, Chuck convinced them to try the bite-size cinnamon buns, dripping with icing and topped with chocolate syrup. Once every crumb was gone, Takoda paid the bill, leaving a generous tip for the great service.

"You have to make this a feature stop on your tours. That was the best pizza I've ever eaten. And those little buns, well, they are to die for. Almost as good as Krispy Kreme donuts." Maddy's eyes popped, and she licked her lips.

Next, Chuck took them to the Republican Palace Museum. It also housed an extravagant car collection, just as Chuck mentioned. The automobiles didn't interest Maddy; she wanted to know more about the culture. So, while Takoda meandered through the vehicles, Chuck gave her a one-on-one narrative of the history of Sudan and of the cultural displays. All of this she'd try to share with Jeneva when she called her later. Along with the fact that Chuck had tried to steal her phone, then turned out to be not a bad kid after all.

When they exited the museum, Chuck told them he needed to get home to take care of his brother because his mother was working the afternoon shift at the dry cleaner and expected him before she left. Takoda told him he did a surprisingly good job and wondered if he'd be able to continue their tour tomorrow. As an incentive, Takoda took a twenty-euro bill from his wallet and handed it to Chuck, thanking him for an enjoyable day. He shook the boy's hand, again commending him on a job well done.

Chuck stuck the money in his pocket.

"I'm sorry, but tomorrow is Sunday, and Mom insists we spent the day together. It's the only time all week we are home at the same time. But! If you could wait till next Saturday, I'd be available all day."

It was agreed, they would continue their city tour next weekend. Chuck pointed them in the direction of their hotel and took off at a full run in the same direction.

When they entered their suite, Maddy asked Takoda if he would mind if she took a nap before they went for dinner. He agreed that would be a great idea.

It was a good thing Takoda set his alarm, or they might have missed their dinner reservation. While Maddy waited for him to freshen up, she called Jeneva to fill her in on the events of their day. By the time she finished telling her everything, and they'd said their good- byes, Takoda had nodded off on the couch. She woke Takoda and told him that Jeneva said hi and that she was feeling about ninety percent but was going mad with nothing to do but exercise, watch TV, and read.

Over dinner that night, the two talked about their day.

"We took what could have been a real downer of a day and made it into a great adventure. I can't wait till tomorrow. Do you think Chuck will show up Saturday?"

"Well, we know he can use the money, and I think he really enjoyed showing us around, so fingers crossed. Otherwise, we may be looking for a map."

The next day Maddy spent on the internet looking for stuff she thought would be interesting to see in the area.

Takoda and Maddy spent the week that followed, organizing permits, hiring his team, setting up barricades and surveying the area around the junction of the White and Blue Niles. Maddy was his right hand. She picked up and copied permits and posted them at designated spots on the site. As well as setting up a file system and shopping for various office necessities. She also rented a jeep for them to use during their stay. She'd called a rental company and had them drop off a small, air-conditioned trailer at the site for the team to use as an office. A large canopy tent for the workers to escape from the sweltering afternoon sun was also erected closer to the bank of the river. It was her responsibility to ensure there was always iced tea in the fridge for Takoda and lots of water in the cooler for the team.

WHEN CHUCK ARRIVED Saturday morning, Takoda and Maddy were waiting on the sidewalk in front of their hotel.

Takoda requested the tour begin at the White Nile Bridge. Chuck pointed out a sign that stating it was the high point of the world's longest river, overlooking the confluence of the Blue and

White Niles. He pointed at the trailer and tent by the bank and admitted he didn't know what was going on over there. Takoda informed him that it was his research site. This intrigued Chuck. He questioned what kind of research he was doing. They found a park bench on the bank, and a discussion of potable water and ancient Native American Indian technology carried on for the better part of an hour. By then, Maddy was looking bored. She put her hand on Chuck's shoulder to get his attention.

She told him she considered visiting a Camel Market. But after reading more about it, she decided it was a long way to go to have some floppy lipped, humpbacked creature spit in your face. All three of them laughed.

"Do people really eat camels?" Her face contorted.

"Most often, it is a meal prepared and served during festivals. Not something we eat on a regular basis." Chuck told her.

When she asked him about going to the Hamed el-Nil Tomb on Friday. He was truly disappointed, and he told her he was writing an exam in the morning and had to watch his brother in the afternoon.

"I think you can watch a ceremony on YouTube.".

"I may just do that."

Suddenly, Takoda's stomach gave out a loud, rolling growl.

"We better get some food into you." Maddy gave his stomach a pat.

Chuck found a little café with a patio that served a variety of local dishes.

After they finished eating, Chuck took them on an alternate route back to their hotel, describing the area sites as they strolled along. They were passing through a grass area, when Chuck came to an abrupt stop. His head dropped, and his eyes fixated on the lush grass that surrounded them.

"What is it, Chuck? Did you lose something?"

"Nope! I found something." He reached into the thick grass and pulled up a four-leaf clover.

"For you, my lady." He bowed and offered her the symbol of good luck.

"Thanks. How'd you do that?" She squinted down at the grass to see whether she could find one. "It didn't even take you a minute to find it. I've never found one!"

"No biggy, I do it all the time." He shrugged nonchalantly.

"There's one more spot I'd like to show you. Follow me." Chuck took them to Nile Avenue, adjacent to Tuti Island. They crossed the bridge linking the fast-paced life of Khartoum to the quiet and calmness of Tuti Island. They sat on a bench and listen to music from a local band. It was the best spot to view the landmarks of the city and watch the sunset beyond the suspension bridge. The perfect ending to a perfect day. It was evident, Chuck had found his calling. Thanks to a second chance.

Chapter 18

Remuneration and Retirement

For the last two weeks, Jeneva had behaved herself, getting plenty of rest and doing the exercises recommended by her physical therapist to strengthen her arm. On her way to the doctor's office for a follow-up appointment, she stopped at the bank to deposit her check from the CERN Control Centre. The young teller was obviously shocked by the amount and discreetly paraded it in and out of the cubicles showing the other tellers, each time receiving the same look of disbelief. She knocked on the door of the bank manager's glassed-in office, went in, and handed him the check. After scrutinizing Jeneva from the comfort of his high-back leather chair, he made a phone call. He spoke for a few moments, and then he put his stamp of approval and signature on the back of the check and returned it to the teller.

"Miss Yassi. Mr. Kostiuk, our general manager, wanted me to thank you for your business and suggested you consider speaking to one of our investment officers."

"I prefer to deposit the whole amount in my account for now." Jeneva was anticipating her need of a substantial amount of money for her trip to Ecuador.

Inquiring eyes were still pointing in her direction as she exited the first set of doors. She pushed through the second set, which were much heavier, with wrought-iron security lattice inlays. A mother struggled to maneuver a baby carriage into the narrow vestibule.

"Here. Let me help." Jeneva held the door. She grimaced as the wheel ran over her foot. "Let me get that one for you as well." She opened the interior door.

Glancing back into the bank, Jeneva noticed everyone had gone back to their tasks at hand. Even the woman she'd just held the doors for had forgotten about her, with not even a thank you. She moved on to her next stop on her list.

There were a couple patients in the doctor's waiting room when she arrived. To pass the time, she opened her pictures on her phone. When she got to the one taken at Maddy's birthday party, the sight of Brian brought back the fact that he was gone. Her heart tightened in her chest. She didn't think she would ever forgive herself for not being honest with her feelings.

After a short time, the receptionist told her to go to Room 2. When the doctor asked how she was doing, she mentioned the dizzy spells she'd been experiencing. He immediately sent her for a CT of her head to check for any abnormalities. The report came back unremarkable, in other words, normal.

"Even though there was nothing evident on your scan, the brain is a mysterious organ and has a mind of its own, no pun intended," he chuckled. "One minute, it remembers your first-grade teacher's name, the next, you can't remember your own." The doctor chuckled again.

Jeneva told him she played some of the brain teaser games on the internet, the ones her specialist encouraged her to use to exercise the brain. He advised her to continue with such activities, along with physical therapy, and suggested she call the office immediately if the dizzy spells persisted. She assured him she would and left the building.

After returning to her car, Jeneva pulled down the sun visor. Thanks to her diligent application of vitamin E, the scar on her forehead was healing quite nicely. If she combed her hair just right, she could totally hide it. Looking at her now, no one would even suspect the harrowing experience she'd escaped. Undeniably, the emotional scars of that traumatic day would haunt her for quite some time.

She pulled her list from her purse. She was finding it most helpful to organize her day on paper rather than trying to remember everything. Bank, check; doctor, check; next stop, grocery store. She drove a few blocks and pulled into the large Co-Op store parking lot and took out another list. She read it out loud as a reminder to herself.

"Milk, bread, eggs, fish. All the experts say fish is a brain food. Better get lots. Apples, bananas, spinach, onions, yogurt and cheese. Maybe I'll grab some berries and make myself a fruit salad for lunch." She stuffed the list in her purse.

She used to shop there every week and was very familiar with the layout and location of most items. Since the accident, Maddy had taken over the task for her. Now, with this memory thing going on, she wandered the aisles as if it were her first time in the store.

It was lunchtime when she wheeled her cart to the front of the store. The tills were backed up four-to-five people deep. Despite the possible longer wait, she always looked for a cashier that was smiling and conversing with their customers. Jeneva took this as a sign that they enjoyed their job. The cashier she chose today was an older woman who looked excited when each new customer stepped up, much like Mrs. Claus might react when Santa returned from his long night of delivering presents, Jeneva mused. It was going to be quite a wait, so she grabbed one of the magazines strategically placed at arm's length. It showed the usual headlines, "Who's divorcing who?" "How to lose belly fat in twenty days;" "What are the latest Paris fashions?" Everything inquiring minds might want to know. In her mind, she decided she didn't need to know and put it back in the holder. Instead, she took another look at her list to confirm she hadn't missed anything. Her phone rang.

"Hello, this is Jeneva . . . Hello, I'm having trouble hearing you. Hang on, I'm going to move outside. Please stay on the line."

Jeneva pushed her cart off to the side and headed for the automatic exit door. She assumed it was either Maddy or Takoda calling to check up on her. Once outside, she repeated, "Hello, are you there?"

The voice that responded was unfamiliar. "Hello, Jeneva, my name is Willy. I'm the volunteer coordinator who is recruiting for the archaeological dig in Ecuador."

"Oh! Hello, Willy."

"I have received your application and was wondering if you would be interested in joining the dig at the Hummingbird Pyramid?"

Jeneva tried to contain her enthusiasm, to no avail.

"Yes! Yes! I mean, can I get back to you in a couple days? I have a few things to take care of before leaving." The big thing would be breaking the news to her dad and Maddy.

The call excited her so much, she drove away, forgetting to go back in for her groceries. After returning to the store, she noticed the cashier she intended to go to must have gone on break and only one customer remained in the line.

A skinny girl with a nose ring and purple hair was at the till. She had an "I can't wait to get out of here" look on her face. Jeneva's head was in Ecuador at this point, and she wasn't letting anyone rain on her parade. To her surprise, the girl was quite friendly, even asked how her day was going. Maybe it was the big clown smile frozen on Jeneva's face that lightened the girl's mood.

"You can never underestimate the impact of a smile," she said, glancing at her own in the rear-view mirror."

When she arrived at her apartment, she had no berries.

"I should have put them on the list," she told herself. "So, no fruit salad for lunch." She found that talking to herself helped deter the feelings of loneliness. She was missing Maddy and her dad's company.

"Okay, new plan. I'll cut up pieces of smoked salmon, and spread creamed cheese on crackers, and garnish with apple slices on the side. Perfect!"

While pillowlike clouds rolled across the midday sky, she enjoyed her small feast, relaxing in her chaise lounge on the patio.

"I could get used this." She closed her tired eyes. These afternoon catnaps were becoming a daily ritual, a favorable perk of her early retirement.

As much as she dreaded making the call to her dad and Maddy, the time had come. If she was going to get her journey underway, she must face the opposition with suitable arguments to back up her decision. Jeneva went to her desk and composed a list. There were two columns: one for their possible questions and the other, her answers. When she thought all bases were covered, she called her father's cell.

"Hello sweetheart, everything all right?" Takoda asked.

"Everything's perfect. I got a thumbs-up from the doctor, and my arm feels pretty good. How are things going with you guys? Is Maddy giving you any grief?"

"I heard that. You're on speaker," Maddy piped in.

"Oops! Well, are you?"

Takoda answered for her. "She's actually been a godsend. Pretty much runs the office. I'm really going to miss her when she leaves for school in a couple weeks."

"I can't believe how hot it is here. Thankfully the trailer is air conditioned." Maddy told her.

"I'm glad to hear you two are getting along so well. I have something to tell you."

"What's wrong! Do you need me to come back?" Maddy hollered.

Jeneva thought she was going to jump through the phone line.

"Nothing's wrong. On the contrary, the doctor has given me the okay to travel." *Time to drop the bombshell and deal with the fallout.*

"I was thinking I'd head to Ecuador to volunteer at that Humming-bird Pyramid. Maddy, I reviewed all the stuff you found, and I'm convinced there is a connection between the symbols on my bracelet and the pyramid itself. I've been in contact with the archaeological department, and they've accepted me as a volunteer on the next dig. I'm so excited."

"It sounds like you have already made your decision, sweetie. I hope you know what you're doing." Takoda's tone told Jeneva he was stifling his reservations.

"I do. I think this is the journey Mom wanted me to take."

Jeneva could imagine how hard it was for them to let her travel alone, so soon after almost losing her.

"I promise to be careful and call every week."

"You better!" Maddy's words sounded emphatic.

"When will you leave?" Takoda asked.

"I'll be booking my flights today for an arrival in Ecuador September twenty-first. That gives me a month to get this arm back into shape. And before you ask, Maddy. I am doing my exercises." She heard her laugh in the background.

"Okay. We love you and understand how important this trip is to you. Safe travels." Her dad said, the reluctance still lingering in his tone.

"Love you." Jeneva heard the sadness in Maddy's voice as the line went dead.

"All in all, that went better than expected," Jeneva reassured herself, letting out a sigh of relief.

"Now let's get this show on the road," she muttered to the smiling reflection on the screen of her computer. Then her fingers went to work on the keyboard booking her flight to Quito, Ecuador, then a quick email to Willy, confirming her flight and arrival time. Once everything was in place, she tucked her hands behind her head and tilted back in her leather chair. Jeneva felt this was the beginning of a wonderful journey. In a moderately exuberant voice, she declared out loud, "Destiny, here I come!"

Chapter 19

One Small Act of Kindness

Chuck had texted Takoda to see if they could meet for lunch on Sunday. He was booked up with tours and it would be the last chance he'd have to see Maddy before she left.

Chuck was waving at them as they walked into Debonairs.

"This is my mom." Chuck put his hand on the woman's shoulder. She was small in stature, with striking features that needed no make-up. Her long auburn hair fell loosely down her back, and she was wearing the new dress Chuck had bought her.

"Hi. I'm Tami. I'm so happy to finally meet you both," she said, shaking hands with the two strangers.

Everyone took a seat.

"I've got great news!" Chuck couldn't contain his excitement. "Now that Owyn isn't sick so much, he has gone back to school, which frees up some time for me to do tours. Debonairs allowed me to put up a sign advertising city tours this summer. Did you see it when you came in? I've been doing them mornings and weekends. So far, I've done six, and with the money I made from them, and what you gave me, I paid last months and next month's rent, and bought Mom this new dress. Doesn't it look pretty on her?" Chuck smiled proudly. And! I bought myself a cell phone. I wrote my number down for you. So, we can keep in touch." He handed her a piece of paper.

Tami gave Chuck a kiss on the check then she reached across the table and put her hand on Takoda's. Tears were welling in the corners of her eyes when she spoke. "Kind sir."

"Please. Call me Takoda."

"Takoda, and you too, Maddy. I can't tell you what your forgiveness and understanding toward Chuck's misguided behavior means to me. I have tried to raise him to be a good boy. He was trying to

110

do the right thing but in the wrong way. Since he met you, he has changed. I can't believe the difference in him. He's become a respectful young man, working here and starting his own tour business. I know he will agree with me that he owes it all to you."

She bowed her head, and her tears fell like silent raindrops on the tabletop. Chuck handed her a napkin and put his arm around her shoulder.

"Don't cry, Mom. I owe you so much too."

Tami dabbed her eyes and blew her nose.

"Enough of this blubbering. I just wanted you to know how much I appreciate the way you handled the situation. If you had turned Chuck in to the police instead of giving him a second chance . . ." She took a deep breath, collected herself, and continued. "Well, let's just say, things would be very different today for me and my boys. Thank you, from the bottom of my heart."

"Yes, thank you!" Chuck said. "You taught me a valuable lesson I will never forget. I hope someday I have the opportunity to change someone else's life for the better, like you did for me."

"There are opportunities all around us. We just have to recognize them and do something with them, like smiling at a stranger who looks sad. It seems like a small gesture, but your smile could have a positive impact you will never know about, and it didn't cost you anything." They all nodded at Maddy in agreement.

Owyn's head was barely visible over the table, and his small frame and quiet nature veiled his presence in the dimly lit eatery. While the others were conversing, the five-year-old listened and saw his chance to interject.

"I can smile," he said with enthusiasm as he climbed up on his chair.

"See!" His two top teeth were missing, making it a comical sight. Everyone smiled back at him.

"And it is a beauty!" Takoda told him. "I hope you share it with everybody."

"I will." He promised.

"Excellent, now let's order that pizza. I'm starving." Takoda said.

"Me too!" Owyn said, sitting back down in his chair.

They looked like one big happy family, huddled around the table, enjoying not only a meal but each other's' company as well, no cell phones ringing and no game playing on a tablet, just friendly conversation.

Being true to his word, Owyn stopped at each table as they were leaving the restaurant and gave everyone a big toothless smile, which to his delight, ricocheted back at him every time.

Takoda went to the jeep to check the upcoming weather reports on his phone, and Owyn and his mom stopped at the restroom. So Maddy and Chuck sat on a picnic table on the patio to wait.

"Well, I guess this is it. I'm heading home soon." She pouted.

The two young friends stood arm's-length apart, unsure of what to say.

"I'm going to," they said in unison, then laughed.

"Miss you!"

"I'll miss you too," Chuck echoed an octave louder. He kissed her cheek ever so gently and gave her another hug that she returned wholeheartedly this time. Neither wanted to let go. They both knew this could be good-bye forever.

Chapter 20

The Divining Rod

When Monday morning rolled around, rather than being sad about leaving, Maddy thought about going back to school and spending time with her friends. She decided the grown-up thing to do was to be happy she had been given this great opportunity and enjoy her last few days as Takoda's assistant.

She tallied up all the accounts receivable and was filing them when Takoda opened the door of the trailer and poked his head in.

"You busy? I picked up a couple pitas for us. Thought we could have lunch on the shore before the interview."

"Yes, thank you, that sounds wonderful, as long as we can find a shady tree to sit under. This heat is horrendous." Maddy closed the file cabinet drawer and grabbed a couple cans of iced tea from the fridge.

It was high noon when they sat down on the bank beside the merging rivers. Surging waves were crashing forward, sending a cool mist lofting over the bank. It was a welcome relief on their hot skin. Maddy pointed out a group of men and women setting up lighting and cameras a little farther up the bank of the main river. She glanced at her watch. It was 12:50 p.m.

"Looks like they are just about ready for you."

After several inquiring calls from the local newspapers and TV stations, Maddy had arranged for Takoda to introduce himself and explain what he was doing there. Several reporters and camera operators were standing by to find out who and why there was so much interest in the Nile, all of a sudden.

After Takoda introduced himself, and his assistant, he told them a little about his background and an explanation of his research.

"What we have here is somewhat of a phenomenon. There is an accumulation of magnetic rocks at the convergence of these two rivers. What we are interested in is the effects they have on the purification of the water. Due to the high temperatures, and in the interest of the welfare of the workers, we have not been able to get much work done." He apologized for the delay and assured them work would commence as soon as possible.

There was a lot of huffing and puffing, and some of the unguarded remarks contained the F-bomb, which Maddy could tell from his expression, did not impress Takoda in the least. As he quickly ushered his young assistant past the disgruntled group of broadcasters and their vulgarities, a thin man in a polo shirt and cargo pants called out to Takoda.

"Wait! Mr. Yassi. Sorry to bother you, sir. I'm wondering when you expect to have more details for us?"

Maddy recognized the man as one of the reporters who didn't curse in disappointment like his colleagues but had just nodded and headed in the direction of the collection of vans.

"I'm sorry, son, with the high temperatures and seemingly more in the forecast, it may be a while. I'll contact you when we have something newsworthy. Do you have a card?"

"Yes, let me grab one." He quickly grabbed a card from the dash of his van.

Takoda took the reporter's identification and handed it to Maddy.

"Can you tack it on the board in the trailer for me? I'd like to reward his professional behavior by calling him first." Takoda didn't lower his voice. Clearly, he wanted him to know exactly how he felt and that his behavior was appreciated and would be rewarded.

"Yes, sir, I'll do it right now." They turned toward their trailer.

"WAIT!" A YOUNG VOICE hollered.

Takoda did an about-face, smiled, and tilted his head questioningly at the young dark-skinned boy who'd appeared from out of nowhere. He stood bold as can be, in front of him, craning his neck up.

"Mr. Yassi, my name is Kenan."

He told them of his life's struggle on the barren desert and that it was his dream to find water for his community. The young boy's story and intensity to help his community touched Takoda's soul. He felt like he should do something to help him, but what? Then it came to him.

"If you could excuse me, I'll be right back." Takoda turned and headed toward the trailer.

Seeing the fatigue on the kid's face, Maddy suggested they sit. She engaged him in idle conversation. He told her he was fifteen, living with his grandmother while his parents worked here in Khartoum because they were unable to grow crops in their village due to the lack of water. She found him very serious and focused for someone her own age.

When Takoda returned, he gave Kenan a gift, a divining rod, and spent the afternoon showing him how to properly use it.

He thanked Takoda and told them he would use the diving rod to help as many people as he could find the water that would change their lives.

On the way back to the trailer, Maddy put her hand on Takoda's arm. He stopped and looked down at her.

"What is it, Maddy?"

"I know you had other things to do this afternoon, but I'm pretty sure what you did for Kenan will someday prove to be well worth your time." She spoke.

"I think you're right. It is important to take the time to listen to people as you travel along life's journey and offer support whenever you can. Small acts of kindness can make big changes in people's lives."

"Speaking of kindness. I want to thank you for your kindness. I know we didn't know each other that well when you agreed to bring me here. I hope I've been more help than hinderance. Being here, working with you, helped me through my grief. You've been like a father to me. Jeneva was right. I will be taking a lot of great memories with me when I leave."

"It's been wonderful for me as well. I'm going to miss you."

Chapter 21

Emergency Landing

It was half past three in the morning, and the cabin of the Boeing 737, on route to Ecuador, was as quiet as the ninth hour of prayer. The lights were dimmed as a courtesy to the passengers who wished to sleep. In the rear of the plane, a couple of night owls were still awake reading. Jeneva was one of them. She was compiling a list of questions for Amir and reviewing the info Maddy had printed for her about the Hummingbird Pyramid.

The day she booked the trip, she considered indulging in the benefits of first class, where she'd gain extra legroom and the elaborate meal service. She came to the conclusion she didn't need the extra room, being a size 8, or need a big meal in the middle of the night. That would only make her stomach-ache, so she booked a window seat in Row 27. Best to let someone who needed the room and big meal sit up front and pay double the fair. To her way of thinking, it really wasn't a matter of need in most cases, but more of a "look at me, I'm special" display of self-importance. Not her style at all.

As Jeneva made her way down the narrow aisle, in the rear of the plane she spotted the fifteen or so young boys she'd observed checking in earlier. Their luggage had a picture of a Viking head wearing a horned helmet and "Vincent Massey High School, Brandon, MB" monogrammed on the side of each one. An identical logo was stamped on the back of the purple jerseys the team was wearing.

When they'd been waiting in the preboarding area, Jeneva had watched as the coach rallied his boys in a circle. They'd said a prayer, asking for safe passage for all. Then, he'd taken center ring and told his team that they were representatives of their families, their city, and their country, and he expected them to do him and them proud. Closing the circle with hands in, they'd given a toned-down version of their team cry, "*Go Trojans!*"

Jeneva had whispered to the older lady sitting beside her, who had also been watching. "That was certainly a refreshing ritual to observe."

The lady had replied in a hushed voice. "That coach is a credit to their school and most definitely having a positive impact on those boys. It's obvious he has their respect."

"Those young men may not know it now, but someday those kinds of gestures will be remembered, and who knows, it could lead them to a decision that could change the direction of their whole life."

She was brought back to the present when she heard a lot of coughing. It was coming from the other side of the curtains at the front of the plane. The cabin lights came on, illuminating a dark gray stream of smoke seeping through the crack in the curtains separating premium from economy seating. A loud voice resonated over the intercom, telling the passengers to please wake up and make sure their seat belts were fastened. The announcer started coughing, then continued with instructions to remain in their seats and stay calm. There was more coughing.

Jeneva felt a wave of anxiety flood her body, and her heart hammered in her chest. Beads of sweat slowly dripped down her temples, her palms felt clammy, and she was certain her armpits were damp. *How can this be happening? I'm so close to discovering my destiny. This can't be where it all ends.*

The oxygen masks fell from their compartments, startling most of the remaining sleepers and causing confusion and panic in the cabin. The two first class attendants, overcome by smoke, made their way to empty seats in coach and started sucking on the dangling yellow cups. Under the coughing, gagging, and screaming from two hundred scared patrons, the captain was making an announcement that no one was acknowledging.

Across the aisle from Jeneva, a middle-aged man, who could have been mistaken for one of the *Duck Dynasty* brothers, stood in the aisle.

"Shut the fuck up! The captain's talking!" The cabin went so quiet you could've heard a pin drop.

The captain repeated, "This is the captain. You are in no immediate danger. The co-pilot has engaged the exhaust fans, so the smoke will be diminishing momentarily. Please stay in your seats with your masks on until the attendants say it is safe to remove them. It appears the galley oven was turned up, instead of off, causing all that smoke. I assure you everything is under control, and you are in no danger. We will be landing in Quito in approximately ten minutes." His microphone clicked off.

Jeneva's eyes closed. She lowered her head and massaged her neck. She inhaled. Then slowly exhaled all the anxiety out of her body. Her shoulders relaxed and her heartbeats seemed to slow. Glancing at the two elderly ladies beside her, she gave their worried faces a reassuring smile.

With some of the flight attendants unable to assist during this emergency situation, Jeneva noticed several of the Canadian boys helping folks with their masks and reassuring them everything was going to be fine. The coach made his way to her row. He stopped to ask whether they needed help. Jeneva said she and the two ladies beside her were all right, and he moved on to the next row. A few more boys from the football team hustled past the coach toward the front of the plane. Twelve staggering first class passengers, with cupped hands over their noses and mouths, were blindly pushing through the curtain, trying to escape the ensuing smoke. There had been a malfunction, and their masks hadn't dropped. The boys in purple assisted the coughing folks to the empty seats in economy, where they collapsed and, frantically, strapped on the dangling masks and seatbelts.

The two flight attendants from coach thanked the boys for their help and asked them to return to their seats and strap on their masks and buckle up. They took their time checking to make sure everyone was settled before climbing into their seats and donning their oxygen masks.

Finally, everyone was seated and breathing relatively calmly, waiting in anticipation of the touchdown. Those who were able watched as the plane banked to the left, then straightened, aligning itself with the distant landing strip.

Out of the silence, a woman's voice screamed, "*Fire!*"

The curtains at the front of the plane turned into a blanket of fiery flames. In moments they were traveling along the roof like the devil's fingers reaching out from hell. Thick black smoke rapidly spread through the main cabin.

Again, Jeneva felt her body tense with anxiety. The flames were getting closer. She was reminded of how it felt when she opened the oven door and the heat hit her face-on. *Not again. This is just like when I was trapped in the lab at CERN.* A tear trickled down her cheek and she bit her lip, hard enough to draw blood.

Multiple screams cut the shocked silence. A baby cried, people prayed, and couples held on to each other. Some had tears rolling down their cheeks as they said what might be their last "I love you." One of the masked flight attendants extinguished the charred bulkhead and managed to foam the burning roof before it reached the back of the plane. The other attendant followed her down the aisle, repeating the order for everyone to remain calm and stay in their seat.

The weight of the plane bouncing on the landing gear as it touched down sent another torrent of gasps and screams through the cabin. And then, the sighs of relief and thanks to God, filled the smoky chamber.

Emergency vehicles waited on the tarmac when the plane came to a stop. The tower instructed the captain to position the plane several meters away from the terminal and recommended the escape slides be engaged. Inside, the flight attendants were wearing their portable masks, giving them Darth Vader voices. They directed the passengers to disembark through the emergency exits and told them to leave all their belongings behind. Most of the Canadian boys evacuated at the rear and made their way to the bottom of the three emergency slides, where they helped the flailing bodies to their feet. The passengers were then ushered away from the plane by airport security. The rest of the team stood at the interior exits, lending a hand to the panicking passengers, who were pushing and shoving their way through the aisle trying to get onto the yellow slides.

When everyone was off the plane and safely settled in a waiting area, the fire chief from the airport fire department was sent into the plane to assess the situation. After the all clear was given, a baggage crew was sent in to retrieve all the carry-on bags. Passengers were given complimentary refreshments while they waited. There was a lot of grumbling and complaining going on in the holding area. Some people were still coughing and threatening to sue the airline for damages.

Jeneva sat with the two senior ladies that had sat beside her on the plane. The older of the two introduced herself as Debra and the other as her little sister, Deanna, who rolled her eyes disapprovingly then said, "Thank goodness I took my anti-nausea pill. I slept through the whole thing."

"I know! I was afraid to wake you for fear that you would have lost it. My heart is just starting to slow down now," Debra said.

"It was something I'll never forget, that's for sure. But we are all safe, that's the important thing," Jeneva said.

Both ladies nodded in agreement.

"We're on our way to celebrate my fiftieth birthday with our older sister, Franny. She runs a bed-and-breakfast on the outskirts of Quito," Debra told her.

The three ladies chatted about the young boys who stepped up to help the panic-stricken travelers. They unanimously agreed the team acted very responsibly and should be recognized for their efforts.

"It was very admirable of them," Deanna said.

"One even offered to ride down the slide with me. I almost took him up on it. He was a cutie," Debra told them, and the trio giggled like schoolgirls.

It was chaotic confusion when the passengers were told to collect their carry-ons from the revolving belt in the next room. A bystander would have guessed it was a rush to a Black Friday Sale. Jeneva was glad her beaded handbag was so unique. She was able to spot it immediately. A short while later, the checked bags started tumbling down the chute of an adjacent belt. The boys from Brandon were standing around the carousel, assisting anyone who seemed to be struggling. Thanks to the big yellow star Jeneva stenciled on her suitcase, it was as easy to spot. One of the boys in purple came to assist Debra and Deanna, who were wrestling through the crowd to get to their luggage. Content that they were well taken care of, Jeneva wished Deanna a happy birthday and bid them good-bye and was on her way out of the airport before everyone else.

Jeneva spotted a familiar face amongst the cluster of drivers waiting for their fares by the exit doors. She recognized Willy from their Facebook video chat and gave him a wave.

"Welcome to Ecuador, Miss Yassi. Your chariot awaits!" He bowed and rolled his arm in the direction of the exit. Relinquishing her hold on her large suitcase to him, they headed outside.

Chapter 22

News Travels Fast

Takoda and Maddy were both on pins and needles, he in Sudan and her in Washington, watching the arrival of Jeneva's flight into Ecuador on the news. She was nowhere in sight.

The reporters maneuver through the crowd, talking to the passengers who were most eager to tell their version of what happened. There had been idle threats to sue for damages. Still no Jeneva.

The GOLTV Sports Channel and LDU Quito TV must have received notice of the arrival of the Canadian football team and had reporters and camera operators on location to welcome them. The news of the boys' actions on board their flight was definitely of interest to the sports fans. The camera operator rallied the football team for a group shot with the airplane in the background.

The female sports announcer said, "These young men are the number-one high school football team in Canada and were invited to play against Quito's reigning champions this Sunday."

She approached the middle-aged man with "Coach" monogrammed on his jacket.

"I'm here with Coach Mills. Coach, everyone is thanking the boys in the purple jerseys. Do you have anything you would like to say to them?"

"I am very proud of our team for working together and stepping up to help. They have always worked well together on and off the field." He quickly turned away from the camera and rejoined his team.

The reporter wished both teams good luck on Sunday, and the segment ended.

Maddy tried calling Jeneva, but she wasn't picking up, so she called Takoda to see if he'd heard from her.

"Takoda, did you see the news about Jeneva's plane? I've been trying to call but she's not picking up."

"I'm sure she's fine. They didn't mention anyone being hurt during the ordeal. She probably had her phone off during the flight and is on her way to her hotel. She'll get in touch with us soon. Try not to worry." She was grateful for his reassuring words, but she couldn't help herself.

Chapter 23

Road to La Maná
    "If you don't mind, Willy, I have to make a couple calls before we hit the road."

"No problem. I'll go get the jeep and meet you here in a few minutes."

She called her dad first and reassured him she had not suffered any injures and would soon be on her way to La Maná.

Next, she called Maddy.

"I have been going out of our mind with worry! We saw the news about your plane catching on fire. Are you okay?"

"Yes, I'm fine. I hate to say it, but there was a moment I didn't think we were going to survive. There was a second set of flames that started heading toward me—my heart almost jumped out of my chest."

"That sounds so scary. Are you sure you're, okay?"

"I am. You can stop worrying. The volunteer coordinator is just pulling up. He's driving me to the hotel."

"Okay, call me soon. Love ya!"

"Love you too. Bye."

Once Jeneva was comfortably seated in the passenger seat and her bags were loaded. they were on their way to her hotel.

Jeneva found Willy to be a wealth of knowledge and noticed he took great pleasure in giving her the fifty-cent tour, as he called it. Which in truth, she figured, would have cost the average tourist substantially more. He informed her of the five-hour drive ahead of them and immediately launched into his life story. He was born and raised on a farm and started his own corporation at the early age of twenty. Five years later, he sold his robotics technology, lock, stock, and barrel for a cool million and a half, which allowed him to head out and explore the world. While he was visiting Newfoundland, he'd met Amir, who at the time was working at an archaeological dig on the Avalon Peninsula. Willy was recounting his story with the enthusiasm of a greyhound chasing a rabbit and stopped momentarily for a short breath. Then he continued.

"While on a tour of an archaeological dig, our group was watching a guy who turned out to be Amir. He was skillfully dusting the ground, slowly revealing pieces of broken artifacts. I found it fascinating that he was unearthing history with a hand broom and a toothbrush. He asked if anyone would like to try their hand at revealing the ancient graphics on a piece of pottery. I jumped in the pit, almost landing on a pile of broken plates. I've been coordinating volunteers and working with his team ever since."

Jeneva and her father had visited Egypt, and she remembered how fascinated she was by the majestic ancient pyramids and the museums filled with artifacts. So, when Willy mentioned that the examination of the basalts of the Great Pyramid of Giza in Egypt revealed ferromagnetic components identical to those found in the La Maná area, Jeneva asked, "How is that even possible? They are so far apart."

Her driver said the La Maná structures were located at one-degree south latitude along Ecuador's Calope River and spread across an area of more than thirty square miles.

"If you look on a world map, you can draw a line eight thousand miles across from one to the other." Willy drew an invisible line in the air, then went on to say, "The ancient monument Amir's team is working on now was named for the great variety of hummingbirds that arrive twice a year. It's quite the sight to see when they shroud the top of the pyramid. Sometimes a bunch of them find their way into the causeways connecting the adjacent structures. The sound that emanates," he said, swaying his head, "is like a beautiful symphony."

"Fascinating!" She made a mental note; *I better look into that. It might be another connection to the symbols.*

Willy noticed her hand move toward her bracelet and commented on its uniqueness.

Remembering her mother's message to keep an open mind to the opinions of others, Jeneva laid her arm on the center console for him to have a better look. She pointed at the hummingbird and told him how Maddy made the connection between it and Amir's story in the symposium pamphlet. He turned his attention back to the road and went on about how thousands of tourists visit the pyramid every year to see the hummingbirds.

Jeneva became distracted by the beautiful landscape they were driving through and momentarily lost interest in Willy's jibber jabber, only half listening.

Likely suspecting his enlightenments were being ignored, he raised his voice.

"So, it begs the question, if a stone falls in one of the monuments, is it possible the noise reverberates off the ferromagnetic surfaces and through the causeway?" Willy turned to face Jeneva. "Well, what do you think, Jeneva?"

At the mention of magnetics, Jeneva's thoughts once again turned to Dexter. She wondered whether he knew about the magnetic properties hidden here. After all, didn't he consider himself an expert in the field? Could there be some connection between him and the symbols on her bracelet? And was it just chance that he and Amir were working in Ecuador? She decided there was no doubt about it; Dexter was a part of her destiny. Whether she liked it or not.

"I'm not sure. Anything's possible when it comes to sound and how far it travels."

The vehicle came to a stop.

"We're here."

"Well, I must say. It's been a very enlightening drive." Jeneva tried to match his enthusiasm. "I can't wait to get started. What time would you like to meet in the morning?"

"Why don't we meet for breakfast about eight. I'll fill you in on what you can expect on-site while we eat."

"I'd like that!"

"You're in room ten, up those stairs."

"Thanks. See you in the morning." She headed up the worn stairs noticing they weren't the only thing worn. The wallpaper in the halls was faded and peeling at the corners and the light fixtures were dust covered. It had been a long day, and she was more than ready to put her head on a pillow and sleep anywhere.

The hotel room was fitted with a small fridge, coffeemaker, and thankfully, a working air conditioner. A basket of fruit and nuts sat in the middle of the bed with a welcome note from Amir and Willy, which was thoughtful of them, she thought. After a quick shower, she opened the cellophane wrap on the gift basket, took out a bag of nuts and slid under the cooled sheets on the comfortable twin bed. She'd barely swallowed her first handful when her eyes closed, and she fell into a blissful sleep. Her dreams were filled with expectations of finally finding her destiny.

Part 2
The Connections
Chapter 1

Volunteering in Ecuador

It was seven fifteen when Jeneva rolled out of bed. She yawned and raised her arms in a star-shaped stretch, welcoming the rays of the morning sun as it shone through the open patio door, warming her naked body. In the distance, she thought she recognized the triangular shape of the Hummingbird Pyramid. Jeneva embraced the realization of finally taking the first step toward the connections between the three bracelet symbols and the destiny her mother had predicted. She decided to waste no time getting her day started.

Willy was already seated and drinking coffee when she walked into the hotel restaurant.

"Good morning! I highly recommend the eggs Florentine," he suggested, as she sat across from him.

"Eggs Florentine it is."

The recommendation had been well founded. They proved to be the best she'd ever eaten. While they were eating, Willy went into great detail about the artifacts he'd helped uncover. He was like a runaway train, trying to describe every detail of every found piece in the time it took to consume a plate of eggs. Jeneva had heard more than enough about what Willy had found; she wanted to start making her own discoveries. Gulping down the last of her orange juice, she suggested they head over to the pyramid. After Willy paid the tab, they drove in the direction of the pyramid Jeneva had viewed from her hotel window.

Willy squinted as he looked in the rear-view mirror and turned the wheel of the jeep to the right, giving way to the parade of red lights fast approaching.

"What the heck?" He stuck his head out the window for a better look.

Jeneva had heard sirens in the distance but had paid them no mind. Soon, though, they were deafening, whizzing past them at top speed, lights flashing, horns blaring. Two fire trucks, an EMS vehicle, and half a dozen police cars. When the way was clear, Willy cranked the wheel and hit the gas.

"This is big. You don't get this much attention unless it's serious. Hang on!"

The jeep raced forward, sending a fishtail of gravel flying out from the rear tires. Jeneva tried to escape the overwhelming cloud of billowing dust but was quickly engulfed. She waved her arms back and forth, choking and blinking as she tried to focus on the road ahead.

Moments later, they leaped from the jeep and rushed to the base camp tent at the bottom of the Hummingbird Pyramid. They approached Amir who was responding with a "Ten-four, Roger that," into a walkie-talkie. The men shook hands, and Willy introduced Jeneva.

"We have a situation here. A kid wandered up the side of the pyramid— we assume to see the hummingbirds and hasn't been seen since."

"That's terrible!" Jeneva said. "What can we do to help?"

"One of my guys is up there already. He just radioed me to bring some ropes and a sling. I have my climbing equipment in my truck. I'll be right back." Amir took off running. Jeneva followed and grabbed her flowery sunhat from Willy's jeep.

"Have you done any mountain climbing?" Amir asked Jeneva, as they walked back toward the camp.

"I've done some wilderness hiking and recreational wall climbs but no mountains."

"I have to warn you, in case you haven't noticed, the pyramid has been engulfed with hummingbirds. It happens a couple times a year. They overtake the summit and find their way inside the caverns. It's really quite amazing, but as you can see, a little too tempting for some."

Jeneva glanced up at the peak. She couldn't believe her eyes. The sky was filled with hundreds of hummingbirds obscuring the summit with brilliant moving colors.

"If you are up for the challenge, you can follow me up there; otherwise, stay here with Willy."

Jeneva grabbed one of the loops of heavy rope from Amir's arm and threw it over her shoulder.

"Let's go!"

They headed for the trail entrance at the bottom of the pyramid.

At the beginning of the climb, Amir warned her not only about the birds but also about the possibility of her having trouble breathing at three thousand feet above sea level. She hadn't had a dizzy spell for a while now and hoped the elevation wouldn't bring one on.

Exploration of this pyramid was still in its infancy, and there was no direct pathway to the top of the pyramid. So Jeneva followed close behind Amir, mindful of the waving sickle he used skillfully to cut through the dense brush and snaking vines. Their greatest obstacles were hidden under the greenery. Large flat puzzle-like pieces of rock had been strategically laid on the rough terrain, like shingles on a roof. Years of erosion had dislodged and shifted them, making the pyramid treacherous to scale.

Amir had glanced back a couple times, and she'd given him a thumbs-up. Jeneva was thankful she'd used the gym in her apartment while she was recovering from her accident. She was in the best shape she'd ever been in, certain that without her diligent workouts, she wouldn't have been able to help with the rescue. When they reached the top, Amir congratulated her on her first pyramid ascension.

She hadn't heard a word he said. The summit was covered with wildflowers, and the hummingbirds were everywhere. The thundering humming seemed to echo all around them, and she thought she felt the ground vibrate under her feet. Before she knew what was happening, they were encircling her flowery sunhat.

Over the sound of the hummingbird's wing song, someone called out, "We've found her!"

Chapter 2

He's My Hero

One of Amir's crew members directed Jeneva and Amir to the northwest side of the pyramid. Pointing to a narrow opening, barely visible beneath the thick overgrowth of weeds and grasses, one of the volunteers told them, "I think she may have gone down here."

Amir immediately went to work, first clearing the thick brush with the sickle, and then digging at the compressed earth with a small hatchet. The heat of the noon sun pounded on his back. Sweat trickling down his torso under his canvas overalls, he feverishly worked to retrieve the little girl.

Lailah's parents had arrived at the base camp at the bottom of the pyramid and, according to an update from Amir's crew on the ground, were drilling Willy with questions. The child's mother, Beth, was beside herself.

Bits and pieces of questions from the worried mother were audible to Amir and Jeneva on the walkie-talkie: "Have they found my little girl yet?" along with her consoling husband's replies, "Calm down, Beth. Let me talk to this gentleman. You go get some water."

Amir clicked off the handset and went back to clearing the opening. Behind him, Jeneva was on the ground with her hat between her knees, hiding it from the noisy birds. She was slowly clearing what now appeared to be a large opening, adjacent to the one Amir was digging in.

"Amir! I hear something," Jeneva said. "Some type of rhythmic vibration is echoing beneath me."

"Lailah, can you hear me?" Jeneva called into the opening. Her voice seemed to reverberate, like echoes in a cave. "Lailah, if you can hear me . . ."

From over her shoulder, a child's voice said, "I can hear you."

133

While Jeneva was preoccupied, Amir had managed to coax the little girl up and out of her trap with only a few scratches. She opened her arms, and the frightened youngster ran to her.

"My mommy has a hat just like yours. She lets me wear it sometimes." She batted her lashes at Jeneva, who couldn't deny her the subtle request. She reluctantly placed it on her head, hoping the curious hummingbirds didn't come and frighten the little girl, as they had her.

"How about we go find your mom?"

From under the big, brimmed hat, the five-year-old asked, "Am I in trouble? I wanted to see the birdies." She looked scared, and her eyes filled with crocodile tears.

"I don't think so, sweetie. Mommy and Daddy are going to be so happy to see you."

A young woman with an EMS jacket on wrapped the little girl in a blanket.

"Come with me." She offered a hand to Lailah.

"I want him to take me to my mommy and daddy," Lailah screamed, pointing at Amir.

Amir bent down and cupped his hands. "Climb aboard, little princess."

Lailah put one foot in his hands, and Jeneva helped her onto Amir's shoulders. Off they went, down the rugged path, with the little girl smiling from ear to ear aboard her trusted steed. Moments later, they came face to face with a half-dozen firefighters, laden with ropes and tackle, cresting the summit. With no one to guide them, they'd taken a wrong turn on their way up and had to double back, making them late to the party. With mixed feelings of embarrassment and thankfulness, the firefighters, laden with all their gear, turned and led the way to the base camp.

As the rescuers came from the underbrush at the bottom of the Hummingbird Pyramid, the crowd started cheering. The firefighters immediately linked arms, surrounding Amir and Lailah, protecting them from the reporters rushing to be the first to interview them. Jeneva followed them to the base camp tent, where Willy, and Lailah's parents, Beth and David, were anxiously waiting for them.

All the happy tears were wiped away, and Beth was convinced her little girl was okay. It was time to face the cameras. Amir led them out of the tent to speak to the reporters, who were patiently waiting for the details.

David held his daughter, while Beth stepped up to the microphone.

"I'd like to thank everyone who came to our daughter's rescue. Because of their quick response, I'm happy to say she is okay. David and I will be eternally grateful to this man." She reached for Amir's hand and pulled him forward for the crowd to see. "This is the hero who saved our daughter from what could have been a life-threatening fall."

She raised their hands in the air, and the onlookers went wild with cheers and applause. Beth took David's free hand and went back inside the tent.

Before Amir could follow them, a reporter grabbed his arm and started probing him for answers.

"What was she doing up there? Did the hummingbirds attack her? Was her life in danger?"

Other news reporters approached, sticking their microphones in Amir's face, waiting for answers.

Amir pulled away from the first reporter, who was still holding his arm. With the diplomacy of a politician, he calmly answered all their questions. He assured them he would be securing the area around the Hummingbird Pyramid to ensure nothing like this could ever happen again. He thanked them for coming and excused himself, ducking inside the tent.

Reports of the little girl's disappearance and rescue were on the front page of every major newspaper, local and international, with headlines like, "Archeologist Uncovers Little Treasure" and "Lost Child Found in Hummingbird Pyramid," as well as "He's My Hero!" Most showed a picture of the little girl with hummingbirds circling her oversized sunhat, grinning happily atop Amir's shoulders. After that, Amir humbly appeared on TV and radio, retelling the rescue of the little girl who went looking for hummingbirds, making him an overnight celebrity.

Chapter 3

Dexter's Memories

Dexter Applebaum was relaxing in his penthouse apartment in Quito, sipping a well-aged Brandy. He'd just watched the weather reports of earthquakes in California, dust storms in Sudan, snowstorms in Canada, and hurricanes passing over the Caribbean Sea, when the station announced they were going live to La Maná, Ecuador. The camera focused on a little girl with hummingbirds flying around her sunhat. She rode on the shoulders of a tall, slender man who Dexter recognized immediately. It was Amir, the archaeologist he'd met at the symposium. He recalled him saying he was going to Ecuador to do a dig at the Hummingbird Pyramid.

What he saw next sent him bolting upright in his recliner. *What is she doing in Ecuador?* The camera zoomed out to include a shot of the Hummingbird Pyramid and caught Jeneva in the background. For the next few minutes, he listened while the narrator told the story of the lost little girl and her rescue. Dexter had forgotten about Jeneva's phone call asking for Amir's number. What exactly were the two of them up to? He pondered the idea of Amir and Jeneva having a romantic relationship. *No way. He's not her type. She's probably on one of her crusades*, he speculated, trying to rationalize their being together. Seeing her again sent a tingle through his whole body that he wasn't at all familiar with. It was usually the women who got all tingly when they were around him.

The interview with Amir ended, and Dexter shut off the TV, staring at his reflection in the blank screen. The memory of Jeneva snatching his cab out from under him, her sheepish look when she saw him again from the stage at the symposium, and the mysterious phone call looking for Amir conjured up even more unfamiliar emotions in him.

The image of her chocolate-brown eyes, long black hair, and be-guiling smile haunted his dreams that night. He had to see her again. He decided to endure the five-hour drive to La Maná the next morn-ing and put an end or beginning to this. Whatever *this* is.

Chapter 4

Hummingbirds' Wing Song

Bright and early next morning, Jeneva and Amir were hard at work in the base camp's large, open-sided canvas tent. They were leaning over a table, shoulder to shoulder looking at a schematic drawing of the area. At a rumble behind them, they first gave a quick glance but then fully turned to watch a vehicle approach. It was hard not to notice a big black Hummer. Or its driver, Dexter Applebaum.

Before anyone could say a cordial hello, the surprise visitor glared at Jeneva, and with a snarky tone in his voice said, "I see you found Amir."

Jeneva was a bit taken aback by the tone of his remark.

"Ah, yes. I did. Thanks to you."

"So. What have you two been up to? Besides rescuing lost kids?" he said, and Jeneva thought she detected a note of insinuation.

In an obvious attempt to lessen the odd tension in the air, Amir offered his hand and suggested they go in the tent, where he could explain what he and his team were working on.

Stretched between two easels was a three-dimensional topographic picture of the Hummingbird Pyramid. Amir explained that the narrow, wavy black lines defined the elevation of the exterior, and the wider black lines illustrated possible fault lines or weaknesses in the interior cavity of the pyramid, which could cause cave-ins or caverns.

"We were looking at the crevasse Lailah fell into, when you drove up. I was telling Amir I felt some reverberations not far from the surface. He thinks it was just the hummingbirds, but he feels it warrants further investigation. We were thinking of heading up there now, before the heat of the afternoon sun overwhelms the peak and the hummingbirds get active again."

"Hummingbirds?" Dexter looked up.

139

"Don't worry. They don't bite." Amir chuckled at the look on his face.

"May I join you? I could use a walk after that long drive."

Amir and Jeneva eyed him up and down. His Gucci sandals, polo shirt, and shorts were hardly suitable attire for the climb.

"Let me see what I have in my jeep. You can't come dressed like that." Amir shook his head and rolled his eyes.

The shirtless man emerged from behind the curtained latrine, wrestling to get his muscular biceps into the long-sleeve shirt Amir loaned him. Jeneva blushed when she saw his hairless chest and six-pack abs. After he adjusted the tight-fitting clothes, he launched into a few bodybuilders poses in front of Jeneva. "What do you think? Perfect fit?"

Not wanting to puff up his ego by telling him he looked like a model from *Esquire* magazine, she asked him about the unusual pendant she'd seen hanging on the chain around his neck.

"What an interesting piece of jewelry you have. May I?" She pointed at his chest.

He nodded, and she pulled it out from beneath the collar of the shirt and cupped it in her hand.

"My great grandfather found it when he was in New Zealand and gave it to my great grandmother on their wedding night. It's been passed down for generations."

"How romantic. Is that a forget-me-not encased in amber?"

"Yes. It's quite an unusual, natural phenomenon. My father gave it to me in hopes that I would be lucky enough to find a wife as loving and kind as he and my grandfather and great-grandfather did."

"Well, if you two are finished jawing, we should get going," Amir spoke up.

After outfitting Dexter in proper footwear, Jeneva grabbed her wide-brimmed hat, and the three disappeared through the opening and ascended the pyramid, shovels, rope, and Amir's trusted sickle in hand.

After all the foot traffic up and down the pyramid the past few days, the path was much easier to follow. They reached the northwest corner in half the time it had taken Jeneva and Amir just the other day.

While Amir was pointing out the spot where he found the little girl to Dexter, Jeneva pulled at the tangled grasses and weeds that camouflaged the opening she'd found.

"A little help, fellas!"

"Coming, your Highness," Dexter mocked, as the two men came and hovered over her.

"Did you bring a flashlight, Amir?" Jeneva asked.

"No, sorry. I was charging the batteries and forgot to put it back in my pack."

"Here, use this." Dexter turned on the flashlight from his cell phone app and put it in her outstretched palm. He was obviously pleased with himself for appearing better prepared than Amir.

THE ARCHAEOLOGIST COULDN'T help but feel inadequate about not bringing a flashlight. *Archaeology 101*, he thought and popped his hand on his forehead. He tried to regain control of the situation by telling Jeneva to get back and let him in there to make sure it was safe.

First, he poked the ground to ensure it was stable, and then, he began clearing the dense ground cover. The audible patter of loose dirt raining down made him pause. Then, without warning, the ground opened up in front of them. A hole the size of a street sewer appeared. Amir hastily backed up. Jeneva fell to her knees and shone the light in the hole. It was pitch black, all but for the beam of the phone's flashlight.

"Can you see anything?" Amir asked.

"No! Only blackness."

Amir grabbed the harness and rope he brought, secured one line to a tree, and slipped into it like the pro mountain climber he was.

"Step aside!"

Jeneva did as Amir asked. She'd seen him in action, so she knew he had confidence in what he was doing.

"Here, take this with you." She handed him the cell phone.

"Are you crazy?" Dexter hollered. "You have no idea what's down there! You could be killed!"

"This is what I do. Now back up and let me in there. And whatever you do, don't let go of this line until I tell you to." He tossed a second line at him.

Dexter grabbed the rope and wrapped it around his waist, thankful that Jeneva stood behind him with her heels dug in and arms tight around his waist for additional anchor.

Amir straddled the hole, then bent down to sit on the edge. He leaned forward, stretched his arms out to the sides, and his legs and body disappeared. "Okay, hold tight, I'm going in."

Amir felt the rope tighten as he lowered into the mysterious darkness, and they held his weight from above. A thin band of light illuminated the cavernous tomb. He shivered as the blanket of dampness wrapped around him.

From up above, Jeneva's voice called, "How's it going down there?"

"Can you see anything?" Dexter asked.

Amir tilted his head upward and replied, "Nothing yet!"

Suddenly, Amir dropped four feet to an abrupt stop on the wet, slippery ground.

"You idiot!" He heard Jeneva yell. Dexter must have been distracted with their conversation and loosened his grip on the rope.

"Amir, are you all right? Amir, can you hear me?" Jeneva called down into the hole.

"I'm fine. No broken bones, just a sore ass. What happened up there?"

"Sorry, buddy! My hands slipped," Dexter said, and though Amir had suspected Dexter had dropped him that last length on purpose, he sounded genuinely sorry. Maybe he'd misjudged the guy.

When Amir made his unexpected drop to the bottom of the cave, the cell phone had flown out of his hand, leaving him in total darkness. Crawling on hands and knees, he found himself on a low wall. He swung his legs over the wall, and they plunked into water halfway up his calves.

With catlike reflexes, he reached for the notebook he kept in the inner pocket of his vest. He exhaled a sigh of relief— thankful it was safe and hadn't gotten wet.

Amir blinked, hoping his eyes would adjust to the blackness of the cave. They did, slightly. Slowly, he turned his head to the left. Nothing but blackness surrounded him. He wondered what mysteries of the ages they'd uncover there.

While his thoughts ran wild with all the possibilities, the ground beneath him started vibrating. Soon, it shook so violently that he grabbed hold of the jagged rock face of the wall he'd sat on. It lasted less than a minute, which was long enough for Amir to have concerns of a cave-in. Without warning, the darkness gave way to a beam of sunlight, shining from through the opening above. The cavern lit up. The hole had been blocked by Jeneva's wide-brimmed hat as she peered down, waiting for his confirmation that he was unharmed.

Now he could see he was, indeed, sitting on a rock wall about two feet high, encompassing a pool of water. The water he stood in was clear, but he had no sense of warm or cold as it filled his boots.

Squinting from the glare reflecting off what he thought might be gold flakes floating in the water, he was both amazed and frightened when they started moving.

"Hey, guys, there is something weird going on down here. I see gold flakes in the water, and they appear to be moving." He couldn't take his eyes off the strange transformation that was happening.

Dexter responded with the immediacy of the scientist he was. He told Amir to grab a sample in his water bottle. Amir complied, stashing the filled water bottle back in his backpack.

Sitting back down on the indented wall, Amir again focused on the strange phenomenon in the water. His peripheral vision blurred, his mind clouded, and he lost all awareness of where he was.

"Get as many of the gold flakes as you can!" Dexter called out, then paused, presumably giving Amir what he considered ample time to get a sample. "Did you get it?"

"I got it. I found your phone too. You might need a new screen." Amir continued gazing, dumbfounded, at the shapeshifting going on in front of him.

CONFIDENT THAT AMIR was safe, Jeneva wandered over to the deep crevasse Amir had pulled Lailah from. Some of the metal security rods had loosened in last night's rain, and she was trying to push them back in place to tighten the yellow ropes that surrounded the area. Dexter joined her and queried her about the incident. "What was that kid doing up here alone?"

"Her parents said they thought she was following humming-birds. Supposedly, they only let her out of their sight for a few minutes. We were all so grateful to find her unharmed that it never occurred to us to interrogate her. I don't think she'll wander off like that again. She was pretty upset."

"Kids! Always up to something." He puffed air threw his lips.

"And what exactly do you mean by that?" Jeneva asked, raising her eyebrows into her hairline.

"I mean just that! You have to watch them constantly." He rolled his eyes.

"You don't like kids?" She gave him a "be careful what you say, mister," look.

"I didn't say that. All I'm saying is that they need constant supervision, that's all."

Dexter must have interpreted her feelings correctly because he changed the subject. "Speaking of kids, we better see what Amir's up to." He turned and stepped closer to the opening.

With pursed lips and squinting eyes, she followed him. Jeneva was pretty certain this guy had an issue with kids. She filed the conversation in the back of her mind; *to be brought forward at a later date.*

"Hello, down there. Anybody home?"

There was no reply. A minute passed. Jeneva pushed him aside.

"Amir?" She was hanging over the edge, calling down into the opening. "Are you okay?" Still no reply. They debated back and forth as to who should go in after him.

"Give him a minute. I'm sure he's fine." Dexter turned his head away, as if enjoying the view.

"Aren't you the least bit worried? Maybe he fell in a hole or something." Jeneva was starting to panic.

Dexter knelt down across from of her. He tried to reassure her. "Don't worry. He probably just found some old bones and is deep in thought."

Still kneeling over the opening, she continued to call to Amir. She gasped when she saw a terrified face appear below. His eyes were filled with fear and his demanding words vibrated off the walls of the cavern and echoed upward.

"*Get me out of here. NOW!*"

Chapter 5

The Magnetic Factor

The three companions made their way down the outer surface of the pyramid and drank water in the base camp tent to hydrate themselves after their hot and exhausting trek. Jeneva and Dexter sat side by side, facing Amir, who hadn't spoken a word, despite their interrogation attempts.

"Are you okay, Amir? What happened in there? You're very pale." Jeneva gave him a concerned look.

He took a big swallow of water. "I'll be okay," he finally said. "I need some time to think."

"So, what did you see down there, the boogeyman?" Dexter probed as if trying to lighten the building tension.

It was apparent they weren't going to let up, and he couldn't blame them for being concerned, so Amir tried to compose himself. But his tactic didn't work for long, Dexter's persistent taunting continued.

"Did you land on your head and don't remember anything? Throw us a bone, will ya!"

"Actually, you dropped me into a pool of water, and it looks like there are magnetic flakes of gold floating in it."

Amir grabbed the water bottle from his backpack and tossed it over to Dexter, who examined it with an inquisitive eye.

"I say *magnetic* because they started moving and came together in an unusual shape." Amir watched Dexter's interest peak.

"I've been doing some research on magnetic energy sources in the area, and oddly enough, the Hummingbird Pyramid has come up. Apparently, the basalt stones that encase these pyramids possess numerous magnetic properties which have also been found in the granite artifacts. It's possible that some gold flakes, as you called them, may have filtered through the iron and ferromagnetic elements, which has shown a pervasive presence in the area. Dexter gave the bottle a shake. "These flakes might be magnetic semiconductors."

"Probably nothing more than iron pyrite, better known as 'fool's gold. What about the reverberations? How do you explain that?" *I've got you now, Mr. know-it-all.* Amir had an interior chuckle.

"I'm glad you asked. Years of exploration of the nearby Calope River has uncovered the hidden presence of several major psychoacoustic stone monuments. The Hummingbird Pyramid is directly linked to an entire complex of similar magnetic structures, all connected by an interior causeway that extends almost seven hundred feet in diameter from the pyramid's apex." Dexter swooped his arm across the horizon.

"How do you know so much about all this? I've been here for two months, and we're just scratching the surface."

"You said it! Archaeologists just scratch the surface looking for old stuff. I on the other hand, was educated in the field of astronomy and have done extensive research into magnetic portals. I don't just scratch the surface. I dig deep, not only into the earth but the universe that surrounds it. The answers we are looking for don't always present themselves without some in-depth excavating, to put it in archaeological terms."

Amir didn't know whether Dexter's expression was smug or whether he was just reading him that way, clearly both were interested in impressing Jeneva.

"And that explains the feelings of reverberation how, exactly?" Amir crossed his arms over his chest and gave Dexter a challenging look.

"I think it has something to do with the elevated levels of ferromagnetic elements in the basalts that encompass the pyramid. When two basalt stones encounter each other, by rubbing or sudden contact, it produces what might be construed as a metallic ringing sound or reverberation, as you've called it. It's possible a single rock falling could be heard all through the causeway." Dexter, in turn, crossed his arms and puffed up his chest.

As the two men faced off like a couple of rams butting heads, Jeneva sat back, listening. She recognized some of the facts as the same information Willy had given her on their drive from the airport. She decided to interrupt after her grumbling belly could no longer be ignored.

"I'm starving! Can we take this conversation somewhere else?"

Amir suggested an Italian restaurant that had just opened in La Maná, but they would have to go without him.

Dexter accused him of being a workaholic, and he snapped. He'd taken all the ribbing he could handle today. The idea of more sparring over dinner with this know-it-all was not at all tempting, especially given the exhaustion and anguish he was internalizing after his frightening experience. First and foremost, he needed to figure out what the apparition he'd seen down there was all about.

"Enough already!" He leaped up and stalked out of the tent, ran to his vehicle and drove off, leaving the couple at a loss.

ON THE DRIVE BACK TO town, Dexter and Jeneva talked about Amir's odd behavior and what might have happened in the cave. After they finished their belated lunch on the street-front patio at Parrilla Restaurante, Dexter assisted Jeneva back into his jacked-up Hummer. The couple took a drive to the nearby community of La Envidia, where they hiked to see the unique Siete Cascadas. He translated for her. "That means, seven waterfalls, in English, in case you were wondering." Dexter noticed Jeneva's thoughts were somewhere other than on the exquisite waterfalls in front of them.

"What are you thinking about?" He gave her shoulder a gentle tap.

"I was thinking about Amir. I hope he's okay. Maybe we shouldn't have left him alone."

"We can head back if you like."

"Thanks. I'd like that."

When they arrived back at Grand Hotel La Maná, Jeneva's hotel, Dexter checked himself into the room next to hers. They both stood at their respective doors, staring at each other. Jeneva finally broke the silence.

"Thanks for the lovely afternoon. It was fun." She gave him a cordial smile and unlocked her door.

"My pleasure." He gave a little bow.

"I think I'll give Amir a call, see how he's doing. I'll catch up with you later." She stepped into her room.

Chapter 6

Bullies Be Gone
      Jeneva had just slipped under the covers, hoping for a quick nap before dinner, when her cell phone rang. Maddy's smiling face appeared on the screen with the familiar theme song from *Friends*.

"Hello there. I've been meaning to call you. Are you glad to be back home?"

"I have mixed feelings. I really enjoyed working with you dad, but it was nice to be back with my new family."

"All settled in at school, I hope."

"You know it. Aunt Patricia is very strict about homework and studying. I feel like I'm at school twenty-four seven sometimes. She gives me advice on study techniques and the best websites to use for research. She even came on our biology excursion last week. And guess what? She lets me drive when we go shopping."

"Well, aren't you the lucky girl to have her devote so much of her time to your education? Maybe you can help repay her by helping your cousin with her schoolwork."

"I do! I cook and clean up too. Did I mention I drive her to the grocery store?" She was very obviously trying to nudge a reaction.

"You what?" Jeneva knew this was the response Maddy was looking for.

"I got my learner's permit a couple weeks ago, and Aunt Patricia lets me drive her everywhere."

"Congrats, honey. Make sure you always drive carefully and *no texting*!" Jeneva raised her voice for effect.

"You don't have to worry about that. I have to keep my phone in my purse, in the back seat. Aunt Patricia's orders."

"You two are getting on all right though?"

"We are." Maddy got quiet.

"Maddy! Everything okay?"

"There is something I want to tell you about that happened at school." Maddy hesitated.

"Shoot! I'm listening."

"Last week, I walked into the changeroom to gather the towels and mop up, just something to do during my spare. I saw a girl huddled in a corner crying. Her hair was hanging over her face, and she was kind of shaking. I almost ran out, but something inside me said she needed me to stay. When I asked if she was okay, she told me to leave her alone, so I offered to just sit with her and not ask any questions. After a few minutes, she told me she wanted to be alone because she had a decision to make. That scared me a bit. So, I told her sometimes it helps to talk to someone, especially a stranger, because they won't judge you. She finally opened up and told me her name was Janet. She told me she'd been bullied in the halls and harassed on all the social media sites. When she tried out for the cheerleading squad, one of the other cheerleaders accused her of being a lesbian and posted pictures of her in the shower, with very nasty comments attached. I was kind of at a loss for words. I'd never heard of anybody being that cruel before."

"Have you told your aunt about what happened?"

"I actually called her that day on Janet's phone. I thought I better call somebody. I was afraid Janet might do something, you know, like kill herself. She seemed desperate enough. Aunt Patricia told me to keep her talking until she got there, but I told her we had talked a lot, and we were just about to head home. Turned out she lives around the corner from me, so I walked her to the door, and she agreed to meet in the morning and walk to school together. I gave her my number and told her to call me if she needed to talk to someone."

"I'm so proud of you, Maddy. You may have saved Janet from making a terrible mistake. Not to mention the pain and suffering her parents would have to go through if they lost their daughter. You did good, kiddo."

"A couple of my friends have turned against me. They've even resorted to bashing me on Facebook and Snapchat. I was really angry with them at first, but now I just feel sorry for them. Guess they aren't really my friends after all. I feel like I'm the better person and they're all cowards."

"It's not always easy to take the path less followed. It took a lot of courage to do what you did. I think you're stronger for going through it together. You should be proud of yourself. Hopefully, your so-called friends will realize their small-mindedness and see what a wonderful thing you did by standing up for Janet in her time of need. How's she doing now?"

"Pretty good, I think. I went with her to see the guidance counselor, and he introduced her to another girl at our school who struggled with her identity too. Her name is Cathy. The two of them have become quite close and spend a lot of time together. The three of us had a sleepover. We ate popcorn and watched movies till after midnight."

"That sounds like fun. We'll have to do that next time we get together."

"Oh! And something else happened! The principal stopped me in the hall the other day and said he was impressed with my selfless act of kindness and wondered if I would be interested in helping with a project he was starting. He's calling it, 'Bullies Be Gone.' I told him I'd have to talk to my aunt, but I really wanted to talk to you about it too."

"It sounds to me like you'd be a perfect fit. You can draw on the volunteering you did at the hospital, sharing your story about losing your mom and all the emotional ups and downs you went through. You were quite successful when it came to encouraging the patients to share their stories. They trusted you, and I think you'll do just as remarkable a job with this task. As long as it doesn't interfere with your schoolwork, I'm all for it."

"I thought you'd say that. I'll let him know I'm in. So, what's new with you, Big Sister? Are you doing your exercises?"

"Yep, and I've never felt better. I just came back from a hike to a fabulous waterfall with Dexter."

"You what? Who's Dexter?"

"Just a man I met at a symposium, I forgot he lived in Ecuador. I almost fell over when he showed up at the Hummingbird Pyramid. He'd seen me on TV the day we rescued Lailah. Did you see the broadcast?" Jeneva wasn't ready to tell Maddy about the discovery they had made in the cavern. She'd save that for another time.

"Yes, I did. It was a miracle she wasn't hurt."

"I think the Ecuadorian government is going to give Amir a reward or something."

"Cool, so tell me more about you and that man from the symposium. Are you guys an item?"

Jeneva gave a little chuckle.

"He's not really my type, but he does grow on you. There's no denying he's very handsome and educated to boot."

"You will have to keep me posted. Remember Chuck? He's the boy who tried to take my phone. We've been talking, and well, we might be an item. I really like him."

Jeneva heard someone calling Maddy from somewhere in the background.

"Maddy! Can you come help set the table, please?"

"Sorry, Jeneva, I have to go. I'm being summoned. Give me a call sometime. I miss you."

"I miss you too. Bye for now."

"Tootles." The line went dead.

Jeneva sat for a moment, mulling over their conversation. She felt so proud of the woman Maddy was becoming, but it was more than that; she truly loved her. She couldn't believe how grown-up her voice sounded. Closing her eyes, she pictured Maddy opening the door the first time they'd met. She was only eight then. Jeneva smiled and shook her head. *How fast time flies.* Her phone was still in her hand, so she pushed Dad in her contacts list.

"Hi Pops, how've you been?"

"Missing my favorite girl. How are you feeling? Not overexerting yourself, I hope."

"I'm fine. Thanks for asking."

"I saw you on TV. That must have been exciting, rescuing that little girl."

"It was, but more exciting than that is what I found when I was looking for her. There's a hidden cavern up there. We're all going back there tomorrow to investigate."

"Someone qualified I hope?" She thought he sounded concerned.

Yes, of course, Amir. He's the archeologist in charge and maybe Dexter will tag along."

"Weren't they speakers at the symposium I sent you to?"

"Yes, they were. I've been following Mom's advice about keeping an open mind and listening to others. It led me to them. I have a good feeling about this Hummingbird Pyramid too. I think it will be a big part of my destiny."

"Wow, that's very perceptive of you. I know Amir had a hand at leading you to the Hummingbird Pyramid, but what's Dexter got to do with any of it?"

"To be honest, he just showed up. I haven't figured out if there's any connection there or not"

"You'll have to let me know," her father said and then paused, "when you make a connection." The subtle implication went unnoticed.

"Before I forget. I was just talking to Maddy."

"How's she doing? I miss having her around."

"She's good. It sounds like she and her Aunt Patricia are getting along."

"That's good to hear."

"And she's driving. Can you believe it?"

"They grow up so fast, don't they?" he laughed, remembering when he taught Jeneva to drive.

"Speaking of growing up, she told me she met a boy there."

"Sorry, honey, but I have to run. I have a conference call with the head of the Smithsonian shortly. He's looking for an update."

"Hey, no problem. Go. We'll talk again soon. Love you."

"Love you too, sweetheart, take care of yourself."

The call disconnected.

Chapter 7

Double Helix
Jeneva heard a gentle tapping on her door. She slipped into the hotel robe and peeked through the hole in the door. It was Dexter. She opened the door.

"Guess you need a few minutes to get dressed."

She saw his face flush with embarrassment. "What time is it?" she asked.

"Almost seven. I'll wait for you at the bar. That is if you are interested in joining me?"

"I am hungry. I'll have a quick shower and meet you there."

Forty-five minutes later, she walked in and sat down beside Dexter on a barstool.

"You clean up good!" He slid a glass of red wine in front of her.

"Thanks! You as well. Looks like we match tonight." She pointed at their attire.

It was obvious they both dressed to impress the other. Coincidently, they were color coordinated. Dexter wore a burgundy shirt, open at the collar, and gray tailored slacks. Jeneva wore a sleeveless burgundy dress with grey pumps. Her beaded handbag hung on her shoulder.

"Have you heard from Amir?" Dexter asked.

A handsome gentleman in a crisp white shirt and dark pants approached them and handed her a note, then took a few steps back from them.

"Is it from Amir?" Jeneva shifted forward in her seat.

"Yes. He says we shouldn't expect him for dinner. He will meet us at the base camp in the morning."

Dexter stood and offered his arm. "Shall we?"

With her glass of wine in one hand, Jeneva hooked her other arm in his and they followed the maître-d' to their table.

Jeneva was pleasantly surprised how smoothly the evening went. The conversation wasn't as one sided as she was anticipating. The man she thought was full of himself impressed her when he mentioned his involvement in several charities that she was familiar with. Apparently, he wasn't as self-absorbed as she thought.

While they ate, they discussed the research they were involved with over the years, the places they traveled, and even enjoyed a laugh or two. Especially when she mentioned his little mishap of dropping Amir into the cavern and their first meeting, when she took his cab. After their meal, the couple stood outside Jeneva's room, talking about what they might find when they all entered the mysterious cavern the next morning.

"Are you scared?" he asked her.

"No! Are you?"

"Hardly! I'm sure there's a perfectly logical explanation for everything Amir experienced. My guess is his imagination got the best of him down there in the dark."

"Maybe so. Guess we'll find out for ourselves." She stuck the key card in the slot and opened the door.

"Thanks for a lovely evening, Dexter!"

"The pleasure was all mine. See you in the morning. Sleep well." He disappeared into his neighboring room.

Later, lying comfortably in her bed, Jeneva reflected on the evening. She decided there was more to this Adonis creature than met the eye. Much to her surprise, they'd made a connection after all.

The following morning, it was Jeneva who knocked on Dexter's door. With tousled hair and only baggy flannel pajama bottoms on, he opened the door and invited her in. Her cheeks heated and she abruptly declined.

"Uh, no thanks. I'll see you in the breakfast room." Her hair twirled around her neck as she made a hasty getaway down the hall. She stood in the closed elevator, staring at her red-faced reflection in the floor-to-ceiling mirror, forgetting to push the L-button on the numbered panel.

"Damn you and your hot body, Applebaum." She'd barely resisted the uncontrollable urge to succumb to his invitation. She knew she wasn't ready for what she suspected he had in mind. Her hand was still trembling when she finally pushed the L-button.

While they ate their breakfast, Jeneva avoided eye contact as much as possible. She was afraid he might see something in her eyes. She wasn't sure what that something might be, but she didn't want to take any chances.

Dexter offered a hand to Jeneva, which she pushed aside as she effortlessly boarded his Hummer. The sun's intense rays shone on the windshield as they approached the pyramid.

"I can't believe how hot it gets here." Jeneva wiped a bead of sweat that ran down from under her hat brim. She was unsure whether it was from the heat of the sun or the proximity to the lean masculine body she'd seen earlier. She couldn't get the sight of him standing in the doorway, half naked, out of her head.

"This is nothing. You should be here in July. You can cook an egg on the sidewalk."

"Look, there's Amir. He still looks shaken up." Jeneva pointed at a figure slouching against the large tent.

AMIR HAD BEEN GATHERING all the supplies and neatly stacking them outside the tent, so they'd be ready to go. While he did, he mulled over what he'd experienced yesterday in the cavern. He was still undecided whether he dared return. He hadn't heard the Hummer approach and jumped at the sound of the doors slamming.

"Good morning, Amir. We missed you last night," Jeneva said in her happy-go-lucky voice.

"What are you waiting for, buddy, an invitation?" said Dexter.

"Very funny, Dexter. I'm not sure we should go back in." Amir stood up and walked inside the tent, motioning them to follow. He pointed at the diagram of the Hummingbird Pyramid layout.

"I'm afraid all that vibrating yesterday may have compromised the integrity of the cavern interior, and it could collapse while we are in there."

Jeneva noticed his hand was trembling. Something really got to him down there.

"Poppycock, if it hasn't caved in after all these years, it's not about to change any time soon," Dexter challenged, giving his hand a flip.

"Maybe he's right, Dexter. After all, he's the expert."

She walked over and put her hand on Amir's, hoping to calm the shaking.

"Do you really believe we would be in danger?" asked Jeneva.

"There's always an element of danger when you're dealing with ancient ruins. Truth is, I'm not sure if it's safe or not."

"I sure would like to investigate whatever magnetic properties are down there. It may be useful in my research." Dexter told him.

"What do you say, Amir? If we get down there and find any sign of collapse, we'll leave, immediately. I give you, my word."

He looked into her pleading eyes.

"I don't know?" He scratched his head.

"I have a strong feeling the answer to the middle symbol is down there. Please, Amir, can we go? I need to know."

He couldn't resist her pleading brown eyes.

"All right! I'll take you, but I'm not going into the cavern. He will have to take care of you down there." He pointed a designating finger at Dexter. "Are you okay with that?" Amir sent him a piercing look that said, 'You better not let anything happen to her!"

"No problem. I'll take good care of her. Don't you worry. Can we go now?"

Jeneva gave Amir a quick hug. "Thanks. We'll be fine."

Amir gave each of them a backpack loaded with water, snacks, a flashlight, rope and tackle.

"Here's some gloves, you'll need them for repelling down the rope." He handed a pair to each of them.

When they reached the crown of the pyramid, the men secured a heavy-duty rope to a large tree trunk and tossed it down the opening Amir had entered through yesterday. To avoid another drop incident, Amir brought along a special harness, complete with a block and tackle system to secure the drop rope.

Dexter stepped into the saddled ropes and positioned himself on the edge of the hole. He gave the other two a quick salute.

"Nice knowing you!" Then he disappeared out of sight.

"Damn his arrogance. I have a mind to leave him down there." Amir shook his head in disgust.

"Now, now, don't be like that. He's just pushing your buttons." Jeneva flashed him a big smile.

"I'd like to push his button, right between the eyes. The fool's going to get himself in trouble and expect me to bail him out."

Jeneva walked over and peered in the hole.

"He'll be fine." From her tone, Amir suspected she had a whiff of doubt in her own mind.

DEXTER FLIPPED ON THE flashlight and directed the beam downward. To his right were the pond and wall Amir had told them about. This was his focal point, his main reason for wanting to get down here. If that archaeologist was right, they might have made a significant find. His knees buckled as his feet hit bottom. He loosened the straps, stepped out of the ropes, and headed straight to the pond. The rock floor was damp and slimy. He slipped and went down like a ton of bricks, right on his tight-fitting jeans.

"Son of a—" he broke off, not wanting the others to hear. He had been reckless and needed to get serious if he was going to be responsible for Jeneva when she got down here. Luckily, only his pride was bruised. He sat for a few minutes, checking out his surroundings by the beam of the flashlight. The walls had a satiny sheen, not unlike the ground he'd slipped on. Everything seemed to be intact, no fallen rocks lying about, no cracks in the walls, and no reverberations.

He got back on his feet, this time being mindful of the damp, uneven surface below him. He stepped up on the low stone wall and looked into the water. Bending over, he waved his hand side to side. In the area he disturbed, the flakes started moving.

"Hmm. That's weird," he said under his breath and stepped off the wall.

Dexter hollered upward, "Everything looks good down here. Take up the harness and saddle up Jeneva. And make sure she's strapped in tight!"

"We wouldn't want to drop her, would we?" Amir took advantage of the opportunity to rub yesterday's incident in Dexter's face.

Inside the depths of the cavern, it was relatively dark. It was early morning, and the sun was still fairly low in the sky. He followed Jeneva's downward movements on the rope with his flashlight.

She tipped her head up. "Don't drop me, Amir!"

When her feet were firmly planted on the surface of the cave, she called up to Amir. "That's good. I'm on the bottom."

Dexter untethered the ropes from around her waist, and as she stepped toward him, the cavern quaked. Not enough to top the

Richter scale, but enough to frighten Jeneva. She wrapped herself around Dexter's neck and hung on for dear life.

"What was that? You said it was safe!" She trembled in his arms.

"I don't think it's anything we have to worry about. At least not until the roof starts caving in on top of us. If that starts happening, I'll get you out PDQ."

"Seriously, you think this is funny?" She released her cobra-like hold on him and cuffed his shoulder.

"Remember those psychoacoustic stone monuments I told you about, with the causeways running through them? Well, I'm pretty sure the vibrations are the effect of the road reconstruction being done along the Calope River. Just the falling of rocks or gravel trucks on the road can cause a reverberation in each monument connected to the causeway."

"I guess that could explain it, kind of like a ricochet of an echo."

"Sure, kind of like that." He snickered at her analogy.

"The ground is very uneven and slippery, so watch your step." Dexter offered his hand. "Look here!" He pointed his flashlight, giving her a beam of light to follow.

"That's the pond Amir told us about."

He helped her onto the low wall. The light from his flashlight illuminated the water and deflected off the small specks of gold.

"Do you think it's real gold?"

"Watch this!" He reached down and swirled his hand in the water. The floating specks started moving. Jeneva gazed into the pond as he continued stirring the water around and around.

"Look at that. They're attaching themselves in a strand, like they're magnetic." She barely had the words out of her mouth when she exclaimed, "Oh, my God, that's it!" She almost slipped off the wall.

"Gold and water, look!" She pointed to the middle symbol on her bracelet. "Dexter! Look! This has to be it, right?" She raised her arm in front of him.

He shone the light on her wrist. "Could be." His enthusiasm was less than she hoped for.

"Could be? Isn't it obvious?" She turned away with a huff of frustration and called up to Amir to validate her hypothesis. "Amir come down here! You're not going to believe it! I was right! The second symbol is here. It's here, Amir. Hurry! Pull up the harness."

Though Amir had been reluctant and nervous earlier, it didn't seem to affect his climbing skills, because he dropped down into the cavern much quicker than they had managed to. After Amir released his restraints, he joined Jeneva on the stone wall.

"What do you think? Doesn't that look like this?" She was pointing to the symbol on her bracelet. "It does, right?"

With a gentle hand, Amir held Jeneva's wrist and looked at her bracelet, then at the particles. "The pieces are lined up in the water, just like they did yesterday. Now that you mention it, it does look the same."

Releasing her wrist, he turned to Dexter. "Hey! Mr. Magnetics. Is it possible these particles are magnetic and came from the volcanic eruption you told us about?"

On the other side of the pond, Dexter sat stock-still, unable to respond.

Chapter 8

Dexter's Vision

The hiking boots Amir had loaned Dexter were a size too small, and he could no longer endure the stinging pain in his heels. He sat in the cut-out of the low stone wall that surrounded the pond and took them off. Crimson blood covered the heels of both socks. He gently slipped them off, grimacing in pain, and tucked them in the boots. He cringed at the sight of the large blisters that were much bigger than yesterday. He slowly eased his feet into the pond. Remarkably, he felt no sensation of warm or cold, only the subsiding pain as the water washed away the blood.

From out of nowhere, Dexter recalled things he hadn't thought of in years. Things oddly out of place, considering where he was and who he was with. Sitting at the edge of the sun-washed, sparkling water, he thought about his great-grandmother's life story, as told to him by his mother. He reached under the neck of his shirt and pulled out the cherished pendant, the one his father gave him. The fossilized forget-me-not appeared to glow in the amber stone. When he looked up, the shadowy enclosed space was losing shape and contorting into something surreal and unrecognizable.

Dexter took a deep breath and tried to shake off the bizarre and unfamiliar feeling that he was coming unhinged from reality. He placed both hands at his sides and clenched his fists, trying to stop the trembling.

What the hell is happening to me?

His fingertips prickled with adrenaline as reality continued to slip from his grasp. Without warning, he transcended into an all-consuming new reality. It was like being trapped in the eye of a tornado. His stomach turned over, and the impulse to vomit caressed the back of his throat. Instead of the anticipated vertigo, a subtle feeling of peace and visual clarity washed over him.

The new surroundings of his altered existence had no shape: no top, no bottom, no end, no beginning. Dexter was confused and disoriented. He buried his face in his hands, so many questions swirling through his foggy mind.

Did I slip and strike my head on the rock wall? Have I been overcome by some lethal gas causing me to hallucinate? Did I die and pass on to the place of exiled lost souls?

Alone in the new reality, he seemed to be drifting even farther from the real world. He raised his head and peered into the swirling mist. He watched a shape taking form, moving slowly toward him. The apparition solidified into an older, tired-looking woman. He watched the facial features take on a somewhat familiar appearance. He stared hard at the advancing figure. It hit him like a hard slap to the face. It was his Grandmother Ester. How could this be?

Grandmother Ester made her way to the stone wall and hovered inches above it. She stood across from Dexter, looking at him with a reassuring partial smile. She wore a full-length pleated skirt, wrapped with a lace-trimmed apron that fluttered in a downdraft that Dexter hadn't noticed before. Partially hidden under the shawl draped around her shoulders, he spotted the familiar amber stone pendant glistening in the beam of sunlight. His hand snapped to his chest—it was still there. When she spoke, her words were filled with purpose and conviction, yet soft and reassuring.

"Dexter," she said, in her dominant voice.

Dexter felt the same shiver he felt as a young boy, when she spoke his name.

"I have a clear understanding of what I have to say to you. It is because I love you and want better for you that I will share something of great importance with you."

Dexter was mesmerized but unable to speak or move. He knew somehow, without question, that what was about to happen, would change his life's direction forever.

The tall, vaporous image of his grandmother continued, "Your grandfather was a good man and had great purpose in his life. I know you and he were very close, and I can tell you he loved you more than life itself. I witnessed your admiration and commitment to your grandfather, and I believe this is a big part of why I have come to you." She held her hands at her middle.

"Isaac was very close to your great grandfather, Abraham, in much the same way you were to your grandfather. During my life, I witnessed these two great men become so obsessed with hunting war criminals that they lost sight of everything else in their lives. Many times, I tried to talk to Isaac about his all-consuming obsession but to no avail. His devotion and commitment to continue with his father's mission was unwavering and could not be influenced. I know you respected your grandfather and remember him as being a perfect role model, but you must know the truth about a long-ago event in his life. When Isaac was in his early thirties, he identified a man named Gunter Weber, whom he thought was a war criminal that appeared to be getting ready to flee. His dedication to his cause drove him to do something he came to regret deeply. In an effort to give himself more time to gather additional evidence, and safeguard the man from escaping, he embellished the proof he had given the police. Acting in good faith that Isaac actually had enough evidence to convict the man, the police made an arrest. The arrest was immediately picked up by the newswires and broadcast around the world. The headline read, 'Suspected Nazi War Criminal Apprehended.' The old woman shifted, from one foot to the other, restlessly.

"After a week of intense interrogation all the while pleading his innocence, the distraught man hung himself in prison. It was eventually proven the wrong man had been arrested. Isaac knew that what he had done directly caused an innocent man to choose death over living a life of suspicion."

"From that day forward, Isaac held remorseful feelings deep inside. The man I married—never returned to me. All that remained was an empty shell. It had left a deep wound in his soul for the rest of his life. Your grandfather made a grave mistake when he let his passion control his better judgment, compelling him to carry out such a bad act. Something he otherwise would never have considered.

"My relationship with your grandfather was one of distance, separated by his all-consuming life's mission and lingering regret. You must make room in your heart for love and passion. Life without passion is no life at all, but life with one all-consuming passion at the expense of all others, is worse.

"Your father is also goal driven with his own obsessions. Some of the same overwhelming sadness that weighed heavy on my heart, I have seen in your mother. She masks her loneliness and concerns in her bubbly personality and perpetual motion, but it is there. It is time to start a new tradition. One you can be proud of. One that generations that follow can learn from."

Dexter's mind was whirling. *How am I supposed to change things?*

"The life of your grandfathers is not the life I want for you, Dexter. I want you to live a full and gratifying life with the freedom to experience all your journey has to offer. Free of obligation. Free of regret. Free of remorse. You must not to be blinded by duty or love. This was their mission. It does not have to be yours. It is time for this family tradition to end!

"The time for guarding your feelings and secrets can be over if you open your heart and share your burden. I know you can accomplish great things if you let down your guard. Never be so consumed by your own needs and fears that you miss the opportunity to show compassion and understanding to all who pass through your life. Some connections will be short, some will be long, but every one of them is important. You won't necessarily know why they are important or what impact you will have on their future but take every opportunity to show compassion to the needs of your fellow man. Rewards for your efforts will come back to you in ways that cannot be measured by monetary wealth but only by the joy that is going to build in your heart."

Dexter tried to speak, but the words would not come. It felt as if they were entombed in his throat. We wanted to tell his grandmother it was too late; he had already done a horrible thing in an effort to carry on the quest of his grandfathers. The deep dark secret that neither he nor his father ever spoke of. He wanted to tell her he understood what drove his grandfathers, and what happened to him still tugged at the fabric of his soul.

Grandmother Ester pointed her bent arthritic finger at her grandson, "Let the things I have told you settle in your mind. Spend quiet time reflecting on the importance of their meaning."

Tears pooled on her lower eyelids then streamed down her cheek. Their eyes locked.

At that moment, he knew—she knew—what he had done.

She turned and disappeared from his view.

JENEVA CONTINUED TO stare at the strange shapes shifting in the water. The tiny elements of gold were now contorting into horizontal and parallel elliptical forms, then stretching into a twisted chain. As Jeneva watched the strange activity intently, she came to a sudden realization of what they reminded her of.

"Amir, are you seeing this? Doesn't that look like the double helix?"

He returned his gaze to the pool of water and gave it a scrutinizing look.

"I'm no biologist, but it sure looks like it to me."

Jeneva looked over at Dexter for a reaction, but he sat silently on the side of the pool with a blank look on his face.

"Dexter! Calling Mr. Know-it-all? No contrary analogies to offer?" she taunted.

The shadowy figure appeared petrified and made no effort to respond. Realizing something peculiar was happening, her humor shifted quickly to feelings of concern. As she made her way around the wall, Dexter's body seemed to catapult from his sitting position and was now crab-walking frantically backward, until he was backed up against the clammy wall of the cavern.

She gingerly hurried across the wet ground and knelt beside him. He was trembling and gasping for breath, almost to the point of hyperventilating. Amir stared at Dexter and backed off to give her room. Jeneva tried to wrap her arms around Dexter's broad shoulders. She couldn't believe this frightened, whimpering, childlike puddle of a man was the same debonair, strong-willed person she'd recently spent the evening with.

She looked over her shoulder at Amir, who was just standing there. She ordered him to bring her the foil heat blanket from his backpack.

"Be right there." He didn't avert his eyes from the water.

"Hurry!" Jeneva said, much louder than her initial request.

Amir, in fact, brought two survival blankets and slowly made his way over to Jeneva and stuffed them both into her outstretched hand.

"The weird shape in the water has disappeared, and the gold flakes are just floating motionlessly in the water again," he said.

"Why are you worrying about that? We need to snap this guy out of this trance."

"Give him a slap across the face. That should snap him out of it." Amir sounded quite eager to do just that.

"Don't be ridiculous. This isn't a movie about some hysterical housewife. This is Dexter!" Her frustration was increasing with every minute that passed.

"All right, already, let's get him out of here and into some fresh air."

"Wait! The trembling stopped!" She put her hands on his cold cheeks and looked him straight in the eyes.

"Dexter! It's Jeneva! Can you hear me?"

At first, his eyes seemed frozen in place, then he blinked, and she saw he was back.

"Where am I?" He blinked several times then quivered.

"You're in the cavern with me and Amir. Don't you remember?"

She was helping Dexter to his feet when he pulled away. He scrambled on the damp ground, fumbling with the dangling rope. His yell echoed in the hollow cavity of the pyramid.

"I need to get out of here, now!"

Chapter 9

A mir's Vision Revealed
Dexter insisted he was quite capable of driving them back to the hotel, and Jeneva sensed it was an argument she couldn't win. Reluctantly, she got into the Hummer with her confused comrade, knowing she couldn't let him leave alone. Not after whatever it was that happened to him back at the pyramid.

Two days, two incidents, followed by silence. What transpired in the depths of that mysterious cavern that upset these two normally loquacious guys? Jeneva was overcome with concern for both Amir and Dexter.

"Dexter! Get your mind back on the road. That's the second time you've almost driven into the back of Amir's jeep!" Her nervous words went unnoticed by the driver.

The two vehicles arrived back at the hotel at the same time. Amir got out of his vehicle and darted over to the Hummer.

"Are you guys, okay? That was some radical driving, Dexter."

Jeneva jumped out of the Hummer and went to the other side. Dexter threw open the driver's door, almost slamming it into Jeneva. He rotated just far enough to slide off the seat to the ground, in a zombie-like motion.

"Anyone for a drink and perhaps a little disclosure?" Jeneva glared at them, hoping to get a response out of one or the other.

Dexter started walking away without looking back, mumbling something about a nap.

"Guess it's just you and me." Jeneva opened the hotel entrance door for Amir.

"Sorry, Jeneva, I'm exhausted too. I need to freshen up and have some quiet time. I'll meet you for dinner if you like, say six thirty?" Amir suggested.

Jeneva stuck out her bottom lip in a childlike pout. "You know what they say about people who drink alone?"

Feeling a bit tired herself, she decided to forgo the drink and watch some mindless TV alone in her room. Maybe it would distract her from the peculiar behavior of her friends.

LATER, JENEVA AND AMIR took a table in the farthest corner from the restaurant door. After the waitress poured them some water, they asked to be left alone until they signaled her to come back for their order.

Dexter's absence at the dinner table gave Amir a sense of ease. It wasn't that he disliked the man, it was his constant needling and that charming personality that provoked a dynamic of rivalry between them. Compared to Dexter's tall, heavily muscled physique, which drew women to him like a magnet, he felt unremarkable and unworthy of Jeneva's affections.

Her gregarious and caring personality made her very approachable. She was used to the attention and admiration of others, which made Amir's infatuation with her go entirely unnoticed. To Amir, Jeneva was a natural beauty with a down-to-earth personality, the perfect woman.

Jeneva looked at Amir with those penetrating brown eyes in a way that made him think she was peering into his soul.

"What did you fellas experience in the cavern, and why are you both unwilling to talk about it? I'm feeling left out. Someone has to talk to me, and you're here now, so spill the beans, mister."

Amir was taken aback by her directness, but there was no doubt he was going to answer her questions. He'd remained silent out of uncertainty and apprehension; had his vision been real? Would she consider him deranged? It was very clear his self-made barrier, built with hordes of anxiety and fear, could no longer stand strong against Jeneva's resolve for answers.

THE EXPRESSION ON AMIR'S face turned to a boyish meekness and uncertainty of the consequences of the imminent disclosure. He shifted in his seat and ran his fingers through his thinning hair. Something he did whenever he was nervous.

"I have not been able to tell anyone about what I experienced yesterday, simply because I needed time to gather my thoughts and let what I saw percolate in my mind. Certainly not because I wanted to upset you! Nothing could be farther from the truth." Amir placed his hand on hers.

"Here goes. When I was sitting on the wall with my feet in the water, the reality of the pyramid cavern dissolved, and I was transcended into what I can only call an alternate reality. The walls around me were gone. I felt like I was staring into the endless night sky of a distant galaxy. I was not afraid but did consider that I may have died and gone to heaven. I even pinched my arm to make sure. I instinctively reached into my pocket to see if my priceless notebook made the journey with me."

Jeneva was on the edge of her seat, totally focused on his every word. It took a great deal of restraint not to ask him about the so-called priceless notebook and why he didn't mention it before.

Amir took a deep breath and ran his fingers through his hair again. She could sense the doubt and hesitation in his cracking voice as he continued his story.

"Out of the endless space, a figure came into focus, walking toward me. He had a long white beard and no hair on the top of his head. When the imposing figure got close, I realized I was staring at the face of someone I'd admired for the bulk of my adult life but never met. I was in the presence of my hero, the father of evolution, Charles Darwin. Initially, I was speechless. My mind was racing with endless thoughts and questions I'd wanted to ask him over the years." He took in a deep breath and continued.

"This Darwin look-alike sat across from me and started asking questions about the progress of science, with respect to the expansion of research he started. He seemed anxious for confirmation of his theories and very interested in what new directions the study of evolution had taken in the last hundred and thirty-five years. Somehow, he knew, I knew the answers. I felt humbled and honored to be updating my hero. All the while, wishing I'd spent more time on my hobby so I could have more intellectual responses to some of his probing questions." He took a drink of water.

Jeneva finally broke her silence as Amir drank.

"Was Darwin everything you expected?"

"He was nothing like my perception of what he might have been like, especially his personality. The numerous questions and continuous need to find answers, were those I would have expected from a scientist. I don't know how to explain it, but he is definitely more real to me now and still a genius. He appeared quite saddened and frustrated that religion was still trying to discredit what he considered to be the undeniable, scientific truth about his theories.

Jeneva was still curious about the mysterious notebook. She wanted to lighten the mood and get an answer. She toyed with the idea of asking, "Is there still something hidden in your pocket, or are you just glad to see me," but decided against it.

"Why do you think he came to you for answers?"

"I'm not sure he only wanted answers. He strongly encouraged me to further my knowledge on the fundamentals of evolution. And to focus on the commonality of where various religions could be in sync with scientific proven knowledge. I won't bore you with the facts, but he did give me a lot of direction. I need more time to reflect on it all and get it on paper."

"Wow! It looks like you have a tough life's mission ahead of you if you decide to go down that rabbit hole. All kidding aside, Amir, thank you for sharing this with me and, absolutely, if it feels right, you should take up this worthy cause. Heaven knows, science is under attack from every right-wing politician in the world."

"There's one more thing." Amir lowered his head in a shameful gesture and ran his fingers over the top of his head. "What I'm about to tell you is difficult to talk about. I have a secret that has weighed heavy on my heart for many years." He raised his head and met her eyes. "I've never shared it with anyone."

Jeneva noticed his demeanor change. He looked like a kid who'd been caught cheating on a test. She sat silent, waiting for the proverbial ball to drop.

"Biology was my minor in university. I made studying Darwin's writings and trying to understand his scientific genius mind a lifelong hobby. I always considered this hobby to be a good distraction. At the same time, it provided good methodologies for my archaeological work."

Jeneva noticed him biting his lip nervously.

"My passion for understanding Darwin's work has grown into what some might call an obsession. His appearing in the cavern was scary at first but has given me some relief. The experience was as real and comfortable as reminiscing with an old friend." Amir took a long drink of water.

It seemed like an eternity to Jeneva before he put the glass down. Was he finally going to talk about the notebook?

"In any case, my passion consumed my better judgment, and I did something I'm very ashamed of. The notebook in my pocket was

Darwin's from the Down House Museum in England. I knew it was stolen when I bought it," Amir blurted out.

Jeneva guessed from the pleading look in his eyes that he needed something from her, understanding, forgiveness maybe. She wasn't sure she could offer either.

"We are all driven by our passions. They make us good at our jobs and can make us better people. It is and should be part of the human experience. Life without passion is a life likely unfulfilled." She said, hoping to appease him for now. "It's been a long day. What do you say we call it a night?"

Chapter 10

Looking for Answers
After tossing and turning restlessly all night, Jeneva's early morning jog was a much-needed distraction. Amir's disclosure of his vision and indiscretion was fascinating and quite disturbing at the same time. The idea of her friend purchasing stolen property seemed so out of character.

An hour later, she impatiently waited in the hotel restaurant for Dexter and Amir to come for breakfast. The anticipation of what might manifest in her cavern experience today had her head spinning. Was it going to be a re-enactment of her mother's visit in the hospital? Would she see someone else? Who? And what the heck did Dexter experience? Patience wasn't one of Jeneva's strong points, and this waiting was driving her crazy.

"Ms. Yassi!" Josué's husky voice disrupted her rampant thoughts. "Here's your special smoothie." He placed a tall glass on the table in front of her.

"*Gracias.*"

"I don't know how you can drink something green."

She couldn't help but snicker at the look on his face. "It's packed with vitamins and minerals. Gets my engine roaring in the morning. You should try it!"

"*No—gracias*! *Que tenga un lindo día!*"

"You have yourself a nice day as well, Josué." She knew a few Spanish phrases, but not enough to carry on a full conversation, thanks to a class she had taken in high school.

Ten minutes later, Amir walked in, alone. Despite her expressing her feelings of urgency to get to the pyramid, he made her wait while he ordered a large coffee and club sandwich to go.

She phoned Dexter from the lobby, to see whether he was up to joining them.

DEXTER AWOKE FROM A deep sleep to hear the *Star Wars* theme playing on his cell phone. Definitely not the nicest sound to wake up to, he decided, making a mental note to change it. "Who's calling so early?" he grumbled. He picked up the phone and glanced at the time.

"What the hell? Nine thirty. I never sleep this late." In a voice that sounded like a forty-year chain smoker, Dexter managed a, "Hello!"

"Hey, Dexter, are you ever going to leave that room, or have you suddenly developed agoraphobia? You left us kind of abruptly yesterday. Seriously, are you okay?"

Dexter sat on the edge of the bed, trying to get his bearings.

"I am still feeling a little out of sorts. Do you mind going on without me?"

Jeneva did not like the answer, and she didn't try to hide her disappointment.

"Have it your way, but when I get back, if you're still in that room, I am going to come up and drag you out."

There was no hesitation from Dexter this time.

"Okay! Okay! I have to do some work stuff that can't wait. You sound excited, so don't let me hold you back. I'm fine! Really! You guys go on. Call me when you get back."

"I would have preferred you see us off on our adventure in person, but I will get over it. Here comes Amir. Ciao!"

Dexter still felt a little disoriented as he set the phone down on the undisturbed bed. Looking around the room, he saw everything was still in order, suitcase tucked away under the bed, all clothes put away out of sight, and nothing visible on the bathroom counter.

Some would call him a neat freak, but to him, tidiness represented a life in control. His arrival back to the room yesterday, after their trip to the cavern, culminated with a four-step walk to the bed and an exhausted collapse onto the vintage duvet.

Now in the light of day, the reality of what happened at the pyramid started to sink in. The memories flowed into his waking mind. It all seemed so real. Even now, safe in his room, removed from the pyramid, there was no doubt his experience had not been a hallucination. Grandma Ester did come to him purposely to deliver a message, and he had received it. Whether he understood it, was another story. Dexter's scientific mind struggled with the concept of anything that could not be recognized as physical or material in nature. He decided the first thing he needed to do was research the one fact that could verified—the arrest and suicide of a suspected war criminal Gunter Weber. He estimated his grandfather would have been in his early thirties at the time.

The next few hours were spent on the internet, searching old newspaper stories he found in the library archival system. Sure enough, he found several articles on the arrest and suicide of Gunter Weber. One of the stories even spoke of his grandfather Isaac Applebaum as a key evidence contributor to the police. Sitting back in his chair, he started to categorize his thoughts. The information Ester communicated to him had all been factual. All the information he researched today was new knowledge to him. There was no way he could have known any of these facts before. After all, science was his passion, not old crime stories. Satisfied after logically assimilating all the facts, Dexter's mind moved to trying to understand the deeper meaning of what Grandmother Ester had said.

She was certainly correct to be concerned that he would carry on his grandfather's quest to bring war criminals to justice. And she did seem to be aware of the tragic encounter with Helmut Von Dresden. But why hadn't she spoke directly about it. The horror of the encounter with the dentist came crashing back into his mind, as if it had just happened.

He shook off the chill of the memory and decided a walk might help him open his mind to the other nagging questions he had. *How could my grandmother have come back from death to speak to me? What scientific phenomena could facilitate such a thing? Why now? The Helmut encounter was in the past now.*

The deserted meandering pathways in the park across from the hotel seemed like a good place to start. The sun was high in the blue cloudless sky, and the air smelled fresh. A wonderful change from the old musty furniture smell of his room. Dexter inhaled the air deep into his lungs then exhaled. The anxiety of all that happened over the last couple days seemed to evacuate from his body. His head seemed clear and ready to make some determinations.

He tried to recall his grandmother's words and determine what the essence of her message was. *You must make room in your heart for love and passion. Life without passion is no life at all, but life with one all-consuming passion at the expense of all else is worse.*

He continued walking aimlessly, without destination, rolling the memory of yesterday's vision over and over in his mind. There must be more to it. Ester would not have presented herself to him in this extraordinary, purposeful way, just to give some philosophical message that could have been written inside of a fortune cookie.

He leaned forward, put his hands on his knees, and hung his head, mentally exhausted.

"What am I missing? There must be something more to be obtained from this profound experience."

He stood up and looked around. Dexter was surprised to see that he'd come full circle back to the hotel. A quick spin of his wrist activated the screen on his Fitbit, showing the time to be 3:20 and the step count 20,120. On the other side of the dusty gravel road, he noticed Amir's jeep pulling into one of the many vacant parking spots at the rundown hotel.

It suddenly occurred to him that he could use some help deciphering Ester's message. Who better than that vivacious woman slowly getting out of the dust-covered jeep, just twenty-five feet in front of him?

As he approached Jeneva, he noticed right away that her normal bubbly personality was not present. His thoughts shifted quickly away from his own confusion to concern for her.

"Is something wrong, Jeneva? Are you okay?"

Jeneva exhaled loudly.

"Not really. Let's go to the bar, I could use a drink." She tossed her arm in the air, pointing to the hotel entrance.

Dexter thought of making a wisecrack about her recent affinity for alcohol but chose to follow her silently into the empty hotel lounge.

A less than enthusiastic Amir tagged along as far as the bar entrance. He poked his head in and proclaimed his intentions to do some work in his room. The old wooden saloon doors flapped in and out behind him.

Jeneva walked over to a corner table in the back of the dimly lit tavern. She dropped in her chosen seat and leaned back, a hair from tipping point, and crossed her arms.

"So! What's up with the bone digger? He seems out of sorts." Dexter asked.

Dexter didn't notice the daggers her squinting eyes were set to release, until it was too late. He felt himself push back against his chair in fright as she leaned forward, banging the front legs of the chair with a deliberate, emphatic bang. With accusing eyes, Jeneva went off on a long, uninterruptable release of frustration and pent-up emotions.

"The last few days, I've been feeling like I'm on the sideline, watching the two of you have some fantastic secret experiences. I thought we were a team. In your absence last night, I was finally able to get Amir to tell me what I believe to be a full accounting of his apparition. I am pretty sure you experienced one too, Dexter. When I tried to duplicate the exact circumstances, nothing happened." Jeneva took a quick breath and continued before Dexter could respond.

"I was getting a little fed up with the two of you and your less-than-forthcoming attitudes. Part of what Amir told me last night is weighing heavily on my mind, so our interactions today have been strained at best. The whole day has been a complete disaster, a far cry from what I imagined this morning when we headed out. Without you, I might add. I had such high hopes." Her emotions were getting the best of her, and she couldn't hold back her tears any longer.

"To add insult to injury, your absence made it very difficult getting in and out of the pyramid. Thanks to you being MIA, Amir had to stay on top to manage the rigging, and I had to get myself out of the harness by myself. I just can't believe you decided not to come. You knew how important this was to me."

Dexter tried to respond, but Jeneva cut him off. "By the time I steadied the rope for Amir to come down, I was exhausted. When I finally made my way over to the exact spot you guys had your visions and settled in with my bare feet in the water—nothing happened. I tried thinking about my mom. I held the bracelet and even tried meditation techniques to clear my mind. Still nothing. I sat on that cold stone wall until my butt was numb. I got up and walked around the cavern for twenty minutes, then back to the *special* spot for another friggin hour. I've never been so disappointed in all my life."

The bombardment of information and follow-up death glare made him feel a little uneasy. He needed a break from it all.

"I'm feeling a bit parched. Think I'll grab a beer. Can I get you something?"

"Make it a double," she said, dropping her head in her hands.

There was no way he was going to ask what she wanted and afford her the opportunity to go off on another rant.

After toweling the dust off the green-tinted glasses, the bartender mixed up two Green Ginny's, displayed as the daily special on the white board behind the bar. The chatty bartender provided for a nice ten-minute break before his return to Jeneva.

As he set the drinks down, he noticed Jeneva's infectious smile was back, so he positioned himself in the chair beside her and quietly waited for the continuing saga.

"Dexter, I'm sorry I dumped all my frustration on you like that, but I needed to unload, and you were unlucky enough to be available. I don't think my non-experience had anything to do with you not being there or anything I did or didn't do. After I begged him, Amir reluctantly tried to duplicate his previous experience and failed as well. We're missing something here."

She turned her eyes to the smoke-filmed window and sighed heavily. Dexter thought her storm of emotion had passed. She looked calmer. He decided he would try to get some answers to the questions that plagued him.

His own questioning mind was still looking for validation of what had happened to him in the cavern. So much so, that his apprehension and fear of asking was overtaken by his need to know.

"You are right. I did have a vision yesterday. Can you tell me what Amir saw in his vision?"

Jeneva's far-off gaze shifted, and she looked straight into his eyes.

"As you may recall, I told you everything about my vision of my mother coming to me and how it was the start of my journey to find my destiny. Now, I'm going to tell you what Amir told me last night at dinner, but you have to promise me you'll fully share your experience with me. Every last detail. Can you do that? I need full disclosure, because it could be important to all of us."

"Honestly, I was planning to tell you everything as soon as you got back today, but you didn't appear to be in a listening mood."

Jeneva didn't appear to be convinced that was true. Nevertheless, she divulged Amir's story as it was told to her last evening.

Dexter listened intently as Jeneva repeated what Amir had told her about Darwin appearing and his questions concerning new developments on his theories of evolution. Details around Amir's recollection of how he felt during the experience came through in Jeneva's impassioned voice. Her demeanor shifted when she went into the details of the stolen notebook. The tone in her voice made her feelings blatantly obvious. Dexter picked up on her anguish and her disappointment in what Amir had done.

"I can tell you are obviously upset with Amir's purchase. Can I interject with some thoughts?"

"If you insist." She again turned to look out the window, which was literally impossible through the film of smoke. She put her elbow on the table, rested her chin in her hand, and held her position.

"You know, it might be good to get someone else's perspective on this. I think you have a tendency to hold people to very high standards." *Careful, Dexter. You're treading on thin ice. She's liable to bite your head off.* He tried to redeem himself. "I am not saying that's wrong, but you have to accept that, occasionally, people are going to fall short of meeting your bar."

Jeneva gave him a slow Linda Blair turn of her head, then returned to her reflection in the window.

"I see this as a typically good person letting his passion for something get in the way of his better judgment. But it sounds to me like he is remorseful and looking to make things right."

"So, you're okay with him being a thief?" She turned to face him head on.

"I don't agree with what he did, but I'm not going to let that get in the way of our friendship. I know I kid him a lot, but I like the guy. I'll deny it if you tell him I said that."

"I'll give it some more thought. No promises, and if you think this philosophical interruption of yours has made me forget about your promise, you are sadly mistaken, mister." She pointed a wagging finger at him.

Dexter initially felt a little taken aback by her response but relaxed when he saw her delayed smile devilishly appear. He was relieved normal exuberant Jeneva was starting to reappear.

"All right, already! I'll tell you." He began with the feeling of losing connection with his surroundings and shifting into what he described as something like another dimension. Then, the manifestation of his grandmother's image and her impassioned advice. Leaving no details out, he told of Ester's plea that he not follow in the footsteps of his grandfathers' obsessive mission to bring German war criminals to justice, at the expense of all else in their lives. The events perpetuated by Isaac that led to an innocent man's suicide. And, finally, her advice on the importance of making meaningful connections with people and allowing people into your life. He told her that today he'd verified Ester's story using newspaper articles available online.

What he didn't mention was his own personal encounter and its connection to the vision.

I just can't figure out the deeper meaning of it all. "What do you think?"

"I think you should have been a storyteller. Your vision recap was much better than Amir's." She gave him a mischievous smile.

"Can you be serious for a minute? Do you think I am trying to overanalyze the deeper meaning of this? Or is there something really significant I'm missing here?"

Just as Dexter finished his eager plea for deeper understanding, a loud group abruptly made their presence known as they flowed into the bar. Jeneva recognized some of them as volunteers from the pyramid.

"What do you say we head to a quieter venue to finish this conversation?"

Jeneva nodded and smiled back to one of volunteers waving in her direction.

Dexter stood and headed toward the front vestibule. Jeneva made a detour over to the group to exchange some quick pleasantries before joining him.

As he pushed open the swinging door for her, an unusually cool evening air greeted Jeneva as she entered the hallway.

"Brr, that's a huge change from today's heat." She shivered and folded her arms in front of her chest.

Apparently immune or perhaps just too distracted, Dexter was surprised at her reaction. "I hadn't really noticed, but I guess the temperature has dropped considerably. I have some fifteen-year-old Cognac upstairs that should warm you up."

"Sure, you look harmless enough to me. Let's head up to your room for a nightcap." She gave him a little push in the direction of the staircase.

She followed behind his slow ascent up the antique stairs, contemplating his strong desire to find meaning to it all.

Dexter swung the door open to expose a room so tidy it could have been featured in a travel magazine. The bed had a small dent in the middle of the mattress, but there was no sign of personal effects anywhere. Jeneva gave the room a quick scan and turned to face him.

"Where's all your crap? The place looks like a forensic cleanup crew's been here and cleaned up after a murder."

"I am really perplexed by these pyramid visions or whatever they are. If I could go back to my earlier question, do you think I am over-analyzing this? You've now had two people's experiences described to you. Do you think we have both gone mad?

The sudden barrage of questions seemed to catch her a bit off guard.

"Why don't you pour us a couple of drinks and let me sit and think on this for a few minutes. My day has not been great either, you know. I could use some reflection time before offering my opinions."

Dexter gently set a couple of glasses on the table, not wanting to distract her with any noise that might interfere with her closed-eye concentration. Generous portions flowed out of the expensive, ornate cognac bottle into the cheap hotel glasses. He sat down next to Jeneva, on what was, a long time ago, an impressive Louis XV needle-point loveseat.

Quietly sipping his libation, he averted his eyes to a faded picture on the far wall. The period piece appeared to be set in the 1800s. There were three women in bonnets and large hooped dresses. They stood beside a wooden-wheeled canvas-covered wagon harnessed to two white horses. It could have been a scene from *Little House on the Prairie*. It was just a place to direct his eyes while he waited. There was no doubt in his mind the intelligent, perceptive woman beside him was going to provide the answers he needed.

Jeneva opened her eyes and sat up. She finished her drink in two swallows and set the glass down on the table, tapping the rim for a re-fill. She wiggled into a comfortable position and took a deep breath, which she let out in a long exhale.

"First of all, I thank you for finally sharing your experience with me. I'd be lying if I said this didn't make me feel more left out of everything than ever. Now that I've listened to both Amir's and your stories, I'm even more determined to be part of this. Having said that, let's focus on your quest for meaning."

Dexter looked anxious, hanging on her every word, waiting to hear more.

"I think the central theme or purpose seems to be the importance of compassion and understanding for your fellow man or woman." A pretentious smile fell over her face.

"I have a thought, but it may be hard to hear or think about."

He tilted his head in her direction and gave her a curious look.

"What is it Jeneva? At this point, I will take anything. I have been going crazy trying to figure this out." He scratched at both sides of his head.

"You may not realise this Dexter, but you can be kind of a cold person. I can see through your facade of dismissive overconfidence, but most people see you as a conceited, shallow pretty boy. I know deep inside you have the same vulnerabilities and needs for human connection as all of us, but if anyone tries to get close to you, you deflect them away with smart-ass comments.

Her blunt assessment made him feel defensive and uncomfortable. He stood up and walked to the farthest point in the room. He was trying to put some distance between him and the person that had just given him such a searing personal evaluation. His hands rubbed his head and face as he paced back and forth, shifting his position closer to the door. Jeneva instinctively jumped up and ran over to him, wrapped her arms around him, and held tight, preventing him from leaving.

"Dexter, your grandmother was just providing you with a roadmap to a more fulfilling life. I think she was just trying to convey the message that you need to break down your protective walls and let people into your life. You may be resisting the meaning because you're afraid to be vulnerable."

Dexter's arms fell limp, tears flowed down his cheeks as he rested his face on her shoulder. He began to shiver. Jeneva grabbed a comforter off the bed and wrapped it around him with the sweeping motion of a cape. She went over to the stone-faced fireplace, turned on the gas, scraped one of the long wooden matches on the mantle, and lit the fire. She stood with her back to Dexter, giving him a chance to compose himself.

When she turned, he was sitting back in the loveseat. "Dexter, I honestly believe we all have the ability within ourselves to make changes and improve the way we live our lives. I didn't mean to hurt you and I hope you understand my frankness. I never knew your grandmother, but I love the gift she has given you in this vision. Please understand, I just wanted to be totally honest and give you my heart felt opinion. I really hope you can accept what I said in the supportive way it was intended.

DEXTER STOOD AND RELEASED the comforter from his grip. It dropped to the floor. As he moved in slow motion toward Jeneva, she thought she could see his unbridled emotions leaving his body and the man she was falling in love with, reappearing right before her eyes. Even with the heat at her back, gooseflesh covered her arms. She stood frozen as the masculine man who, moments ago, had been weeping like a child, opened his arms and pulled her to his chest. She let herself collapse against him and felt her own frustrations of the day slip away. Without releasing their hold on each other, they shuffled backward as one, and a rush of passion overtook them. Frantically, they unbuttoned, unzipped and tossed each other's clothes to the floor.

Dexter slowly lowered Jeneva's naked body onto the bed. A calmness flowed through her as she closed her eyes, enjoying the warmth of his kiss on her partially open mouth. A whimper escaped her parted lips as the back of his hand stroked her cheek and slid down her neck to her shoulder then to her hand. Dexter raised her soft hand to his lips like a Knight of the Round Table and gave it a chivalrous kiss.

From his seated position on the side of the bed, he started to explore her body from head to toe with his fingertips.

Jeneva felt like butter melting under his erotic touch. When he rolled her aroused nipples between his fingers, she uttered a soft "ouch!" He immediately released his grip.

"Sorry. Is this better?" He was gently tickling the hard tip with his tongue.

She inhaled with an erotic "Ah!" Her eyes widened. He saw a definite expression of pleasure infuse her face. He slid his lean, sculptured body in beside hers, tucked his arm under her head, and ever so slowly rolled over and slipped his stallion-like hardness between her parted legs. Jeneva closed her eyes and surrendered herself to Dexter's manly desire.

JENEVA AWOKE TO THE morning flood of sunshine warming her face through the pale worn sheers in Dexter's hotel room. Opening her sleepy eyes, she saw him kneeling beside the bed, elbows on the mattress, his head in his hands. The big grin made him look like the cat who swallowed the canary. She gasped, and then grinned back.

"How long have you been watching me sleep, oh, great lover of mine?" She thought she saw him blush at her praise.

"For what seemed like an eternity, my dear. I thought you would never wake up. Actually, I've been awake for hours, pondering your puzzlement."

Jeneva pulled the blanket around herself in a modest gesture to conceal her nakedness and sat up against the headboard.

"Have you really? And what puzzlement is that my competent lover?" She continued to poke at his ego.

Dexter stood up abruptly, striking a pose with crossed arms.

"Competent, you say. I demand a do-over! I dare say, I think I was quite outstanding!"

Jeneva tightened the blanket around her in a graceful motion and rolled out of the bed into his arms.

"Stop bragging and tell me what you've been up to."

"Well, I have been thinking about your frustration of not being able to share in Amir's and my mystery dream, for lack of a better definition. As you know, I have done substantial research in magnetics and its effects in the universe, as well as here on Earth. I was thinking about how you interrupted my important work and compelled me to come to this place." His turn to tease her.

Jeneva gave him a stern questioning look of disbelief.

"Hold on there. My recollection is you just showed up without invitation."

"Potato, patato. As I was saying before your rude interruption, I have been doing some extensive research into the effects of magnetics, and I am currently focused on the impacts of the magnetic fields at the equator during equinox periods."

"Is this going somewhere, or are you just going to showcase your wealth of knowledge and try to overwhelm me with your great intellect? After that workout last night, I'm famished."

Dexter laughed and gently sat her down in the loveseat they shared last night.

"Can you be serious for a minute? I am really trying to help you."

Jeneva faked a Betty Boop pout but remained silent.

"The interaction between the solar system and the earth changes with the seasons and, as such, has unique characteristics during the spring and fall equinox events. This morning, I woke up to a revelation. Maybe the pyramid mystery dream and the equinox have a connection. I did some checking on the computer this morning, and coincidentally, the peak time of the equinox interaction was during the time of Amir's and my visions. So, my dear, my hypothesis is that you missed the chance to have a mystery dream by about eight hours. It would appear you will now have to wait for the March event. Also, I have one more revelation for you. The last symbol on your bracelet just happens to be the sun and moon, split fifty-fifty, half day, half night, or wait for it—the equinox!" He raised his arms in the air and made the sound of a crowd cheering.

She glanced at the bracelet on her wrist.

"OMG! Dexter! You're a genius. I think I love you." She quickly slapped her hand on her lips. Then she jumped up and started dancing circles around him.

As she raised her arms wrapping them around his neck, the blanket fell to the floor. He picked her up and carried her back to the bed. With the morning sun warming their naked bodies, she expressed her gratitude, twice.

Chapter 11

Vacationing in Cayo Coco

After months of volunteering with Amir, Jeneva called her landlord back in Switzerland and asked him to put all her belongings in storage and sublet her apartment for the remainder of her lease. She was enjoying the experience in Ecuador so much; she couldn't imagine being anywhere else.

The March equinox was only days away and it was all Jeneva talked about. The morning they were to head back into the cavern for her chance at having a vision, the weather had taken a turn for the worst. High winds were downing trees and torrential rain had caused mud slides on the pyramid, making it impossible to climb. Jeneva was heartbroken, once again she had been robbed of the experience she so desperately had been anticipating. The sky's cleared three days later. The window of opportunity had passed.

Dexter headed back to Quito to tie up some unfinished research, reluctantly, leaving Jeneva with Amir in La Maná to do her volunteering. When he returned two months later, Jeneva proposed they take a vacation.

"We've diligently analyzed and rationalized the significance of the symbols and the whole mystery-dream-vision thing. I think we need a getaway to clear our heads. I think Cayo Coco would be the perfect place for us to relax. May is the perfect time to go, not too busy but still comfortably warm." She tried using her irresistible batting eyes to entice him.

Dexter was quite compliant with the idea of vacationing in Cuba, boasting his fluency in Spanish would come in handy.

Jeneva told Dexter about her volunteering with Global Volunteers after Hurricane Irma devastated the island and how anxious she was to see how things turned out. She was hoping to meet up with the many staff members who volunteered their time to help clean up their broken place of employment. She told him she'd never before witnessed such devotion.

Over drinks at the hotel the evening before the couple were leaving for the Caribbean, Amir told them it was best he stayed behind and guard their precious secret. They wholeheartedly agreed.

He turned his head and glared directly at Dexter. "And you are in charge of guarding this precious lady." He pursed his lips sternly.

Dexter responded with a tap to his brow. "Aye, Aye, Captain. I won't let her out of my sight."

As Amir stood to leave, he put his hand on Jeneva's shoulder and gave it a gentle squeeze.

"You guys have a safe trip, and don't worry about anything back here. I've got this!" He bid them farewell and left the room. The next morning, they got up early and drove to Quito to board their flight to Cuba.

THE BUS ARRIVED AT the Iberostar Mojito Resort shortly after nine in the morning. When their check-in was completed, the friendly receptionist told them their bags would be delivered to their room around eleven and suggested they go for breakfast.

Everywhere they went, the smiling faces of the staff greeted them.

"*Hola*! Good morning!" They asked if you were having a good time with sincerity in their voices. Everyone appeared to be happy in their position, be it a maid cleaning rooms, the bartenders serving drinks, or the gardeners trimming the flora and cutting the grass. They were all in motion, as a team, keeping the resort in tip-top condition.

After a lovely breakfast buffet, the couple walked the loop around the resort and found their bungalow. Their luggage had arrived, so they changed into their bathing suits, grabbed towels from the towel shack, and settled into chairs at the quiet adult pool.

White silk-like material draped the pergolas, blocking them from the intense sun. Dexter put some light jazz on his cell phone, which added to the tranquility of the surroundings. They lay back and relaxed without speaking.

A tall gentleman with a white shirt, blue cotton pants, and a friendly smile approached them and asked whether they were ready for a drink.

"Well, this is a nice touch. I'll have one of your signature mojitos." He placed his hand on Jeneva's shoulder.

"Did you want something, dear?"

"That sounds good to me. *Gracias*, Chicho! How have you been?" Jeneva asked.

He was caught off guard but immediately recognized Jeneva when she removed her sunglasses.

"Miss Jeneva. So happy you returned. I heard you checked in this morning."

"I must say, the place looks great. Oh! I'm sorry!" She turned and put her hand on Dexter's chair.

"This is Dexter Applebaum."

"Pleasure, sir." The men shook hands.

"I hope you enjoy your stay. I'll be back with your drinks."

When he returned, he bowed, handing Jeneva a red rose and kissed her hand.

"For the pretty lady."

Dexter gave him a five-peso tip.

"*Muchas gracias*, senor."

The rest of the afternoon was spent sipping cocktails, reading, and relaxing, with the occasional dip in the pool to cool off.

After a fabulous à la carte dinner, the waiter met them at the door and thanked them for coming. Dexter dropped a generous tip in the jar that sat on the talented pianist's keyboard. She mouthed a "Thank you," while continuing to play Elvis Presley's, *"Can't Help Falling in Love."*

The couple agreed it had been a long day and decided to retire early, in their home away from home.

AT BREAKFAST THE NEXT morning, Dexter told her the waves were ripe for the picking, and he was going to try his hand at kite surfing.

"Want to join me?"

"Thanks, but I don't think I have the arm strength to stay upright. I'm going shell hunting. You have fun."

Jeneva walked along the white sandy shore, enjoying the cool water rolling over her toes, picking up the odd polished shell. She stood on the shore, watching the skillful kiters dancing their boards through the boiling waves of the Cayo Coco shoreline. Every once in a while, one of the thrill-seeking teenagers would flip up in the air, land, then continue to ride the rolling water with ease. She thought they looked like ballet dancers pirouetting across the Caribbean sky in a rainbow of colors. She squinted, trying to pick out Dexter. He should have been the novice, struggling to master the moves, but they all looked as if they knew what they were doing. It occurred to her that he might have been pulling her leg about it being his first attempt. Out of nowhere, a kite went flying past her, cascading a spray of saltwater. She shivered from the sudden coldness. She wiped her eyes, and there he was, grinning from ear to ear, one-handing the motion bar and blowing her a kiss.

"You bugger!" she hollered as he waved and continued down the shoreline. Jeneva admired the fact that, at his age, he was still trying to hold on to that youthful mindset of indestructibility and childish pranks. But she hoped he knew his limits.

After several laps along the beach, waving as he passed her, he returned the board and kite to the equipment shack.

Jeneva was sitting in the snack-bar wrapped in a towel, sipping a cappuccino. Her eyes were affixed to his bronzed physique as he nonchalantly made his way toward her. She thought he looked like a Greek god in a Speedo, with those pumped-up muscles and that erect stature. Hers were not the only eyes sharing the view.

"That was pretty impressive for a first timer."

"Wasn't it though." He gave her the devilish grin she adored.

"Be right back, I could use one of those to warm up. Can I bring you another?"

"Maybe a latte this time."

Moving to one of the sunshades, they stretched out on lawn chairs, watching the remaining kiters zipping back and forth. They were giving the sunbathers memorable photo ops to share with friends and family when they returned home.

"Dexter, I've been thinking about my mom a lot lately and her message about the bracelet symbols helping me find my destiny. Now that I, I mean *we*, have figured out the meaning behind them, what do you think our next step should be? They were all connected. Maddy finding the hummingbird on the symposium brochure led me to Ecuador, where I reconnected with Amir at the Hummingbird Pyramid. Then the rescue of Lailah led me to the opening of the cavern, where we found the gold in the water. Then you made the third and final realization that the timing of the visions was connected to the Equinox. I couldn't have done it without the three of you, and I am so grateful. But where do I go from here? Surely there's more to my destiny than that."

"I'm not sure. Maybe it's more about your journey and the experiences you've encountered along the way."

"Maybe so. When Mom came to me during my unconscious state in the hospital, she said that all would be revealed if I kept an open mind to what I see and hear from others and not to focus on where I think I'm supposed to go. What the heck does that even mean?" She threw her hands in the air.

As if he could sense her level of frustration elevating, Dexter suggested a walk on the beach might bring them some clarity.

As they strolled, Jeneva was the first to speak. "Maddy is a prime example of a small deed making a big difference in someone's life."

"Who's Maddy again? Is she your Little Sister?" Dexter scrunched his brow slightly.

"Yes. Maddy's my Little Sister. I've been acting as her Big Sister since she was eight. She's sixteen now and smart as a whip. I can't wait for you to meet her. When I last spoke to her, she told me about an incident at school. She stopped to talk to a fellow student who was crying, and it turned out she was struggling with her sexual identity and was being bullied by her peers. With the help of the guidance teacher, they possibly saved the girl from committing suicide. The principal got wind of the incident and has started a program called, 'Bullies Be Gone,' and asked Maddy to be the head of it."

"She sounds like a very special young lady. I look forward to meeting her."

"She sure is! I'm very proud of her. You know, Dexter, there are many people out there doing good deeds of kindness every day. Can you imagine if everyone did something nice for someone else, expecting nothing but personal gratification in return? Wouldn't that change the world as we know it?"

They returned to their chairs and her frustration faded and was replaced by total euphoria in minutes.

"No doubt about that." He finally answered.

"What can we do to make this happen? Help me out. This could be big. This could be my destiny!" She was on the edge of her seat now, pleading for his input.

"I don't know. Maybe propose a challenge to see who can do the most, good deeds?"

"You're a genius, a challenge could work. All we have to do is in-still our intent that small acts of kindness can change the world. Can you imagine the impact that could have if not only people, but whole countries banded together, helping one another, instead of waging war on each other? Oh, my gosh!" She raised her hands in the air, re-joicing. "Hallelujah! Peace on Earth!"

"Take a breath, and give your head a shake, girl. That would take a miracle!"

"I believe in miracles!" She gave him a resolute sneer. "I think it was Francis of Assisi who said, 'Start by doing what's necessary; then do what's possible; and suddenly you are doing the impossible.'"

"That sounds great, but what's the incentive? There has to be more than a warm fuzzy feeling to entice people." Dexter was clearly trying to be the voice of reason.

"Unfortunately, you are right about that. It needs to be some-thing unique, definitely not money. I don't want it to be a contest of chance or luck, and it must be affordable to whoever wants to partic-ipate."

Probably in an effort to calm Jeneva's exuberance and put her no-tion of world peace on the shelf for a while, Dexter suggested they relocate to the pool to relax. Maybe have a mojito and a swim. It took some doing, but he eventually convinced her take a break from their exciting plans to save the world.

Ice cold minty drinks in hand, they listened to the water roll over the concrete wall in crystal clear cascades. Mourning doves flew ever so close to the surface, causing a turquoise reflection on their bel-lies from the tiles in the figure-eight-shaped pool. Couples came and went, some took a quick dip, and some just dangled their feet, enjoying a beverage and friendly chitchat amongst themselves.

Jeneva reminded Dexter that they hadn't made any reservation for their evening meal. "And if you don't mind, can you stop at the bar and get me another mojito, no extra sugar, *por favor*, amigo?"

He returned with the reservation slip for that evening, along with two tall glasses filled with the rum mixture and fresh mint leaves.

"So, where are you taking me tonight?"

"Tonight, my dear, we will be dining at the beach chalet."

"That sounds perfect."

"What do you say we put the contest discussions on hold until tomorrow and enjoy a nice romantic evening under the stars?" She supposed he'd had his fill of her wild idea.

"Okay. On one condition. You have to take me to the disco after dinner." She put her chin on her shoulder and gave him a coy look.

"I'll think about it."

Later that evening, they walked hand in hand along the boardwalk, guided by swooping rope lights. At the top of the aluminum bridge, Dexter stopped abruptly. He pulled her around to face him, with less than a finger's width between them.

"Look up!"

What she saw were millions of glittering stars painted across the black velvet sky as far as the eye could see. A crescent moon overhead was so close she thought she could reach out and touch it.

"So. What do you think?" Dexter looked into Jeneva's eyes.

"Have you ever seen anything so magical?"

"It's . . ." She was unable to speak; he'd wrapped his strong suntanned arms around her and was kissing her. His lips were soft as silk and just as slippery. After a few seconds, he loosened his masculine hold on her feminine frame. The strap of her sundress fell off her shoulder, and with the gentlest finger he put it back in place.

When she caught her breath, she continued her response, "It's spectacular, and the kiss was pretty spectacular too."

Dexter linked Jeneva's arm in his, and they continued down the boardwalk to the beach.

When they reached the open-air dining area, they were greeted in the familiar friendly fashion they received from all the staff. A waiter seated them at a candlelit table. There was a whisper of a breeze, just enough to push the ocean to shore in a passive ripple, giving their surroundings a romantic ambiance.

Dexter had paid the surcharge for the lobster meal when he made the reservation earlier in the day. He'd recalled Jeneva mentioning her love of seafood and wanted to give her the perfect night.

Jeneva was pleasantly surprised when the large, hand-painted platter with two cheese-topped lobster tails were placed in the center of the table. The aroma of garlic butter hung in the air and moistened their mouths with anticipation. The orange of the fresh pumpkin and green broccoli heads that surrounded the tails rivaled the brilliant colors on the decorative plate.

When there was nothing but two empty shells remaining in front of them, they sipped their last swallow of white wine and headed to the beach for an after-dinner stroll. Jeneva admitted she was too full to show off her *Saturday Night Fever* moves at the disco and was okay with heading back to their bungalow.

She was hanging her sweater in the closet when Dexter came around the corner, wearing nothing but his Calvin Klein briefs. She gasped at the sight of his near nakedness. The sweater dropped from her weakened grasp. As her eyes met his, he reached out his hand. She couldn't restrain the urge that had been gnawing at her all day and put her hand in his.

A light breeze from the balcony fluttered the sheer drapery back and forth. Jeneva quivered from the cool ceramic tiles on her bare feet. Or was it the gentle stroke of Dexter's finger's removing her sundress in one skillful movement? She wasn't sure.

Gingerly, she caressed his brawny shoulders and slid her hands down his back. Her fingertips slid under his CKs until they fell freely to the floor. The couple tumbled onto the bed with Jeneva on top, straddling Dexter's hips. He reached up and cupped her breasts gently. Raising her head, she took in a vivacious breath. After several minutes of rhythmic moves, they moaned boisterously in unison. Jeneva rolled over and snuggled in against his sweaty body. He smiled as if he knew that he'd given her the perfect night, and she fell asleep in his arms.

ON THE THIRD DAY OF their vacation, Jeneva awoke to find the other side of the bed empty, except for a large pink hibiscus and a note that read, "Gone for coffee. Be right back." She took a quick shower and heard the door slam as she finished drying off.

"Need any help in there?" She knew where this was going and let him in.

When they were finally dressed, her in a white tank with flowery capris and he in a flowery shirt and white cropped pants, they went for breakfast. They looked like two people in love as they held hands and sipped their mimosas, lost in each other's eyes. They'd worked up quite an appetite back in the room and ravished their way through a buffet fit for a king.

As they were leaving the breakfast building, Jeneva noticed a quaint little cat house beside the walkway and ran back in to get some scraps off their plates. Next time she'd plan better and salvage more scraps for the eight felines that sat in chairs and lingered on the roof, waiting for their next meal. None looked to be malnourished.

The couple decided a long walk along the beach would be good for their digestion. Thankfully, the sun hadn't yet reached its full potential.

It was still early when they got back to the lobby. It didn't go unnoticed by Jeneva that Dexter was still looking for ways to distract her from her obsession to save the world; he suggested they check out the excursions. As it turned out, there was one leaving in half an hour, just enough time to gather hats, sunglasses, and such, and be out front when the tour bus arrived. The sales rep offered his best tour, "Especial Deluxe San Miguel Tour." The price was more than reasonable. It included a horse-drawn carriage ride, visit to a sugar mill, speed boat ride through a mangrove forest, and a stop at a silversmith artisan shop. The creator himself was on the premises and told them he used silverware the Germans left behind for his exquisite pieces of art. They also took a ride on a working steam train, and of course, a quick stop for souvenir shopping.

It turned out to be a very enjoyable and enlightening trip. Jeneva had been totally distracted and hadn't thought of "The Challenge" the whole trip. She chuckled to herself. Dexter's "plan" had worked like a charm, but she'd talk to him about it later. The reception manager approached them and told Dexter she knew they were away and had made a reservation at the international à la carte restaurant for seven. He thanked her for her thoughtfulness and offered her a tip, which she refused.

"My pleasure, Mr. Applebaum. Enjoy your evening, Miss Jeneva." She turned and made her way behind the front desk counter.

"It's little things like that, that will bring folks back here," Dexter remarked on the way to their bungalow. They decided to conserve water, in the interest of Cuba's posterity, by showering together. At six o'clock, they were sitting on the balcony, wrapped in cozy white robes, sipping cold beers.

"Thank you for another wonderful day, Dexter."

"I should be thanking you for picking this place. I've never felt so at home, away from home."

"I know what you mean. These folks have so little but appear to be so happy and appreciative of what they do have. Did I ever tell you the story about gratitude I read in a book called, *The Secret* by Rhonda Byrne?"

"I don't think so?" He gave his head a little shake.

"Well, it's kind of a self-help book of sorts, about the power of positive thinking and the law of attraction. Long story short, I put a load of laundry in the washer and sat down to continue reading. This guy carried what he called his "Gratitude Stone" with him wherever he went. Anyway, he gave his stone to a man whose son was gravely ill and told him if he thought positive thoughts, positive things would come to him. Months later, the father contacted him. He told him his son had recovered. He said, he'd sold over one thousand gratitude stones and donated the money to charity.

I just finished the story when the buzzer went off on the washer. When I was loading the dryer, I heard something hit the floor. You're not going to believe me, but lying at my feet was a maroon stone, the size of a fifty-cent piece. I'd never seen it before, and to this day, I have no idea where it came from. I take it with me everywhere, and at night, I thank the Universe for everything good in my life. You probably think it's nonsense, but that book has changed a lot of people's lives.

Dexter took the last gulp from his can and set it on the patio table. Straddling Jeneva's chair, he leaned in, putting them nose to nose and eye to eye.

"It may surprise you to know, my little Cuban cupcake, that I very much *do* believe in the law of attraction. Did you forget I'm an expert on the subject of magnetics? And that, my dear, is precisely why you can't resist my magnetic personality?"

"Yeah, right." Jeneva rolled her eyes.

He lowered himself close enough to nibble her ear.

"Mmm, chocolate," he purred, assisting her to her feet.

"You have five minutes to dress. *Rapidez*!" he ordered in Spanish, giving her bottom a little tap.

The international cuisine was a buffet of familiar dishes, plus a few Cuban originals. Jeneva continued the conversation of their plans for the how, what, when and where this idea she was calling "The Challenge" might progress. She always carried a notebook in her beaded bag, and she made a lot of notes before, during, and after dinner. Later, back in their room, they reviewed what they'd discussed.

"That's a good start. Can we go to bed now?" Dexter yawned.

A RELATIVELY YOUNG woman in a crisp white uniform, holding a clipboard, stopped the couple as they approached the door to the morning buffet. She handed Jeneva a brochure from the nearby AquaVita Spa and asked whether they would be interested in a couple's massage.

"Will you be here for a while? I'm starving. Can we let you know on our way out?" Dexter asked impatiently.

"My name is Yusnaisy, and I would be happy to wait. Take your time."

As promised, she was sitting in one of the wicker chairs just outside the buffet entrance when they came out. Before she finished explaining the inclusions in the different packages, much to Jeneva's surprise, Dexter said, "Sign us up."

They picked the four-hour Cleopatra deal: transportation to and from the spa, a milk bath in a jacuzzi tub, hot mud detox, a half-hour massage in the outdoor gazebo, hydroponic pools with an ocean view, and an open bar were all included. Yusnaisy told them they were to meet the van at the entrance of the resort at two o'clock sharp. She took down their names and bid them "Adios."

The couple headed back to their bungalow where they decided to spend some time discussing Jeneva's save the world project.

Out on the balcony, Jeneva got comfortably seated, opened her laptop to the Word file she'd started, and recapped the bullet points she and Dexter had discussed last night.

- Do good deeds, self-gratification
- Make it affordable, everyone can participate
- Don't have a cash prize, what is reward?
- Promote world peace

"What if we establish the average income of each country and set the cost to participate accordingly? That will cover the affordability issue," Jeneva suggested.

"Maybe we can convince some wealthy philanthropists to invest.? Between the sign-up fees and investment money, we should be able to cover the operating costs."

"That's a great idea. We're going to need some money, but I'm hoping for volunteers to help out in some administrative areas along the way."

"The big question remains. What is the reward? People won't do anything without incentive. What is worth more than money?" Dexter queried.

They both shrugged their shoulders and stared at the ocean in front of them, hoping the answer would wash up on the beach.

Jeneva broke the five-minute silence.

"Anything?"

"Nope, I got nothing." He gave a huff of disappointment.

"How about this, Mr. Applebaum? If you could have anything, what would it be?"

He scrunched his brow, trying to come up with an answer.

"I guess it would be another visit with my grandmother to get a better understanding of her message."

Jeneva jumped to her feet. "That's it! You've done it again. We offer them a chance of a vision with connections past. I bet a lot of people wish they could talk to someone who's passed on. Maybe to apologize for something they said or did or just tell them they love them." She was practically vibrating with excitement.

"I don't know about that." He gave her an apprehensive look. "It was pretty scary. Some people might get freaked out. It sure did a number on my head."

"We can brief them on what to expect and walk them through the possibilities beforehand. It's the perfect reward! I'm still upset about last March's equinox, when that Dragon storm hit. I was so looking forward to the experience and so disappointed when we had to cancel because of the torrential rain and destructive winds." She lamented.

Three and a half hours flew by like minutes. They developed a rough outline of the rules and regulations and started a list of associated words that could be used for the official contest name.

"We better get going. Yusnaisy will be looking for us." Jeneva closed her laptop.

When they arrived at AquaVita, they were given a tour and ushered to the changerooms. After their spa treatments, they stretched out on the loungers, sipping a complimentary beverage at the cliff's edge, listening to the crashing waves below. They both agreed the view alone was worth the price of admission.

When they were back at the resort, neither were in the mood to get dressed up. So, they decided to have a late dinner at the buffet. Before heading to the open-air theatre to watch the entertainment, Dexter grabbed a Brandy for himself and a Spanish coffee for Jeneva. When the show was over, they strolled past the colorfully lit adult pool on their way to their bungalow. Dexter was looking down, watching his footing on the cobblestone path and hadn't noticed Jeneva had stopped.

"Do you remember those two guys at the symposium?"

He turned when he heard her voice.

She was staring at the changing colors in the pool.

"Sure, Alex and, who was that quiet fellow?"

"Nelson Jones. They invented a machine that projected people's thoughts onto the screen. What if we could use it to project people's visions to the world from inside the cavern?"

"What are you talking about? That's really out there." Dexter took hold of her hand. "I better get you to bed, where you can continue this dream."

"I'm serious, Dexter! We need incentive, right? Seeing is believing."

"If you say so. Can we talk about this tomorrow, please? I'm exhausted." He hung his head and slowly dragged his feet over the cobblestone path.

Chapter 12

Nelson Jones
At five o'clock in the morning, the resort coffee bar was vacant, except for Jeneva. She was searching the internet for Nelson's phone number, not having much luck. Alex and Nelson didn't seem to have a website devoted to their project, so she resorted to checking Facebook, Twitter, and Instagram. She found nothing. It finally occurred to her that because of his disfigurement, he likely wouldn't have any interest in posting or sharing with anyone on those platforms. She was able to find Alex Belle on LinkedIn. When they'd met at the symposium, she'd detected a dominance in his character that she didn't much like. Nelson was more laidback and approachable. After scouring his profile, she found the info she was looking for.

NELSON JONES WAS SITTING alone in his one-bedroom flat in London, England, thinking about today's heated argument with his partner. Alex and he used to be close. They'd enjoyed an exhilarating quest together, designing and perfecting the Visualization Technology (VT) apparatus. The machine had evolved to a finely tuned mechanical marvel, since their debut presentation at the Washington DC symposium last spring. Nelson felt great pride in their collective accomplishments, despite their diverse personalities. Their very different skill sets worked well through concept, design, testing and debugging. He'd found his partner's disciplined approach and organizational skills to be a definite asset during the invention's development. And they agreed, Alex's teaching skills and outgoing personality better qualified him to be the VT presenter at events.

Which allowed Nelson to remain in the background, sheltered from scrutinizing stares. But recently the relationship dynamic had changed. As they ventured into the marketing phase of the VT, their goals had started to fork in very different directions. Now, they were at a crossroads.

Alex received his education in British military engineering programs, so of course, he had a predisposition to think in military terms for everything. Alex was of the opinion that the best uses for VT would be in military application, like combatant interrogation.

Such an idea went against Nelson's very peaceful nature.

Nelson's mind wandered to thoughts of the kind, attractive woman who'd taken the time to talk to him personally when he and the other speakers met for drinks. The vision of Jeneva was indelibly imprinted on his mind and often crept into his dreams.

Nelson was an electronics geek and a passionate gamer, who enjoyed being around people about as much as one enjoys dental surgery. His twenty-nine-year life on this planet had been challenging, to say the least. At the age of nine, he'd lost his entire family in a devastating accident. Their car had been broadsided by a transport truck, which rammed it through the guardrail and down an abutment. Nelson had been thrown from the vehicle, landing in front of an oncoming bus, that unknowingly, dragged his crushed body fifty feet down the highway. The clothes on his back had quickly been shredded off, exposing his bare skin to the rough asphalt. He'd sustained many broken bones, a ruptured spleen, and a severe contusion. All of which healed in time. It was the raw, open gouges on his face and left side of his body that, although attended to with plastic surgery, had left him horribly disfigured. With no relatives available to take him in, he was designated a ward of state. The young boy's life at the orphanage was very difficult. During one of many physical bullying incidents, he had been pushed down a flight of stairs, leaving him with a permanent and noticeable limp, on top of all his other disfigurements.

Nelson jumped up, startled out of his reflective state of mind by the loud ringing of his desk phone. He snatched the handset as quickly as a child sneaks a cookie from the cookie jar.

"Hey, Nelson. This is Jeneva Yassi. You probably don't remember me, but we met during a symposium in Washington DC last spring."

The phone fell out of his trembling hand. He grabbed the cord just before it collided with the floor. Words escaped him. Nelson stood silent, clenching the phone in his sweaty hand.

"If I remember correctly, you and your partner invented a cool machine that displayed people's thoughts."

Still silence on the other end. She must have wondered whether they'd been disconnected.

"Nelson, do you remember me?" In her best cockney accent, she said, "I thought of a way you blokes might put that apparatus to good use."

The horrible attempt at an East End accent was enough to bring Nelson out of shock, and he broke into spontaneous laughter.

"Hey, Jeneva. That's the worst fake accent I have ever heard, and to answer your question, yes, I most certainly do remember you."

"Have you boys got that what did you call it, visualization something or other, perfected yet?"

"We do indeed. The Visualization Technology, VT for short, is working flawlessly." He smiled proudly at his reflection in the window.

"Do you remember Dexter from the symposium? Well, he and I are working on a project that could really use an innovative device like yours. Would you and Alex be willing to meet with us to discuss the details?" Jeneva's excitement was evident through the phone.

"You there, Nelson?"

Nelson too was excited. He could hardly contain himself on the other end of the phone. Ever since their first meeting several months ago, it was all but a hopeless reoccurring desire of his to see her again. Was this fate? He had been thinking about her, and out of the blue, she called him. His legs went limp, and he flopped back down in his chair. He tried not to come across as too eager.

"Sounds fascinating. I would be very pleased to meet with you!"

Nelson was selfishly hoping Dexter wouldn't be at their meeting. He hadn't liked him in Washington and disliked him even more now, knowing he was working with Jeneva.

"I know you probably want to hear more details, but I'm afraid this project is just too complex to discuss over the phone. We are still in the early stages of development but wanted to touch base with you now, just to see if there was any interest."

"I see." Nelson's heart was racing, contemplating seeing her again.

"Why don't you mention our call to Alex. I'll give you a call back in a couple of weeks to set up a date and place we can all get together and discuss the details in depth."

"That sounds great Jeneva." Just speaking her name made him feel like a teenager on his first date.

"Smashing, I will give you a ring on the telly around teatime in a fortnight."

Nelson chuckled at her playful attempt at the English language. It made her even more endearing.

"That's a bit better, but still awful. And the 'telly' means television not telephone." He chuckled again. "We'll talk soon. Good night, Jeneva, I can't wait to see you again." He hung up the receiver and closed his eyes, picturing her beautiful smile and big brown eyes staring lovingly into his.

Nelson knew Alex was in negotiations to sell their invention to the British Armed Forces. Which he didn't agreed with. And now that there was an opportunity for him to win Jeneva's affections, he wasn't about to let anyone stand in his way. Alex would have to be dealt with sooner, rather than later.

SETTING HER PHONE ON the table, she felt a twinge of apprehension. Nelson had been awfully enthusiastic to meet, eager even, considering she'd given him so little information about what they were looking for.

"Who was that?" A voice asked from over Jeneva's shoulder.

She turned and saw Dexter fully dressed in long pants and a light jacket, ready to leave their island escape.

"It was Nelson Jones. He's going to talk to Alex about letting us use their Visualization Technology. He sounded quite eager to talk with us. I told him I'd call back in a couple weeks."

"Excellent. We can put it to good use producing our proof-of-concept trials during the next equinox. Shall we grab a bite to eat, or would you prefer to pack first?" He pulled her chair out.

"Let's eat, it won't take me long to throw everything in my suitcase. I'm sure going to hate leaving. Five days just wasn't long enough," Jeneva said, hooking her arm in his and putting her head on his shoulder.

"Me too! We'll just have to come back sometime."

"The Challenge was more or less born here. Maybe, after we have changed the world, we'll come back to celebrate."

THE FLIGHT BACK TO Ecuador was a noisy one. Everyone was milking the last hours of their vacation with drinking, dancing and singing. The attendants shut down the dancing posthaste. But by the time they exited the plane in Quito, they knew every word to the song "La Bamba."

While they were waiting for their luggage, Dexter turned to Jeneva.

"I was thinking. If we want to keep what's happening in the cavern confidential, should we tighten security around the Pyramid even more?"

"You're probably right, but how do we do that without drawing attention?"

"Leave that to me. My parents are very influential people. I'm sure they can help us out. I'll call and see if we can stop by."

After dropping their bags of at Dexter's condo, they drove to his parent's estate. The Applebaum's were more than happy to have them visit and insisted they stay for dinner. Dexter's mom was ecstatic to finally meet Jeneva. She and her husband were hoping their son was finally going to settle down and get married and give them grandchildren.

Business was never allowed at the Applebaum dinner table. Once they were all comfortably seated in the den, the couple told them about their plan to bring more kindness to the world and what they needed from them.

Dexter informed Jeneva, that despite his mom's affiliation with her woman's institutes and her sitting on several committees, this project was definitely something she would want to be a part of.

"I'm telling you; she'll be running the show if we aren't careful."

It didn't take long for Jeneva to realize just how right Dexter was about his mom

"THE FIRST THING YOU should do is set up a foundation. It needs a catchy acronym, something relevant to your cause. Hmm!" She scrunched her brow in thought. "KIND, Keep It Nice Day; BEST, Be Ever So True." She stood for effect and paced in front of them.

"Come on, people! Help me out."

Jeneva raised her hand. "How about Cherish and Respect Every-one? CARE!"

"I like that," Mrs. A. said, "or maybe CARE, Charitable Actions Reassure Everybody?"

"If I may?" Dexter's dad asked, smiling at the couple hold-ing hands in an antique love seat. "I think I have a good one! Charitable Acts Reform Everything!" Mr. A. raised his eyebrows questioningly.

Dexter and Jeneva looked at each other and nodded.

"By George, I think he's got it!" Dexter said.

"I love it too!" Mrs. A. clasped her hands together in front of her chest. "I can't wait to get started."

"Looks like we have a winner! What's next Mrs. A.?" Jeneva leaned forward, putting her elbows on her knees and her head in her hands.

The tall, handsome Mr. Applebaum stood and spoke to his son. "What do you say we step into my office and discuss how we can manage security around your pyramid?"

Dexter stood and embraced his mom in a hug, giving Jeneva a wink and a smile. She assumed that was his way of saying, "I told you so."

A little while later, the men entered the den with a plan.

"I've made some calls," Mr. A. announced to the women after he and Dexter returned to their seats.

"We're going to meet with the National Institute of Cultural Heritage and convince them the area around the Hummingbird Pyramid needs to be secured. I think it's doable.

"Amir has agreed to come with us once he's finished some dig he's being pressured to complete. That Humanitarian Award they gave him for rescuing the little girl, will carry a lot of weight when he pleads his case. Once he meets with the university, they're his backers, and shows them what he's been finding on his digs, they too will want things under cover." Dexter informed them.

"That sounds very promising. Jeneva took hold of his mom's hand.

"We ladies have drafted a plan for the CARE Foundation that should take care, no pun intended, of all the financial matters of the Pyramid Challenge."

"We should celebrate!" Mr. A. gave his hands a sharp clap.

"What's to celebrate? We haven't done anything yet!" Dexter says.

"Sure, we have!" He stood and helped Jeneva to her feet.

"We have finally met your wonderful girlfriend, and we are all about to make some big changes in the world. Right, Jeneva?"

"Right you are, sir!"

The afternoon visit turned into a week-long CARE Foundation planning and get to know each other session.

THE NEXT MORNING, DEXTER headed back to his office to do work on a project he'd left unfinished before their vacation. Jeneva left as well, traveling back to La Maná aboard a Wanderbus, Ecuador's equivalent to Greyhound.

As she gazed out the window at the rolling hillside, a shiver ran up her spine. The memory of the day Lailah was rescued popped into her head. She could almost feel the encapsulating sensation of the symphonic sounds on her body that day, when the hummingbirds congregated around her. What a wondrous, magical place it was. She felt a sense of shame that they were keeping it from the world, and worse yet, withholding the whole truth about the hidden cavern. Total honesty was at the core of everything she believed, and this deception was eating at her soul. She couldn't wait to share their secret with the world.

When she arrived at the hotel, she was surprised to see Willy come walking over to the bus.

"Hey stranger! Amir sent me to get you. I think he missed you." He reached into the belly of the bus for her bag and carried it to her room.

"I'll be right down. I just want to splash some water on my face and freshen up a bit."

"Take your time. I'll grab a couple burgers; you must be starving." He tipped his tilly and went downstairs.

As usual, Willy talked all the way to the camp. He told her all about the great things they found and how demanding Amir had been lately. Still maintaining it was the best job he'd ever had.

The head archaeologist was overseeing his volunteers cleaning their latest acquisitions when the jeep pulled up. Amir sauntered over and opened the passenger door. He looked past Jeneva and thanked Willy for his service, then offered his hand to her.

"Welcome back. Ready to get to work? As you can see, the volunteers are busy cleaning the artifacts we discovered on the west side. Hey, Willy! You're in charge!" Amir hollered, then turned back to Jeneva.

"I was on my way back to do some more digging before calling it quits for the day. Want to join me?"

"Sure!" She grabbed the backpack Amir packed in anticipation of her arrival.

She was anxious to tell him about the CARE Foundation and the help Dexter's father offered with security issues. After all, as one of the finders of the cavern, he was an integral part of their team. But she had a feeling he wasn't in the mood to talk about anything but his latest find. Hence, she decided to wait until she had his full attention.

They made the arduous climb up and around to the west side when her cell flashed Maddy's smiling face and played their chosen theme song.

"Welcome back. Did you and Dexter have fun?" Maddy giggled mischievously.

"We sure did. Most of our time was spent on the planning of what we are calling *The Pyramid Challenge*. I think I finally found the destiny my mom was guiding me to."

"You mean the Hummingbird I found, led you to your destiny, don't you?"

"You're right. I probably wouldn't be here if it wasn't for you. Funny how one thing can change the direction of your life. So, tell me more about Chuck, is he your destiny?"

"Time will tell. We haven't been in contact much. He's pretty busy with tours, school, working at the restaurant, and watching Owyn."

"He sounds like quite a resourceful young man."

"He is and he cleans up nice too!"

The girls laughed.

"I better get over there and see what the bone digger has uncovered. We'll talk soon, okay. Love you. Miss you!"

"Miss you too. Toodles."

During her phone call, Amir had been giving her disgruntled looks, so she put on her cheeriest face and knelt down beside him.

"How's it going? Found anything interesting?"

"Actually, yes I have, and I'm ready to take it back to the camp to clean it up and see if it is what I think it is."

"That sounds ominous. What do you think it is?"

"I won't know for sure till I can run some tests, but it appears to be shards of a magnetic earthenware pot. There's a possibly it contains pulverized quartz, tourmaline, pyrite, nickel, iron and laterite. See how it reflects the sunlight." He held it up to the sky.

"Congratulations, that sounds like quite a find."

"The University of Quito wants me to bring them up-to-date on my findings so far, and this just might be the golden egg that gets me continued financial backing and tighter security around here." He wrapped the artifact and put it in his backpack. "If you have no other calls, can we get going?"

It was very apparent that he was upset with her. She couldn't imagine her taking a call was the root of his disdain. It must have been something else, but what? She followed him back down to the camp in silence.

When they had the pieces laid out in the tent, Amir asked her whether she and Dexter had had a good time lying carefree on the beach, drinking margaritas.

"So that's why you're upset with me. Your jealous?"

"Hardly! Who you spend your time with, is no concern of mine. Right now, your time is mine, so I'd appreciate if you started dusting off some of these piece's." He handed her a brush.

She went to work; certain this was not a good time to engage him in a conversation. She'd wait for a better time to enlighten him on what she and Dexter were organizing and the developments they'd made with his parents.

It was six o'clock when Amir dropped her off at her hotel, with no mention of getting together later, which was fine with Jeneva. She needed to call her dad and tell him her news.

She grabbed a club sandwich from the restaurant and headed up to her room to make the call.

"Hi, Dad. Got a minute?"

"For my girl, I've got two."

"Very funny!"

"So, what's new with you? Found your destiny yet?"

"As a matter of fact, I think I have." She gave him a lengthy explanation about what she and Dexter had come up with on their trip.

"The first thing I recommend is to set up a foundation that will handle all the financial and administration departments."

"I was just about to tell you Dexter took me to meet his parents, and his mom suggested we do just that! They're well connected and anxious to help. Mrs. Applebaum and I are working on the details of the foundation, and Mr. Applebaum and Dexter are coordinating with the government on the security issues."

"I have no doubt you are going to make a big difference in the world, honey, and I want you to know, I am here for you, whatever you need."

"Thanks, Pops, for everything. I'm pretty sure The Pyramid Challenge is my Destiny! Wish me luck!"

"Luck!"

Chapter 13

G ood News
Amir was convinced the west side of the Hummingbird Pyramid held the key to gaining continued financial support from the university. So much so, that he insisted the volunteers scour the area from sunup to sundown, looking for more artifacts.

Jeneva worked diligently by his side, giving her ample time to fill him in on the CARE Foundation and discuss the security measures needed in preparation for the secret Pyramid Challenge events.

It appeared that he might have gotten over his jealousy of her and Dexter's relationship. That was until the morning he was leaving for his meetings in Quito, his jeep laden with the unique finds.

"I think that's everything." Jeneva slammed the tailgate.

"I hope these latest pieces impress them enough to throw some more cash at our project." Amir stepped close enough to smell her sweat.

"They're going to beg you to keep digging, once they see those magnetic pieces."

"From your sweet lips to the board's ear." His eyes were fixed on her lips.

Quite by accident, he lost his footing and fell forward. Their mouths momentarily touched as his lanky body pinned Jeneva against the back door.

"Whoa there, Cowboy! Are you all right?" She gently pushed on his shoulders.

"I'm good. Just lost my footing on this bumpy ground." Trying to hide his embarrassment, he quickened his step around the vehicle and jumped behind the wheel.

"Any messages for Mr. Wonderful?"

"Just tell him I miss him."

"Sure thing!" He knew full well he wouldn't be telling Dexter anything. He pushed on the gas, and the jeep disappeared down the road in a cloud of dust.

He watched Jeneva waving goodbye in the rearview mirror. Did she believe it was a loss of footing, like he said, or did she think it a deliberate advance?

AMIR WAS HALFWAY TO Quito when he got a call.

"Hey, buddy! Ready to razzle dazzle the powers that be? We're counting on you. My father and I will meet you on the front stairs of the building around three."

"Sounds good, Dexter. I should be done with the heads of the Archaeological Department at the university by then."

"Good luck!"

WILLY HAD DROPPED JENEVA off at her hotel where she was enjoying a glass of white wine. Her cell phone rang, frightening her from her bliss. It was Dexter.

"Amir did a fabulous job. He convinced the Ecuadorian officials that the Hummingbird Pyramid should be deemed an Ancient Historical Landmark. And any findings will be protected by the National Institute of Cultural Heritage and donated to the University of Quito, to be distributed as they see fit."

"Excellent!"

"I didn't recognize him. He's a real tyrant when it comes to his precious artifacts. He took control of the meeting and made it clear he wasn't leaving until he got everything he was asking for. With the financial backing the university just gave him and his award for rescuing that little girl, they didn't even put up much of a fight. He got us total control of who goes in and out. I should say, he will have control, as head of security. He even convinced them to cover all costs of five thousand yards of fencing around the perimeter."

"I guess I know what I'll be doing for the next while. Hopefully, Amir and I can mend some fences while we're putting them up."

"What's going on with you two?" Dexter asked.

"Oh, he's got a bee in his bonnet about our relationship. I think he's a little jealous of you, that's all."

"Do you want me to talk to him?"

"No thanks, I can handle it. More importantly, when are you coming back? We have a lot to talk about if we're going to get the Pyramid Challenge rolling."

"I'll be there by the weekend, maybe late Friday if I can swing it."

"I miss you. Drive safe." She smacked her lips, imitating a kiss.

SOMETIMES THE DRIVE from Quito to La Maná took him four hours, sometimes five, never without some challenges. He was getting more than a little agitated today, waiting for slow-moving cattle to cross the road in front of him. He'd put Quito three hours behind him at this point, and his anticipated reunion with his Jeneva was now going to be later than he'd promised. The farmer seemed totally oblivious to the line of vehicles and horns honking. Dexter's impatience was growing by the minute. Closing his eyes, he could see and hear Jeneva saying, "Dexter, you need to work at calming yourself. Here's an easy method you can do anywhere to release tension. Take a deep breath, then plug one side of your nose, and exhale slow-

ly through the other nostril. Then repeat, plugging the other nostril."
Jeneva's little yoga trick was actually working. Maybe there was something to this yoga business.

Dexter pushed his phone cord into the truck's USB port and fired up an audio book. The remainder of the trip went off without further interruption. About a mile from the hotel, he sent a text to Jeneva using voice command.

She was waiting for him in the hotel lobby with open arms, just as she promised. It was hard to tell whose embrace was the most intense as the warm feelings of passion washed over them.

"Sorry I'm late. I missed you so much."

Jeneva gazed into his tired eyes.

"Shut up, and kiss me, lover boy."

Amir was the only one left at the table when Dexter and Jeneva walked into the restaurant. Amir rose to shake Dexter's hand.

"Hey, Dexter! Welcome back. You missed a great steak dinner. He summoned the waiter.

"Andre! Can you bring this weary traveler an Old Fashion? Light on the ice."

"Hey, buddy! I understand you've been a bit hard on your team." He put an arm around Jeneva and pulled her close to his side.

"You know, they didn't volunteer to be your indentured Pyramid building Egyptian slaves, right!"

"You couldn't wait five minutes before bustin' my balls?" Amir rolled his eyes.

"Perhaps I have been a little intense, but we needed to secure the perimeters if we are going to keep outsiders away from the cavern. Jeneva and I have been talking and the equinox is fast approaching. If we want to move to the next phase of our plan, we should test the idea of displaying the vision on a monitor. This is going to be key to getting the engagement we want for the Pyramid Challenge."

"So, we all agree? Nelson and Alex's Vision Technology would be pivotal in getting worldwide engagement in The Pyramid Challenge?" Jeneva looked at the men for confirmation.

"I honestly believe that this is the only way to bring the cavern phenomena to the world. Sorry, I can't think of a better way to put it, but that's some weird shit that happens down there," Amir's face contorted. No one's going to believe it without some kind of tangible proof."

Dexter acknowledged Jeneva's, "and what do you think, Applebaum?" glare.

"I don't disagree with either of you. My big concern is confidentiality. We have to keep the location a secret, or every news agency from here to China will descend on us like vultures on roadkill."

"Nice simile, Dexter!" Jeneva grimaced at his colorful comparison.

"In any case, I think you should both be a little more concerned. The more people we bring into our confidence, the more risk of the word getting out. You!" He nodded at Jeneva. "Always with the positive, 'everybody's good' philosophies, and the bone digger over there, he only thinks about the mysterious ancient worlds. That leaves me as the voice of reason." The two recipients of Dexter's opinionated outburst looked a little stunned for a minute. Then, all three broke into knee slapping laughter.

"Seriously though, we need to look at this practically. We need a plan. Here's a suggestion. Let's have the two Brits sign a nondisclosure agreement."

"Okay! So, we call Alex and Nelson, ask them to haul all the vision gear down here at their expense, and tell them, oh, by the way, you need to sign this nondisclosure agreement because we don't trust you. But you can trust us. Sure, who wouldn't jump all over that offer?" Jeneva mocked.

"Yep, that pretty much summed it up." Amir said.

"Well, I think it should be a video call and I happen to know a persuasive young woman that might just be able to pull it off. Because, to my knowledge, no one has ever said no to her." Dexter eyes turned to meet Jeneva's.

"You know what? I'll take that challenge. Heaven only knows you two couldn't pull it off if your lives depended on it!" She gave them an overexaggerated full-toothed smile.

"You two wait here. I am going to go to a quieter place to call and I don't need any peanut gallery wisecracks in the background." She gave a backward wave as she left the bar.

Dexter looked at the time. It was almost midnight, so it would be just before six in the morning there. "It'll be pretty early in the morning there."

Jeneva winked. "I'll take my chances. Cheerio, boys!" She waved over her shoulder as she left the bar.

ONCE SHE WAS OUT OF the restaurant, Jeneva did a quick check of the internet speed, opened her Facetime app, and clicked on Nelson's contact info.

Her grinning face popped up on the screen and the repeating ring tone sounded. It took almost a full thirty seconds, but finally, the surprised but tired face of Nelson shared her screen.

"Hi there, Nelson. What's happening in jolly old England?"

"To be honest, a little shut eye. How's my acquaintance from the colonies doing?"

She saw him masking a yawn.

"Oh gosh, I am so, so sorry. Can I call you back later in the morning?"

"You most certainly will not. I'm awake now, and I want to know what's on your mind. I've been waiting for a follow up call to our last conversation. You left me with a lot of intrigue but also a lot of unanswered questions." He repositioned himself on the side of the bed.

"Again, Nelson I am sorry for the early call. I guess I let my enthusiasm cloud my judgment. I should have been more respectful of the hour. Anyway, I am, if you can believe it, in South America. We are continuing work on a fantastic world-changing discovery."

"Can you be a little more specific than your continental location?" His eyebrows rounded up in an expression of annoyance at the whole cloak-and-dagger scenario.

"I really empathize with your frustration, Nelson. But I have to maintain my clandestine persona for a little while longer." She gave him a sincere look of sympathy.

"Nelson, this is really world-changing stuff. Having said that, it needs to be rolled out over time and in a way that provides the best opportunity for change. We're not in this for monetary gain. To us, it's a labor of love. I don't mean to imply we won't pay you for your help. You will totally understand once you have all the details." She watched for a reaction.

"Okay! Like I said, I am intrigued, but as you can appreciate, also very perplexed. I have to say, your enthusiasm cannot be denied. What else can you tell me?"

"Well, that brings us to the sensitive part of the call." She took a deep breath. "Dexter, Amir, the archaeologist you met at the symposium, and I are the leading participants in this adventure. We would like to bring you and Alex into our confidence, but the boys want additional security in the way of a nondisclosure agreement before we do that. I'm sorry to have to ask, but to be honest, I agree with them. We really do hope you guys will be part of the secret group." She was surprised at how emotional she was getting.

Nelson's eyes seemed fixed, like he was lost in a daydream. It seemed to take him a second to pull himself back to the moment and respond.

"Oh! Sorry. I can see you are being very up front with me, and I respect that. I will sign your nondisclosure agreement, but first, I have some sad news about Alex."

He seemed to gulp down a lump in his throat. "I am very sorry to say, my partner and close friend Alex Belle has passed away."

"Oh, my gosh. I am so very sorry, Nelson. What happened?"

"He was diagnosed with a very fast-growing type of pancreatic cancer a couple months ago and passed away two weeks back."

"I didn't know Alex well, but he seemed like a really nice person and extremely intelligent. I'm sure he will be missed by many people. I am sorry for your loss. It must be hard to go on without your close friend and professional partner. Such a loss."

"Thank you, Jeneva, for your kind words. In any case, please go ahead and send your NDA, and I will get it right back to you."

His sudden snap back to business shocked Jeneva, considering how emotional the subject of Alex's death had left her. She hesitated long enough to regain her composure, then agreed to email the document.

As if he'd seen the look of surprise on Jeneva's face and sensed she might have found his response a little abrupt, Nelson quickly told her, "I've been moping around, grieving for Alex since his death, and I think it is time I start to move on. You will have the NDA in hand when you get up in the morning. Can I video call you back tomorrow evening, say twelve noon your time and we can discuss the next step?"

"Yes, of course, and again, I'm sorry for your loss." She gave him a subtle wave goodbye.

Jeneva opened the door and walked back into the room.

"Well boys, Nelson has agreed to sign your NDA. I have a call scheduled with him tomorrow, where I'll see if I can talk him into coming to Ecuador. I'm guardedly hopeful. It's a lot to ask."

"What about Alex? Will he sign?" Amir asked.

"I am afraid I have sad news about Alex."

NELSON LET HIMSELF drop backward onto the mattress. The warm feeling from the call still lingering in his now fully awake body.

Staring up at the ceiling he said, "It won't be long now my love; til we will be together."

BACK IN THEIR NOW SHARED hotel room, Dexter was stretched out on the bed in his birthday suit.

"That sure was a shock, hearing what happened to Alex. I guess you never know how much time you have left to get things done in life."

Jeneva came walking out of the bathroom brushing her teeth and talking at the same time. "What's that, Dexter? I couldn't hear what you were saying."

"I was saying, you should get your ears checked."

Jeneva jumped on the bed, straddling Dexter, and gave him a big toothpaste-laden kiss.

"What's that, Magnet Man? Did you have something to say worth hearing for a change?"

"Actually, to be honest honey bun, I still am a little bit concerned about bringing Nelson into our little circle of trust. Every time we add a person to the equation it comes with some risk."

"Equation. Is that what we are to you? An equation! Do you always have to turn things into a mathematical probability of outcomes?"

"Yes, I do! I wonder what the probable outcome will be if I do this?" Dexter pulled her oversized T-shirt up over her head and threw it to the floor.

"It's hard to say, Applebaum. We'll just have to see what comes up."

The two lovers fell into a passionate embrace.

JENEVA AWOKE EARLY to the sound of a pleasant but somehow still annoying songbird perched close by the open window. She quietly grabbed her clothes and went into the sitting area of the small hotel room to dress. After putting on her running gear, she took what was left of yesterday's smoothie out of the refrigerator and headed out for her morning jog.

Dexter's concern about bringing Nelson into their confidence rolled around in her mind as she made her way through the old cobblestone streets of La Maná. The little town was just starting to come to life as the sun made its first appearance over the Hummingbird Pyramid. Grabbing her sunglasses out of her pocket, she turned and started up the incline toward the town's modest but impressive cathedral. The building stood high above the town like a great sentinel, protecting its people from the outside world.

It would be a shame to see the quiet life of this town interrupted by throngs of inquisitive people and news-hungry journalists. The solitude and slow-paced way of life of the townspeople quite possibly could be at risk.

Jeneva stopped at the crest of the hill and sat on the wooden park bench just in front of the old cathedral. Taking a large drink from the travel bottle, she tried to catch her breath. The concerns rolling around in her mind had driven her to run up the steep hill, which had brought her to the point of overexertion. Her stomach heaved as she leaned forward and deposited part of her smoothie on the ground between her sneakers.

Once her stomach had settled, she rehearsed under her breath what she'd tell her partners. "We have to make sure our goals of the contest are not in conflict with the best interests of the people living around the pyramids. Our presence needs to be controlled and rolled out in a way that has the least impact on the people and the environment."

Jeneva walked slowly around the park and cemetery surrounding the cathedral until she felt rested enough to head back to the hotel. Her pace back was much more leisurely. She even stopped to sit in the town square for a while and observe the morning pursuits of the villagers. A quick check of her Fitbit showed eleven thousand steps and ten twenty. Time to head back.

The hotel was deserted when she got back. All guests, including her comrades, apparently were off taking on the day's tasks. Dexter left a note that said he and Amir received a call back from a message they left yesterday. They were at a meeting with a group of local tribal leaders to update them on the upcoming activities in the area.

After a quick shower and change of clothes, Jeneva grabbed her phone and headed downstairs. The first email was from Maddy, giving her an update on stressed-out studying and final exam challenges. Jeneva responded with an encouraging message to her Little Sister.

The second message was trying to sell some useless products that, apparently, she could not do without.

Message three was from Nelson. The completed NDA was in an attachment, along with a message reconfirming he'd be calling at noon, her time. Jeneva turned her wrist to check the time but realized she'd forgotten her Fitbit on the sink in the bathroom. Looking past the desk clerk, she could see the antique wall clock indicating five past twelve. Panicking, she pulled her phone out of her back pocket to check whether it was turned on. To her relief, the phone was live with four bars, and the display read eleven fifty-nine. The phone started to shake in her quivering hand, accompanied by the Facetime ring.

Taking a couple deep breaths, she answered, looking directly into the phone's camera. "Hello, Mr. Jones. I hope all is well across the sea this evening."

"All's well! But I think the Mr. salutation doesn't quite fit, now that we are entering into the world of NDAs, secret agents, and espionage."

"Not quite espionage but very important to many innocent people that are at risk if this isn't managed properly. Sorry for all the secrecy, but we have an obligation of confidentiality that must be maintained until the time is right."

"I assure you I will respect the NDA and confidence you have afforded me. I can't wait to hear what you are up to. So, for starters, where in South America are you?"

"We are in Ecuador, about a few hours south of Quito. We have discovered a very exciting natural phenomenon here that's hard to explain but if used right, as I said last night, has the potential to change the world."

"Not sure I have ever heard such a profound statement in my life, but now I need the details to back it up. Go on please."

"Nelson, seeing is believing, and I have a big ask. Would you be willing to pack up your Visualization Technology equipment and bring it to Ecuador? I know it's a lot to ask, but your VT is going to play a big part in the success of this project. We need you to help us bring it to the world. I'd like to give you all the details in person. If you can just trust me for a little while longer and make the trip, all will be revealed."

"Bring it to the world? Another big statement. I can see the intensity in your expression and have little doubt that you are a woman of your word. By Jove, I am going to make the journey, just to see what the blazes you have gotten yourself into."

Jeneva could see the excitement on Nelson's face. To keep the enthusiasm rolling, Jeneva replied with equal fervor.

"Oh, Nelson you have no idea how happy that makes me. We have some work to do around the site, but we should have everything under control by mid-September. Does that work for you?"

Nelson's face seemed to flash with pleasure. "Jolly Good! It gives me plenty of time to put some finishing touches on the VT to make it a bit more portable."

"Perfect! We will pick you up at the airport. Don't worry about booking any lodging. We will take care of all that at our end. Also, Amir will be sending you some paperwork confirming you are a volunteer at our site, and your equipment is for research."

"Great! More espionage. I love it." He was smiling from ear to ear.

THE LARGE HUMMER MADE its way through the streets at a speed that made Amir feel more than a little nervous. Dexter's call with Jeneva ended, and he set his phone on the console.

"Dexter, would you mind slowing down a touch and maybe try a little hands-free action next time you're on the phone? These streets are not made for a tank-size vehicle like this, and it's starting to get dark."

"Okay! okay! My mind is pumped from our productive meeting and that call from Jeneva confirming Nelson's on board. Thanks to you and your personal equity with this community that meeting with the Indigenous leaders went better than I expected. What's it like to be a celebrity child-saving hero?"

"Frankly, I don't enjoy all the attention. We bone diggers, as you like to call us, are more into the solitude of studying ancient civilizations. This whole thing got so blown up on social media, it's a little unnerving."

"Right! Zero to hero in a couple posts." Amir was not amused with Dexter's comment.

"With federal approval, I know we really didn't need the local tribe's permission and support to extend the archaeological site to include the Hummingbird Pyramid. I just didn't want to upset anyone and create a newsworthy protest reaction. Now we can complete our preparations with no disruptions.

Dexter pulled the Hummer up in front of the hotel and jumped out.

"Unfortunately, I have to head back to Quito for a few days to clean up some things at work and hand in my resignation."

"Okay, no problem. I will head back to the pyramid, and with the volunteers help, I should be able to finish that final section of fence we talked about. We need the area totally secured before Nelson arrives."

"Sounds like a plan. See you later, Magnet Man." Amir laughed loudly at the out-of-nowhere-inspired nickname he'd come up with.

Dexter didn't seem to share Amir's amusement. He grunted something superlative and headed up the stairs to the second floor, two steps at a time.

OPENING THE DOOR JUST far enough to stick his head in, Dexter gave his best Jack Nicholson impression to tell Jeneva he was home.

Jeneva laughed at the reference to her favorite Stanley Kubrick movie.

"Am I to take from your good mood that your meeting was a success today?

"Yes, indeed, I did have a very productive meeting, and you, my dear, managed to coerce our British friend into coming to La Maná. Well done!"

"Actually, the only destination he knows so far is the Quito airport. I thought it best to fill in all the details in person. I'd like to think of it as *persuaded*, not coerced."

"Okay, maybe coerced is a little strong. There is something about that little guy that makes me uneasy though."

"Dexter, you only met him that one time in Washington. Give him a chance. I'm sure he is just self-conscious about the disfigurement and uncomfortable around people."

"Maybe so. Enough about Nelson. My boss is starting to push back at all the time I have been taking off. Apparently, there's something urgent he needs me to do that can't wait, so I've committed to help this one last time. I've made a decision. Once this job is done, I'm going to hand in my resignation."

"Dexter! Are you sure? I know you really enjoy the work."

"Yes, I am sure. It's time to move on. I want to focus all my efforts on this adventure, our adventure. This Pyramid Challenge is going to take all our focus if we're going to pull it off. I'm not sure how long I'll be gone, so I was thinking, you might come along."

She looked at him with an expression of disappointment. Sorry, Dexter, I already made a commitment for next week. A volunteer's daughter has a big exam that will likely determine if she'll get into university. I promised to tutor her on some physics concepts she's struggling with. I just can't let her down. And Amir is counting on me to help him get things in order."

"I understand."

"Do you have to leave so soon? You just got back?"

"I'm afraid so. We can video chat every night. I promise."

"All right, but this is the last time we separate for more than a couple days, agreed?"

Jeneva took Dexter's hand.

"Agreed!" She led him toward the bedroom.

"You know? I really liked Jack Nicholson in *A Few Good Men*.

"Is that so? Let's see if you can handle the Magnet Man."

It would appear she could.

Chapter 14

Disappointed Passenger
        The project Dexter had agreed to do ended up lasting two month. He called Jeneva almost every night for a video chat, but she still missed him terribly. She had busied herself working with Amir and tutoring the volunteer's daughter.

Nelson had been in touch to let her know the VT was ready to go, and he'd purchased his ticket to Quito. He would be there in time for the next equinox.

THE AIRPLANE PA SYSTEM played a pre-recorded message in Spanish, then English. "Attention passengers, as we start our descent into Quito Airport, please make sure your seat backs and tray tables are in their full upright position and all carry-on luggage is stowed underneath the seat in front of you or in the overhead bins. Thank you for flying with us."

The long flight from London had included a stop in Madrid, making it a sixteen-hour trip. The anticipation of meeting up with Jeneva prevented Nelson from feeling the fatigue that was evident in the other passengers' faces.

No woman ever gave him the time of day, yet this beauty had sought him out and sat right next to him. Their interaction was seared into his memory. It felt like only yesterday. Nelson had little memory of any other events at the symposium, only his time with Jeneva.

Nelson broke into a fast walk on the debarkation ramp, almost a jog. He narrowly missed banging into a little girl walking sideways to the flow of passenger traffic. He had never been to this airport, but he knew exactly where to go. The information card in the seat back provided maps and the history of the new airport. It stated that it was completed in 2012 and had become one of the busiest airports in South America. The map showed every exit, restaurant, washroom, and the pick-up markers on the outside of the building.

Nelson's high-speed trek to the baggage claim put him there ahead of all the other passengers. To his disappointment, the belt was empty and motionless. Trying to relieve his restless legs, Nelson shifted from one leg to the other, then started pacing up and down the length of the belt. At every pass, he stopped to look into the dark tunnel coming out of the wall. When the belt screeched to life, he jumped back in surprise. Looking around, he saw some of the other passengers giggling at him. Normally, he would have considered the notion that they were laughing at his disfigurement, but not today. Today was going to be the start of a new chapter in his life, and no insensitive stares or whispered comments were going to dampen his spirits.

A few minutes later, his cart was overflowing with luggage and equipment. Nelson arduously made his way to pick-up post 20, as instructed in Jeneva's text. Seeing the post on the other side of the driveway made the fatigue of the long jaunt through the airport evaporate. In his excitement, he drove the cart off the curb. The contents slid off onto the roadway, causing cars to swerve and horns to blare. A large muscular man ran to his assistance and shouted at the drivers to show a little patience. Nelson kept his focus on picking up the precious cargo while the Good Samaritan held traffic at bay.

"Let me help you with that, Nelson. I'll carry these two, so the cart isn't so top heavy."

Nelson looked up in surprise at being addressed by his name. His mouth went dry at the sight of his rival. He cleared his throat and forced the words out. "Thank you, Dexter. The cart is definitely over-loaded. That's probably why it tipped over."

"No worries, Nelson. Let's get this gear into the Hummer, and we'll be on our way." Dexter nodded in the direction of the black beast.

We? Nelson's heart skipped a beat, then pounded as if it were going to explode. *Jeneva must still be in the Hummer.* He abandoned the cart at the back of the Hummer and walked to the passenger door. The dark tinted glass blocked his vision. His hand trembled on the handle as he opened the door. The interior was vacant. Nelson's knees buckled at the disappointment of Jeneva's absence. Struggling to regain some composure, he grabbed the holy-shit bar on the door post for support. The adrenaline rush from running through the airport in anticipation of seeing Jeneva again and then the fall from that euphoric high when she wasn't there to greet him was heartbreaking. The suppressed weariness from the flight and this big letdown put a painful ache in his stomach, and his head started pounding.

"Hey, Nelson! Can you come back and give me a hand to lift this trunk in?"

"The transfer through the airport has me knackered. Can you give me a minute?"

Once the vehicle was loaded, they headed into the hectic morning traffic, which was backed up with departing travelers. As if sensing his passenger's exhaustion, Dexter turned some relaxing music on the radio.

"You must be weary after your long journey. Why don't you push your seat back and relax?"

"You can say that again." Nelson huffed.

"Why don't you push your seat back and relax?" Dexter laughed at his own little joke.

Nelson ignored the subtle attempt at humor and turned his head toward the window.

His heartbeat felt irregular, and his left leg started twitching uncontrollably. He put his hand on the previously broken bone and massaged it in an effort to contain the aggravated muscles.

An hour out of Quito, the traffic became lighter. The morning sky was clear, and the sun shone brightly as they made their way down the open highway in silence.

DEXTER HAD BEEN INSTRUCTED to brief Nelson on the cave phenomena and also provide some explanation around the Pyramid Challenge during the five-hour drive to La Maná. So far, no opportunity to do either had presented itself. He kept glancing over at the balding man for some sign of life. Seeing none, he focused his attention on the late summer farming activities along the roadway. Dusty combines and grain bins dotted the gold-colored fields. About three hours into the drive, the open fields started to transform into rolling hills, and pasturing cattle replaced the farm implements.

Dexter shifted his thoughts to the weary traveler beside him. There was something definitely off about the guy. He was finding it hard to engage Nelson in a conversation. They'd exchanged maybe ten words since meeting up at the airport. Why was talking to him so awkward? *Maybe it's a cultural thing. I've heard those Britts can be stuffy.*

Nelson stirred in his seat and cleared his throat. "Are we almost there?"

"You were out for quite a while. Another two hours or so should do it."

Dexter reached down into the deep center console and handed Nelson a thermos.

"It won't be hot but should give you a caffeine bump."

Nelson accepted the offer and poured a half cup of the dark contents into the lid. Two large swallows, and it was gone.

"Will Jeneva be meeting us at the hotel? I am very interested to hear more about this little adventure you guys are cooking up. She has been very cryptic, only saying, world-changing discoveries and alike." Talking about Jeneva appeared to rapidly bring him out of his groggy state.

"She and Amir will be meeting us in the lobby. I will text them just before we arrive. Let me give you some of the missing details while we finish the drive."

Dexter started with an explanation of how they accidently discovered the hidden cavern while searching for the lost girl, Lailah. He hesitated for a minute, then went into an explanation of his vision experience. Even after all this time, he still found it hard to talk about, and Nelson's expressionless reaction didn't help. He tried to keep the explanation at a level that would hold Nelson's interest, without disclosing too much personal information. A trickle of sweat ran down the side of Dexter's face as he moved on quickly to the easier conversation about his understanding of Amir's experience. Next, he went into a scientific explanation of the importance of the equinox and the sun's magnetic interaction with the earth during the critical two days when the associated visions were possible.

Nelson seemed to find the story hard to believe. He sat silently through the entire summary, shaking his head occasionally, as if he thought the whole thing absurd. Well, he'd see for himself soon enough.

Dexter paused to send Jeneva an update on their arrival and to give Nelson a few minutes to think about what he'd told him so far. He wondered whether he'd given him too much, too fast. It was a lot to digest.

"Hey, Nelson. You must have some questions."

Nelson looked straight ahead, clearly trying to avoid eye contact.

"So, it looks like I am in for quite the adventure here in La Maná. From what you just explained, I think my vision technology is meant to display these visions."

"Exactly! Welcome to the experience of your life."

The Hummer was pulling up in front of the hotel. Jeneva was standing out front, smiling at the site of Dexter waving out the window.

Even from the corner of his eye, Dexter couldn't miss Nelson's face lighting up when he saw Jeneva.

The Hummer was still coasting to a stop as Nelson opened the door and jumped out. Walking right past Amir's outstretched hand, he threw his arms around Jeneva. As if not wanting to offend their newest team member, she somewhat awkwardly returned the hug.

"WELCOME TO LA MANÁ, Nelson. I am so glad you were able to join us."

Over Nelson's shoulder she saw a peeved look on Dexter's face. She pushed back slightly to break the embrace. Dexter came forward and put a firm hand on Nelson's shoulder.

"My good man, I'm sure you must be famished. Let's head into the restaurant. You remember Amir from the symposium?"

Nelson turned to accept Amir's outstretched hand.

"Good to see you again, Nelson."

He gave Amir a weak, one-pump shake. But Nelson's attention remained solely on her.

With the briefest of glances at the men, Nelson said, "Hey, would you guys mind

unloading my gear and dropping it at the front desk? I'll check in later. Jeneva and I will meet you inside."

Nelson nudged Amir out of the way and put an arm around Jeneva's shoulder. Before she knew what was happening, he was ushering her through the front door.

Nelson pulled a chair out for her and sat down next to her.

"Dexter told me all about the vision experiences."

"Actually, later this week will be my first time. I'm really excited but a little apprehensive. I'm going to be the guinea pig for the testing of your Vision Technology system."

Nelson seemed ecstatic that Jeneva would to be his first test subject. He visibly beamed up with pride.

"You are the prettiest guinea pig I have ever met." He caressed the side of her cheek and gave her an adoring smile. "My vison technology is very safe, and I will be there to make sure nothing happens to you. You have nothing to be concerned about."

Jeneva recoiled and shifted in her chair uncomfortably.

Dexter came to the table, giving Nelson a scornful look of annoyance behind his back. Amir looked just as pissed and sat between them.

"Bellboys are back. Tips will be gladly accepted in any currency or denomination."

Jeneva was glad for the opportunity to look away from Nelson's adoring stare.

"I hope you guys didn't overexert yourself. There's a lot of equipment to haul up the pyramid tomorrow," she said.

"So, I'm nothing but a workhorse to you?" Dexter gave her an Atlas pose, flexing his muscles.

"I think beast of burden might be a better description for you, my dear."

"If I'm not mistaken, I believe the jackass is part of the workhorse family." Amir never let an opportunity to needle Dexter pass him by.

The waiter broke up the group's laughter when he requested their food orders.

OVER THE NEXT HOUR, Jeneva passionately went through the goals and intent of the Pyramid Challenge. Nelson sat transfixed on her, though Dexter doubted he was actually taking in a single word she said.

Amir was watching Dexter's reaction to Nelson's attentiveness toward his girl with some amusement, which was not lost on Dexter. Amir remained silent, to his credit, probably content to take in Dexter's aggravation while holding back from his favorite pastime of pushing his buttons. Nelson was doing it for him. Dexter chewed his food a little too hard and drank a little too much, not wanting to interrupt Jeneva.

While enjoying mouth-watering pecan pie, the group shifted the conversation to the plans for the week. The beginning of the equinox was fast approaching. Nelson proposed tomorrow should be the set-up and preparation day to ensure everything was ready. At ten fifteen, the group agreed it was time to head to their rooms for some rest.

Dexter unlocked the door and waited for Jeneva to step inside before he started venting his frustration.

"I hope you realize Nelson is totally infatuated with you. He hasn't taken his eyes off you since we got here. I don't think he ventured more than three feet from you all night."

"Do I sense a little jealousy in your words? He was just very interested in hearing about our challenge, and of course the whole idea of the vision experience has to be a little unnerving. I think you might be overreacting."

Dexter sat on the side of the bed, undressing.

"Think what you like, but I am going to keep my eye on him tomorrow. There is something about that guy that makes me nervous."

Jeneva clicked the light off and crawled into bed next to him.

"You're probably tired after the long trip back from Quito. Let's get some rest, we've got a big day tomorrow.

Chapter 15

Testing the VT Machine

In anticipation of the equinox, the group of four snuck up the pyramid under the light of a full moon and headlamps. The climb was taking twice as long as usual because of the equipment they were carrying on their backs. Nelson insisted he carry all the VT equipment himself, which he was regretting. He gladly relinquished an armful of cords to Dexter, who'd noticed him lagging behind.

At the crest of the pyramid, Amir and Dexter set up the block and tackle and loaded large canvas bags with the supplies while Jeneva and Nelson looked up at the star-covered sky.

"This is amazing. I've never seen so many stars, and that moon is huge." When he looked for a response from Jeneva, he noticed she was still breathing heavier than normal and was shivering. He helped her to a seated position on the ground and snuggled in close, wrapping his jacket around her shoulders.

"Thanks. I think the lack of sleep and little food consumption today might be why I'm exhausted. That and maybe a bit of anxiety." She took in a deep breath of the cool night air. "If you think that moon is amazing, you should be here when the hummingbirds descend on the area. Now that's amazing."

"Will they be here tomorrow?"

"No, you just missed them. They come a couple days before the equinox and leave before it starts. Which is a good thing. We don't want them swooping in on us while we're doing our thing down in the cavern. I do have videos if you want to see them sometime."

"I'd like that." Out of the corner of his eye, he saw Dexter coming their way and quickly stood, offering Jeneva a hand up.

"Time for your descent, honey. I've sent Amir down with the first load. Nelson, you stay up here and help me fill the rest of the bags."

247

Once everyone and everything was safely in the cavern, they began setting up for the next morning's trial run. They'd brought a four-by-four rubber mat to go under a small folding table where they planned to put a laptop for displaying the VT visions. The rubber would act as a shield from the damp floor. Two industrial-size, battery powered, halogen lights on stands would illuminate the whole area.

Nelson was diligently inspecting the VT apparatus, knowing it would be Jeneva on the receiving end of its substantial energy, when Dexter approached him.

"That thing looks a lot like the old projectors they used to show home movies on, back in the fifties and sixties."

"I can see why you would make such a comparison, but believe me, there are very few similarities. Inside this cast-iron box there is a complex computer hard drive, which will be recording what the participant is seeing in their mind, simultaneously sending that image through this chrome silicon cable to another computer or other chosen device, for viewing said vision."

"Cool. I better get back to work before the bone digger sees me schmoozing with the help."

Nelson wasn't sure if he should be offended or not. He chose to ignore Dexter's comment and went back to the task at hand.

The men told Jeneva to relax, but boredom seemed to set in quickly. She gathered empty boxes and the canvas bags and put them in a corner. She must have been apprehensive about her opportunity to finally experience the phenomena Dexter and Amir had told her about.

Dexter was watching her and must have also noticed the frustrated look on her face.

"Why don't you sit over there and watch Nelson set up the VT equipment? Amir and I've got this." Dexter was placing one of the big lamps on a stand.

"He's right. You need to preserve your strength for tomorrow. We know, only too well, how the experience is going to drain you." Amir was unfolding the table on top of the rubber mat.

"Sit here, by the wall, and I'll get the headpiece sized to fit you." Nelson was excited to have her attention. Ever so gently, he slipped the mesh netting with its conglomeration of colored wires on Jeneva's head. She grabbed hold of Nelson's slender forearms.

"Don't you turn that thing on! I may only get one chance at this, and I don't want to blow it."

Placing his fingers under her chin, he tipped her head to meet his eyes.

"I wouldn't think of it. I know how important this is to you, and I would never jeopardize your chance of having the best experience possible." Though his words were simply reassuring, could she feel the sexual attraction in his stare?

Once everyone was satisfied that the cavern was secure and ready for the morning's test, they made their way down the pyramid to the hotel bar for a nightcap.

Nelson ordered a large pitcher of Guinness and filled everyone's mugs.

"Dexter! How does the equinox fit into all this, and what was the rush to get my machine set up?"

"Well, Nelson, the earth's interaction with the sun during the equinox period creates unique magnetic fields near the equator. The magnetism in this area is very concentrated because of the distinctive geology of the rock formations found all around the pyramid. Gold and silver nanoparticles . . ."

Nelson lost interest and was discreetly admiring Jeneva while Dexter rambled on with his explanation.

"In summary, the pyramid has a very high level of magnetism that is particularly strong during the equinox periods. I will bring my gauss meter tomorrow, and we can take some measurements of the magnetic field emanating from the rock formations if you like.

"The equinox is key to the visions," Jeneva told him. "That's why we wanted you here as soon as possible. We have a small window to run our testing."

"Okay, but it still all sounds like abstract science to me. Maybe I will get a better sense of it all tomorrow." Nelson took the last swallow of his Guinness.

"I don't know about that, Nelson," said Amir. "I've read that on a spiritual level, the equinox is thought to represent the struggle between darkness and light, and death, and life. Which might explain our visions being with someone who has passed."

Dexter rolled his eyes and scoffed at Amir's conjectures. Jeneva nodded and agreed there might be something to that theory. Nelson ignored them both. He just smiled at Jeneva and asked if she would assist him with his check-in. Before saying their goodnights, they agreed to meet for breakfast at six.

JENEVA WAS ALREADY seated, drinking a cup of coffee, when the men filed through the swinging doors.

"Morning, sweetheart!" Dexter leaned in and kissed her cheek, taking a seat to her right.

Amir gave her shoulder a squeeze. "You're up early." He walked behind her and took the seat to her left.

"I couldn't sleep. Too excited, I guess."

"You should have called me! I've got some pills that knock me out in minutes," Nelson offered. He pulled out the chair on the other side of the table, giving him a straight-on view of Jeneva. One he never got tired of seeing.

"Thanks, I'll remember that. Are you guys ready to order? You know what I want, Dexter." She stood and ran her fingers through his thick hair. "I'll be back in a sec."

The three gentlemen watched as she sashayed to the ladies' room.

Nelson wasn't the only one green with envy over Dexter's relationship with Jeneva. Amir was also clearly affected. Despite her acknowledgment of being their friend and collaborator on the Pyramid Challenge project, they continued trying to please her and win her affections.

Nelson was quick to push her chair in when she returned and just as quick to pull it out when they were ready to leave. This got him an evil eye from both Amir and Dexter. He just smiled and held the front door for them all to leave the hotel.

DEXTER INSISTED THEY take two vehicles. He quietly told Jeneva he wanted to be alone with her and make sure she was still okay with being the guinea pig for the VT testing.

"Are you sure you're up for this?" He reached over and held her hand. "You look tired." He was giving her an easy out if she wanted it.

"Sleeps overrated. I'll get plenty when I'm dead. If I recall, both you and Amir went to bed and slept for hours after your visions. I'll probably do the same."

"We sure did. I felt physically and mentally drained, but it was worth it. I hope yours is just as fulfilling."

"Do you have any advice for me?"

"Not really. No one seems to know what's coming, so I'd just relax and let whatever's going to happen, happen."

"I should have had a double shot of Baileys in my coffee. Hindsight, right? Speaking of hindsight. I forgot to tell you, Maddy called last night. She was asking when she gets to have her vision. It sounds like she's hoping to see her dad. I tried to explain that the visions experienced so far could not be predicted or willed to happen."

"I'm not sure she's old enough quite yet. Maybe in a couple years?"

"I promised I'd get back to her after I'd been through it, and that seemed to pacify her for the moment. Looks like those guys are packed and ready to go." She pointed at the two figures standing outside the camp tent.

Before getting out of the Hummer, Jeneva reached into the back seat and grabbed her purse. Something was snagged on the blanket Dexter kept back there for emergencies. She carefully untangled the wool and noticed it was the pin that Brian had given her as a thank-you for being his daughter's Big Sister. A series of fond memories raced through her mind as she checked to make sure the clasp was still secure. Then she joined the men.

Nelson and Amir were waiting with much lighter loads in their backpacks than last night. Nelson added a couple extra CDs and a portable hard drive for emergency backup. Dexter grabbed his laptop from the back seat of the hummer and stuffed it in his.

"Where's mine?" Jeneva looked from the ground to Amir.

"I've got it. You go ahead and lead the way."

"Gee, thanks, Amir!" She gave the others a cheeky grin and plopped her sunhat on her head.

Amir told them he'd stationed his trusted guards around the perimeter of the Hummingbird Pyramid to ensure them plenty of undisturbed time in the cavern.

"I've instructed them to be discreet, so if you see them in the shadows, don't be alarmed."

There had been a lot of up and down traffic over the past while, and the path to the top was easy, compared to the first time she and Amir went up in search of the little girl. In order to save time and effort, the block and tackle were left in place at the summit, ready for their morning descent into the cavern.

Once the halogen lights were turned on and the laptop was plugged into the VT unit, Nelson started it up. They all stood still, watching. Waiting. Dexter put his arm around Jeneva. A low hum filled the air. A green light blinked on, and the screen on the laptop glowed blue.

"Looking good, so far!" Nelson said. "Let's get you hooked up, *little lady*." Was that supposed to be a John Wayne impersonation?

Jeneva gave Dexter a kiss on the cheek and sat straddled on the low wall facing Nelson. He fitted the mesh cap on her head and inserted the connection cord into the VT machine.

"This is just a precaution." Nelson stuck a couple suction cups on her upper chest, so he could keep an eye on her heart rate.

Her hands trembled as she removed her shoes and socks, swung her legs around, and slowly slipped her feet into the water.

"Everyone ready?" Nelson put his hand on Jeneva's shoulder.

"Ready as I'll ever be." She took a deep breath and exhaled trying to slow her racing heart.

Dexter and Amir nodded and turned to focus on the laptop screen.

While Nelson slowly rotated the power knob, sending energy to the mesh cap on her head, she focused on staying calm by fixating on the gold flecks in the water.

"Hey, you guys! The gold flakes are attaching themselves into the shape of a double helix."

"That's what happened just before my vision came. Nothing to worry about. How's my girl doing?" Dexter asked.

"She's good. Just staring into the water."

Jeneva sat still, waiting and worrying. *I hope there won't be those horrendous vibrations Amir told me about or a ghost floating out of the mist like in Dexter's vision.* Her head was itchy. She suddenly remembered Nelson's warning. "Do not touch the mesh skull cap, unless you want electricity rushing through your body and into the water, killing you instantly." Scratching was definitely not an option. She looked up from the pool of water for a distraction and saw something. It was as if a big room had been cut into the wall of the cavern at the end of a long hallway. It started moving closer and closer, until she recognized not only the room but the people in the room. It was a scene from Maddy's sixteenth birthday party. A familiar feeling of being part of their family washed over her, and she was at the table with Brian and his daughter, eating macaroni and cheese. She saw the birthday cake with the big one and six candles on top and a half-empty bottle of ginger ale on the kitchen counter behind them. They talked about the birthday girl's presents and how she was doing in school. There was some chitchat about charity events they were looking forward to, especially the Christmas one.

She and Brian exchanged looks across the table. She assumed, looks of gratitude, after all, he'd mentioned how grateful he was for everything she'd done for Maddy on several occasions. But she was certain there was something else.

When they were alone in the kitchen, Brian handed her a small box and said, "Just a little token of thanks for everything you've done for Maddy as her Big Sister.

She fastened the small broach on the side of her purse. They embraced, and the look in his eyes was more than gratitude. Then he kissed her. Maddy came in with her report card, and the moment of truth was lost forever.

DEXTER TURNED HIS HEAD. "How is she now Nelson?" He was wondering what she was feeling and just how close she had been to Brian.

"Her heart rate spiked a bit a minute ago, but it's back to normal now. Is the projection coming through clear enough for you to see what's happening?"

"Very!" There was no denying the anger in Dexter's voice.

"I hope we don't lose the clarity when we try to project on a larger screen." Amir elbowed him.

"Dexter, look here, something's happening!"

The room started slowly moving away, back where it came from.

Without warning, she was encompassed in black billowing smoke that choked the breath out of her. She started coughing and gasping for air. She pulled her shirt up over her mouth and nose and squinted her eyes. The air had a wavy appearance, as if she stood in sweltering heat, but Dexter couldn't see any fire.

"Dexter! What's happening? She's choking!" Nelson hollered and reached to turn off the machine.

Dexter grabbed his arm.

"Wait! Give her a minute. It's starting to clear." He watched the smoke on the laptop screen dissipate.

Then, as quickly as it had started, the coughing stopped, and Jeneva pulled her shirt away from her face. Her eyes were open wide. The smoke curled and parted in the center, where a large figure appeared. She gasped.

SHE COULDN'T BELIEVE her eyes. It was hard to see through the smoke-filmed oxygen mask, but she was sure it was Brian. He was in his full firefighter's gear and held a little boy in his arms. She wanted to go to him and help, but she couldn't move. She tried to call out to him, but her lips were glued shut. All she could do was watch. Another firefighter ran up to Brian and took the little boy away. Brian collapsed to his knees; his head fell limp to his chest. Two more firefighters came and picked him up and laid him on a gurney, a few yards in front of Jeneva.

He turned his head to face her. His voice echoed in the mask when he spoke. "Jeneva."

She rushed over to him.

"Brian! The little boy is okay. You saved him." She was glad she could move this time.

For a moment, his eyes seemed to come alive, and she saw him smile. Even covered in black soot, he was a handsome man. The truth was, she'd fallen in love with him. Not because of his looks but because of his charitable personality and big heart. She'd thought they might have a future together, but things had turned out differently.

He struggled to remove the mask from his head. The weight of it pulled his arm downward. It fell from his weak fingers to the ground with a loud thud. Then, he took Jeneva's hand and placed it over his heart. She felt helpless standing there, listening to his dry wheezing breaths.

"Tell Maddy I love her." He coughed, then gasped in a little air. "Tell her I'm proud of her." Tears rounded from the corners of his bloodshot eyes, leaving trails of white through the soot.

"I will. I promise." Jeneva felt the warmth of a tear on her own cheek.

He pulled her closer.

"Jeneva, I'm sorry. I should have told you, I . . ." His chest heaved. He gasped for air.

Then his eyes closed, and his hand loosened on hers, then drooped over the side of the gurney.

Jeneva picked it up, held it in her two hands and kissed it.

"I loved you too," she whispered.

Slowly the scene disappeared in a milky mist. Her eyelids were heavy, and she struggled to open them. She felt like a rag doll, limp and weak. Someone was lifting her from behind, under her armpits. She opened her eyes a crack as Amir reached for her ankles and lifted her feet over the wall. Nelson was laying an emergency blanket out on the ground. Dexter and Amir gently laid her on it.

"Jeneva! Jeneva!" Dexter was leaning over her.

"Nelson! How do I get this thing off her head!" Amir hollered, placing another rolled emergency blanket under her neck.

"Step aside! I'll do it!" Nelson gave him a shove. He pulled the connection cord out of the VT machine and went to work. As he was gingerly removing the mesh cap, he looked down into Jeneva's glossy eyes.

"Was it everything you'd hoped for?"

"And more." Her head fell to the side, and sleep pulled her under.

When she woke a few minutes later, her eyes met Dexter's discerning glare. "Can we get out of here? I'm ready for that sleep we were talking about earlier." She rolled on her side, and with Dexter and Nelson's help, she was able to stand.

"We're just waiting for the VT to cool down, then we'll get you back to the hotel. From what we saw, you've been through a lot."

Amir pulled himself up and was waiting when Jeneva crawled over the top of the cavern opening. He untethered her and tossed the gear back down the hole. He helped her get comfortably seated while they waited for Dexter and Nelson.

"So, how're you feeling? Things got a little intense. Nelson almost shut the machine down when you started coughing, and Dexter's jaw dropped a few inches when you kissed that guy. I thought he was going to shut you down himself."

"That's enough, Amir! Leave her alone!" Dexter was stripping off the ropes. He tossed them back down the hole for Nelson. "Don't you remember how pissed you got when we tried to interrogate you after your vision? Come on, honey! I got you." He helped Jeneva to her feet.

"I'll call you later and let you know if we're meeting for dinner. It depends on how long this one sleeps."

"Sure thing. Sleep well, Jeneva."

Dexter assisted Jeneva into the Hummer, buckled the seat belt for her, then pushed the recline button.

"How's that?"

"Good, thanks." Before he shut the door, she asked, "You mind if we don't talk? I'm feeling a little wonky."

"I understand. Close your eyes and rest. We can talk whenever you're ready."

SIX HOURS LATER, DEXTER called Amir.

"Hey, buddy! Jeneva's having a shower. We'll be down for supper in about ten minutes."

"How's she doing? Have you guys talked about what we saw?"

"Not really, she just woke up. Let's wait till after we eat to talk about it. Unless she brings it up."

"Got it. I'll fill Nelson in. He's been chomping at the bit to talk to her. He hasn't stopped raving about how wonderfully the VT worked and says he wants to be next. We can talk about that later too. See you in a few."

When Jeneva walked into the dining room, Amir couldn't believe how beautiful she looked. From Nelson's wide eyes, he seemed to think the same. She'd left her long black hair down and was wearing a plaid shirt, tight jeans, short cowboy-style boots, and a smile that lit up the room.

"Good evening, gentlemen!" She took a seat between them.

"You look rested," Amir said. "Can I get you a drink?"

"I'll wait for Dexter. He's making a call. He shouldn't be long."

With Dexter delayed, Nelson jumped on the opportunity to ask Jeneva a few questions, despite Amir's warning. He leaned forward.

"You look better than you did when you came out of your trance. How did it feel, while you were hooked up, I mean? Was it like being hypnotized? Other than being tired, do you feel normal? I just want to know what to expect." Nelson glanced at Amir, so there was no way he could have missed the infuriating look he was giving him.

Amir held his hand up, almost smacking Nelson in the nose.

"That's enough! If you insist on knowing how it felt, I'll tell you. It was like nothing I have ever felt before. Let's leave it at that." He turned to Jeneva. "Wouldn't you agree?"

She just nodded.

Dexter showed up shortly after Amir shut Nelson down. Amir didn't mention the audacity Nelson had shown by going against Dexter's request. He felt he'd handled it.

Jeneva appeared to be back to her jovial self and very at ease, so after they finished dinner and ordered dessert, Dexter opened the conversation.

"I think the VT machine is going to suit our needs very well. The system seemed to produce a very clear picture of what Jeneva was seeing. Just to confirm, at first, you were at Maddy's birthday party, right?"

"That's right."

"Then you were overcome by smoke."

"Yes. It was so thick I thought I was going to choke to death. Then it was gone."

"That part scared us too! You were coughing so hard I almost shut the VT off!" Nelson told her.

"I'm so glad you didn't."

"I bet you are." As the words passed Dexter's lips, he scrubbed his hand across his mouth as if he knew immediately, he should have swallowed them.

"What exactly do you mean by that, Dexter?"

"Just that . . ." Dexter trailed off. Amir could see the tortured look on his face as he tried not to finish the sentence. But he did. ". . . if he shut it down, you wouldn't have hooked up with Brian again."

"For God's sake. Don't be ridiculous! The poor man died saving a child."

"I get that, but ..." Again, Dexter visibly fought his impulse to finish his sentence and lost. "What did he say to you at the end? We didn't have the mic turned up loud enough to hear your whispers." He was giving her a pinched-eyed glare.

Amir felt for Jeneva, suddenly finding herself in an interrogation session, like a criminal being accused of a crime. She started to cry into her hands, and if she'd been hooked up to the VT right now, Amir was sure they'd see the sad image of the man lying on the gurney.

Nelson and Amir excused themselves and went to the bar. They watched Dexter and Jeneva's reflections in the mirror behind the rows of liquor bottles. This was the catalyst they'd been hoping for. They watched in anticipation.

"I'M SORRY, HONEY. YOU don't have to tell me right now if you don't want to." Dexter wrapped an arm around her shoulder.

She wiped her eyes and blew her nose into her napkin and turned to face Dexter head on.

"I don't appreciate your accusations one bit. It was very personal! But I'm going to tell you anyway. Because I trust you enough to share every part of my life with you, even my past." She sniffed.

"First, he asked me to tell Maddy he loved her and was proud of her. Then, he said he was sorry he didn't tell me he loved me."

A lump formed in her throat, and she swallowed it down.

"Then—I told him I had loved him too." She turned and lowered her head, waiting for the fallout.

Dexter's arm fell abruptly away from Jeneva's shoulder, and he stiffened in his chair. He got up and approached the waitress at the other end of the bar.

"Any idea when we might get those desserts?"

Jeneva rose from the table and looked over to her comrades.

"I think I'll skip desert. The day's events are starting to catch up with me. I'm going to bed."

Amir's and Nelson's heads followed Jeneva as she walked right past Dexter and out the exit. An uncomfortable silence filled the room as she departed.

JENEVA STRAINED HER eyes, trying to make out the time on the alarm clock sitting on the other side of the bed.

"Twelve thirty in the afternoon, that can't be right." When she turned over on her side to exit the bed, her eyes met Dexter's. He was sitting on a chair facing her.

"I have been waiting for you to wake up. I am sorry! I was a real jerk last night. Your life did not start when we met nor did mine. We both have pasts, and we should be able to share those experiences freely.

"No argument from me. I want to hear all about your past. You can tell me anything you want, and I promise there will be no judgment. You've been acting a little weird around Amir and Nelson as well. There is no positive side to jealously, you know. After I got back to the room last night, I was wondering something. Have I done anything to make you feel insecure? I try to be the kind of person people find easy to talk to. Consequently, I'm always going to interact with men and women in an outgoing and genuine way. I love people, Dexter, and that's not going to change."

"I don't want you to change. You are perfect just the way you are. Keep being you. I wouldn't want you any other way. I have never loved anyone like I love you, Jeneva. I've never experienced such sole dedication to anyone, ever. Can you be patient with me as I learn how to live with these new emotions?"

Jeneva got up and threw her arms around him.

"I'll try, but you know patience isn't my strong suit. One more thing, buster, the next time I walk out on you and leave without saying goodbye, that doesn't mean you should hide out in the bar for a couple hours. It means you need to get your thoughts together and come and talk to me."

"Got it. Like I said, I'm still learning."

"While you were hiding out with the boys last night, I got a call from Maddy. No surprise, she wanted to know how my vision went. She also mentioned coming to Ecuador for a week during spring break to start writing her university entrance essay. She's interested in volunteering with Amir while she's here. She feels getting away from all her friends will help keep her focused. To be honest, I kind of like the idea. I really miss her, and with all that has been going on, I haven't been able to spend any time with my Little Sister." For extra emphasis, Jeneva looked into Dexter's eyes and gave him her special pout.

"How can I say no to that face? I think it is a great idea. Go ahead and ask Amir to get the paperwork sent to her."

Chapter 16

N ew Reveals
       Dexter and Jeneva were under tremendous pressure preparing for the worldwide broadcast. It was reassuring to know Amir was primarily focused on managing the security of the site and keeping the archaeological finds significant enough to satisfy the university. Nelson had informed them he was enhancing safety functions on his equipment to limit the risk of electrical overload from all the television equipment.

However, today, Jeneva, Dexter, and Maddy were taking a break from their all-consuming undertakings. It was sunny and warm on the peak of the pyramid. A light wind carried the hummingbird wing song.

Dexter sat on a blanket, feeling more at peace than he'd ever imagined he could. He watched Jeneva and Maddy, laughing and spinning like tops amongst the swooping and diving birds, surrounded by wildflowers. Dexter focused on the beauty of the moment, permanently imprinting the memory of the scene in his mind.

When Dexter lay back on the blanket, hypnotized by the puffy cumulus clouds rolling across the sky, his thoughts automatically went to the Pyramid Challenge. The sound of the girls' laughter seemed to move farther away, and his eyelids closed.

The last couple months had been busy beyond description. Jeneva and Dexter spent almost all their waking hours working on the upcoming worldwide broadcast of Nelson's vision.

To their knowledge, no one had ever tried to roll out a worldwide event as big as Jeneva's Herculean goal of world peace. There was no reference material, no road map, and no one with the experience to help them. Preparing for and producing the visions in the cavern added a layer of complexity they could not have imagined back in Cuba. It was a whole lot easier to muse about it on the beach, sipping mojitos. Dexter might have given up if it hadn't been for Jeneva's persistence and unwavering commitment to the ultimate goal. They were breaking new ground here, and the outcome was far from assured. Drafts of their plan were written, rewritten, and rewritten again, and still, there were uncertainties.

Jeneva's Little Sister was growing on him, maybe because she shared Jeneva's zeal for life. She too was committed to filling her days with productive and fulfilling endeavors. There had been times when he noticed a sadness about her. He assumed she was missing her dad. For the most part of the trip she volunteered with Willy, discovering and cleaning up artifacts, followed by essay work in the evenings. To both Dexter and her Big Sister, it seemed an overcommitment when she was only there for a short time. He was glad they were able to convince Maddy to set the essay aside until she went home, but she insisted on being Willy's assistant archaeologist every other day.

Dexter's head had been resting on Jeneva's purse when the ringing jolted him back to reality. He opened the makeshift pillow and grabbed the phone. The number was a Washington exchange. Jeneva was too far off to get her attention, so he answered.

"This is Dexter. If you can wait a minute, I can run over and get Jeneva."

"Oh! Hi, Dexter. This is Maddy's aunt, Patricia. I am actually trying to get a hold of Maddy. I think her cell phone must be turned off. Can you get a message to her?"

"I can do better than that. I can get her for you." Jeneva and Maddy had spotted Dexter's wave and were on the run. Dexter met them halfway.

"Hi, Auntie. What's wrong?" Her face arranged itself into an expression of disbelief. "Thanks. I can't wait to tell Jeneva. Guess I'll see you in a couple days. Thanks for calling. Love you."

Jeneva and Dexter couldn't tell from the look of shock on Maddy's face whether it was good news or bad.

"Is everything okay?" asked Jeneva.

"My school is giving me the Humanitarian Award for leadership in the 'Bullies Be Gone' program!"

The night before Maddy returned to Washington, they celebrated her recognition at the local restaurant, Papa Locas. Maddy chose the large funnel container filled with fries and fried chicken. Something she had never seen back home.

THE BIG DAY FINALLY arrived. The Hummingbird Pyramid was crawling with people going up and down and in and out of the cavern. A hush came over the group as the director counted down to the long-awaited worldwide broadcast on top of the Hummingbird Pyramid.

"Three, two, one, and we're live!"

"Good evening, my name is Jason Bonner. I am coming to you live from an undisclosed location, somewhere in South America. I am standing next to the entrance of the mysterious cavern. We are going to take you inside to witness what has been described to me as something beyond description. Let's move closer to the opening and talk to one of the original discoverers of this phenomenon, Dexter Applebaum.

"Mr. Applebaum, can you give us some hint of what we can expect to see tonight?"

"Well, Jason, let me start by thanking everyone for tuning in tonight for what is going to be a very exciting evening, and for some of you, perhaps the start of your own adventure. You see, we have brought you here tonight to share a very unique and exciting experience that I am sure many of you will want to participate in some day. We will be following up tomorrow night with the kick-off show, which will explain all the details around how you might get the opportunity to experience this for yourselves."

"What exactly is this experience? You still haven't given us any hint of what this phenomenon is."

"Let me just say, what you are about to witness is a demonstration that will likely change how you think about life and potentially transform how you might live your life."

"That is all very cryptic. I guess we will just have to wait and see. I don't think I am going to get any more details out of you, am I?"

"Seeing is believing, my friends. All will be revealed over the next couple hours," said Dexter.

"When we come back, we will all be inside the cavern. Stay tuned! This is going to be some night. With that, we will go to a break."

Dexter dropped down to help Nelson with the final touches on the VT setup. Nelson checked the output from the main control box to verify it was properly connected to the television crew's equipment. One camera was set up close to the participant's location, with the second and third overtop of and on the opposite side of the glimmering pool of water.

The lighting inside the cavern was so bright you could see the reflection of the camera operators standing around it. The interior of the cavern was exceptionally humid and damp today, which produced condensation on the ceiling. Occasionally, drips fell into the pool, forming donut-shaped ripples, giving the water a hypnotic affect.

A nervous Jason was being slowly lowered into the cavern in a cable chair. Amir had assured him the newly installed access rig was safe. As well as being belted into the chair, a backup cable was attached to the harness, securing the passenger's body.

The entire television crew had been whisked directly from the private jet at the airport to the site in a windowless van. Dexter's father had used his political influence to secretly bring them into the country through diplomatic channels. Each member of the crew, including the network president, had signed the extensive nondisclosure agreement in return for the rights to televise any future shows relating to the CARE Foundation or The Pyramid Challenge events.

Down below, amidst the bustling activity of the numerous TV personnel, Nelson maneuvered his way over to his partners.

"I don't think I can go through with this. I'm nervous about not having any control over what will be broadcast to the world."

"Relax, Nelson. You've got this," Amir assured him.

"You're positive, only things related to these wedding rings will show up in my vision, right?" He held up his right hand to Jeneva, who took the thin gold wedding bands from him.

"Yes! We are quite sure. Everyone who has experienced the visions had some memento that connected them to the event they witnessed. Turn around. I'll put your parents' rings on your chain for safekeeping. I don't want them dropping in the pool accidently."

"You've just got the wedding day jitters. It will be all over before you know it. Let's get you hooked up. Looks like they are almost ready to start the show." Dexter led him over to the wall and helped him with the headpiece.

When Dexter returned, Jeneva said quietly, "I'm surprised at how well he's handled things this far, considering what an introvert he is."

The television crew's broadcast director blew a whistle to get everyone's attention.

"Camera one, you will zoom in, on the water, then pull back to focus on Mr. Jones's face. Camera two, pan the cavern, and then focus on Jason. Jason, you will set up the scene as rehearsed. Controllers, you will be recording the three cameras and the feed coming from the VT. Nelson, I'm not going to direct you in any way. I want this to be spontaneous and unrehearsed. Hopefully, it all works out." From the tense expression on the director's face, Dexter guessed that memories of every live broadcast flop were filling his head.

As instructed, everyone in the cavern went silent, and the director counted down.

Jason provided the introduction to the audience, then the director hand signaled for a zoom in on Nelson.

NELSON SAT IN HIS ASSIGNED location with his bare feet in the pool. From this position, he could see the gold flakes suspended in the water. He closed his eyes and clutched the rings in his right hand, trying to think about something other than the thousands of people scrutinizing him. The shift in mindset was not coming. He opened his eyes and looked into the glimmering water again. This time, the gold flakes were moving in circles. They appeared to be aligning themselves in a pattern he was vaguely familiar with. It looked like a ladder, complete with rungs, spiraling in a twisting motion. The image made him dizzy, so he looked up, beyond the pool.

The camera operator was gone, and the cavern was completely empty, except for a cold haze lingering in the air. A feeling of complete abandonment swept over him. The cavern walls started to distort and take on new shapes as the space around him closed in. The wet, glistening walls transformed into a rural landscape with a vertical two-lane road up the center. In the distance, a car was coming toward him. Suddenly, Nelson was inside that car. His mother and dad were singing along with a duet on the radio, "I Got You Babe." His father sang Sonny's line, leaning to his right. In the back seat, his brother tried to grab a toy out of his obstinate sister's hand. Through the windshield, the road ahead wound through a hilly terrain. This place felt familiar, and then he saw the bullet-riddled sign: Watch for Falling Rocks.

This was the location of the accident that took his family from him. His heart tightened in his chest, and he tried to warn his father about the oncoming transport truck. A feeling of impending doom fell over him, and tears rolled down his cheeks. No matter how hard he tried, he was unable to shout out or move in any way. He was frozen in time. He was there but not there, in the vision but not an active participant. Terror gripped his whole being as the oncoming truck crossed the median and headed directly at them. Again, Nelson tried, desperately, to warn his father, but the words were wedged deep in his throat. He closed his eyes and leaned back against the seat. It was gone. He felt himself fall backward through space in a rotating tumble. He gasped for air and expelled an earthshattering scream.

As quickly as it had come, the terror disappeared. His ears were filled with a steady beep and the gushing sound of a pump. Something was wrapped tightly around his head and face. Squinting to see through the narrow opening, he looked around. He was back in the hospital where he'd spent so many months recovering from the car accident. There were no walls or ceiling, only medical equipment and sparse furnishings.

The memory of the excruciating pain that had plagued his battered body was back. This was too painful. Inside his head, he screamed, *Get me out of here*!

All of a sudden, he saw his mother and father walking toward him. It looked as if his brother and sister were between them, and all four were holding hands. As they drew nearer, he saw they were smiling at him. Nelson's father took off his old plaid cap and placed it under his left arm as he approached the bed. Nelson knew then that it was definitely his family. His father never went anywhere without his cap.

"Hello, son. Unfortunately, we left this world long before expected. I know it has been tough for you, and I regret that I didn't make any plans in the event of my death. Your mother and I were young, and there didn't seem to be any urgency to organize our affairs. I don't know what happened to us, but I do know you were left alone in this tough, unforgiving world without parental love or guidance. And for that, I am deeply sorry."

Seeing the torment in his father's face moved him deeply. His heart pounded, and a large lump formed in his throat. Frantically hoping he could speak this time; he took a deep breath and opened his mouth.

"Mom, Dad, it was an accident. I don't blame you. I miss and love you all so much. Many times, over the years, I desperately wished I could be with you all again. Never in a million years did I think it would ever be possible."

His sister and brother ran over to him and jumped up on the bed, hugging and kissing their big brother.

"It's okay, Nelson. We love you too." Their round little faces beamed.

Nelson's parents came closer and put their hands on his shoulders, encircling his siblings between them in a family hug.

"Nelson, we are so proud of you and the things you have accomplished on your own. We knew you were special from the day you were born, and you have more than lived up to our expectations."

"Our love and admiration for you is without bounds. Your secret doesn't change the way we feel about you." His mother caressed his bandaged cheek and smiled tenderly at her boy.

"Son, we have to leave now, but be assured we are with you always, in your heart. Embrace the times you sense our presence and let them give you strength to carry on."

His siblings gave him another big hug before jumping off the bed. His family walked back into the haze, hand in hand.

Nelson's heart ached as he watched them leave him once again.

The cavern slowly transformed back to the present. Nelson's body quivered from the damp surroundings. He blinked his eyes back into focus, and with little effort, he stepped out of the water and onto the low wall. He looked at his reflection in the pool, and an overwhelming sense of contentment and newfound self-esteem instantly replaced the insecurities and loneliness he had lived with all of his life.

His legs relaxed, and he collapsed into the waiting arms of Jeneva and Amir, who sat him gently back down on the wall. A tired but smiling Nelson looked up at Jeneva.

"That was the best experience of my life."

Jason and the television crew broke the silence with enthusiastic clapping and cheering.

The camera was zoomed in on Jason's face. He hesitated for a second to compose himself, then cleared his throat. "Well, my friends, as you just heard, we have witnessed the best experience of a life. I need a moment to set up the interview with Mr. Jones, so why don't we go to break?"

The director was dabbing her eyes when she motioned the controller to go to commercial.

Jeneva and Amir helped Nelson disconnect all the wires and remove the VT gear. Nelson remained silent, staring into the glimmering pool. Amir and Jeneva, who obviously understood what he was going through, didn't try to engage him in conversation. They knew the adrenaline would slowly dissipate, but the euphoria of his experience was going to last a long time.

JASON WAS WALKING TOWARD Nelson to prepare for the live broadcast coming back online in one minute. Jeneva intercepted him.

"Mr. Bonner, Nelson is going to need some recovery time. Why don't you interview me first? I can give some background on what my vision experience was like."

Jason nodded in agreement as the director started counting down. "Three, two, one, and we're live!"

"Welcome back, viewers, we're going to give Nelson some time to collect his thoughts after what must have been a very intense encounter. In the meantime, I would like to introduce you to one of the board members of the CARE Foundation, Jeneva Yassi. Jeneva, I believe you have also had the opportunity to sit where Nelson just sat. What can you tell us about your experience?"

"Thank you, Jason, and thanks to everyone tuning in to our presentation. I know all this must be a little unbelievable. It was to us at first as well. We discovered this phenomenon accidently, and to our knowledge, it's something very special and unique to this cavern. I can also tell you it's time sensitive. Visions are only possible during the two-day spring and fall equinox periods. Several of us have experienced a vision, and each time, it has been very unique and special to the participant. I can say without hesitation, for me it was the most enjoyable and heartwarming experience of my life. Our goal tonight was to present this to all our viewers in a way that would stimulate their imaginations. And encourage them to think about what their vision might reveal. I should also mention, the technology that let us see what Mr. Jones was experiencing was actually coinvented by Mr. Jones himself and his late partner, Alex Belle. A big thank-you to them both. This broadcast would not have been possible without their expertise and Nelson's willingness to be the subject of the presentation."

"Thanks, Jeneva. It looks like Nelson is up and walking around. Let's get a few words from tonight's vision participant, shall we? Nelson, what can you tell our viewers?"

The normally reserved Nelson smiled and looked directly into the camera.

"It was absolutely awesome." He pulled the mic in Jason's hand closer. "Mind blowing! I feel so relieved and liberated from the anguish I've always felt about not being able to spend time with my family or not being there to say goodbye to them. There was a large hole in my heart that has now been filled with love and gratification. Reuniting with my family again seemed an impossible dream, but as everyone saw, dreams do come true."

Nelson's legs appeared to be weakening again as tears of joy washed down his cheeks. Jeneva moved in quickly to provide some support to the wobbly man. Jason turned back to face the camera.

"Well, my friends, there you have it. Directly from our Vision Star of the night. We will be right back after the break to wind up the show and give you some specifics about tomorrow night's broadcast."

Jeneva and Amir eased Nelson over to one of the crates used to bring the television crew's equipment down. He dropped down on the well-worn black box, tears still lingering on his cheek and chin.

"I think I need to get back to my room. I am totally exhausted."

Amir motioned to one of the crew to come over.

"Can you get the chair elevator ready? Mr. Jones needs to go up for some fresh air."

Dexter and Jeneva walked back over to Jason in preparation for the show's close out.

"Three, two, one, and we're live!"

Welcome back, folks. Dexter and Jeneva have joined me now to provide some background on tomorrow night's show. What can our viewers expect to see?"

"Thanks, Jason. Dexter and I deliberated about this a lot. We weren't sure how this discovery should be rolled out to the world. We feel this incredible find does not belong to us but to all people. Having said that, access to this sensitive area is very restricted, and the window of opportunity, short. To that end, we've come up with a challenge, open to all people around the world. Tomorrow night, we'll introduce you to The Pyramid Challenge, but in the interim, you are invited go to the webpage showing at the bottom of the screen, to acquaint yourself with the goals, rules, and of course information on how you can participate. The website will also provide you with details about the neutral governing body called the CARE Foundation that oversees all aspects of the program."

"Okay, folks, I'm afraid that's all the time we have tonight. Hope you enjoyed the show as much as we did. See you all tomorrow evening for what I promise you is going to be equally thrilling. On behalf of this network, we'd like to thank the founders for allowing us to be a part of this worldwide adventure. This is Jason Bonner signing off from who knows where! Good night, citizens of the world."

THE NEXT MORNING, NELSON packed his bags. He told the group that he was eager to get started on a second VT machine in the event they needed a backup. The truth behind his hasty departure was much more ominous. Being around Jeneva for the past while had only made him want her more. He was convinced that Dexter's presence was blinding her from seeing how much she meant to him. He had to find some way to discredit the cad and win her love, once and for all.

Still drained from yesterday's experience in the cavern, he took advantage of the five-hour bus ride to Quito airport and slept. His reoccurring dream about Alex haunted him, as it often did.

Chapter 17

Maddy's University Essay
Several months had passed since the broadcast of Nelson's vision. The show had been rebroadcast in over one hundred additional countries that hadn't picked it up live. Major issues with the Pyramid Challenge website crashing from all the traffic were now resolved. Currently, the Challenge was still receiving the highest level of traffic on most social media platforms.

The CARE Foundation was up and running in a small section of the office complex owned by Applebaum Enterprises. The entrance door was labeled Special Projects and required a security card to gain access. The staff working in the rest of the building had been informed that this area was off limits for confidential government contract work.

Jeneva was busy scanning emails, doing a quick review of those flagged as important.

This one was from the CARE Foundation's accounting desk regarding a breach in one of their accounts.

Attention CARE Foundation Board Members:

We are happy to announce that the financial concern we notified you of last week has been dealt with, thanks to our new internet security company, Arctic Shield.

Jeneva put her hand to her mouth, considering the worst possible scenario. Sooner or later, they'd have to set up a much bigger office to handle all their finances as well as the documentation of the entrants that would be pouring in. As she read on, it looked like this company would be able to manage all their upcoming security needs. It was signed by Mrs. R. Applebaum. "Thanks Mrs. A. Looks like you got this handled." *Dexter was right. You do take charge.*

Jeneva frowned at the vibrating intrusion of her phone. I thought I turned that thing off!" The anger flushed out of her voice when she turned the phone over and saw the face of one of her favorite people.

"Maddy! What a pleasant surprise. How is my soon-to-be high school graduate doing?"

Jeneva's Little Sister replied with such excitement she was on the verge of screaming. "I know you'll be here for my graduation, but I couldn't wait to tell you the good news. I heard from Chuck. He got promoted to assistant manager at the restaurant."

"Good for him. Maybe he'll be the manager someday."

"That's not all. I finished my university entrance essay. I sent a draft to my friend, Cathy. She thinks it's great. I think you'll love it too, but I need you to check it for accuracy."

Jeneva heard what sounded like Maddy falling back on her bed with a huff. She waited for a second to see whether her overjoyed caller was out of breath before responding.

"So, you are finally going to let me in on what this masterpiece is all about. I have to be honest with you, the anticipation has been driving me to distraction. What's it about? Can you give me the *Reader's Digest* version?"

"What's a *Reader's Digest* version? That must be some old school terminology." The young girl laughed.

"Smarty-pants. How about a CliffsNotes version? Is that something you're familiar with?"

"Wait for it!"

The little tease made her wait fifteen whole seconds.

"The title is, The Pyramid Challenge."

Jeneva was surprised and delighted that Maddy chose her and Dexter's creation as the topic for her essay. She sat back in her chair, smiling and crying at the same time.

"I love it. I can't wait to read it. I'm shocked you've been able to keep this from me all this time. When are you emailing it?

Maddy toyed with Jeneva's obvious excitement and spoke in a slow, robotic voice.

"Well . . . I . . . guess . . . I . . . could . . . send . . . it . . . now."

"You little teaser. I'm hanging up. It better be there! Love you, bye."

"Love you too."

Jeneva turned back to her computer in anticipation of Maddy's email.

"That little sneak! She sent it half an hour ago." Jeneva shook her head and smiled at how Maddy had duped her.

"I'll get you for this." She loved the back-and-forth pranks they played on each other. It reinforced her belief that having a good sense of humor is good in a relationship.

Jeneva opened the file and did a quick scan of the document before going into a thorough read of the details.

The Pyramid Challenge
and
Its Sociological Impact on Society
By Madison Cartwright

Essay Statement: How a simple challenge is changing people's attitudes and moving the world order in a positive direction.

The Pyramid Challenge is open to all citizens of the world to participate in, regardless of economic position or standing. This was one of the key priorities of The Pyramid Challenge creators. To accomplish this goal, they connected the entrance fee to the average income of each contestant's country of citizenship. I think this was a great way to level the playing field for everyone.

The contest is ingenious in its simplicity: Contestants post good deeds to a website to accumulate points. All good deeds must be endorsed by someone who benefited or witnessed the act.

The Pyramid Challenge defines a good deed as: An act that has no personal benefit, costs you something and benefits someone else.

For the first round, countries only compete against each other. You could think about it like the Olympics, where a contestant competes in their own country for the honor to go to the Worldwide Championships. Each country has a governing body that oversees fairness, rules, and compliance of its own national Pyramid Challenge activities. Ultimately, each country will follow a voting process to select one entrant to represent it in the next phase of the challenge.

At the international level, again like the Olympics, a neutral governing body oversees the worldwide competition.

All the rules and regulations details are posted on: ThePyramidChallenge.org website, but in summary, the Challenge winner is ultimately chosen by worldwide voting after it is narrowed down to the final three nominees.

My research indicates The Pyramid Challenge is unique, in that no program has ever reached such a high level of engagement on an international scale. Of the 195 countries in the world, 163 are currently actively participating.

Financial standing and political status will have no influence on the outcome and are not recognized in any way when becoming a contestant.

The non-monetary prize is an interesting alternative to the usual financial motivation for people to get involved in most contests.

The impact of The Pyramid Challenge can be seen in the nightly newscasts and news feeds online, heralding the good deeds of ordinary citizens. People are going about their daily business but in a way that opens their eyes to the opportunity of helping others.

Violence and crime have statistically decreased as the citizens of the world have shifted their focus in a more positive direction. For example, the overall crime rate has decreased in the US by 25 percent, and physical disputes reported to police are down 35 percent.

The Pyramid Challenge has definitely had a measurable, positive impact on the sociological fabric of society. To prove out my conclusion, I will provide some actual examples of sociological shifts.

JENEVA WAS AMAZED AT the wisdom and understanding her Little Sister exhibited in her essay. That obstinate eight-year-old she'd met almost ten years ago had turned into a wise, insightful young woman. Jeneva spent the next hour working her way through the practical examples Maddy used to prove her conclusions. The essay concluded with some factual appendices taken directly from the CARE Foundation Guidebook. Jeneva read through the technical sections carefully, checking for 100 percent accuracy.

When she finally looked up at the clock, it was eleven o'clock. Her suggested edits turned out to be minor, a couple corrections to some factual statements only.

She included a smiley face and an A+ in her reply email. It was too late to call her now. Congratulations of this magnitude needed to happen in person, with a big hug.

I might just have a job for a soon-to-be political science graduate.

DEXTER AND JENEVA LEFT the condo early and headed to the airport in Quito for her flight to Washington DC.

"You'll never guess what came in my email last night!"

"Wouldn't be the long-awaited and highly anticipated Madison Cartwright essay, would it?"

"It was indeed. She wanted to tell you about it herself. I thought I'd call and put her on speaker. It would give us something to do on the way to the airport.

"By all means, give her a call." Jeneva suggested.

"Hey there, kiddo, Jeneva tells me you have finished your essay. What's it about?"

"It's called, The Pyramid Challenge and Its Sociological Impact on Society. It's about how The Pyramid Challenge has changed people's attitudes and moved the world in a positive direction."

Dexter's head snapped right to give Jeneva a wide-eyed look of surprise.

"Dexter, it's absolutely insightful. She totally captured the essence of what we're trying to accomplish. I think you're going to love it. The essay is a marvel from the opening statement, through the practical examples, to the fact-based conclusions. She researched this and found the positive to negative ratio has completely flipped from 20/80 to 80/20 in favor of positivity."

"Hey, I thought you were going to let me tell Dexter what it's about. Just kidding. Keep telling him how great it is."

"Sorry, I'm just so impressed. You go ahead."

"Well, I also included impactful stories that were forwarded to the CARE Foundation. One story is about a nurse in Australia who stopped to give a vagrant water, and her good deed ended up taking Alzheimer's research in a new and exciting direction. I try to explain how the totality of the small deeds were instrumental in shifting societies in a positive, more compassionate direction. I used social media metrics from before and after the Challenge to illustrate the change in tone of the exchanges and the paradigm shift in the direction the interactions have taken. Jeneva already covered that."

"I always knew you were a smart cookie. What I've heard so far is remarkable. We are both so proud of you."

"Thanks. I'll email you your very own copy. Listen, I have to go. Auntie just popped in and pointed at her watch. You guys drive carefully. See you soon, Jeneva. Good night."

"Sweet dreams. Love you!"

DEXTER STOOD IN AN impassioned trance, thinking, as the love of his life headed through the security lineup. *I can't believe the effect that woman has on me. She has such a blithe spirit that it's hard to believe she is as earthbound as the rest of us.*

Jeneva turned and blew him a kiss, then a backward wave before she disappeared in the crowd heading to their departure gates.

JENEVA TOOK A CAB FROM the airport to the address Maddy had texted her. Her aunt Patricia's house was on a quiet crescent encircled by mature trees and brick bungalows that looked as if they might have been built in the seventies. Maddy was smiling and waving from the living room bay window as she pulled in.

"I'm so glad you came. We've made up a bed in the den for you. How long can you stay?"

"First things first! I owe you a big 'Congratulations' on that fabulous essay. I'm confident you'll be accepted at any university of your choosing. And here's a big hug to go with it."

Jeneva handed Maddy her carry-on, and they looped arms and headed for the front door. "Now, to answer your question. Mrs. Applebaum offered to hold down the fort at the CARE Foundation for a couple days, so I'll probably head back Sunday. I don't want to take advantage of her generosity. If you don't have plans for tomorrow night after the grad ceremony, I'd like to take you all to my favorite restaurant on the pier."

"Let's check with Aunt Patricia. She's making a snack in the kitchen. Then you have to see my dress. Auntie bought it. It was my graduation gift. Plus, she gave me some cash."

Jeneva could always tell when Maddy was on a fishing expedition, so she pulled an envelope out of her purse.

"What a cool card!" There was a picture of a young girl tossing her mortarboard up in the air. Maddy gasped when she saw the amount on the check inside.

"Dad and I thought you could use a little money for books and such."

"Thank you so much and thank Takoda for me too.

AFTER THE GRADUATION ceremony, they all went for supper at The Olde Marine Restaurant, the one Jeneva liked to meet her dad at when she was in town. When the platters were licked clean, she ordered one of their famous key lime pies to go. They all agreed that a walk on the pier was needed after such a filling meal, and maybe then, there would be room for pie.

As the group hustled through the front door, Jeneva's phone vibrated in her purse.

She recognized the number; it was the Smithsonian. "Why on earth is the Smithsonian calling me?"

Chapter 18

I ssues of the Heart

Jeneva sat quietly in a yellow paper suit and blue gloves, listening to the shallow breathing of the sleeping man she barely recognized. His face was gaunt and pale with dark half-moons under his eyes. Suddenly, the cool hand she was holding clenched hers.

She was devastated to hear her dad was in a hospital after having a heart attack. The Smithsonian had contacted her and told her they were airlifting her father from Sudan back to DC after he'd experienced a second heart attack.

Takoda opened his eyes and immediately smiled at his daughter. Above her mask, he noticed her red puffy eyes.

"Why so sad, my angel? I am not going anywhere. I have too much work to do. Come, help me into the chair. I can't be lounging around like an invalid." He pulled the covers back and swung his legs to the side.

Just then, the doctor came in and reported that, although Takoda needed to remain on the monitors and oxygen overnight, he was sending him home tomorrow. The cardiologist explained in detail what the next few months would entail; a change in diet, moderate exercise, some more tests, and appointments at the cardio rehabilitation unit located in the old red brick building behind the hospital. Takoda gave her a grand smile and the doctor a thumbs-ups. "That sounds doable. Thanks for everything, doc."

Once the doctor left, they sat chatting about her visit with Maddy and how pretty she was in her grad dress. Jeneva, of course, had pictures. She also showed her dad the essay on The Pyramid Challenge.

"Once I'm back on my feet, I'd love to come and help out."

"You're something else, Pops. After what you've just been through, you should be thinking about retirement." She put her gloved hand on his.

"Tell me what's been going on with you, honey." He obviously wanted to change the subject, quick. Jeneva knew he didn't feel ready to retire.

"I've been thinking about Mom a lot these days and what she said about me finding my destiny and changing the world. I think she was right. First, I figured out what the symbols meant on the bracelet, which led me to create The Pyramid Challenge, which is changing the world, one good deed at a time. I couldn't have done it without the help of so many others."

"I never doubted you for a minute."

"Thanks to Dexter's dad, the security around the pyramid couldn't be tighter. That's taken a weight off our shoulders. And since the worldwide broadcast of Nelson's vision, the media and our website are just exploding with nominations for the thousands of people who have started doing good deeds for other people. We couldn't have gotten this far without Nelson's VT machine. You'll have to come to the pyramid during an equinox and try it."

Takoda's head fell back against the chair, and he tried to conceal a yawn behind his hand.

"I couldn't be happier for you. I hate to say it, honey, but I'm ready for a nap."

Jeneva helped him get comfortably back in bed and kissed his cheek. They hugged and squeezed hands.

"See you tomorrow." She gave a backward wave as she left the room.

Driving back to her dad's apartment, she noticed a voice mail from Dexter had come in while her phone was off at the hospital. He just wanted to know how Takoda was doing. She made a mental note to call him later.

After being closed up for months while her dad was in Sudan, the apartment was musty. She opened all the windows to air the place out. Jeneva finished her late lunch of Greek yogurt and fresh fruit, sitting in the comfortable reclining chair in her father's living room. A refreshing breeze was lofting over her, and she closed her eyes, ready to meditate. Instead, her thoughts turned to tomorrow's tasks: go shopping for food, pick up Dad, stop for medication at the drug store, get him settled into his apartment, and call Dexter back.

So much for meditating. Her thoughts were too overpowering to block. She pulled up on the handle of the recliner and headed to the bathroom for an Epsom salt Jacuzzi bath. She still experienced some discomfort from her injuries back at CERN, and the massaging jets helped relax the stiff muscles.

When her cell phone vibrated on the vanity, Jeneva begrudgingly climbed out to take the call, just in case it was the hospital or Dexter calling back.

"Hi, Jeneva! It's Nelson. I wanted to call and find out how your dad is making out. It must be scary for you. How are you holding up?"

Jeneva took a breath before responding to the unexpected caller. "Actually, he is getting out of the hospital tomorrow, and we're expecting a full recovery. I appreciate the call, but I was just about to head to bed."

"Oh." Nelson's disappointment at her subtle brush off was clear in his tone. But he persisted in trying to pique her interest. "I do have some things to show you with respect to the VT."

"Yes, of course, Nelson. I didn't mean to be so abrupt, but I have a lot on my mind. Could you give me a call back tomorrow evening?"

"I am actually in town on business. Could we meet at the bar in the Harbor Hilton Hotel for a drink, say eight p.m. tomorrow?"

"Sure!" She was surprised at her quick response.

"That should work. I will call you if I have to reschedule, okay?"

"Sounds good. Talk to you later."

ACROSS TOWN, IN A DIMLY lit hotel room, Nelson started searching the internet, determined to find something he could hold over Dexter's head. Something that would hopefully open up the playing field for him to win over Jeneva's affections. He was convinced she had feelings for him. If they only had more time to get to know each other, who knows where their relationship could go.

His initial findings showed Dexter's education and credentials as an astronomer, and magnetic portal researcher to be admirable. Nothing helpful there. Next, Nelson punched in: Applebaum family history. Once he located Dexter's lineage, he found references to his great grandfather Abraham and grandfather Isaac. There was an article about Isaac in reference to an arrest that led to the man dying in jail. Too dated to be anything interesting. His father Jacob Applebaum appeared to be a very successful businessman but again nothing controversial.

"Bloody hell!" Nelson slammed his fist on the desk. Exasperated at his failed effort to sabotage Dexter and Jeneva's relationship, he stood up, ready to slam the lid of his computer. He took one more, quick glance at the screen, and spotted a news clipping on the bottom of the page that read: "Murder or Self-Defense?"

"Blimey! I've got you now, Dexter."

WHEN JENEVA ARRIVED at the hospital to pick up her dad, he told her the doctor forgot to sign his release papers and wouldn't be back till later in the day. She confirmed the doctor's time of arrival with the nurse and went back to her father's room.

"Guess you're stuck here for a while. I grabbed you some snacks from the kitchen to hold you over." She set a can of iced tea, a muffin, and a pudding cup on the bedside table.

"Thanks, honey." He slid off the bed into the reclining chair beside the bed.

"I'll go for groceries and pick up your meds. Why don't you try and sleep till I get back?"

"I just might do that." He yawned under his cupped hand.

"I won't be long." She placed a kiss on his cheek and closed the door behind her.

Sitting in her car at the grocery store, she searched the internet for heart-healthy foods. After making a list of the food she knew her father would enjoy, she headed into the store.

Hearing of Takoda's heart attack had made Dexter feel a bit melancholy, so he went to visit his parents at their villa, not far from his condo in Quito.

His mother greeted him with a kiss on each cheek and warm motherly hug.

"Dexter, I am so excited to have you home. Will you be staying for a while?" She didn't wait for an answer.

"I saw the huge crowd of admirers at the airport on the news. Sorry to ruin your surprise visit. I asked Nellie's daughter to program my phone to send me notices whenever The Pyramid Challenge shows up in the news. So far, I've been able to keep our little CARE Foundation office running smoothly. I have two full-time and three part-time volunteers at the moment."

Dexter gazed in awe at his mother as she frolicked around the kitchen like the silver ball in a pinball machine. He hadn't seen her this happy in a while. She was making his favorite sandwich, brisket with lettuce smothered in wasabi mayonnaise. Her excitement and passion were out of control, and she continued to ramble on as enthusiastically as an auctioneer calling for bids.

Her nervous housemaid, Rosa, jumped aside to avoid a collision with her fast-moving employer.

"Senorà, can I help you with that? Why don't you visit with your son? I can take it from here."

His mother spun around, her long gray hair swooping back and forth, struggling to keep up with the exuberant sixty-year-old's pace.

"No, no, I have to do this. It needs a mother's touch to make it just the way he likes it. He's a world-famous celebrity, you know." She gave Dexter a big smile. "Why don't you vacuum or something?"

Rosa quickly disappeared through the stone archway.

"It looks like this Pyramid Challenge is going to be a point in world history that will be recognized as a paradigm shift. I think it could shift civilization to a kinder, more compassionate place. You know, everyone at the synagogue is talking about Mr. Jones's experience in the cavern. Even Rabbi Abraham incorporated it into his sermon last Saturday."

When his mom stopped for a quick breath, Dexter jumped in. "It's actually a group of us running it, which you know, so I think you might be overstating just a little."

"No, I don't think I am. Since you and Jeneva initially came to us, your father has become a kinder, more thoughtful, loving person. I love it. He's no longer that singularly obsessed company-focused tycoon. You won't believe the change. He turned much of his business responsibility over to your uncle and spends the majority of his time on things to help your project, as well as my needs of course." She gave Dexter her signature smile and eye blink with feigned embarrassment.

"He's helping you with security stuff, and with Jeneva busy taking care of her dad, I'm helping with the CARE Foundation. We're a team. This project has been like a whole new beginning that's brought us all together." She was overcome with emotion and wiped her eyes with the tea towel she had slung over her shoulder.

Dexter tried to change the subject, but his mother's proud tête-à-tête freight train had left the station and was not stopping for anything or anyone.

"I won't steal your father's thunder, but he has some great news. I think you are going to be very pleased, dear. He worked hard during the last election; you know. The country was ready for change, and he seized the opportunity to campaign. Spending a ton of money, I might add, supporting candidates he felt would be sympathetic to your cause. The old guard was swept out to sea, allowing for a tidal wave of change. I can tell you this much, the new group of congressmen and congresswomen are sympathetic to the environment, Indigenous rights, and our country's heritage. They are also very focused on improving the economy of the country. These people are long-term strategic thinkers, like your father."

They heard Rosa, greet the master of the house in the front hall.

"Bienvenido de nuevo, senor. Tu esposa e hijo están en la cocina."

Dexter jumped up and hurried to the front door. The two men exchanged a firm handshake and then embraced in a bear hug with numerous back pats.

"I had a great day today, and I think you are going to be very pleased, my boy. I have started something in motion that has now come to fruition, and it is going to secure your site now and well into the future. The legislature has passed into law a bill designating the Hummingbird Pyramid and a fifty-mile radius around it a Historically Sensitive Archaeological Site. The HSAS is to ultimately become a National Park, under joint control of the federal government and the local Indigenous peoples. Access will be controlled and restricted. Only visitors with permits will be allowed on the site. The Indigenous population is going to be given much-needed jobs." His father offered his hand for a high five, and Dexter followed through.

"Congratulations, that's an amazing accomplishment. Calls for a brandy, don't you think?"

They relocated to the den, where his mother joined them with a glass of sherry and Dexter's sandwich.

"We were so sorry to hear about Jeneva's father. How is he doing? Poor dear, she must be worried sick. Let her know I have things under control at the foundation, will you?

WHEN JENEVA STEPPED out of the hospital elevator, the clock on the wall read two thirty.

As she rounded the corner, she saw a doctor and nurse standing outside her dad's room. She panicked and bolted in their direction.

"What's wrong? Is my dad, okay?" She grabbed hold of the doctor's arm.

"He's fine. We needed his room, so he offered to wait at the nurse's station. I've signed his release. He's free to go."

She gave a sigh of relief and headed back the way she'd come. In her haste, she hadn't seen Takoda sitting in a wheelchair behind the reception desk, chatting with the nurse.

"Hey, Pops, you've been sprung. Shall we go?" She stepped behind the wheelchair and placed Takoda's overnight bag in his lap.

He thanked the nurse for her excellent care and gave a wave to the doctor down the hall.

When they arrived at Takoda's apartment, he looked tired, so Jeneva sent him to his room for a nap before dinner. Once the groceries were put away, she sorted her father's pills into the daily slots in the week-long container purchased at the pharmacy. She set them beside his recliner along with this month's copy of *World Water Projects Magazine* she found in his mail.

"I'm starving. What delicacy, have you cooked up for us tonight?" Takoda was shuffling cautiously into the kitchen.

"Almond-crusted salmon and wild rice. Your timing is impeccable. Have a seat."

As she was pulling the steaming platter from the oven, she noticed him struggling with the chair. He obviously didn't have the strength he used to. She placed the fish on the table.

"Here, let me help you with that."

"Thanks, honey. Guess I better hit the pool before my muscles start to atrophy."

"I don't know about that, but a little physical therapy wouldn't hurt. I'll call the doctor and see if we can have someone come in until you get your strength back."

"Sounds good. Now let's eat." He rubbed his hands together in glee and licked his lips.

Takoda had not only lost weight and strength, but his appetite also wasn't what it used to be. There would be enough leftovers for tomorrow's dinner.

"I've cleaned up in the kitchen. Can I get you anything before I go, Dad?"

"I'm good. You better hustle, or you're going to be late for your meeting with Nelson."

Nelson's eagerness to meet with her made her wonder whether his motives were honorable. Just to ensure she didn't give him any false impressions, she wore a blue high-neck dress, covered with a knee-length sweater, and a yellow and navy scarf around her neck. She pulled her hair up in a messy bun, slipped into a pair of black leather ankle boots, and headed to the bar.

She quickly regarded her reflection in the window of the Harbor Hilton Hotel before entering the double doors. *Not too shabby, not too sexy, just right*, she decided.

The after-work crowd had gone home, and the room was all but empty, except for a couple in the corner and Nelson, also in a dimly lit corner. As she made her way to his table, Jeneva watched his face turn from gloomy to euphoric when he saw her. He stood and pulled the chair out for her.

"Such a gentleman."

"My pleasure, and may I say you look smashing this evening."

"Thanks, and how have you been, Nelson?" She tried to keep the conversation light.

"Pretty good, thanks." He looked as if he couldn't contain his smile.

"Well, shall we get down to business?" She pulled a notepad and pen out of her beaded bag.

Nelson opened up his laptop and showed Jeneva an updated PowerPoint demonstration of the Visualization Technology HD features and the modified headpiece.

"Very impressive. Having that conglomeration of wires wrapped sure makes it a lot tidier." Jeneva snapped a few pictures of the screen to show Dexter.

Nelson slammed the computer lid shut, making her jump.

"Sorry about that. I'm a bit gutted at the moment. I need to tell you something."

"For goodness' sake, spit it out, Nelson. How bad could it be?" She hoped it didn't have anything to do with backing out on them. She crossed her fingers under the table.

"It's about Dexter."

As Jeneva looked at him, she could swear he was struggling to hide a look of jubilation. But Nelson was no fan of Dexter. Her heart skipped a beat.

Nelson slid a news clipping across the table. The headline read, "Murder or Self-Defense?"

She gasped when she read that Dexter Applebaum had been a key suspect.

DEXTER LOUNGED ON HIS penthouse balcony in Quito, admiring the spectacle of flickering night stars. Ice cubes tinkled as he rocked his Old Fashion back and forth. He thought about how his carefree bachelor lifestyle was changing into one with purpose, centered around a shared mission. It was transforming him. At the core of it all was the woman who snatched his taxi a few short years ago. He thought it a cliché, but she actually had stolen his heart. Now he was counting the days, the hours, the minutes, until he'd see her again. Just the mention of her name or the touch of her hand filled him with passion and love beyond his wildest dreams. This type of all-consuming desire was a new and exciting experience for him.

A quick glance at his wrist showed 9:07 p.m. on his Fitbit. That meant it was 10:07 p.m. in Washington DC. He surmised Jeneva should be back from visiting Takoda in the hospital by now. He opened the FaceTime app and touched the name at the top of the list.

It took Jeneva an uncharacteristically long time to accept the call, and the face that popped up on his screen was not a happy one.

"Hi, gorgeous! Is everything okay? How's your dad doing?" It was apparent Jeneva was not at her father's apartment. She appeared to be walking through a noisy, crowded room.

"Dad's fine. Hang on! I'm on my way to my car. It will be quieter in there."

There was a sharpness in her tone that Dexter had never heard before. The screen did a wavy dance over the indistinguishable surroundings. Her frowning face reappeared.

"Where are you?"

"I stopped by the Hilton to meet with Nelson. He wanted to show me the modifications he's made on the VT machine. He also showed me a very disconcerting news release about you, titled 'Murder or Self-Defense?'" She was biting her lip as if trying fiercely not to cry.

At that moment, Dexter wished he'd opted for a voice call instead of a video chat. *What must this beautiful, trusting woman be thinking, looking at my guilt-ridden face?* His mouth went dry, and a lump formed in his throat, making it impossible to speak or swallow. The room started to spin, and he fell back into his chair. Beads of sweat were forming on his forehead.

"I know I've caught you off guard, Dexter, and I can see by your reaction that this is serious. This probably isn't a conversation we should get into right now. I haven't even read through the whole article yet. Why don't I call you tomorrow, and we can discuss it then? I have to get back to the apartment and get Dad settled in for the night."

"Jeneva, can I ask you not to read any more about this?" Dexter's throat was as dry as cotton. "There is a lot of unfounded speculation and misrepresented information out there. I'd like to explain everything to you before you come to any conclusions." His soft, beseeching voice trailed off in a hoarse cough.

"Okay, goodnight." The video call ended, without the customary kiss and blow exchange.

Dexter gulped down his drink and started shaking. The short phone call instantly stripped away all the happiness and euphoria he'd been feeling. Now he was shrouded with fear of losing his first true love. His body felt airborne, as if someone had just pushed him off a cliff. Suddenly, he was recalling the long-suppressed memories.

JENEVA UNLOCKED HER car, slipped in behind the wheel and buckled up. The events of the day had exhausted her. She wrapped her arms around the wheel and dropped her head on her hands.

"Dexter, Dexter, Dexter. What on earth have you done?" She raised her head and turned the key. She caught a glimpse of someone peering around the corner of the building.

"What the...is that Nelson?"

Chapter 19

Ten Years Earlier

Grandfather Isaac believed it was important for everyone, including Dexter, to know the horrible crimes that were committed against their fellow Jews.

Isaac dedicated many years of his life to hunting down Nazi war criminals just as his father Abraham had done before him Many escaped to South America after the second world war, with Brazil being the most popular destination. Isaac was surprised and outraged, when he found one living in Quito, Ecuador, posing as a dentist. By the time Helmut Von Dresden was discovered, Isaac's failing health kept him from apprehending him personally.

Helmut had worked at Auschwitz, with the Angel of Death himself, Dr. Mengele, the worst of the worst. The two conducted horrible experiments on the concentration camp prisoners before sending them to their deaths in the gas chambers.

His grandfather had asked Dexter to take up the torch and confront the dentist, who was using the alias, Henry Weidman. His need to honor his grandfather and continue his mission outweighed his apprehension and misgivings.

Dexter disguised his voice to sound much older and gave a fictitious name when he made the appointment with the dentist's assistant for a checkup.

As fate would have it, there was a cancellation. She instructed Dexter to come the next day at three thirty, the last appointment of the day. She told him she wouldn't be there but would leave a questionnaire on the counter, and she requested he please fill it out before seeing the dentist.

Dexter tossed and turned restlessly all night, in anticipation of finally confronting the man his grandfather so desperately wanted brought to justice.

The next day, Google maps led Dexter to a run-down, impoverished neighborhood, which made him very uncomfortable. The streets were narrow, hardly enough room for him to park his pickup truck. When he spotted the Dentistry for Seniors, Henry Weidman, DMD sign, he pulled over and straddled the curb. His palms were wet and clammy on the steering wheel, and despite having turned the AC dial to high, beads of sweat covered his forehead. Inside the large center console, he found several fast-food napkins. He used a couple to wipe his brow and hands, then tossed them in the small half-full garbage basket behind the passenger's seat. Then he sanitized his hands. Part of his OCD ritual. He surveyed the area, and when he was sure it was safe, he got out and locked the doors.

The proprietor's sign creaked overhead on its rusty chains. Cautiously, he walked around his vehicle to the sidewalk where he observed the same caption as the hanging sign, etched in the glass panel of the door.

Dexter's hand shook like a leaf as he reached for the doorknob. He was nervous as hell. His heart started pounding so hard, he thought it was going to jump out of his chest.

When he entered the empty reception area, a musky smell lofted over him, and a bell tinkled overhead. From the back room, a male voice called out.

"I will be right with you!"

Afraid he might lose his nerve, Dexter burst into the treatment room and shouted, "I know who you are, Mr. Dresden, and I am going to see you are brought to justice!"

The dentist turned to face his aggressor and responded in a polite voice. "You must be mistaken! I am Henry Weidman." He placed both hands on his chest and bowed curtly. When he raised his head, there was a cryptic glare in his eyes that made Dexter very uncomfortable.

This man was not at all the intimidating monster Dexter had envisioned. Instead, his aging complexion was pitted and etched with wrinkles that made him almost mousy looking. He was clean shaven, except for a waxed handlebar mustache that curled at the tips. Under his white lab coat, he wore a black turtleneck and a pair of sharply pressed black pants. Thick lensed spectacles sat on the end of his long, narrow nose. His feet were sockless in brown leather loafers. To an unknowing stranger, he could be mistaken for exactly what he aspired to be, a kindly old dentist.

Dexter elevated his voice and waved a pointed finger at the dentist. "You committed horrible crimes on helpless captives, and you must pay for your crimes!"

"I am just an old dentist taking care of poor people in the neighborhood. What you are suggesting is absurd! I insist you leave before I call the authorities!" His German accent surfaced in his threatening words. He turned back to face the cabinet and opened a drawer.

Dexter was taken aback for a moment by Helmut's personal exoneration and threat to call the police, but he knew the evidence was clear. There was no mistaken identity here. And there was no way the police were being called by anyone but him.

"I'm not quite ready to leave, Dresden!" Dexter squinted his eyes and tightened his brow, trying to appear fearless.

"I have all the documentation needed to prove you are Helmut Von Dresden. I'm going to see you are arrested and put on trial as the despicable war criminal that you are." Dexter took a step closer to the old man.

Helmut swung around, pointing an old Ruger at Dexter's chest. Dexter lunged forward, impulsively grabbing the old man's boney wrist with both hands, raising it to the ceiling. They both lost their footing on the shiny linoleum floor. Their contorted bodies tumbled over the reclined dental chair onto the floor. *BANG!* A single deafening gunshot resounded in the small examination room.

Chapter 20

Interpretations Vary

Dexter felt as if he had sleepwalked through the past three hours, barely remembering anything. Somehow, he managed to book himself on a flight to Washington DC, pack an overnight bag, and arrive at his gate at the airport in Quito with his boarding pass in hand. He put his elbows on his knees, dropped his head in his hands, and closed his eyes. Because of the snail's pace through security, he'd had to make a mad dash to get to his gate on time. His chest was still heaving. His mind was focused on his one and only goal: *Get to Jeneva! Make her understand!*

A flight attendant's husky voice, offering drinks to the passengers behind Dexter, woke him up. He looked out the small window of the plane and saw beads of water dancing across his reflection on the glass. That he'd fallen asleep before the flight even took off threw him for a loop. *How long have I been out? I don't have time to sleep! I need all the time I can get to figure out how and what I'm going to say to Jeneva.*

He looked at the large TV screen hanging on the bulkhead. The map showed that they were halfway to their destination. He ordered a coffee, hoping to numb what felt suspiciously like a bourbon hangover. He tried to focus on his explanation. *How do I make her understand it was just an accident? She has to believe me!* He laid his head back on the comfortable seat.

The hard contact of the landing gear on the runway made his body twitch awake.

"Damn it! I fell asleep again!" he said under his breath. He massaged his neck to get the kinks out and rehearsed his intended explanation in his head. He clenched his fists and took a deep, right to the bottom of his lung's breath. Then in a hushed voice, he said to his reflection on the window, "She has to believe it was an accident," believing that saying it out loud could make it so.

THE LOUD NOISE OF CUPBOARD doors banging in the kitchen aroused Jeneva from her restless sleep. The green display on her nightstand clock had shown three fifteen when she had finally stopped trying to fathom what Dexter had or hadn't done and had given in to sleep. As she rolled over, the bright sunlight peeking through the curtains stung her eyes and made her head feel as if it were going to explode. She turned her head away and massaged her temples with two fingers, then moved to the tightness in her neck. To her relief, the banging stopped in the kitchen. Then, she heard her name being called. Slowly rising from the bed, she ran one hand along the wall to steady herself. Her head ached like hell, but it was her aching heart that dominated her thoughts this morning. Combing her tangled night hair out of her face with open fingers, she twisted it in a knot and headed for the kitchen. What she really needed was a cold shower pulsing on the top of her head, but that would have to wait.

She leaned on the doorframe leading to the kitchen.

"Morning, Dad. You're not going to find any coffee, I hid it. You know you're not supposed to have any caffeinated beverages. If you want, I can pick up some decaf next time I'm out. For now, it's herbal tea for you, I'm afraid!" She was on her way to the sink with the kettle in her hand.

"Good morning! You're right, honey. But it's going to take a while for me to get used to this post heart attack lifestyle. I'm sure going to miss my morning java. Old habits will die hard." He stuck his bottom lip way out.

They both shared a somewhat subdued laugh as he reached to turn on the morning news.

"I don't know why I torture myself with the events of the day. All they want is to raise their ratings with sensational stories of disaster and despair. Never a positive story to be found." He shook his head in dismay.

As if to answer his challenge, the morning anchor introduced a YouTube video of an NYPD officer rescuing some baby ducklings in Central Park. Apparently, Officer Max was patrolling the park on his horse and was alerted to the tragedy by the distraught mother goose, who was sitting on top of a grate, honking and refusing to leave.

The video showed him guiding the goose away from the grate and dismounting, leaving his horse to keep her at bay. He picked up a large fallen branch, used it to remove the steel cover, and pulled eight wet goslings out of the storm drain. He put them in a box an onlooker brought him. Then he took them over to their mom. She did inventory, then led them into the nearby lake. The crowd that gathered cheered and applauded the officer as he walked back to his horse. The man who continued to record the event approached him.

"Can I get a selfie with you?" He snapped a pic before getting an answer. "That was very kind of you. I hope you're okay with this video going viral!"

"I guess. I was just doin' my job. There was a crisis, and I helped them out. Sometimes those in danger can't speak for themselves. Sometimes they aren't even human. Now, some folks may not see this small act as anything significant, but for one mother goose and her babies, it made all the difference in the world. You all have a good day and help one another whenever you can." He tipped his hat and mounted his horse.

"Well, there you go, Dad! A story about dedication to the job and well-being of your fellow . . . *geese!*"

Jeneva dropped heavily into a kitchen chair and blew out a huff. "Sorry about that. I didn't get much sleep last night." Her body hung like a wet rag over the chair. "I'm exhausted, physically and mentally. I have something on my mind, and it's driving me crazy. I could use a second opinion if you're up for a father-daughter chat."

"Of course, dear. Let's go to the living room and drink our lovely caffeine-free tea. Sorry, now I am being sarcastic. Tell me what's troubling you."

"Well, it's about Dexter. Last night, Nelson showed me a disturbing article. It was titled: 'Murder or Self-Defense?' So far, I've only skimmed it. The story is centered around Dexter and some encounter with a Nazi war criminal getting shot. Dexter happened to call just after I read part of it. When I questioned him about it, he asked me to let him explain before I read the rest. He said he doesn't want me jumping to any conclusions. I got up several times in the night intending to read it all but couldn't bring myself to go against his wishes. It seems so impossible that the man I know, and love could have acted so recklessly." She tightened her lips together and blinked back tears.

"Honey, I'm inclined to agree with Dexter. He should have the opportunity to explain what happened in his own words. You know these sensationalized stories are often very slanted to the writer's point of view or prejudices. Just look at the title: 'Murder or Self-Defense?' It could easily have been titled: 'Self-Defense or Murder?' See what I mean? Right off the bat, the writer is organizing the article to put the idea of murder first. I have no idea what happened, but I can tell you that many stories reported by the media that I've had direct involvement with were falsely represented by the networks. I am not saying they were complete fabrications but definitely slanted in a way to sell more newspapers and increase ratings." He patted her knee. "I recommend you set the article aside for now and wait for Dexter to tell his side of the story."

"I don't disagree, Dad. What concerns me is, after all this time, he's never mentioned anything about this. We made a pact to tell each other everything about our pasts. The fact that he kept this from me scares me to death." She dropped her head on his shoulder to hide the fact that she couldn't hold back her tears any longer.

"I'm sure you two will work this out, kiddo." Takoda wrapped an arm around her.

JENEVA RETURNED FROM her shopping trip to a quiet apartment. She looked through the crack in the bedroom door to check on the patient. He was sound asleep. She still found it hard to believe that her father, the invincible giant she'd looked up to all her life, could be taken down so hard.

She'd gone to the kitchen to put the decaf coffee and sugar-free cookies away when a knock sounded at the door. When she opened it, she was stunned. Dexter was the last person she expected to see. The man looking back at her was an alarming site indeed. With a two-day scruff on his face, dark rings under bloodshot eyes and his wrinkled clothes, he could be mistaken for a homeless bum.

"My God, Dexter! You look terrible!" She grabbed his arm and hauled him into the apartment.

"Thanks. I got here as fast as I could. To be honest, I don't remember much since we talked last night." He sounded as exhausted as he looked.

Jeneva turned away without giving her guest a welcome kiss or hug. She walked back to the kitchen and whispered over her shoulder.

"Why don't you head into the bathroom and freshen up." She pointed to a door as she passed by. "I'll make coffee."

Dexter turned into the bathroom.

When he'd finished cleaning up, he entered the kitchen. Jeneva had chosen to sit at the end of the table, leaving no opportunity for him to move in close to her. His freshly brewed cup of coffee was at the opposite end of the table, waiting for him. Sitting at his assigned spot, Dexter made a couple throaty noises and began to articulate, in full detail, the events that transpired on that fateful day at the old dentist's office, ten years ago. Over the next thirty minutes, he managed to curb his emotions and deliver his complete recollection of the events that had led up to the moment a bullet found its way into the cold heart of the Nazi.

"Jeneva, you have to believe me when I say that this was an accident. My intention was to confront Helmut and let him know I knew who he was and what he had done. Then, hand him over to the cops. That horrible, evil man needed to be brought to justice. Believe me, I never meant to kill him. It was just a freak accident. You could say I shouldn't have gone over there that day, and if I hadn't, he might still be alive. But I did what I did, and I can't change what happened." He buried his face in his sweaty palms. "I will admit that I'm glad he's dead."

Jeneva sat there staring at his bowed head for a few minutes. Then she picked up her cup and walked over to the counter. After refilling it, she stared out the window into the courtyard.

"Dexter, the thing I find most disturbing about all this is that you never felt you could tell me about it. We have been together almost two years now, and you chose to keep it to yourself. I don't think anyone would describe this as a minor event in someone's life. Definitely not something you just forget to mention. Remember our talk after my vision of Brian? I revealed everything in my life to you, so you could understand me totally, and our relationship could grow and evolve in truth and honesty. You know you had the perfect opportunity to disclose this whole thing when you detailed your vision experience back in Quito. I feel like maybe you didn't trust me enough to be totally honest and forthcoming." She turned and stared directly into his tear-filled eyes.

"Is there anything else you're keeping from me, Mr. Applebaum?" She crossed her arms and gave him a demanding look.

"No! That's it! I have no good explanation for not telling you. I did want to tell you during my vision explanation but somehow, I just felt so distraught and confused. This is not an excuse, but for the past ten years, not even my father has ever brought up his involvement. It was an unfortunate turn of events that we chose not to revisit." You are right, I should have been totally honest and forthcoming with my past. I love you more than anything in the world Jeneva and I promise no more secrets.

She could feel the honesty and conviction in his voice as she moved her chair closer to him this time.

"Did the police believe you? Did they write it up as an accident or self-defence? What happened in the end?"

Dexter took a deep breath as if he'd hoped the talking was over.

"Actually, I was arrested and taken to the police station for some very unpleasant interrogation. They found my grandfather's notebook in my pocket, and after reading it, felt it was potentially an act of premeditated murder. The whole thing spiraled out of control quickly. When I sensed where they were heading, I refused to answer any more questions and asked for a lawyer. To them, that made me look even more guilty. I was scared shitless! With no witnesses to corroborate what actually happened, I thought I was going to be charged with murder and sent to jail for the rest of my life!" His voice strained, and his body tensed as if he were back in the interrogation room.

"Holy crap! How were you able to convince them it was an accident?" The anger she'd felt earlier was gone, and an eagerness to hear the rest of the story took its place.

"I'm not sure they ever really did. My father showed up with one of the town's well-known lawyers, who was also a part-time law professor at the university. Some calls were made to my father's friends in high places and the lawyer's connections. At one point, I overheard Dad talking to the mayor, I think. He said something like, 'You know, public opinion is never going to side with that murdering so and so. You're going to be very unpopular if you choose to go forward with this ridiculous action against my son!' I was released that same night, but I think one of the skeptical cops that interrogated me leaked the story to the press. I was never actually charged with anything. A couple months later, the case was dismissed as an accident and closed. Rumors of there being a cover-up have persisted ever since. It probably would have been better to go to trial, but I was young and scared and just wanted it over with. So, I let my dad deal with it. I guess there will always be this dark cloud hanging over my head." Dexter finished with a shrug.

"Just so you know, there isn't any doubt in my mind. I believe you just made a bad decision and unfortunately orchestrated the events that lead to Helmut's death. You're not completely innocent, but you are no murderer either. If you are guilty of anything, it's that of being an overly enthusiastic young man, trying to please his grandfather. Mistakes we make in youth should not be used to judge the worth of the person. You and I have a lot of good work to do, so let's get on with it." Jeneva wrapped her arms around his neck and held him tight for a few minutes.

"One more thing. Don't you ever hold anything back from me again, mister." It was a moderately threatening tone, but the intense glare told him she meant business.

Dexter tried to respond, but Jeneva held a finger to his mouth and escorted him to her bedroom.

Chapter 21

Relocating to Zurich

Maddy was excited when Jeneva asked her to join her and Dexter on the trip to Zurich to find a new office for the CARE Foundation. Jeneva told her it was her reward for the outstanding achievement of finishing her first year of university with a GPA of 4.0. "You're one of the team now and I think you are going to find this experience will teach you life lessons you don't get in school," she'd told her.

They walked along the concrete walkway that bordered both sides of the river with decorative wrought iron railings. The color of the river could rival the surf of any Caribbean coastline. The air was filled with the chiming of bells from cathedral steeples that towered over the rows of buildings layered with windows that provided a panoramic view of the city.

Dexter and Maddy gave their approval, and Jeneva signed the rental agreement for a three-story building in downtown Zurich. There were two apartments on the second floor, one for Takoda and one for Jeneva and Dexter. The full-length windows offered a picturesque view of the central Old Town, *Altstadt*, and the Limmat River. Maddy immediately fell in love with the third-floor loft and claimed it as hers.

In less than a week, the street level concourse of their rental building was filled with desks, phones, TVs, fax machines, and file cabinets. Fortunately, the company who vacated the building last month left a long oak table and several black leather chairs in the boardroom. T. J. Buttenham, the wealthy Canadian industrialist, donated a big screen TV for video conferencing. Everything was coming together at a rapid pace.

When Jeneva told them Takoda was interested in the position of CEO of the foundation, Dexter and Maddy agreed he would be a good man for the job. After being cleared for travel by his doctor, Takoda raced head on into his new position. The morning he arrived at the new office, the desks were filled with volunteers, the phones were ringing non-stop with good deed reports, donations, questions, and nominations.

"Where do I sit?" Was his only question.

After a busy morning of conference calls with the board members and dodging the constant hounding from the press, Jeneva, Takoda, Dexter, and Maddy went for lunch in a small café off the beaten track to avoid being noticed. The media was relentless in their quest to get an exclusive interview with the people who had started the phenomenon, known worldwide as, The Pyramid Challenge. It was the lead story on most TV news channels, and it was the most discussed topic on social media.

The whole world was waiting for the final counting of the votes. Everyone hoped their pick would be one of the finalists. With the new sophisticated computer system in place, the numbers were tallied in no time. When the group returned to the office, the final three contestants' qualifying stories were awaiting their review.

Part 3
The Final Three
Contestant 1
Rachael Watkins: Teacher

The drumming of the helicopter propellers was loud, even through the bulky headphones that she was required to wear. The machine rocked and vibrated like an off-road vehicle on some bumpy, forgotten trail. In other circumstances, the thrill of Rachael Watkins's first-ever chopper ride would have been appealing to her outdoor-loving, adventurous nature, but today, it was simply a means to a destination.

The smoke jumpers sitting across from Rach wore orange coveralls and could have been mistaken at first glance for prisoners on their way to incarceration. However, on closer inspection, these handsome, well-groomed, physically fit specimens were more like firefighter calendar candidates. On a normal day, these lads would have been very attractive to Rachael. The kind of men she would have eagerly engaged in flirtatious conversation. However, today was no normal day. Nor was her life likely to return to normality anytime soon.

Rachael's twin sister Reba had burned to death a week ago while trying to warn some campers about an approaching forest fire.

REBA'S SUMMER JOB AS a forest ranger had been the perfect complementary learning experience for her environmental science

312

studies at the University of California, Berkeley. This had been her second summer working as a ranger, and she'd loved every minute of it.

Because of this season's budget restraints, cutbacks had been made, and all experienced rangers were patrolling the massive park alone. Each ranger had a walkie-talkie and a GPS beacon on their belts when on solitary expeditions–often far from the park office.

That fateful day, Reba had left her ATV and headed up the marked trail to the designated campsite. There had been reports that the fire started on the opposite side of the mountain near the base, presumably not putting the campers in imminent danger.

The report Rachael and her father received stated that when Reba reached the family of campers, they told her that while packing up the night before, some backpacking teenagers had stopped at their site. Apparently, the intruders had headed toward the peak with some food and beer they had stolen from them. The ranger told the group to go down the hill and wait for assistance by the ATV. Reba radioed the ranger station to inform them the family was safe and indicate where they could be picked up. She'd also advised the operator that she was pursuing an unregistered group of teens north of her location, promising to check in regularly.

Reba had labored upward through the dense forest, searching but never finding the second group of teens. During her efforts, the wind had shifted direction, quickly advancing the fire up the drought-stricken mountainside, trapping her near the summit. With no visible escape route, she'd quickly put her survival training to work. The young ranger had dug a hole big enough for a fetal-shaped body, using a small spade she'd had in her backpack. Then she'd covered herself with a thermal emergency blanket.

The parched landscape and dry foliage had provided plenty of fuel for the fast-approaching fire. The heat and smoke racing up the mountainside was later described as an inferno. The fire inspector speculated that Rachael's twin sister succumbed quickly to Forest Fire #249.

REBA'S SUPERVISOR, Steven Dolson, was apprehensive about allowing Rach to travel unaccompanied to the location of her sister's death. Rach's insistence forced him to reluctantly come up with an alternate plan. After filling a large backpack with everything he felt she might need for such a dangerous endeavor, he contacted the smoke jumpers and asked them to drop her as close to the area as possible.

Their evening flight left promptly at six to work on the now out-of-control Forest Fire #249, nicknamed "The Beast." The Beast was now fifty miles from Rachael's drop site, which was directly on the helicopter's route, so they agreed to shuttle an additional passenger. Steven restated his concerns, but Rach insisted it was something she needed to do for closure.

One of the smoke jumpers pointed out the marked area as they approached the blackened mountainside. It was a daunting sight, and a lump formed in Rach's throat. She managed to slip her sunglasses on before the tears started to percolate in her eyes. The sun had already set, so it was unlikely her move to camouflage her emotions fooled anyone. The pilot set the helicopter down expertly, and one of the men helped her leap to the ground and handed her the backpack.

"See you at eight a.m. tomorrow. Take care." She gave him a thumbs up.

Rachael hunched over, focusing on the ground as she moved cautiously forward. The large rotors accelerated, and the helicopter lifted in a tornado of dry leaves and branches.

When she thought it was safe to raise her head, she was surrounded by hundreds of charred poles. The once majestic, lush leafy trees, with fragrant foliage blanketing the ground beneath them, were no more. Only the pungent smell of burned wood lingered in the air.

She was all alone now. Dusk was closing in around her, but she was able to see the red-staked area Steven told her about, about one hundred and fifty feet up the mountainside. Burdened with her backpack and heavy heart, she walked slowly toward the location. Tears rolled down her cheeks, and her throat started to constrict, making it hard to swallow. The chill that she'd experienced a week ago, at the moment of Reba's death, came back to encase her body like an Egyptian sarcophagus. Her legs weakened as if inhibited by her internal emotional collapse. Nearing her destination, she fell to her knees, weeping uncontrollably.

With the location of her twin's death in view, the realization of never seeing her again felt unbearable. With clenched fists, she pounded the ground, but the physical pain could not make the gut-wrenching agony subside. Ravished with grief, she crawled to the taped area, lay down on the cold ground between the stakes, and closed her swollen eyes.

WHEN RACH OPENED HER eyes, night was now completely upon her. She stared up at the clear starlit sky. From this mountain vantage point, it was breathtaking. She had no idea how long she'd been pondering the many reasons she had come to this place; her mother's struggle with asthma, her sister's declaration to improve the environment and the camping trips she had taken with her father and Reba. The campsite was not set up yet, but lying there, staring up at the mesmerizing vastness of the universe, she felt at peace.

From the corner of her eye, she could see the moon coming up in the east, but her focus remained on the overhead marvel for a couple more minutes. As she turned her head back toward the rising moon, she suddenly realized something. She wasn't alone.

There was a wolf about twenty feet from her. The gray silhouette cast a long shadow from the moonlight at its back. The wolf sat with its front paws vertical, looking straight at her.

Not wanting to startle the animal, Rach remained motionless for what seemed to her an eternity. The wolf looked very gaunt, and its fur appeared to be scorched, but it was hard to be sure how badly in the dim moonlight. Its small size made Rach think it most likely was a female, which raised an alarming question. Where was the alpha male? The creature's eyes continued to focus on the intruder. Surprisingly, its demeanor seemed docile and curious, not what Rach expected from a wild animal.

She sat up slowly, feeling more pity than fear for the poor thing. She gradually reached into her backpack, looking for some food. Scant pickings in a vegetarian's bag for a carnivore, Rach speculated. Her drive to be a vegetarian was more about the carbon footprint of raising animals for consumption than animal rights issues. At this moment, she wished she'd made a different culinary choice, at least for this trip. She located the one thing that some would consider non-vegetarian. A hungry wolf was an unlikely candidate to enter that debate. Breaking the cheese block into several chunks created little reaction from the wolf. However, when she stood up, it also stood and started walking gingerly toward her. As the wolf came closer, the extent of its injuries became more apparent. Her left hind quarter was scorched bare, and she walked with a limp favoring the right paw. Around her neck was what Rach believed to be a GPS tracking collar. As the pitiful creature drew nearer, Rach's heart raced, and she seriously considered running away. Suddenly, the apprehension of being so close to this wild animal vanished, and compassion replaced her fear. Rach sat on a stump, encouraging her unlikely companion to sit beside her. The wolf took the cheese gently from her outreached hand and sat down at her feet, content as a pet dog sits by its master.

Seeing the burned skin and deep gash on its leg, Rach wondered if this once magnificent animal would survive. Rach cautiously stroked its back. Big golden eyes looked despairingly up at her. The hours passed and breathing became more labored for the waning wolf. Rach didn't understand the overwhelming connection that had come over her. It was as if she could feel its pain. She lay down next to her mountain companion, and they slept.

Rach awoke to the sound of the approaching helicopter. Startled by the sudden break in silence, she frantically jumped to her feet and looked around the site. The area was empty. Last night's companion was nowhere to be seen.

A weary-looking smoke jumper exited the chopper to provide boarding assistance. The black smoke-coated face of her escort looked at her backpack.

"I see you're all packed and ready to go. I hope you had a peaceful night."

She didn't feel like getting into a long explanation about how she never actually unpacked. Extending his hand, he boosted her up into the chopper. He threw her backpack behind his seat and jumped in. The helicopter lifted vertically, then moved horizontally over the desolate forest.

Rach was surprised to see Steven sitting in the rear passenger seat. She put on her headset.

"What are you doing here? Are they transporting you somewhere as well?"

The ranger explained that he'd been worried about her all night and tagged along to make sure she'd come through the experience unscathed.

"I felt bad after you left, and I just couldn't stop thinking about you. It must have been very lonely, and I am guessing quite scary. Before I went home for the night, I noticed wolf *R* was roaming the area. I hope she didn't give you a fright. Of course, she wouldn't have bothered you in a tent."

"No," said Rachael with an internal smile. "It was a peaceful night, and I got my closure. My sister mentioned you weren't supposed to, but often gave the wolves a name. Did wolf R, have a name?"

Steven's eyes were filled with emotion. "I called her Reba."

RACHAEL'S LOVE OF KIDS sent her in a different career direction than her twin chose. She became a teacher. Thanks to her Korean mother's encouragement, she learned to speak Korean fluently. After graduating teacher's college, she did a two-year teaching assignment in Seoul Korea and volunteered at the Winter Olympics. She thought it a thrill to witness the world engaged in a focused, peaceful demonstration of their athletic skills. By-way of social media, she was able to organize a get together for teachers attending the games. They spent evenings chatting with old and new acquaintances and over time, started an association between their schools.

They called it the Worldwide Network of Teachers for Change. Rach was grieving the loss of her sister shortly after she returned home from Korea and lost touch with the group.

Recently that she had applied for a job at one of the local middle schools.

RACH WATKINS SAT ACROSS from Principal Skynyrd, who was giving her his standard new teacher welcome speech. His over-sized backside was snuggly wedged in the wooden armchair behind his old well-worn desk.

"Welcome to our academy of learning, Ms. Watkins. May I call you Rach?" His words sounded somewhere between sarcasm and disdain.

"You may."

"Excellent! This is an inner-city school, and most of our students come from what you would call poor to lower-middle-class families. As such, they have a host of external issues and challenges that you would be best advised to stay clear of. You can't change their circumstances, so don't beat yourself up trying." The words came out from under his Ned Flanders mustache, sounding more like warnings than professional advice.

He wore a dark brown suit that probably looked good on him, thirty pounds ago. The straining buttons appeared to be holding but could easily have turned into projectiles at the slightest wrong move. Rach wondered whether he'd been a dedicated, caring teacher at the start of his career. There was no evidence of it today.

"I see you're teaching Science and English, good solid subjects. Don't worry too much about following the prescribed curriculum. No one expects our students to score high in the standardized test-ing." A nasty frown came over his face as he looked up from his desk.

"Ms. Watkins, there will be times when you feel more like a babysitter than a teacher. Whatever you do, don't let them pull you down to their level. Send the problem ones my way. I'll deal with them."

When he stood, his chair followed him up a couple inches, then crashed to the floor. Rachael assumed, hoped actually, this meant their meeting was over.

"One more bit of advice. If you want to have any hope of getting their attention, collect their damn cell phones at the door. Welcome, and good luck." He led her to the open door.

The less than satisfying experience ended, and Rach left the office without having asked any of her list of ten questions. She concluded that she was on her own.

Rach arrived at her classroom forty minutes before class to review the unfamiliar class schedule. It appeared that she had double science classes on Mondays, Wednesdays, and Fridays in this room. The rest of the week was filled in with regular-length English classes, scattered throughout the school in different classrooms.

The kids started to file in without acknowledging her presence or missing a word in their conversations. Rach was a little intimidated by their amplified laughter and nonchalant demeanor. These kids were definitely a far cry from her uniformed, disciplined, and always respectful Korean pupils. Some thirty boisterous students slowly made their way to the science lab stations. The loud bell had little impact on stifling their conversations. Nor did they look away from their cell phones.

"Class, my name is Ms. Watkins. I am looking forward to what I hope will be an engaging experience for all of us." She mustered her loudest voice, in hopes of getting their attention.

The noise level went down considerably, but there were still some low-level conversations going on that she ignored. The blinds had already been pulled down, so when she flicked the light switch off, the room fell into complete darkness. It also went quiet. She flicked on the overhead projector, and the picture of a large glacier under the arctic sun shone on the screen. It was so brilliant, it lit up the whole room.

"This magnificent, natural phenomenon is dying. If things don't change, your grandchildren will never have the opportunity to see this view in anything other than pictures." She switched the picture to a sequenced collage of historical satellite photos of the previous area.

"This is what it looked like in 1968, and this is what it looked like in 1975, in 2005, and in 2012. And this is what it looks like today. This iceberg has receded by some 65 percent in the last fifty years. What do you think has caused this?"

She flicked the light on, which caused the students to fidget restlessly.

"Anybody? Come on! Let's get the dialogue rolling. It's going to be a long semester if you have to listen to me talk for eight hours every week."

A girl in the back raised her hand and meekly suggested, "Global warming?"

"Excellent answer! Global warming, or as we refer to it now, climate change. The climate is changing, but why? Anyone?"

The same girl hollered, without raising her hand, "Pollution!"

"Yes! But from what source?"

A boy in the front row raised his hand. "My dad says it's a natural cycle of nature."

"Could be. What do the rest of you think?" Rachael kept prodding.

Answers started rolling out as the exchange accelerated enthusiastically from every corner of the classroom.

One of the students rattled off a list, "Factory smokestacks, cars, trucks, power plants, buses."

From the back of the room, a loud-voiced jokester yelled, "Cow farts."

The class broke into uncontrollable laughter.

"Yes! As funny as that sounds, he is correct."

A tall well-groomed girl raised her hand. "Ms. Watkins, this is science class, not environmental studies. Why are we talking about this?"

"That's a great question. If we're going to understand pollution, we need to understand the science of how it's created. So, if we're going to fix it, we need to understand the science behind our solutions. We can go back to the prescribed curriculum if you want, but I was thinking we could work together to bring science into the real world. Your world."

"That sounds good, but what is the curriculum? I usually read ahead." A heavyset girl confessed.

A loud "moo" came out of the cow fart boy at the back of the classroom. Rach ignored his outburst, making a mental note to speak to him later.

"How about we write the curriculum together?" The room went silent, and the students looked from one to another, confused by the suggestion. Rach let the thought settle into their minds. Deciding their own curriculum was surely a new concept they were not accustomed to.

"Think about it, and we'll talk about it later. Right now, I want to stop pointing and start calling you by your names."

She walked over to a girl in the front row.

"I don't see your cell phone. Where is it?"

"It's in my backpack. I don't use it in class."

"I don't know why you wouldn't. It's a useful tool if used correctly."

Looks of shock were visible on every face in the room.

"Okay. Who has a cellphone?" Almost every hand raised.

"Good. Get them out and take a selfie. Use Edit to print your name on it, then text it to the number on the board. Please share your phone with those who don't have one. Give me a couple of minutes to review your responses. After it's sent, go ahead and check your messages or emails while you're waiting."

She checked each of the responses quickly and looked out over the classroom to verify she had full compliance.

"It looks like I have everyone's picture and name. That's great. It's nice to meet you, Mr. Donny Trump. Glad you could join us." She shook her head and chuckled.

The classroom broke out in loud laughter again.

"I see a couple other suspicious-looking names, but no worries. I already have a class list of your real names. Mr. Trump, should I address you by your alias, or would you prefer Donny?" The room filled with laugher again.

"One important point before I chat with each of you individually." She raised her voice slightly, hoping for their full attention. "We have had some good laughs today, and I encourage you to keep things light. Laughter is a great outlet, and I have no issue with you joking around. Only caveat I have is, please do not disrespect any of your classmates. In other words, no jokes at anyone else's expense. Agreed?" Rach heard mumblings and hoped for their cooperation. "Thanks, everyone!"

THE NEXT WEEK, WHEN Rach entered the classroom, she noticed there was significantly less chatter and even a few, "Good Morning Ms. Watkins."

The first thing she did was introduce herself to every student, addressing them by name.

"Over the weekend, I used my student list to connect your face to a name. Since then, I have spent some time searching you out on the internet."

Their faces grimaced, and their eyes widened in shock.

"In the past, I have found this to be a mutually beneficial technique. In order to be a better teacher, it's important to me to know as much about each of you as possible.

There was some talking and huffing of disgust flying around the room when she finished, but she did notice a few understanding faces smiling back at her.

They were halfway through a two-hour, double class and recessed for a fifteen-minute break. Everyone returned promptly.

"Class! During this class, our phones will be your primary research tool. "For your first assignment, I want you to individually research one way humankind is impacting the environment negatively. By negatively, I mean changing its natural course of progression in a way that affects any or all life forms on this planet. Please make your choices based on what interests you and something you want a better understanding of. After making your choice, do some digging. Find out details around the source, mitigations underway or contemplated, impacts, quantities, growth rates, et cetera. You can email me your responses by the end of the class. On Wednesday, we are going to review your answers as a group and have a lively debate on the relevance of each. Out of that debate, as a unified group, we're going to develop the course outline. Take it seriously. Your responses to this assignment could determine your learning destiny for the next four months."

WHILE WAITING FOR DINNER to cook, Rach checked her emails. Much to her surprise, she'd received responses from every student in the class. Some were better than others, and some didn't come until later in the day, but 100 percent response, nonetheless. She corralled her father at the kitchen table after supper.

"Rach, this is amazing. I think you are doing good work here, and I know Reba would be proud to see you taking up her gauntlet like this."

"Thanks, Dad."

"Some are way out there, but I see some really good ones like, water shortages, smoggy air, poor packaging choices, herbicide and pesticide use. So, what's the next step?"

"Well! I'm expecting a lively debate during our discussion on Wednesday. They'll probably use their competitive instincts to defend their own opinions, so the challenge is going to be in uniting them in one direction."

Rach finished organizing the submissions into one document to be used on the computer projector. She was watching her dad out of the corner of her eye, and noticed he looked a little less melancholy tonight. Perhaps the time had come to share her experience on the mountain with him.

"Dad, can we talk? I have something I want to tell you." She was as nonchalant as she could be, under the circumstances. She gave him a detailed description of everything that had transpired that evening on the mountain, including the wolf encounter and the intimacy and comfort she experienced with the animal.

Her dad was very attentive through the long, detailed story, but his eyes opened wide on hearing the name given to the wolf wearing the *R* tracker collar.

"Really? He named her, Reba? After our Reba?"

He sat in deep thought for a minute or two before speaking.

"Rach, I think throughout our lives, we see, hear, and feel things that can't totally be explained. Most choose to ignore or dismiss the occurrences. I believe you should open your mind and accept them as legitimate signs or wake-up calls."

"Funny you should say that. On the drive back, I experienced an epiphany of what my life's work is going to be." She stood for effect, bent forward, and put her hands on the table looking her father square in the face.

"I'm going to use my skills as a teacher to create a paradigm shift in the way that the next generation looks at the environment. They are our best hope for the future."

"I think your encounter with, let's call her "R," really got to you. Was it a sign? Who knows? If you feel that strongly about those feelings, I think you should go for it. I know you will accomplish great things, whatever you do.' He gave her a hug, excused himself, and headed to bed.

The Wednesday discussion was every bit as lively as Rach had anticipated. It was great to see the enthusiasm and transformation in her students. Some of their debating sounded more like arguments. Nonetheless, the new curriculum was hammered out, and a consensus was reached.

A lanky brunette with pink-framed glasses raised her hand in the air.

"Yes, Jeannie."

"We have been talking, and we don't want to just learn about the environment, we want to start doing something about it. We've done a little digging, and we see your environmental interests are linked to losing your sister in a forest fire. Can you tell us more?"

Rach was caught off guard. It never occurred to her that they would look into her online presence as she'd looked into theirs. After deliberating in her own mind, she decided there were lessons to be learned here. This was going to be tough, and she hoped she could keep her emotions in check. She took a deep breath in, then slowly let it out.

"Okay, I'm going to share something very personal with you. Only because I feel it is relevant to our environmental science studies." Rach gave a very brief summary of Reba's death, trying to keep focus on the environmental impacts that were making the forest fires more frequent and more intense. She did include some abridged details of her wolf encounter because she knew it would have an impact on their recollections going forward. As she told the story, she could see the immersive effect she was having on the room.

"In summary, my sister's death had a huge impact on my life. I'm curious though. What was it you ladies were interested in doing, Jeannie?"

"Well, some of us girls were brainstorming last night, and we thought about the impact it could have if we started an environmental movement here in this school, and maybe use your Teachers for Change group to help spread it out all over the world. We know it would be a huge undertaking and wondered what you'd think."

"I think you might be on to something, but it's going to take a lot of time and effort from all of us to start a movement like that. Let's begin small, see what we can get up and running right here in this school first. I commend you on your vision. Most people your age, aren't that forward thinking. Having a strategic direction will help us develop the foundation for growth."

Aka Donny Trump suggested they have a wolf as a mascot. "We could call our movement REBA."

Rach's heart stopped momentarily, and she fought to hold back her emotions from her students' benevolent united approval.

Grabbing a tissue from her purse, she forced a grateful smile.

"Thank you, Donny. I love your idea." She wiped her cheek.

Donny looked as if he felt very proud of himself, having pleased his teacher.

"Cool! Now we just have to come up with words to represent each letter, R, E, B, A."

"An acronym! That sounds like a great idea. We will definitely come back to that another day. Right now, we're working on our environment. I want you to text me the things you want to do that will change things for the better, right here in your school. I'll mirror them to the TV monitor."

A long list of possibilities began popping up on the TV.

- Organizing tree planting in the community.

- Removing all soda vending machines from schools, replacing them with reusable water containers and water fountains.

- Adjusting classroom temperatures 1 degree.

- Organizing ride-sharing programs for students who live farther away from the school and cannot bicycle.

- Rainwater collection for landscape irrigation around the school.

- Preferred parking for students and teachers with electric cars.

- More classes conducted remotely on a biweekly basis, to prevent crowding.

- Conducting all schoolwork on tablets, including testing.

- Rolling out more community-based green days organized by students.

- Meatless Mondays. Animals fart methane.

- Installing beehives in some city-owned sections of property that are not commonly used by the public.

- Planting flowers to increase proliferation of butterflies.

- Petitioning cities for more green space and protection of public parks.

- Weed digging days in the schoolyard to illuminate the use of chemicals.

- Vegetable gardens in school yards and public city property.

The room went quiet. It seemed they'd run out of ideas.

"Wow! That's an impressive list. I must say, some of these ideas are quite ingenious. On Friday, we'll start looking at ways to implement some of them. A lot of these suggestions only require some attitude adjustment. Unfortunately, that can be one of the hardest obstacles to overcome."

Nancy jumped up, waving her hand at the teacher.

"Attitudes would be a great A-word in REBA."

The bell rang, ending the double period. No one moved.

"Ms. Watkins, do you mind if we stay longer and work on the acronym now?" Judy was tugging at her too-short skirt.

"Well, if there is enough interest?"

A series of yeses and count me ins affirmed there was an abundant amount of interest.

"All right, throw out some ideas, and I'll start another list on the screen."

Environmental, Eco, End, Ecosystem, Everyone.

"Okay. Let's get some R-words."

Rid, Reject, Remove, Rescue, Repel Reason, Reasonable.

"Anyone have a B-word?"

Suggestions flew at her like darts at a Rotary Club tournament.

Better, best, beginning, behavior, breath, breakdown, believer, banish, bubble, boomerang, brotherhood, breakdown.

"Now, let's see if we can put something together. I think from our discussion so far, we all like Environmental and Attitudes, but that may change as we go forward. Let's start throwing out some other words that fit in."

And they were off again with more excitement than ever. This time, they just hollered them out.

"Replace Environmental Bad Attitudes."

"That's a good one."

"Remove Environmental Bad Attitudes."

"Another good one!"

One of the usually quiet students decided to join in with, "Remove Environmental Breakdown Attitudes."

"Reject Environmental Bad Attitudes."

"Powerful, I like it."

After several more imaginative ideas were thrown into the ring, they took a vote. After tallying the votes, the teacher announced the winning name.

"And the winner is! Your very first idea: Replace Environmental Bad Attitudes. This was a great discussion and a very constructive debate. Thanks everyone for participating. Great job! Now, you better get going before your parents start calling the school and I get in trouble. See you all Friday, and again, well done, everyone."

Donny was the first to start the high fives as the cheerful group exited the classroom. When the last high five was hit, Donny approach Rach at her desk.

"Ms. Watkins, at break we were all talking, and . . . well, we think you are the best teacher we've ever had." He offered her his raised hand. The slap of their high five echoed in the now-vacant room.

"Thanks, Donny, that means a lot to me. Now get out of here!"

Rach leaned back in her chair, reflecting on what had just happened. What a gratifying and exhausting day it had been. Walking in the classroom earlier, she'd had a lesson plan, but she could never have anticipated it ending like this. There was happiness and satisfaction in her heart that sent a warm sensation throughout her body. The missing piece to her life's mission was revealed by her students. A new movement was about to be born—REBA! It was in its infancy, but she was certain it would become a driving force for change. One Rebecca would have embraced wholeheartedly, if she was still alive.

Contestant 2
Harvey Mills: Cartoonist

Harvey Mills, coach of the Trojan football team, was sitting alone in the boys' locker room. The number 7 sweat-stained jersey on the bench beside him would never be worn by the team's star quarterback ever again. How could this have happened, and what could have been done to stop whatever it was that drove Chris to take his own life?

Chris was his son Jamie's best friend, and because he practically lived with them, Harvey considered him part of the family. Relentless guilt weighed heavy on his heart. For the past few days, he'd sensed himself slipping back into depression. Harvey was no stranger to the gut-wrenching pain of losing someone close. Over the last couple years, he had tragically lost two loved ones. Determined not to let the tormenting anxieties take hold of him again, he fought to pull himself back from the brink of a total breakdown. He closed his eyes and let his mind wander back in time.

JUMPING FROM THE HIGH-level barn rafters into the freshly filled hay mow provided the three brothers that adrenaline rush young boys crave. Sunday afternoon bike rides to the lake for fishing and swimming adventures would provide a break from his everyday routines. The daily chores of collecting eggs, feeding livestock and filling water troughs somehow never felt like a hardship. His dad, a short stocky man with a great sense of humor also had a flare for motivation. He used to tell his sons, 'Hard work builds character and laughter is good for the soul. And everything in moderation makes for a happy and healthy life."

From a very young age, Harvey showed a talent for drawing, usually cartoon characters. Any time he wasn't in motion, he would be drawing. Scrap pieces of paper, napkins, workbook covers, or the back of school assignments were often covered in his artwork. His middle school teachers encouraged him to include art in his high school class choices. His artistic passion was not encouraged nor discouraged by his parents, who thought it would never amount to anything more than a hobby, if that.

In high school, he was an accomplished athlete, earning him the leadership role as Captain of the football and baseball teams. His outgoing personality made him one of the most popular students on campus, never short of friends at his side. As a jock, he was unique amongst his peers, in that he always made time for anyone that approached him, regardless of their age, gender or social standing. Everyone looked up to Harvey.

It was a forgone conclusion that his oldest brother would take over the farm and that was fine with Harvey.

Expected to graduate with no more than average marks, the guidance counselor's advice was in line with his parent's thoughts. Harvey had begun his career as a millwright. For ten years, Harvey had traveled to remote job locations before settling down and marrying his high school sweetheart, Rita. To be close to home, he took a job in his chosen trade at a large local meat processing plant, where his hard work and dedication moved him up through the ranks and into the position of Maintenance Manager.

As a member of the Joint Health and Safety Committee, he was constantly looking for ways to improve plant safety. While he sat doodling, waiting for his shift to end, an idea came to him. What if he developed a series of comic strips that spoke to different elements of safety and accident prevention? To test his idea, Harvey sketched a funny picture that spoke to the issue of people walking past trip hazards. In most cases, issues like this were only recalled later, during the accident investigation. The health and safety manager loved the concept and insisted the humorous but meaningful comics be posted on walls throughout the plant. The impact was immediate. There was an increase in all types of potential hazards being reported to supervisors throughout the plant.

Over the next year, Harvey authored twenty new comic strips. The acceptance and excitement generated by the postings put safety front and center. Accident rates fell to the lowest level in the history of the plant. The program was implemented in all facilities of the multinational company with equal success. Everyone anxiously anticipated the next comic strip posting by Harvey Mills.

DADD

Life took an unexpected, tragic turn for Harvey. On his way home from football practice, his only son was struck and killed by a drunk driver. The loss of Jamie took Harvey and Rita to a dark place of depression and isolation. Realizing they were in trouble, Harvey searched for help. While reading the local Sunday newspaper, he saw an ad for a self-help group for people in bereavement. It was sponsored by a local funeral home. He and Rita attended a couple of meetings, but the group was primarily composed of people who'd lost older relatives, not children, so they stopped going.

Rita's grief was becoming so debilitating that her family doctor sent her for psychiatric counseling. She was immediately prescribed medication to help her cope with her grieving emotions. Harvey had no interest in psychiatrists or medication. He chose to suffer in silence, all the while searching for something that could help ease the pain of losing his son. A co-worker told Harvey about MADD, the Mothers Against Drunk Driving group.

Harvey called the chair of the local chapter, explained his situation, and followed up by attending a couple of their meetings. Out of his interaction with mostly mothers at the MADD meetings, he had an awakening. Men need help too! DADD, Dads Against Drunk Drivers seemed the perfect name for the group. His intention was not to compete with MADD, but to provide a male-specific group. He knew men tend to compartmentalize emotions internally and find it difficult to talk openly about their feelings. The research he found pertaining to his own issues explained that emotions get pent up internally, and if not released, can lead to long-term mental issues, heart attacks, and strokes.

Harvey posted an ad in the local newspaper, promoting DADD and received two calls. The three men met, reluctantly shared their stories with each other, and Dads Against Drunk Drivers was born. Using a similar format to MADD, the newly minted group flourished, even with its small member size. With his newfound purpose, Harvey found it a little easier to cope with his loss. *The Brandon Sun* ran a story on the group, which was then picked up by the *Winnipeg Free Press*. Harvey received some desperate calls from bereaved fathers in Winnipeg and knew he had no choice but to help with the formation of another chapter.

Forming a new chapter would be a demanding challenge, and he was torn between the desperate need in Winnipeg, two and a half hours away, and his personal priorities. Was there another option? Perhaps he could lead the new group in the evenings from home via video conferencing. He decided his attendance was important for the kickoff meeting.

During one of his drives home from work, it occurred to Harvey how he could capitalize on two goals. First, he could drop Rita off for a visit with her favorite aunt in Winnipeg. Maybe a familiar face and change of scenery would help with her depression and failing health. Then, he could attend the critical kickoff meeting of the new chapter in person and interact with the participants face to face.

During the Friday morning trip to Winnipeg, Harvey tried to engage Rita in conversation. The interaction was limited, with most of the dialogue one sided. Harvey desperately hoped Rita's jovial Aunt Mavis would be able to bring his wife out of her downward spiral.

After a superb supper, Harvey left Rita in the capable, loving hands of her aunt. When he walked into the Legion Hall, he stopped dead in his tracks, astounded at the size of the group. There were at least twenty men sitting in wait. He made his way to the podium, introduced himself, and welcomed the men to the first Winnipeg Chapter of Dads Against Drunk Drivers. An embarrassed flush came over him when the walls echoed with applause. Thankfully, his past experience leading large maintenance staff meetings quickly kicked in and gave him the reassured confidence he needed to deliver a motivational speech. After he'd finished, several of the men approached him, shaking his hand and thanking him for his inspiring talk. The meeting, to Harvey's assessment, went very well, and he was pleased with the inaugural start-up of the new chapter.

As he walked in the door of the cozy cottage-style house, he was greeted with a very despairing look from Aunt Mavis. Harvey's heart sank. He knew her bubbly personality and cheery nature did not achieve the desired effect they both were hoping for. Despite Rita and her aunt's close, life-long relationship, Mavis described a very strained and limited interaction between them while he was gone. Tears filled her eyes.

"It was as if I just spent two hours with a stranger."

Harvey understood only too well the worry and concern he heard in her voice. He thanked her for her hospitality and assisted his wife to the car.

Blowing snow swelled over the highway as they made their way back home. The blanket of white surrounding the car epitomized Harvey's world closing in around him. He felt like a mouse in a live trap with no way out. For most of the trip, Rita sat motionless and silent, oblivious to the merciless winds and snow. Tired and emotionally drained from the long day, Harvey was thankful for the blue flashing light of the snowplow to follow. Rita's head dropped to her chest, and she slept the rest of the trip.

Over the next couple weeks, there was little or no change in Rita's emotional state, even her passion for quilting had vanished after Jamie's death. Harvey took a family emergency leave of absence from work to tend to his wife's increasing needs. Arrangements for home care to come once a week afforded him the opportunity to take a break and attend the Brandon DADD chapter monthly meeting. But that night, he received a call from the agency telling him that no one was available. He'd keep the meeting short.

Harvey was a bit surprised to see only one other member show up. He'd kept the meeting date on the calendar, recognizing Christmas can be a trying time of year for people coping with the loss of a loved one.

After the short half-hour meeting, he stopped at Tim Hortons to get the seasonal peppermint latte Rita loved, in hopes of making her smile. He missed her smile. They used to have such fun together, sharing every aspect of their lives. All their friends thought of them as the perfect couple.

He entered the house, bellowing, "Ho! Ho! Ho! Santa has brought a special surprise for you."

The living room was dark, and the bedroom door was closed. It was never closed. A cold shiver ran up Harvey's spine as his sweating palm reached for the doorknob. Every nerve in his body tensed as the knob turned. Slowly, he opened the door inwards, squinting to see into the darkness as he moved toward the bed. The glow from the full moon shone through the sheers, giving just enough light for him to see his wife's profile. Rita was sitting upright, her back against the headboard, and her feet outstretched on the bed, uncovered. Harvey moved closer and whispered, "Honey, I'm home." He was hoping for a response that would immediately wash away his fears. There was none. He turned on the night table lamp.

The latte dropped from his hand, splashing his legs as it erupted on the floor. He sank to his knees and wrapped his arms around his wife's cold legs, crying uncontrollably. His life had just taken another dark, horrible turn.

It was a fast spiral downward into a nervous breakdown that followed. Certainly, this was not unexpected after the loss of two close family members.

The following two-month stay in the psychiatric hospital was very difficult for Harvey. The treatments offered little help at first but did ultimately have some impact. The deep depression had eased, and he was coping, but far from his normal self. It felt good to be released, but now what? He was on long-term medical disability leave from work, which stated his official diagnosis as "Stress Reaction." He was told he could expect the disability checks for two years max. After that, it was a forgone conclusion that he would retire.

The DADD organization had flourished in his absence. He was a welcome sight when he returned to his first meeting after Rita's death. Thankfully, the group knew not to ask the stupid questions or provide generic condolences most well-meaning people felt obligated to offer. Over the next few months, Harvey took up his leadership role, traveling to Winnipeg monthly to help where he could. DADD expanded across Canada, with Harvey as the key driver of its success. He was elected the chair of the board and continued to be the primary managing force of the organization. A regular person would likely find it odd, but Harvey still needed more in his life.

During his son's short time on the Vincent Massey football team, he was a part-time, assistant coach. He missed the satisfaction he got from helping the boys learn their skills. It had been rewarding. The memories of those good times started to lift his spirits, so he decided to stop in and see the principal. Maybe there would be an opportunity for him to volunteer. The long-tenured principal remembered Harvey and recalled the boys' admiration for their assistant coach.

Fortunately, the timing couldn't have been better, the full-time coach had taken seriously ill and would not be returning this year. To Harvey's great surprise, he was offered the Head Coach position, starting immediately. The next day, he was standing on the football field, providing guidance to an eager group of boys trying out for a position on his team. A new adventure began, and Harvey's life was finally taking a positive turn.

The previous coach never did return, and over the next couple years, Harvey was able to put together a championship team.

A remarkable season of wins culminated into a trip to Quito, Ecuador. where they played in the World High School Football Tournament. The tournament turned out to be the least memorable part of the trip. Near disaster had almost cut their trip short.

Their plane had caught fire while preparing to land at Quito Airport. If not for the quick action of Harvey's well-disciplined team helping passengers escape, lives might have been lost. The team and Harvey were hailed as heroes, and their story received worldwide recognition. The media jumped on the human-interest aspect of Harvey's tragic life and made him an overnight celebrity.

• • • •

BACK IN THE LOCKER Room

His walk down memory lane did little to provide answers to his questions. Nor did it relieve the agony of losing his son, his wife, and now Chris. He clenched the jersey in his hands, held it to his chest, and bowed his head.

"I'm so sorry, Chris. I didn't know."

Just before he gave in to a full-blown breakdown, he heard a gentle knock on the door. There was a chafing creak as the locker-room door was pushed open.

"Coach! Are you in there?" A familiar female voice called out.

Harvey tapped into the depths of his soul to pull himself together enough to respond. "Yes, I'm in here."

"It's Angel, Chris's girlfriend. May we come in?"

He wiped his eyes and cleared his throat.

"Yes, I'm the only one here."

Three girls entered the boy's changeroom and sat down on the well-worn wooden bench across from the coach. The girls had always found Harvey very approachable, and they'd talked to him about many issues, some of which bordered on the edge of Harvey's comfort zone. The unique coach, player, and player's-girlfriend relationship inspired them all to have respect and compassion for one another.

Angel, Chris's bereaved girlfriend, remained quiet, while the head cheerleader, Cheryl, stood.

"Coach, we're in crisis and have nowhere else to turn for help. I know you're going to ask. So, yes! We have talked to our parents, guidance counselors, grief counselors, and even a minister. We thought you might understand what we're feeling, as you're so close to the boys and us."

Harvey maintained his composure while second-guessing his decision to let the girls come in. He knew they'd have questions he couldn't answer.

"We're all cried out, grieved out, and very angry. We want this problem to be taken seriously before we lose another student." At five foot ten, Cheryl towered over Harvey with a demanding look on her face.

Harvey looked at the three determined, wide-eyed faces staring at him. He wasn't sure how to respond.

Emma, the third cheerleader, broke the silence. "This is the second student suicide this year, and there was one last year too. No one is doing anything to stop it . . ." Her voice trailed off in a hard choke, barely getting the last word out.

"Coach, we're hoping you'll know what to do. Please! Can you help us with this? You're our last hope," Cheryl pleaded, her hands together, tapping her chin.

"We're begging you. There has to be an answer!" Emma was close to tears.

The girls joined hands and sat waiting for his response.

Somewhat unnerved by the directness of the girls, the coach impulsively replied, "You're right. I'll find some answers." Harvey was shocked at his own knee-jerk reply. His heart reacted to their pleas with the answer they needed to hear.

"Give me a couple days to come up with a plan of action." He wanted answers just as much as the girls did, but he doubted any existed.

The girls' expressions immediately changed from desperation to relief. They jumped up and gave Harvey a group hug.

"Thank you, Coach," "Thanks, so much, Coach," "You're a Saint," "We love you, Coach Mills."

Harvey sat there a little dazed, listening to their grateful words and wondering. *What have you done? How am I going to explain to these hopeful girls that answers to difficult questions don't always exist?*

Harvey gave them a composed smile, which he hoped masked the internal storm of regret churning inside him. Without a word, he stood and made a quick exit. Hoping to quiet his pounding head, he went outside for some fresh air.

He spent that night tossing and turning. The girls' pleading words played over and over in his head. At four in the morning, the inner turmoil erupted into a dry heaving event in the bathroom.

IT WAS LATE AUGUST, and the mosquitos were thankfully gone, allowing Harvey to enjoy his morning coffee outside, free of their annoyance. Sitting on his back-porch swing, he let his mind wander.

It had been three years since he'd sat in this very spot, fretting about the locker-room meeting with the frustrated girls, when from nowhere, like a wave shocking an unsuspecting swimmer, an inspirational idea had hit him. He could develop a booklet of cartoons to prepare students for what life would be like in high school and what to do when pressures mount, and stresses lead toward depression.

Three hectic years later, the little pocketbook of comic strips was readily available in hundreds of high schools. The impact had been extraordinary. The scenes depicting life in high school were the perfect blend of humor and much-needed orientation. The easy read provided the students with thought-provoking ideas on how they might find their place in this new, sometimes difficult environment.

Harvey was the author and comic strip illustrator, but the issues went far beyond his understandings and depth of knowledge. He included an honorable mention page, thanking all the contributors for their support and help: guidance counselors, youth sociologists, psychiatrists, parent-teacher organizations, and most importantly, the students.

Due to the overwhelming popularity of the first booklet, requests poured in for other themes. The list of different subjects displayed on the fridge provided inspiration and purpose to his life. Harvey proudly checked each one off as it was published.

- Bullying
- Social media stresses
- Making the most of high school years special interest programs
- Popularity
- Intolerance
- Racial identity
- Physical appearance and body shaming
- Family issues, divorce, and violence
- Gender identity and sexual pressure
- Varying levels of maturity
- Personal identity: where do I fit in?
- "A"-listers and hierarchy perceptions
- Peer pressure, smoking, sex, and drugs
- Self-discipline and taking responsibility for your own destiny
- Sibling rivalry
- Home, school, work, and social balance

The doorbell rang at nine, sharp. Harvey opened the door and greeted his assistant, Angel, and her little boy.

Losing her boyfriend Chris to suicide was devastating but finding out she was pregnant added a whole second layer of pressure on the poor girl's shoulders. Christopher Jr. was almost three years old now and added a welcome handful of childhood antics to Harvey's workday. Angel organized the daily activities and managed the finances of the budding publishing company. Harvey did all the heavy lifting and shipping on top of his drawing.

They were distributing the little handbook both in hard copy and electronic formats to an estimated 60 percent of the high schools

FAYE & GEORGE CHAMBERLAIN

in North America. The book was experiencing remarkable acceptance in England, Australia, New Zealand, and just this week, a ship-
ment was sent to South Africa. It seemed the humorous comic strip
messages had universal appeal. The worldwide acceptance was wonderful, but now inquiries were coming in for translated versions.

So far, the proceeds of the book paid Angel's wages and their
overhead costs. The publishing costs were kept as low as possible to
put the little notebook in as many adolescent hands as possible. Getting rich had never been Harvey's plan; this was a mission of love for
both of them.

"I'm concerned with going global. Humor doesn't always come
across the same in different cultures. I believe the desire for, or the
enjoyment of, humor is universal, but the interpretation and delivery
can vary immensely. The newspapers hire political cartoonists who
seem to be the best at it. Maybe we should consider hiring a pro."

"You're the one with the funny bone, so I'll let you deal with the
hiring of cartoonists. Personally, I think you're pretty talented."

Angel had set up a meeting with a representative from a newspaper publishing company, and he was coming today.

"Angel, I'm a little apprehensive about meeting with this big
company. So far, this has been just our little self-controlled enterprise. I'd hate to lose it to a huge conglomerate."

Angel started organizing some of Harvey's works, along with the
financial ledgers. "I agree totally. Let's hear him out anyway. We can
decide later if this is something we want to pursue."

At the prearranged time, Harvey opened the door to accept his
visitor. The surprised look on his face must have been evident. The
unexpected man at his door was the owner of Fisher Publishing. P. J.
Fisher was a well-known Canadian businessman and philanthropist.
Harvey wasn't sure whether he was on the top-ten list of wealthiest
Canadians, but he was up there for sure. P. J. was from third-genera-

tion money and as close to an aristocrat as you could get, this side of the ocean.

"I am very pleased to meet you, sir." Harvey was so excited, he feared he might slur his words. He turned his head and brought Angel forward, with Christopher at her side.

"I'd like you to meet my office manager, Angel, and her right-hand man, Christopher." Harvey was relieved that he was able to insert humor into the strained introduction. It was his go-to thing, when confronted with any stressful situation, but this was a more stressful situation than most.

The tall man crouched and shook the little boy's hand. "Very pleased to make your acquaintance, young man."

P. J. Fisher was a slim, distinguished, and handsome man of six foot six, with wavy gray hair. He possessed a commanding presence that could be intimidating at first glance. He seemed well aware of his impact on people and moved very quickly to put his hosts at ease. "Mr. Mills. Can I call you Harvey?"

"Yes of course, Mr. Fisher." Harvey realized he sounded a bit contrite after just being addressed as Mr.

"Please, call me P. J. And this guy here is my right-hand man, Bill."

"Pleased to meet you, Bill." Harvey shook his hand and walked them over to the sofa.

"Harvey, I feel like I am meeting an old friend. I've read your 'Little Handbook,' and I have to tell you—I love it. You are doing a great service to the young people of today with what I would describe as a little book with a giant message. I have to confess I have been following your journey into the world of publishing for quite some time. Bill has kept me up to date on your progress for the past two years. You have taken a small kernel of an idea and grown it into an international phenomenon. What you have accomplished with the resources you have at your disposal is absolutely astounding. I follow many new publishers from afar. You could call it an old man's hobby, I guess. My grandfather, Edward, started the Fisher Publishing enterprise. It is his pioneering spirit and drive to succeed that still lives in the Fisher Publishing Company DNA today. You have that same spirit, Harvey. I've been planning to get in contact with you for some time but held back. Frankly, it didn't look like you needed any help or advice. You can imagine my surprise when Bill came to me with Angel's letter forwarded from our local paper asking if it would be possible to have a meeting. I don't have papers in every country, but I sure as hell know people that do. So, what do you say? Shall we get this thing rolling?"

Harvey was taken aback by the cordially direct delivery of his proposal. He tried to get a bead on Angel's impression, but she was preoccupied with tying Christopher's shoe in the other room.

"Well, P. J., not to put too fine a point on it, but we actually were somewhat concerned about approaching your paper for help. We don't want to lose our identity and control of what, for us, is more of a labor of love than a source of profit. I hope I don't sound like a preacher, but we started this to make a difference, not a profit. Sorry if I'm being too blunt, but I'm just a regular guy being honest."

"Well, Harvey, my good man, I often wish people could be more straightforward with me at times, but this is not one of them." A long awkward pause came to an end when P. J. started laughing.

"I'm kidding. I apologize. I shouldn't do that. My wife says it's a bad habit to act serious and then laugh about it. Sometimes, I just can't help myself. I just love the look on peoples' faces. It never gets old. Here is what I am thinking! What you are doing is, as I said, a great service to the young people of the world. I see this as a non-profit endeavor that I want to support in any way I can. I will instruct my editors to make their cartoonists available for the translations as soon as possible, so consider that a done deal. As you know, all things come with a cost."

Harvey's body tensed as the clock behind him ticked. One, two, three seconds.

P. J. enjoyed watching people squirm; this was evident to Harvey, who was clearly no exception.

"Relax, Harvey. It's only going to cost you some time. I expect you to meet with me for dinner twice a year, my treat, and update me on how things are going. Are you ready to shake on it?" P. J. offered his hand.

Harvey snapped his forward, quick as a whip.

"Let's do it!"

P. J. laughed and starting walking toward the door, then turned into the adjoining room.

"Pleasure to meet you, Angel and Mr. Christopher." He gave a low wave to the boy.

"Harvey, I hope your passport is in order and you are available next week?"

Harvey stood with a dumbfounded look on his face.

"My associate will call you with all the details. I'd like us to meet with my editor in Poland to get this train on the tracks. Cheers!"

As P. J. Fisher walked out the front door, it felt as if a vacuum of charisma had just been pulled from the room. Harvey sat down and loudly exhaled, feeling like a coach who'd just won the Super Bowl. There was no doubt in his mind, small town football coach, Harvey Mills, had just met his new best friend. Who just happened to be a Trojan in the publishing world!

Contestant 3
Kenan Alazhari: Young Boy in Sudan

Kenan Alazhari was a slender dark-skinned fifteen-year-old boy, living on a small parcel of land outside Atbara, Sudan, in the Nubian desert. The bone-dry fields and lack of water to grow crops left his parents no other choice but to seek employment away from their friends and family. With anguish in their hearts, they left their son Kenan with his grandmother and relocated to the capital city of Khartoum to work in the struggling textile industry. Kenan stayed behind to care for his widowed grandmother and continue his schooling.

Kenan sat in the sweltering heat of the one-room school. Along with the hot desert air, flies found their way in through the small openings at the top of the cinder block walls. They circled the heads of the children, who took no notice as they worked at their desks. There would be the occasional *swish* or *smack* as the teacher used her flyswatter to scare the pests away. If she was quick enough, there would be one less.

From her table at the front of the class, Miss Neufield scanned the room. Every desk was occupied, forty-two at last count. Five desks across and eight desks deep, with two tagged on the last row. There was no definition between the ten grades in her charge, which made organizing daily tasks for each grade a challenge. Thankfully, the older children would assist her with the younger ones, freeing her time to spend with the those who needed supplemental assistance.

More often than not, Kenan was bored with his own lessons and would lend a hand. He was one of the more promising students. His teacher delighted in hearing about his ambitions to make a difference in his community and encouraged his dreams in any way she could. Fittingly, she challenged him with intriguing and inspirational tasks, often sending her prize student home with books on the environment, agriculture, and anything pertaining to research being done on water treatment. He told her he hoped to find a solution to the scarcity of water that plagued his and so many other local communities. It appeared that reading books had opened his mind to the many possibilities and opportunities this world offered to anyone who had the initiative to do something with them. The severe shortage of water plaguing his community was uppermost in his mind.

Miss Neufield looked at Kenan the same way his granny did, with pride and hope. They both told him to study hard and use his gift of intelligence to help others. Out of respect for them both, he intended to do just that.

With no eye-level windows to view the outdoors, there was nothing to distract Kenan from his thoughts that afternoon. Oblivious to his surroundings, a solemn look fell across his young face. It had been a rough morning. His lip started quivering as he remembered watching his frail granny trudge in aguish to and from the well. A tear rolled down his cheek. He brushed it away before anyone could see it. The defeated look on his granny's face that morning weighed on his mind.

The wind had blown strong, and the sun was unrelenting, slowing their progress as they'd made the two-hour walk to the well in Shendi. An arduous journey they were destined to make every day. The sand had pelted their faces and stung their eyes, with only their bare arms as a shield. The fine grains had felt like porcupine needles pricking in their pores. Hot and thirsty, they'd taken their spot in the long line of weary travelers, also there to collect fresh water for their families. After a boring but restful hour, they filled the four buckets with fresh water and placed them over their shoulders.

Today the walk back home had taken its toll on his grandmother. Halfway, she collapsed on one knee. Kenan had recognized the pain in her timeworn face as she'd struggled to get back up. He'd held her arm in his until she steadied. As he watched her walk on, her head hung down from the weight of the water buckets across her weakening frame. He noticed a tear roll down her dust-covered cheek. She looked so frail and tired. *What happened to the granny who used to play kick the can? Tell stories about the old days and race me to the outhouse?* He knew he had to do something . . . but what?

The old woman had made this tiresome journey to the well every day since the local well had dried up nine months ago. After his grandfather had passed from a sudden illness, her life was riddled with many hardships. Cataracts in both eyes impaired her vision, and the degenerating discs in her back were hindering her ability to move around and do chores. Nowadays, her movements were slower, and she grimaced with every step. The daily walk to the well was becoming more than her frail body could withstand. Kenan knew she hated being a burden on him. She knew he felt responsible for her because of the promise he had made to his parents before they left.

KENAN WATCHED AS A drop of sweat fell on his wooden desk, or was it another tear? It evaporated on the warm surface almost immediately. Salty sweat ran down his forehead, stinging his eyes. His shirt was dripping wet and hung heavy over his boney shoulders. When the beam of sunlight finally hit his desk, he was thankful. That meant it was almost time to head home. It wasn't that he didn't like school, quite the contrary. He considered it a privilege to be there, and he was eager to learn. But today, he was worried about his granny. The final bell rang, and all his classmates jumped to their feet. The skin on his legs stuck to the seat as he tried to stand. He winced as he peeled himself upright. With his mind focused on getting home, he hurried for the door.

Before he could make his escape, Miss Neufield called him over. She'd come across an article in a magazine she was certain would interest him. Kenan took the magazine and read the title, *World Water Projects*. He thanked her and headed out the door. There was a cloud of dust billowing behind him as he ran barefoot down the sandy road to his beloved granny. She would be waiting on the front step of the small shack Kenan called home.

His concern for her and the anticipation of reading his recent acquisition had his adrenaline flowing through his veins like a babbling brook after a rainstorm. His chores were over and done in record time that afternoon. His grandmother, who appeared to be rested from the morning walk, noticed how excited her grandson was and agreed to tidy up after supper. Kenan only had an hour or so of daylight left to read by.

The studious young boy scanned over the pages of the magazine, searching for the article Miss Neufield thought would interest him. He finally found something near the end of the issue. A Takoda Yazzi, the head of WWP was coming to Khartoum. Apparently, there was something of interest to him at the confluence of the White and Blue Nile Rivers. That night, Kenan read and reread each page until his eyes fluttered like the flame in the old oil lamp. When the candle went out, the room went dark, and he surrendered to sleep.

The next morning, the weather was much more tolerable. He bubbled over with enthusiasm on the way to the well, filling his grandmother in on the things he'd read the night before. The time went by quickly, despite the slower pace Kenan set for his granny's sake. Before they knew it, they'd arrived at the well. Kenan told his granny he was going to the market and would be back shortly.

There was only one phone booth in the main building. He was in luck. Only one person was at the phone, and they hung up just as he approached. The coins jingled as they fell into the coin box. Kenan pushed the numbers that would put him in touch with his parents.

"Hi, Mom, I only have enough money for a one-minute call. Can I visit on the weekend?" He asked hopefully.

"That would be wonderful! I'll pack a picnic lunch. Where can we meet you?"

"In the park, close to where the Nile rivers come together?"

"Sounds perfect. Love you, bye, bye."

"Bye, Mom. Love you too."

He was looking forward to seeing them, but even more so, he needed to meet Mr. Yassi.

SITTING ALONE ON THE porch the night before the big day, he gazed up at the twinkling blanket overhead. He pondered a life where food and water were plentiful. Where men, women, and children worked hand in hand to create a better world. Over the boy's head in the ebony Sudan sky, a falling star floated gracefully downward, disappearing into the horizon. Was this a sign? Kenan made his wish.

The boy was up at the rooster's first crow and on his way to the city before the sun crested the horizon. He couldn't wait to meet Mr. Yassi. With his knowledge of water, this could be the beginning of a new life for his family and his village. His dream might finally come true.

The sound of an approaching vehicle brought Kenan back to the reality of the dangers that lurked on these desolate roads. Not knowing if they were friend or foe, he threw himself into the ditch and laid motionless in the tall, dehydrated grass. He closed his eyes and prayed he would not be discovered. Two vehicles slowly rumbled past his hopefully barely discernible body, leaving curling clouds of red dust hovering over the stretch of road behind them. Kenan tucked his face in the crook of his arm to filter the descending dust. He was petrified of an unwanted sneeze or cough.

A gunshot rang out, echoing over the desert. It seemed only yards away from him. A cold chill of fear and panic rushed over him as he waited for the rebels to come down on him. Minutes passed, nothing happened, no pain, no angry faces peering down on him from the roadside. Instead, men's loud laughter erupted up on the road.

Five minutes passed, then ten. He lifted his head just enough to see down the road. It was clear. His big sigh of relief sent a puff of sand up his nose, and he sneezed. Kenan climbed out from his hiding spot and cautiously proceeded on his way.

There was a dead gazelle on the side of the road. Killed from a shot to the head. He closed his eyes and exhaled deeply. Fear of torture and death came to his mind. *That could have been me!* A cold shiver went down his spine, despite the extreme heat of the midmorning sun.

For the final hours of the trip, Kenan's mind flipped back and forth between fear of another encounter and anticipation of meeting Mr. Yassi. The image of the gazelle and his thought, *that could have been me*, kept his eyes and ears on high alert. Once in the city limits, he relaxed and headed straight for the park.

Cresting the hill, he saw the welcome blanket covered with an abundance of fresh fruit, breads, and cheeses awaiting his arrival. He was starving and could feel the saliva filling his mouth as he ran down the hill. His parents jumped up immediately at the sight of their son, plainly relieved he was safe and sound. He fell into their welcoming arms, and they all wept happy tears of joy.

The encounter with the rebels never entered the conversation over lunch. The boy felt no need to burden his parents with any more concerns about his well-being. He told them all about Takoda and pointed to the barricades set up by the rivers. They listened intently to his hopes and dreams of a better life for them and their village.

A large crowd gathered on the adjacent bank, and as much he wanted their visit to continue, his thoughts were elsewhere. Kenan couldn't restrain himself any longer. He hugged his parents, thanked his mom for the meal, and kissed them goodbye. With an apparent skip in his step, Kenan headed toward the goings-on across the river. As he reached the outer edges of the crowd on the other side of the river, he gave one last wave to his parents. Standing on his tiptoes, craning his neck, he tried to see over the reporters obstructing his view. Just as his ankles were about to give out, he heard someone in front of him call to Mr. Yassi. Kenan was determined to meet this man. With bull strength, he shouldered his way to the front of the crowd.

The picture in the magazine did not do justice to the height and stature of the figure towering in front of him. Staring up at the man with a gray ponytail, something Kenan had never seen the likes of, he felt small and insignificant. This was the moment he'd been waiting for.

Takoda must have noticed the stubborn look of determination on his face.

"Mr. Yassi! My name is Kenan. I read all about your research in this magazine." He pulled it out of his shouldered backpack and opened it to Takoda's story.

"I have come all the way from my village just outside Atbara to seek your advice." His pleading eyes were fixed on Takoda's.

"With all your research and experience with water, I was hoping you could help me. You see, sir, my village doesn't have any fresh water close by, so every day my granny and I have to walk six km's to a well and return home carrying the heavy buckets on our backs."

He was hoping his request wouldn't be dismissed by this man, who surely had better things to do than help a stranger. Let alone a young man such as himself. When Takoda offered his right hand, Kenan took a frightened step back.

"A pleasure to meet you, Kenan. This is Maddy. She's, my assistant."

The girl who appeared to be around his age smiled and offered her hand.

"Hi, Kenan. Where did you say you come from?"

Kenan told her he traveled many kilometers from his village outside of Atbara.

"You must be exhausted. Can I get you some water or something to eat?"

"No thanks. I just ate lunch with my parents. We try to meet once a month."

"They live here?" Maddy looked confused.

Kenan explained the reasoning behind their separation and turned to face Takoda. "I'm hoping you can help me find water in our village, so they can start farming, and we can all live together again as a family."

"You seem to be a very determined young man, and your willingness to help others is very commendable. I like that in a man." He placed a hand on Kenan's shoulder.

"I am a firm believer that one small act of kindness can make a big difference. Wouldn't you agree?" Takoda held a keen eye on the boy, as if watching his reaction.

"Yes, sir! I agree." He could feel the excitement welling up inside of him with every word Takoda spoke.

"This is an extreme challenge for a young person to undertake. Are you sure you are up for the task?" Takoda put one hand to his chin, squinting his dark eyes sternly down at him.

Kenan bobbed his head up and down several times.

"Yes, sir! I sure am!" He stood as tall and proud as he could.

"All right then, wait here with Maddy. I have an idea. It may take me a few minutes, but I will be right back after I find what I am looking for." He turned and walked over to the trailer and started digging through the equipment.

Maddy and Kenan chatted like best friends, probably because of their closeness in age. With a little coaxing from the pretty girl, Kenan went into detail about his community and their need for the everyday things most people take for granted. He told her the lack of water was the hardest thing to bear in their desert location. Maddy listened with a sympathetic ear as Kenan spoke of the hardship he and his community were enduring.

When Takoda returned, he was holding something similar to a large metal wishbone. He told the two kids it was called a divining rod.

"Follow me." A few feet away from the river, Takoda demonstrated the proper way to hold the apparatus. There was an immediate reaction. The rod, slowly bent down, toward the ground. The tall man with the gray ponytail explained that this was a possible indication of an underground source of water, fingering out of the river.

Kenan's eyes just about jumped out of his head. He could hardly keep his feet on the ground. Inside, his heart was jumping for joy. Was this odd-shaped rod the answer to his prayers?

Takoda clarified that it wouldn't always be that simple and mastering the art of dowsing would involve a lot of reading and even more practicing.

"You will need this to master your skill." He handed Kenan the divining rod and a stapled bundle of age-colored sheets of paper. I wrote this paper when I was in university, Kenan. You see, my people pass down ancient knowledge through word of mouth, from generation to generation. I thought it important to write down what the elders were telling me so it could be preserved for future generations.

I don't know for sure, but today I think I have found another reason. Perhaps our paths were destined to cross. I wish you all the success in your worthy undertaking.

"I thank you, sir. My family and my community thank you." Kenan bowed his head for a moment, then looked up into Takoda's eyes. "I will be forever grateful for your generosity and counsel. My granny and I have a small place outside of Atbara. It would be our honor to have you as our guest. You will never taste a more delicious goat stew than the one my granny makes."

Takoda and Maddy thanked him for the offer and wished the boy good luck.

Kenan made it home just before dark to find his granny in bed. Her breath was labored, and her strength diminished. Her voice too was labored and hard to understand. Apparently, on the way back from the well today, she was accosted by some rebels who took one of her jugs of water. They joked that they were just trying to lighten her load. Kenan was furious and even more determined to end this water hardship.

For the next couple weeks, he cared for his grandmother and did everything around the house, including the long trek to the well, leaving him little time to practice the art of dowsing.

Just before dusk, a neighbor spotted him meandering back and forth over the barren fields. He approached Kenan, questioning his peculiar behavior. With the enthusiasm of someone sharing a big secret, the boy explained the unique process of finding water. Realizing the importance such a discovery would mean to the community, Theodore, offered his family's services. Kenan accepted the offer and requested help with the care of his granny.

"If someone could bring us water, that would free up a considerable amount of my day to continue looking for water here."

The better part of the next morning Kenan spent walking back and forth in the new quadrant he'd staked out. First, he traversed horizontally and then vertically, pointing the rod to the ground as instructed in Takoda's writings. The recorded methods were clear but also warned of false positives. His heart jumped a couple times when the rod reacted, but each time when he retested, the rod remained motionless.

Midafternoon of day three was different. The rods reacted more violently than before. The area Kenan moved to, was a half kilometer due south of the village. Could this be it? Had he really found water?

The excited boy ran as fast as an Olympic sprinter to his neighbor's house.

"Theodore!" He tried to catch his breath. "I...think...I...found...water."

The village was suddenly abuzz with exited men grabbing shovels, picks, and buckets. The whole community descended on Kenan's marked location with the enthusiasm of bees to honey. The women screamed encouragement as the men dug.

The work went on late into the torchlit night. The women's screams had long since quieted, and fatigue was starting to show on the diggers' faces. No one had left, but some were complaining, and you could sense the doubt engulfing the group.

As the night turned to dawn, the sky glowed a crimson red and purple over the horizon. Some of the diggers stopped to take in the beauty of the moment.

As the red sky lost its color to the bright yellow morning sun, screams of the men in the hole broke the daybreak silence. Without warning, water came streaming into the hole, forcing the men to scramble to the surface.

The village celebration that followed could have put Mardi Gras shame. If the villagers were tired after their sleepless night, it was not showing in their enthusiastic dance and song. The bright colours of the traditional tribal costumes adorned the revelers, heralding the coming of a new prosperity to the village.

Kenan smiled and waved to his granny as he passed by on the shoulders of the village leaders. His grandmother's face beamed as she watched the celebration of her grandson's success from their porch.

The party went late into the night, finally going silent just after three in the morning.

Kenan lay in bed thinking of well stabilization and irrigation plans. Yes, tomorrow was going to be a new day.

The merciless crow of the rooster came too early for tired Kenan's liking. Apparently, the party didn't keep the king of the coop awake. Kenan rolled out of bed, rubbing his sleepy eyes, and headed to the kitchen to boil water for his granny's tea.

Strangely, the full cup was still there when he came in from doing his chores. She never slept this long. *Something's wrong!*

Nervously, he slowly pulled back the curtain hanging over the doorway of her room. She was lying on her back with her arms stiff at her sides. He stood there, listening for the wheezing sound of her breathing he was accustomed to hearing through the paper-thin walls. Nothing! The room was as soundless as a tomb. Kenan went to her side and checked for a pulse, even though he was certain she was gone. He bent and kissed her cold, weathered cheek, then covered her lifeless body with a sheet.

He sat at her side, holding her hand, letting his sadness bleed out of his eyes and run down his face. He was alone now. Only his memories of the strong, hardworking, selfless woman who spent her whole life looking after her family remained. Glancing around the dimly lit room, Kenan noticed something on the crate beside the bed. It was a note.

My dearest boy, in the event I do not wake to the morning sunrise, I want you to know how proud I am of you and your efforts to bring water to this barren land of ours. I believe with all my heart you are destined for more great things. Try not to mourn my passing. I had a full and satisfying life. Thank you for being you and for all the time you spent with me these last few years. I will always be with you. All my love, Granny.

WORD OF KENAN'S ABILITY to find water, facilitating the successful growth of crops on the barren lands around their village spread like wildfire. In the months that followed the passing of his beloved granny, the young man and his divining rod were sought after like gold. To ensure only good came of his work, Kenan insisted that no one but him would ever use his divining rod.

The word was out that wealthy and corrupt warlords were hoping to find him and duplicate his methods for their own profit.

In appreciation for supplying water to his fields, Theodore gave Kenan one of his donkeys to help speed up his travel time. Kenan packed a small bag with only necessities for the journey to Khartoum to visit his parents.

There were three villages he intended on stopping at along the way, hoping to find a water source for each one of them. His dream was coming true. He was bringing water and new life to the people of his country.

His determination was unwavering, even with the imminent danger of a rebel encounter along his route. Kenan kept a watchful eye out for anything suspicious.

However, without warning, the ambush that would change everything appeared in the form of two machine-gun–toting men. They stepped out from behind a rockpile and confronted him. With no regard for the young age of their victim, they brutally pulled him from the donkey. One of the rebels punched him in the stomach so hard he dropped to his knees and bent over in agony.

Four other horsemen appeared in a cloud of dust.

Kenan felt a lone tear roll down his cheek as the butt of a pistol was pushed hard against his temple.

"Stand down!" One of the horsemen hollered. "Face me, boy! Where are you going?" He glared down at Kenan, kneeling beneath him and trembling.

"Khartoum, to see my parents." He kept his head lowered.

"Have they money to pay for the return of their son?"

"I don't think so. In exchange for my life, you can have my donkey."

"I have no intention of killing you. You are of no use to me dead."

"Tie him to his ass!" He bellowed.

Boisterous laughter erupted.

"He can walk, like the rest of you."

Kenan ran alongside his captors, tethered to his donkey, relieved his life was spared.

When the group arrived at the tented village, Kenan was untied and shoved in a hole. A heavy grate of steel was dropped over the opening. Several hours later, dehydrated and weak, he was hauled out to a large tent where he came face to face with the man who'd spoken to him earlier. Lying across the desk in front of him was the divining rod. Kenan's heart sank. *Is this the end of my journey?* The rebels would no doubt use his faithful rod for evil rather than good.

"It would appear you do possess something of value after all." The bearded man leaned in and picked up Kenan's prized possession.

"I can explain."

"No need! I know who you are, Kenan Alazhari!"

"Word of your divining rod and how it finds water has spread across the countryside."

Kenan reached for the divining rod.

"Did you want me to show you how it works?"

"I don't think you can. When the blanket was pulled from your mule, it dropped out and fell to the ground. We've been trying to make it work, but nothing happens."

Kenan examined it for damage. It appeared to be unscathed. He was confident he could make it work. In an effort not to discredit their attempts, he asked if he could take it outside and give it a try.

With proficient hands, Kenan guided the rod over the desolate surface. Still very dehydrated and exhausted from the walk, he tried to focus the apparatus on the ground. Using the same back-and-forth pattern he'd used back at his property, he prayed he wouldn't have to wait too long before feeling the pull of water. He was tired, scared, and skeptical that there would be water this far from civilization. Moments passed, and nothing was happening. His hands and brow began to show signs of sweat. The bystanders scoffed and called Kenan names. He tried to ignore their vulgarities and stay focused on his task.

The cool air of sundown was a welcome change to the sweltering heat that plagued the long days in the desert. Kenan surmised he'd zig-zagged about two acres of the dry barren landscape, without a single twitch of the rod. It was getting dark and hard to tell what ground he'd already covered.

From the corner of his eye, he spotted a withered shrub sticking out from a clump of weeds in the sand. He slowly turned and steered toward it. Then he felt it. That subtle downward pull. Continuing in the direction of the shrub, the rod visibly started bouncing up and down, a few steps more, and it was nose down in the sand. Kenan watched as the skeptical stares of the spectators turned to those of shock and anticipation.

Kenan stopped and pointed at the ground.

"There! If you dig there, you should find water."

The leader signaled to several men, who pushed Kenan aside and immediately fell to their knees and started burrowing through the

sand. They'd dug down about four feet when the sand started showing signs of dampness. A couple men appeared with shovels, and the
hole got larger and deeper more quickly with their efforts. Several of
the younger men took turns digging. The opening had reached well
over their heads. All of a sudden—there it was. Water!

After the oohs and aahs turned to cheers, the big boss raised his
arm in the air. A hush came over the crowd as he stood looking into
the fast-filling hole. "Bring him to me."

Two men seized Kenan by the arms, lifting him off the ground,
another took the divining rod from him. They pushed him to his
knees and handed the rod over to their superior. The head rebel cast
a dark shadow over Kenan, who knelt trembling in fear.

"Well, young man. It would appear the rumors of your talent to
resurrect water from the depths of our barren land are true.

Kenan kept his head down in silence, waiting. They had what
they wanted, so there would be no need for him anymore.

"Your talent for finding water could finally put an end to the rivalry and fighting that ravages our country. With a supply of fresh
water, crops can be grown, livestock fed, and all could prosper." The
rebel leader stared down at Kenan, but the scowl disappeared.

"Stand up, young man! I have a proposition for you. We will accompany you from village to village, assisting in the search for water.
We are just one of many rebel groups. You will need security if you
plan on traveling around this country. You have built up a reputation
of goodwill that we can use to negotiate our way across the country.
I would rather not fight our way from village to village. That would
serve no purpose other than more death and destruction of property.
What do you say, Kenan? Will you be our Goodwill Ambassador?

Part 4
Full Circle
Chapter 1

The Finalists' Summations

The new location of the CARE Foundation was up and running like clockwork. After the airing of Nelson Jones's experience in the cavern, philanthropists from around the world wanted to contribute to the foundation. There was Opal Winston, a Hollywood celebrity, Derek Swanson, an environmentalist, T. J. Buttenham, a wealthy industrialist, and S. W. Sanchez, a human rights activist. They all made substantial donations and volunteered at the foundation, offering their expertise wherever needed.

Jeneva smiled at the shenanigans going on between Takoda and Maddy. Maddy was re-enacting her childhood prank of sneaking up on the gentle giant from behind while he worked on his computer. Jeneva suspected her dad was pretending to be totally engaged in his review of the monthly financial report on his laptop. Before she popped the bag, Takoda jumped to his feet and leaped over the small desk in a single motion that defied his age.

"Dad! Aren't you a little old for hurdling over a desk?"

"Who are you calling old? I'm as spry as a teenager."

The two girls looked at each other and started to laugh so hard tears poured down their cheeks.

Dexter looked up from his laptop. "Quiet down, you guys. I thought we were supposed to be hard at work compiling the summations of the final three contestants before tonight's presentation. I'm only half finished, and the live TV broadcast is not going to wait for any of us. I don't imagine you guys are done either."

Maddy walked over to the table and picked up the stapled sheets between her thumb and forefinger, waving them back and forth as she sidestepped in Dexter's direction.

"Well, Mr. Appelbaum, you imagine wrong. I am afraid my Kenan Alazhari summary is all done. Furthermore, I have done such a good job, he is likely to win. Why don't you save your energy and cut your summation short as it will likely make little difference to the outcome. It's all over but the crying, Dexter." Maddy turned, reached out with her other hand, and dropped a pen on the floor. Grinning like a rock star dropping the microphone at the end of a well-done song.

Dexter banged his fist on the desk for emphasis and also a little shock treatment.

"I admire your confidence, young woman. Unfortunately, my contestant, the honorable Mr. Harvey Mills, has a pretty compelling story to be told, and I intend to tell it in a way that will *illustrate*. Get it? Illustrate, a greatness never exhibited in the history of all of mankind."

"Really, Dexter? The history of all off mankind?" Jeneva looked over the top of her new reading glasses. "Any chance you could be a little more grandiose?"

She slid her glasses up onto her head and looked around the room.

"Remember, guys, this is about the contestants. It's not a writing contest between us. The life story of each of them and their selfless acts are what this is all about. We are just the messengers bringing their fantastic stories to the world."

Just as she finished her discourse, Amir walked into the room. "What's all the noise about? I heard a couple of loud bangs. You folks are disturbing the whole office. Some of us actually have some work to do. Keep it down, will you?"

Dexter threw a crumpled wad of paper at Amir, who reached out with a one-handed shortstop catch and returned the projectile, causing Dexter to duck.

"Nice catch and release, buddy."

"Anyone for a game of dodgeball?" Amir gave Dexter an evil smile.

"Count me in." Takoda closed the lid on his laptop. "I think there is a basketball in the closet." He chuckled.

"Enough fooling around. I told you guys I have to finish my summary." Dexter sat down and turned back toward the computer screen.

"Well, I don't know what the problem is. I finished Rachael Watkins's summary yesterday," Jeneva teased. "Looks like you are the only procrastinator, Dexter."

Dexter apparently did not see the humor in the group's needling at his expense. "Thanks for ganging up on me, people. I'm more of a technical report kind of a guy than an advocate endorsement writer."

"We're just having some fun with you, honey." Jeneva walked over and put her arms around Dexter's neck and peered over his shoulder at his computer screen.

"Let me see what you have so far. I am sure it's great."

THE NEXT DAY, JENEVA'S head was spinning between the anticipation of finally knowing who received the most votes in The Pyramid Challenge and what she would do when it was all over. She needed an escape and offered to do a coffee run. Dexter was the only taker.

This coffee shop was a favorite of the foreign banking crowd. The financial district was always the busiest part of the city, and today was no exception. It was shoulder to shoulder this Friday afternoon, and all eyes were on the TVs scattered around the room.

Lost in her thoughts, Jeneva waited patiently for her low-fat latte and Dexter's double shot espresso. She could tell she was being recognized and pointed at by some of the patrons. Thankfully, the Swiss citizens of Zurich where too polite to approach and bother their famous resident.

After two years of searching for and finding what she thought was her destiny, mixed feelings of satisfaction and anxiety were bouncing around in her head. The all-consuming passion and focus of The Pyramid Challenge provided little opportunity to think beyond tomorrow. Plans for starting the next challenge were already in the works, with the program systems and a competent management group in place. Should she be thinking about a new adventure? The competing thoughts of staying or moving on had her in the middle of an emotional tug of war. She knew it would be hard to walk away from something she loved doing and start something new and unfamiliar. What to do? What to do? She was brought back to the moment when her name was called out for order pickup.

Turning toward the exit, she stopped suddenly, causing the man behind her to crash into her back. Which in turn, caused her to drop Dexter's coffee onto the tile floor.

"I'm so sorry, sir! I shouldn't have stopped like that. I thought I dropped something."

"No, I am the one that should be sorry. I was staring at the TV when I should have been watching where I was going." He reached down and picked up the empty cup, then stood, making eye contact for the first time.

"Oh my gosh! It's you! From that show last night! I can't believe it! This is so crazy! I really love Rachael! I hope she wins!"

Jeneva stepped aside as the manager arrived with the mop.

"I have re-ordered your double espresso. If you want to wait over there, someone will bring it to you. I am not sure we have ever had someone in the shop that was actually on TV at the same time. The Pyramid Challenge has done great things for the world. You should be very proud."

Jeneva apologized to the owner again and moved over to a table near the window, away from the action.

A smiling barista brought Jeneva's replacement coffee. Reading the pretty girl's name tag, Jeneva smiled and thanked Mia by name.

"My pleasure. I can't wait to see who wins. It's all everyone is talking about today." She rushed back behind the counter.

Just as she stood to leave, Jeneva heard the loud pitter patter of rain beating on the window beside her. With no raincoat nor umbrella, she decided to wait and see whether it would ease up before heading out.

Jeneva's sideline presence became less of a distraction as newly arriving patrons put their orders in and waited out their deliveries looking up at the TV.

The BBC network was airing clips from last night's show in the background while the announcer summarized the key elements of the show.

Jeneva saw her smile reflected in the window as she thought about what a great job Maddy had done summarizing Kenan's accomplishments. She'd ended with, "This young man has brought peace between the rebels and the citizens in a very violent part of the world. And is fulfilling his dream to bring much needed sources of water to his community and beyond."

A gentleman with a heavy English accent thanked the waiter for his coffee and requested the TV volume be turned up.

Jeneva turned and looked up when she heard Takoda's deep voice bellowing out of the speakers. Everyone's attention was on the TV screens.

"I think you would agree, the final three contestants are all winners in their own right. They have made a wonderful difference in people's lives. I would like to leave you with one final thought. I think they have taught us something we can all take into our daily lives. You do not have to be a person in a position of great power. Nor do you have to be a person of great financial resources or hold certificates or degrees from multiple institutions of higher learning. All you need is the desire and the drive to want to make a difference. We all have it within our abilities to do something impactful for our fellow citizens.

"From all of us at the CARE Foundation, we thank you for joining us on this wonderful quest. Now, let's all go out there and continue making positive differences in our lives and in the lives of those we encounter along the way. I look forward to sharing the results of The Pyramid Challenge with you tomorrow evening. Thank you, Jason."

He handed the mic back and Jason.

The coffee shop patrons had all been fixated on the screen and applauded as the video clip ended and the commentator went to the weather map.

Jeneva recognized the older balding man approaching her table from the spilled coffee incident.

"Excuse me! Do you mind if I sit with you? My feet are aching, and I am not ready to head out into the rain yet."

"No problem, please sit. I'm waiting for the rain to lighten up as well."

"Allow me to introduce myself, I'm Tomas, the klutz who bumped into you earlier. I think I came off a little strange before, proclaiming my admiration for the Rachael Watkins story. I believe I used the word *love*. I felt rather weird after that."

Jeneva tried to respond, but Tomas just kept on talking.

"Do you know what I love about Rachael? Oh, there I go again. It is her deep dedication to her pupils. I plan to incorporate many of her unique approaches with my students. Such as encouraging them to use their cell phones as a tool to enhance their learning experience. I love, *hoopla*! There is that word again. I'm impressed with what she has done for the environment as well. Students all over the world are making a great impact on this planet of ours. All thanks to her unique way of bringing out the best in her students. She has made me proud to be a teacher. I hope that she wins. I am glad I bumped into you, figuratively and literally. I am an English teacher, you know, but not nearly as good as Rachael." Tomas laughed at his little joke while rising from the table.

"Nice chatting with you Jeneva. I have a class in twenty minutes, got to go. Cheerio."

Chapter 2

Will You Marry Me?

Lighter rain and dark heavy clouds greeted Jeneva as she ventured out into the street. A raincoat would have made good sense, but the overwhelming need to get out of the office to clear her thoughts had prevailed over good planning.

She heard someone call her name from across the street. It was Dexter, waving and running out into traffic with a big black umbrella flailing in the wind. A couple horns expressed their displeasure at his shortcut. Certainly, something you would never see a Swiss citizen do.

"I was starting to get a little concerned. You have been gone a long time."

Jeneva gave him the full rundown of the coffee shop encounters as they headed back toward their apartment.

"What did the TV show say about my presentation?"

"I took a detour on the way to get coffee, and I'm afraid it must have played before I got there. I did hear dad close the show. No doubt they will rerun the whole thing later. We'll catch it then."

Dexter looked a little disappointed at the response.

"Allow me to give you my personal critique of your performance, Mr. Appelbaum. Let me see. Where to start? The life of Harvey Mills. You know, Harvey was probably the most tortured of all the contestants by his life's struggles. Loosing his son to an accident caused by a drunk driver, his wife's suicide and then losing his star football player to suicide. You really presented well how Harvey was able take all the feelings from the adversity in his life and channel them into his little book of informative cartoons. Your portrayal of his impact on students struggling through those challenging high school years was truly inspirational. Dexter, you did a fabulous job.

"Thank you, my dear. I too think I was quite inspirational."

"Well, my cocreator of the greatest challenge ever, four hours from now, the outcome of the worldwide voting will be announced."

The red-brick-faced building came into view as the light shower turned into torrents of pelting raindrops.

"We better get going then. Last one to the door is making dinner."

Their fast walk turned into a full run.

HAVING BEEN A BACHELOR for years, Dexter had become quite a good cook. Tonight, he was offering seafood linguini with white wine sauce. While they waited for the pasta to temper, they cuddled on the sofa with a glass of wine.

"You looked a bit distraught when you left the office, something bothering you?" Dexter rubbed her thigh.

"You know me so well. Actually, my head was reeling. When we started this adventure way back in Cayo Coco, I was sure it was my destiny. Now that it's all coming to an end, I don't know what to do with myself. I feel lost. I have no direction."

Dexter wasn't sure what to say. It was true, they had done what they said they were going to do. Now what? He had a surprise for Jeneva, which he'd planned for after the final votes came in.

"I'll be right back." He jumped up and hustled to the bedroom.

"Where do you think you going! You can't just leave me hanging like this!"

Dexter felt his heart pounding as he returned with the surprise behind his back.

"Sorry, I needed to get something from the other room. I want you to know I understand your feelings, and I might have the answer. I have to ask you a question."

He got down on one knee and held out the black velvet case that her bracelet had come in.

"Your mom said your bracelet would lead you to your destiny, and it did. I'm convinced that you are my destiny." He opened the case. The ring had three diamonds inlaid side by side. Later, he would tell her they represented the three symbols on her bracelet.

"Jeneva Yassi, will you marry me?"

Her eyes widened, and her jaw dropped.

Dexter was trying to read her face. It wasn't the happy look he'd been expecting.

"Well, will you?"

"I don't know what to say."

"Say yes, silly!"

She looked into his pleading puppy dog eyes and gave him the smile he'd been looking for.

"Before I give you my answer, I have one question for you, Mr. Applebaum."

"Ask me anything!"

"What the heck took you so long?"

"So that's a, *yes*?"

"That's a *yes*! Now slip that gorgeous ring on my finger, and let's eat."

Chapter 3

And the Winner Is!

"Good evening viewers, and welcome to The Pyramid Challenge big reveal show. My name is Jason Bonner, and I will be your host for tonight's exciting announcement. This show is being broadcast all over the world, and tonight, we are coming to you live from Zurich, Switzerland."

There was loud cheering and whistling from the crowd.

"We started this exciting journey twenty-two months ago with our first show at the Hummingbird Pyramid in Ecuador. This never could have happened without the support of the Ecuadorian government and its people. The world thanks you for allowing us access to your beautiful country and for your willingness to share the rich experience of your wonderful pyramid. Your support has contributed in a big way to the success of this worldwide challenge."

Again, the crowd applauded and cheered.

"From what I have been told, of the one hundred and ninety-five sovereign countries of the world, one hundred and fifty countries submitted a final contestant. I can also tell you that a staggering three and a half billion people officially entered the contest. I think it is pretty safe to say that never in the history of the world has there been any contest or challenge with this level of engagement."

More cheering.

"With your entry fees, the CARE Foundation was able to provide grants to countries that needed to upgrade their internet infrastructure. They also provided financial assistance to poorer countries to help them get the contest up and running. Your entry fees helped ensure The Pyramid Challenge provided all countries and all their citizens an equal chance to participate."

Jason motioned for Takoda to come to the stage.

"It is my pleasure to introduce you to Takoda Yassi, the CEO of the CARE Foundation. He has something to share with you."

"Thank you, Jason. And thanks to everyone who entered the challenge and to the dedicated volunteers all over the world who donated their time. It is because of you that we have covered all the overhead costs to run The Pyramid Challenge and have a substantial surplus of funds left in the account.

"So, how much is the surplus? You are probably wondering. Well, I can tell you it is projected to be a staggering two and a half billion euros. That's *billion*, with a *B*, my friends."

I know you thought your vote last night was your last official duty, but we have one last request. Please, go online to our website. There you will see a new menu choice named Charitable Acts of Kindness. When you're asked to enter a code, please use the same one you used to submit your vote for tonight's winner. A new web page will open with a list of fifty international charities. This is where you are going to vote for your favorite five. All fifty charities will receive donations from the surplus based on the percentage of the votes they receive. So please, don't forget to go online after the show and make your choices. The outcome will be published on the home page Monday morning. Thank you."

Takoda walked across to the wings, waving to the crowd as they cheered. Jason took center stage again.

In a couple minutes, Jeneva Yassi will be announcing the winner of The Pyramid Challenge. But before we do that, please direct your attention to the big screen behind me for live shots from around the world.

"First, let's go to Times Square in New York City. Jane what's happening in the Big Apple tonight?"

"Have a look at this crowd, Jason. It's like New Year's Eve around here."

A drone camera panned overhead and zoomed in on the crowd of people cheering and singing along with the live band.

"There's a real festive spirit here at Times Square tonight. We're anxiously awaiting your big announcement."

"Thanks, Jane, it won't be long now. Let's go to Tiananmen Square in Beijing. Good evening, Lin. What's the excitement level like where you are?"

"Jason, we have the largest crowd I have seen here in a long time, considering the early hour. We have a big screen set up, and we are watching you live. Everyone is very excited."

"Thanks, Lin. Now, let's go to Red Square. Yuri, what's happening in Moscow tonight?"

"Jason, people started gathering here hours ago. The Red Square is about eight hundred thousand square feet in size, and it is full to the point of overflowing into the side streets. I can't recall an event in recent history where so many people came together in peace."

"Thanks, Yuri, this is a wonderful event for sure. Well, folks, that gives you a sampling of what is happening around the world. During the show, we will be flashing live scenes from different countries on the TV screens behind me."

Everyone started screaming, whistling, and waving when Zurich came up on the screen behind Jason.

"I see a very important person standing in the wings with a sealed envelope in her hand. I think it's time we call Jeneva Yassi to the stage for the big announcement. Come on up Jeneva."

The building shook with wild enthusiasm.

Jeneva slowly walked across the stage, giving a queen's wave to the crowd. She was wearing a short green velvet dress and matching pumps. A beaded headband held back her long, shiny black hair. Jason handed her a microphone.

"No need to be nervous. It's not like everyone in the world is watching." The crowd laughed at his joke.

"So Jeneva, this has been quite the journey for you as well. First, you discovered the mysterious cavern in the Hummingbird Pyramid. Then, you established the CARE Foundation.

"That's correct, Jason. CARE stands for Charitable Acts Reform Everything, in case people weren't aware. We felt that was the perfect acronym to capture the essence of our mission. You could say the foundation is the heart and soul of the challenge. It's where all the fees and nominations were collected."

"Then you had to figure out how to bring the experience to the world."

"Right again, and we couldn't have done that without the expertise and knowledge of Nelson Jones and his Visualization Technology."

"It must have been exciting to watch everything come together. All that positivity building up momentum around the world and then climaxing tonight with the unveiling of the winner of The Pyramid Challenge."

"It certainly has been a wondrous journey for us. You have also been with us for a lot of the journey. So, thank you for hosting these well-organized live events. I'd like to say a few words about how happy I am with the positive engagement from all our contestants, volunteers, government officials, local boards, and everyone at the CARE Foundation. This complicated, worldwide challenge would not have been possible without all their help and unrelenting support. I'm very proud, and so should you be, in celebrating our great success."

"Jeneva, is this the conclusion of Pyramid Challenges, or will there be more to come?"

"I can't say for sure at this time, but I can tell you this: we are weighing all options for what might come next. For now, I think we should stay in the moment and open up this envelope."

"I think that's a great idea, Jeneva. Can we ask all of our finalists to come out on the stage, please? Viewers, your final three: Rachael Watkins, Kenan Alazhari, and Harvey Mills."

As they paraded across the stage toward Jeneva and Jason, the crowds in-house and on the TV screens roared with cheers and loud applause.

"Jeneva, I can't stand the suspense any longer. Will you open the envelope, please?"

"I couldn't be prouder and happier than to do just that. One last thing. All of our contestants deserve to win, and in fact, you could say have already won the challenge to make a positive difference in people's lives. Thank you, everyone, well done. Here we go, Jason!"

The crowds were cheering, lights were flashing, and drumrolls echoed over the airwaves.

"The finalist who received the most worldwide votes is . . . . . . Kenan Alazhari!"

Streamers, balloons, and confetti fell like rain from the ceiling. The Zurich studio audience erupted with loud cheers and clapping. Kenan's humble smile was broadcast around the world for all his many fans to see. All the contestants shook hands and hugged each other. Some were even crying, but all were smiling and truly happy for Kenan.

The camera shots on the big screens around the world also exploded with loud cheers from the crowds. The director raised the volume and let the sound cascade into the studio. Security struggled to hold back the well-wishers from rushing onstage.

Jeneva and Dexter went over to shake Kenan's hand and were interrupted when Maddy ran over and grabbed his hands jumping up and down happily. Takoda stepped in to give the young man he had encouraged to pursue his dream a firm handshake.

Dexter and Jeneva made their way to the other contestants, of-fering their congratulations and thanks for all their contributions to the contest and to humanity.

Jason shuffled through the streamers, balloons, and confetti to bring Jeneva back to the front of the stage.

"Well, Jeneva, it has been an honor to be part of this great experience, and the world thanks you for making this all possible. Is there anything else you want to say before we go?"

"Thank you, Jason. As the winner of The Pyramid Challenge, Kenan will have his pyramid experience broadcast live next spring. You won't want to miss that! I'm so happy to announce Harvey and Rachael are also invited to Ecuador for the fall equinox to have their own pyramid experience."

"Wow! That's great news, Jeneva."

"I have more announcements. This came to us yesterday, but we didn't want it to influence the voting, so we kept it a secret until now. Kenan, can you join us, please?"

The young man gave her a questioning look. She waved him over, and he came and stood beside her.

"I have been given the honor of letting you know that you, Kenan Alazhari, have been nominated for a Nobel Peace Prize for your contributions to peace talks among your countrymen. in South Sudan."

Kenan's face lit with a smile on all the TV screens. The crowd was calling his name and cheering again."

"That's absolutely amazing. Congratulations, Kenan, for that outstanding achievement." Jason shook his hand.

"Well, folks, that concludes our show, but before I go, I'd like to leave you with something a wise man told me."

Jason looked over at Takoda and gave him a two-finger salute.

"The totality of our sameness is greater than the sum of our differences."

He paused for a moment. "This is Jason Bonner wishing you a good night."

Chapter 4

S cotland Yard

"Jeneva, I am going to head back to the apartment. I'm feeling a little worn down. I guess my ancient warrior bones can't stand up to the pace anymore."

"I am ready too, Dad. Why don't Dexter and I drive you? The crowd has thinned, and I think we have touched base with everyone we need to for now." Her father's pallor was concerning to Jeneva.

"Excuse me, Miss Yassi. Can we have a word with you?" Two men came out of nowhere and flipped open wallets, revealing gold badges.

"I am Chief Inspector Escott, and this is Inspector Sims. We are with Scotland Yard. Would you accompany us to the theater manager's office, please?"

Dexter stepped in front of Jeneva and her father.

"Hold on! What's this all about? I am not sure you have jurisdiction to question anyone in Switzerland."

"Dexter, it's okay. We should cooperate. Let's go and see what this is all about. Maddy, can you take Dad home, please? We'll meet you there shortly."

The couple followed the two well-dressed inspectors to an office just off the lobby. The theater manager unlocked the door and walked away.

Inspector Sims closed the door behind them and opened his notebook.

"Please, have a seat. We would like to inquire whether you know the whereabouts of a Nelson Jones. We understand he is a colleague of yours, and we need to talk to him immediately."

A troubled look came over Jeneva's face. "Nelson was supposed to be here tonight, but we haven't been able to reach him for a few days."

"I knew there was something off about that guy," Dexter interrupted. "What has he done?"

"So, neither of you has seen or talked to Nelson in the last couple of days?" the inspector continued.

"We already answered your question. Again, what is this all about? We are not answering any more questions until you tell us what's going on." Dexter demanded.

"Dexter, please, I'm sure the inspectors are just trying to do their job." Jeneva reached out and grabbed his hand.

"I think it might help if you tell us what this is concerning," she said.

"We have reason to think your lives may be in danger. When we searched Mr. Jones's computer, we found some disturbing photos." Inspector Sims opened a file folder and handed some printed photos to Dexter.

"What the hell! He's been following us?"

Jeneva took them and saw what appeared to be surveillance pictures of her and Dexter in different locations. There were big X's on Dexter and hearts all around her.

"I knew he was fond of me, but this looks more like an obsession. What do you propose we should do?" She handed the pictures back to the inspector.

"Until we can locate him, I suggest you don't let your guard down and keep an eye out for him everywhere you go," he suggested.

A long pause followed as both the suited men stared at them, as if preparing to judge their reaction to what they were about to tell them.

"There is something else." The chief said. "A dredging crew discovered a Mr. Alex Belle's body in the Thames River three days ago. He was a business partner of Nelson Jones's. There were obvious signs of trauma. When the local police couldn't find Mr. Jones in his lab or flat, they contacted us, speculating that he might have left the country."

"There must be some mistake. Nelson told us Alex died of cancer." Jeneva told them.

"There's been an autopsy, and the bruising on his wrists, along with blunt-force trauma to his head, proves differently," Inspector Sims said.

"We didn't know Alex that well. Only met him once, actually, but he seemed like a great guy. Inspector, you have our full cooperation. What can we do to help?" Dexter offered.

Chief Inspector Escott stood and spoke in a demanding voice.

"If he calls you or you hear of his whereabouts, you are to call us immediately. If you do speak to him, let him know it would be in his best interests to get in contact with us right away. And by no means, tell him where you are. He can't hide from us. We will find him, eventually."

The two inspectors handed over their contact cards and headed for the door.

"That's all for now. If you decide to leave Zurich for any reason, please notify our office," Inspector Escott said opening the door.

Inspector Sims stopped at the door and turned back to face Jeneva and Dexter. "There's one other thing. Did you ever get the impression Nelson was nervous or maybe hiding something?" he asked.

The couple thought for a moment and shrugged.

"No, I can't say that I did. But there was something about him I didn't like," Dexter said.

Dexter took hold of Jeneva's hand, and they followed the men across the lobby to the exit doors. When they were driving home, Jeneva told Dexter about the conversation she'd had with Nelson before his vision.

"You know, now that I think about it, he was really apprehensive about what was going to show up in his vision."

Chapter 5

Freddie's Cigar Bar

Dexter marvelled at the multitude of pastel shades in the Cuban sunset as he headed toward the ocean. With every barefoot step he took, the boardwalk creaked and swayed under him. To his left and right were cottages in various degrees of construction, all mounted on posts in the shallow lagoon. It felt good to be back in Cayo Coco where the idea of The Pyramid Challenge was born. Everyone was so friendly and welcoming it felt almost like coming home.

Finalizing all the next day's wedding plans had made for a full day. Jeneva was too busy to join the stroll tonight because of some last-minute dress alterations. The early evening solo walk provided for a nice break and an opportunity to reflect on the future. Dexter took a deep breath and exhaled slowly as he leaned on the railing overlooking the rolling waves in the turquoise water. Just as he was drawing in a second purifying breath of sea air, a voice called out from behind him.

"Dexter! Hey, Dexter! Come up this way. Let's go in the cigar bar for a cocktail."

Even with Dexter's back to the beckoning, there was no mistaking who it was. Takoda was a good distance away, but his deep, thundering voice reverberated across the lagoon as if he were ten feet away. Dexter turned and waved as he started heading in the direction of the rustic-looking building with its open shuttered windows. "Well, I guess quiet reflection time is over," he muttered to himself.

The bartender was standing on the porch as the two gentlemen climbed the stairs.

"*Buenas noches!* Welcome to my bar." The middle-aged Cuban man bowed and swooped this arm for them to enter.

Loud music was blasting from the speakers, but no one seemed to be bothered. The sound of billiard balls crashing came from a small room to the left of the entrance, partially open to the rest of the bar. Takoda gave Dexter's sleeve a tug when he spotted two open stools at the bar.

"Freddie, my good man, I hear you make a great Old Fashion. What do you say you mix a couple for me and my soon-to-be father-in-law?"

"Welcome back, Dexter, and your name, sir?" Freddie asked.

"My name is Takoda, father of the bride. Pleased to meet you, Freddie."

"Well, Dexter, it has been quite the journey you and my girl have been on. I am so proud of both of you. The way you were able to present an opportunity for change to humanity and get individuals all over the world to embrace it is unprecedented." Takoda gave Dexter a broad smile. "Ready for act two?"

"If you are referring to the marriage, absolutely! If you are asking about where we go from here, that's a totally different question. Jeneva has been very reflective since the contest and a bit distressed about what she wants to do next. The Pyramid Challenge itself will be a hard act to follow. She is focused on the wedding right now, but I often see her staring at the bracelet when she thinks no one is looking. I think she feels lost and without purpose or direction. I am not sure how to direct or help her."

"Your role now, Dexter, isn't to provide direction, only to support her through this transitional time. Give her time for quiet reflection and soul searching. I am confident she will find her path to the next chapter in her life. You could do some soul searching yourself. I am confident that together you two have more terrific things to offer the world as a couple and individually. Jeneva has a driving force within her that will have to come out. Your life, my soon to be son-in-law, is not going to be boring. I can promise you that!"

Dexter raised his glass to meet Takoda's. "Of that I have no doubt. I can't wait. Cheers."

FREDDY SMILED FOR A moment, watching the two men take a big drink of his expertly prepared beverages. But suddenly, his expression became one of despair. Takoda picked up on it immediately.

Amir shouted over the loud music as he approached the bar. "Hey, guys, what's going on? Mind if I join the party?"

Dexter got up and met his friend with a handshake. "Let's shoot a game of pool. I want to talk to you, pal."

Takoda caught Freddie's attention. "I hope you don't mind my forwardness, but I feel you are not at peace tonight, Freddie. You look troubled."

"I am sorry. Is it that obvious? I was trying to be a good host. To be honest, I am a little distracted. You see, it's my wife. She just lost her close friend to cancer, and she is really struggling with it. I have my faith to guide me through these times, but she is no longer a believer. I am afraid she has gotten very disillusioned with all that has happened in the church and has lost her faith. For her, death is an end not a beginning, like I believe. I can't imagine why I told you all this. I'm sorry. I shouldn't be burdening you. I'm the bartender, I should be the one providing comfort to my patrons."

"Not at all, Freddie, you are not a burden, just a man in pain. Do you mind if I tell you how Native Americans view spirituality?"

Freddie looked up and nodded politely. He felt the situation was hopeless, but he listened anyway.

"Freddie, we do not look at the real world and the spiritual world as two separate levels of consciousness. They are one in our eyes. We believe you can be part of the spiritual world by simply appreciating and valuing Mother Earth and everything she has to offer. Like watching a bird soar in the sky, and you feel the wind on their wings. Or thanking the deer for giving itself as food to nourish our bodies. We believe the conscious and spiritual worlds exist together in harmony not as two separate entities.

There are no written doctrines or prescribed ways you must follow in order to enter into the next world. For me, I believe that the spirit leaves our physical body when we die, but trust that part of the person remains with us forever in spirit."

Freddy's expression changed to one of astonishment. "Takoda, you are a very wise man. Because of my strict religious upbringing, I wouldn't have looked at life and death that way. I think it's something I can take back to my wife for her to consider. Actually, she is working tomorrow morning. I'd really appreciate it if you could speak to her directly. My explanation wouldn't have the same impact as it would coming from you." Takoda saw the desperation in the man's eyes.

"Not at all. What is her name?"

"Benita." Freddie flashed a picture of a woman in his wallet.

"I have my daughter's wedding tomorrow morning at ten, but I would be happy to meet with her earlier."

"That sounds great. I really appreciate this, Takoda. She works in the buffet serving breakfast. We could meet you there before her shift, say six o'clock."

Takoda stood and set a generous tip on the bar. "Six it is. I'll stop in on my morning walk. Goodnight, Freddie."

Takoda bumped Dexter's elbow just as he was about to take a shot. The white ball made its way into the corner pocket.

Amir laughed at the miss placed shot. "Bad luck, Magnet Man."

"Well, boys, I am off to my room. Don't stay up too late. I don't want to see any bloodshot eyes at my daughter's wedding. It's going to be a very proud and happy day for me."

"Hey, Takoda, you'll never guess who just got asked to be the Best Man?" Amir said.

"I have a pretty good idea. Goodnight, boys."

Chapter 6

Wedding Crasher

       He could hear lively music from the lobby bar reverberating through the hallway. Nelson was crouched in the corridor alcove behind one of the maid's cleaning carts. His legs were starting to cramp up, and the music was an annoyance to his already agitated state. And the custom-made composite gun in his waistband was pushing uncomfortably against his ribs. From his hideout, Jeneva's hotel room was in his direct line of sight.

The flight to Cuba had provided plenty of time to come up with a plan but organized thought was eluding him these days. Staying just one step ahead of Scotland Yard and the constant threat of being caught, was wearing on his nerves. Nelson longed to return to his solitary life of an inventor but not until he completed his mission of winning the affections of Jeneva. His mind remained fixated on the one obstacle in his path to happiness. *Dexter Applebaum!*

A young women opened the door of Jeneva's room, and he heard her say, "I will be right back. Just going to grab a few things from my room, or should I say, the groom's room for night." The girl giggled. "It's going to be so much fun having a sleep over. Last night of being single, Big Sister." She said as the door closed behind her.

Nelson lowered his head to insure complete concealment behind the cart. The young women walked swiftly past his screen and attempted to unlock the door, not six feet from him. His heart was pounding, and his chest felt as if it were going to crack open from the convulsing compressions of his labored breathing. *Calm down Nelson. You're going to give yourself away.* The girl tried two more times, and the door finally unlocked. It made a loud bang behind her as she entered. Nelson's body jerked in response to the thundering echo that amplified on the concrete walls of the corridor. His stomach contents erupted into his mouth. He bent over, releasing them into the mop bucket. His head was throbbing, and he felt dizzy. His knees gave way, and he dropped hard to a seated position behind the cart. *I may be on a secret mission, but I am no international spy. What am I doing here?*

Before Nelson could gather his thoughts, the door flew open, and the girl came out with a small, flowered suitcase, passing again directly in front of him and back in through Jeneva's door. As she wrestled to hold the door open and drag the suitcase across the threshold, Nelson impulsively leaped from his hiding spot and pushed her into the room, causing her to stumble over her suitcase. She fell face first onto the marble floor. There was a loud thud as her head hit the floor, causing Nelson to gag momentarily, then he stepped over her motionless body. The door slammed shut behind him.

Jeneva stepped out of the bathroom, hairbrush in hand. "What's all the ruckus about, young lady? Where are you?" Walking around the bed, Maddy's body came into view. "Oh, my gosh! What happened?" Still oblivious to Nelson's presence, she knelt, cradled Maddy in her arms, then lifted her up and set her on the bed. She ran to the bathroom and came out with a wet towel that she dabbed on Maddie's forehead. "Sweetie, wake up! Please, open your eyes and tell me what happened. Are you okay?"

Nelson stepped out of the shadow and into the light. "Jeneva, I am so sorry. I didn't intend to hurt her. It was an accident. She fell over the suitcase."

"Nelson! What the hell are you doing here?" She pointed a finger at him. "Move over there. Get away from us."

Nelson backed up against the wall. Jeneva leaned back over Maddy and continued to apply the cold towel to her forehead, keeping a keen eye on Nelson.

"Scotland Yard has been looking for you, and they've made some very troubling accusations."

Nelson opened his mouth to speak just as Maddy moaned and opened her eyes. Jeneva held a hand up in Nelson's direction. "Don't you move!"

"Are you okay, Maddy? You fell and bumped your head. Hold this towel on your forehead while I go for a fresh one."

Nelson bolted and cut Jeneva off at the entrance to the bathroom. She shoved him out of the way. "Stay out of my way mister, or suffer the consequences."

From inside the bathroom, Jeneva hollered at him. "Nelson, what do you think you are doing here? Have you gone completely mad? You bust your way in here, hurting Maddy in the process, and now what? Are you going to hurt me too?"

Nelson was sitting on a chair beside the bed, pointing an odd-looking gun in Maddy's direction when you returned from the bathroom.

"Is that another one of your inventions?"

"This, my love, is an undetectable, airport-proof gun that I brought along as ahh, shall we say.... a present for Dexter. More correctly, a delivery mechanism for Dexter's present."

"Are you going to kill him too? You know I can't let you do that. Then what? You kill us too?"

"No, I would never hurt you, Jeneva. I love you and would do anything for you. You'll see. I will be the most important person in your life soon. Dexter is no good for you. He is a murderer and a very selfish person. Everything I do is for you, my love. We are destined to be together forever. Fear not, for I have come to rescue you and save you from the biggest mistake of your life. You can't marry that scoundrel."

He could hear the desperation in his own voice. It felt like his insides were going to explode. Perspiration was dampening his whole body and dark stains appeared on his shirt. He felt like a man unhinged and disconnected from reality, but he had passed the point of no return.

Maddy sat up on the bed and threw the wet towel at the intruder. "Get out of here, you jerk. Leave us alone!" she screamed.

Nelson brushed the projectile away and released the gun's safety switch. "No more of that, or your will be sorry, young lady," he threatened.

Jeneva held her hand up in front of Nelson and turned to Maddy.

"Maddy, please, stay calm. Everything is going to be okay. Don't make any sudden moves."

A light knock sounded at the door.

"Ladies. It's Takoda. I just wanted to say goodnight."

Nelson jumped onto the bed and held the gun against Maddy's temple and put a finger to his lips."

Jeneva glared at Nelson, "Thanks, Dad. We're all tucked in. Goodnight."

Maddy hollered, "Goodnight, Takoda. Ómakiya yo!

Nelson looked sternly at Jeneva and whispered, "What did she just say?"

"It means *sweet dreams* in Native American Sioux. Something my dad taught me as a young girl. I didn't realize he taught it to Maddy. Great pronunciation, sweetie."

HEARING MADDY'S PLEA sent a chill down Takoda's spine. What could be wrong? His first instinct was to crash down the door. *What if it's just a pre-wedding day joke? It can't be a joke. Maddy would never say,* goodnight . . . help. *Plus, I taught her to use this secret word only in an emergency.*

Takoda moved around the building to the patio door to get a better look into the room. The black-out curtains where open but the sheers blocked his visibility. He momentarily considered going back to Freddie's bar to get Dexter and Amir but decided it would take too long. He was on his own.

Between the walkway and the patio door, a series of pools offered private swimming for the guests. He took off his sandals and, not to waste a second of time, entered the water fully clothed. Wading through the chest-high water, he made his way to the steps leading to the patio. He stealthily climbed the steps and made his way to the midpoint of the patio door. The sheer window covering was pulled back slightly. Peering into the room, he could see a man with his back to him, pointing an odd-looking gun at Maddy. The situation was obviously desperate and needed immediate intervention. He looked around the patio for something to use on the assailant. Two big heavy chairs, a glass-topped table, and a hammock. Nothing useful here. Takoda closed his eyes momentarily and silently asked the Great Spirit for strength.

JENEVA COULD JUST MAKE out the silhouette of her father on the patio behind Nelson. *Is he alone? Is the door unlocked?* Jeneva stood and walked slowly towards Nelson in an effort to keep his attention.

"So, what's your plan? Are going to keep us here all night. Tie us up? Drug us, maybe?"

She walked over to the dresser, picked up the complimentary bottle of rum, and poured a large drink. "Whatever it is, I'm sure it is not going to be pleasant. Mind if I have a drink? Do you want one, Nelson?"

As Jeneva turned back to face him, she saw her dad pulling the doors apart and quickly threw the drink in Nelson's face. Takoda wrapped his arms around Nelson, pulling his arms to his sides. Nelson struggled to free himself. Takoda turned, rotating Nelson to face toward the wall, away from the girls. Water poured off Takoda's clothes, soaking the tile floor. The two men lost their footing and went tumbling down on top of each other. The gun went off. The bullet went into the wall, spraying chunks of concrete into the air. A piece of concrete flew into Takoda's eye. He managed to grab the gun and toss it across the room. Nelson freed himself and started to crawl toward the gun. Just as he was about to reach for it, Jeneva smashed a porcelain lamp over his head.

The front door came off its hinges, and Dexter and Amir came crashing into the room.

Jeneva stood over Nelson, still holding the stem of the fractured lamp in one hand and an empty glass in the other. Her hair hung wildly over one side of her face. She turned and said, "A little late for the party, aren't you boys?"

Chapter 7

The Wedding Day

Takoda was glad everyone had agreed, that despite the events of the previous evening, the wedding day plans should go forward. The National Revolutionary Police Force had Nelson in custody, awaiting the arrival of Scotland Yard. Thanks to Jeneva lamping him, he'd needed eight stitches in his head. A doctor had attended to Takoda's eye and assured him there would be no long-term damage, but he would have to wear an eye patch for a couple of weeks, until the scratch healed. He'd met with Benita later in the day, and after talking with him, she appeared to be feeling better about losing her friend.

WHEN DEXTER AND AMIR entered the adult pool area, they saw one of the pergolas was draped with white ribbons and colorful flowers. Dexter thought it was the perfect setting for the couple to recite their vows. As he looked around, he saw the pool and waterfalls were also adorned with various shades of hibiscus flowers and palm branches. Chico was at a makeshift DJ stand and bar, setting up for the after-ceremony mimosas.

"I don't know about you, but I could sure use a drink." Dexter said.

"Count me in." Amir said.

THERE WAS A KNOCK ON the bungalow door.

"Miss Jeneva, I have your bouquets and your headpiece. They look beautiful."

"Come in, Anna, we're just about ready." Jeneva told her.

Maddy set the bouquets on the bed and placed the wreath of yellow sweetheart roses on Jeneva's head.

"Perfect!" Maddy said, giving Jeneva a big smile.

"You think so? They were my mom's favorite flower."

"I hate to rush you, but I saw the men waiting for you at the pool when I passed by." Anna told them.

Jeneva and Maddy were standing in front of the full-length mirror. Jeneva's white strapless chiffon dress was knee length in front and draped to the ground in back. The only jewelry she wore was the bracelet with the three symbols and her engagement ring. Maddy was wearing a short flowery dress with pink ribbons intertwined through her braided blond hair. Both were wearing white sandals.

When they left the bungalow, she saw her father waiting on the bridge to escort her. As she walked toward him, she wondered whether he was envisioning her mother on their wedding day. She felt a twinge of melancholy as she took his offered arm and gave his hand a gentle squeeze.

Maddy had gone ahead and stood opposite Amir under the pergola, with Dexter and the Cuban officiator between them.

As they slowly walked toward the pergola, a hummingbird appeared and encircled her headpiece. At first, she was tempted to swat at it, but something told her to let it be.

Takoda smiled and whispered, "I think Mom's here."

They continued their slow walk, serenaded by a Cuban wedding song Chico had picked out for them. The Hummingbird perched itself on the top edge of the pergola.

"Who gives this woman to be wed to this man?" The officiator asked.

"I do." Takoda kissed her cheek and put her hand in Dexter's. He looked up and blew a kiss to the little bird. It fluttered in the air for a moment, then returned to its vantage point.

The officiator read a passage from the bible, and then Dexter and Jeneva read what they had written to each other. Jeneva was thankful Maddy brought Kleenex. She needed them to dab her tears after Dexter read his emotional expression of his love for her. She noticed Dexter tear up after she finished her statement of love and devotion to him as well.

After the exchange of rings, they were pronounced husband and wife.

The officiator joined their hands and held them up in the air. "Go in peace and love and forever be as one."

During the long, drawn-out kiss, the small group of tourists who'd gathered on the sidelines applauded, then made their way to the loungers around the pool.

Chico turned on some cheerful music and offered a tray of mimosas to the wedding party with his congratulations.

Jeneva glanced up at the pergola just as the hummingbird took flight and disappeared into the palm trees.

Chapter 8

Reminiscent Lunch

The Olde Marine Restaurant on the Potomac River looked much as it had so many years ago when Jeneva and Takoda last met here. Their favorite seafood platter for two sat in front of them, teeming with shrimp, scallops, cod bites, and steaming clams.

"I can't believe it has been five years since we were here together. I was heading back to my job at CERN, and you were leaving for Sudan. It was Maddy's sixteenth birthday, remember? And you saved that poor boy from drowning that day." Jeneva recalled. "I have missed you so much. I am so glad you're here."

"Dexter and I are so happy, and we're still very much in love. Did you hear the latest about Nelson? He got twenty-five years for killing Alex Belle. It's hard to accept that he was capable of such a horrible act. He never liked Alex's idea of selling the VT to the military for combatant interrogation. I wish they could have made some kind of compromise, instead of . . ." Jeneva gave an exasperated huff. "I really hope that's the reason, Dad. Sometimes I wonder, if I hadn't contacted him about the Visualization Technology, would Alex still be alive?

"I look at it this way; the VT machine helped bring a lot of good change to the world. And Nelson turning all the rights to the VT invention over to me and donating every cent in his bank account to the CARE Foundation, now you have to admit, that was very charitable of him."

Jeneva sighed as she cracked open a clamshell and slurped it down, then continued. "I wonder if one bad act erases all the good people have done in their lives.

"Anyway, enough about Nelson. Dexter and I are off on a new adventure. Amir has been working in Indonesia on some archaeological site and has something to show us. He's being very cryptic about the whole thing. So off we go again, into the wild blue yonder."

"Don't worry, I'll call and show you videos, so it will be like you're right there with me. I'm so excited to see what life brings me next."

"You have some sauce on . . . Here let me get that for you." She dapped at the side of her father's mouth and continued.

"Did I tell you, GWG Studios called? They want to make a miniseries about my journey to find my destiny and, The Pyramid Challenge. They're calling it Jeneva's Journey."

"Dad, did you hear me? Dad!"

Jeneva could hear a voice in the background, calling her name. She tried her hardest to block it out.

She felt a warm hand on her bare shoulder.

"Jeneva, honey, our airport limo will be here in an hour. Time to rise and shine."

Dexter gave her a kiss on the cheek and left a coffee on the nightstand.

Tears welled up in her eyes as she rolled over and sat up, pulling her knees to her chest. It felt like yesterday, but he had been gone for 6 months. She looked at the pictures on the dresser.

"I miss you, Pops. Say hi to Mom. Love you." She blew a kiss. " Until we meet again."

Authors Final Note

Four years ago, our initial inspiration to write a book came from these four statements:

- *The totality of our sameness is greater than the sum of our differences.* George Chamberlain
- One small act of kindness can make a big difference,
- Sometimes the journey is more important than the destination,
- Finally, from Alex Trebek: *We are trying to build a kinder, gentler society. If we all pitch in a little, we can get there.*

We wanted to bring these messages to the readers in a way that is entertaining but also inspirational. Although it was a challenging task, we enjoyed working together, brainstorming for hours, compromising, and analyzing every plot line until we were both satisfied that we had accomplished what we had set out to do.

Which now leads us to Book 2, coming soon.

Jeneva and Dexter are off to visit their archeologist friend, Amir, in Indonesia.

What adventures will they find there? Visit us for updates at. https://www.chamberlainbooks.com